Mother Goose

Also by Gloria T. Delamar

Children's Counting-Out Rhymes, Fingerplays, Jump-Rope
and Bounce-Ball Chants and Other Rhythms:
A Comprehensive English-Language Reference *(McFarland, 1983)*

Rounds Re-Sounding: Circular Music for Voices and Instruments;
An Eight-Century Reference *(McFarland, 1987)*

Mother Goose
From Nursery to Literature
by
Gloria T. Delamar

McFarland and Company, Inc., Publishers
Jefferson, North Carolina, and London

Library of Congress Cataloguing-in-Publication Data

Delamar, Gloria T.
Mother Goose, from nursery to literature.

Bibliographies: p. 281.
Includes index.
1. Children's poetry, English — History and criticism.
2. Nursery rhymes, English — History and criticism.
3. Folk-poetry, English — History and criticism.
4. Mother Goose.
5. Popular literature — Great Britain — History and criticism.
I. Title.
PR507.D45   1987   398′.2′0941   87-42504

ISBN 0-89950-280-6 (acid-free natural paper)

Manufactured in the United States of America.

McFarland & Company, Inc., Publishers
Box 611, Jefferson, North Carolina 28640

From Mommy Goose
to
the Gander...Bill
and the Goslings...
Graelie
Keltcie
Keallie
Dawson
Crohan

Acknowledgments

Any research project involves a certain intimacy with earlier works on the subject. Those are points to start from. How can one adequately emphasize the importance of libraries to such work? I am deeply grateful for the private libraries of collectors who shared their valuable volumes with me, the Philadelphia Free Library, whose various reference departments helped in finding important isolated pieces of information, and, especially, the dedicated staff of the Elkins Park Free Library of Cheltenham Township, Pennsylvania, whose knowledgeable use of the Inter-Library Loan network brought to my doorstep book and magazine resources from all over the country.

I acknowledge a debt to the illustrators of long ago who drew the pictures scattered through the book—their art lives again with each reprinting.

For emotional support—there were friends, especially other writers who understood the sometimes fatiguing task of absorbing research to turn it into a personal style and viewpoint—and there was my family, always present with encouragement—and in particular, there was my loving husband who could always be counted on to be supportive, to help proofread, to give up part of *his* time at the word-processor, and above all, to inject a sense of humor into this writer's workday.

G.T.D.

Table of Contents

List of Illustrations

Foreword

Something happens in the soul of a compulsive researcher when a random tidbit of information nags like a burr in the brain. I'd worked with Mother Goose materials many times before, and knew there were political implications connected with some of them, that some had roots in religion and elsewhere, that many were also fingerplays, rounds, or other songs, and that some were by authors who rarely got credit for writing them.

But one day, someone remarked that "Ring-a-round a rosie..." was really about the Great London plague of 1665. It piqued my interest and I couldn't rest until I checked the veracity of the allusion. I did—and the verse is *not* about the plague—but in the process, I became enamored with the many other curiosities connected with the traditional rhymes. After that, there were numerous paths of fact and fancy to wander through.

Everyone finds a personal voice in writing a reference book. I found mine in the many items that made my heart race at new discoveries about old verse-friends. Perhaps only others with the affliction will empathize with that research high that comes when hours of work turn into one or two sentences that validate a statement. There were some difficult decisions — counterbalancing the inclusion of additional material with the caveat against giving more information than anyone would reasonably want to know — and leaving out some favorites whose bland histories didn't fit the theme of the book. Throughout, the decision about what to include or exclude was based on a foundation that said, "Ah, yes, this interpretation is reasonable — this is relevant — this is fascinating history — this has additional import on a verse that others might like to know — and here's something that others can use."

As I began to work with the long chapter about the many known authors of nursery works, I realized that the inclusion of their "Mother Goose" verses was more meaningful if placed beside the context of their other work, so I added brief biographies. I figure I'm not the only reasonably literate person who remembers some of these dates and accomplishments more in the general than in the specific. And it was exciting to realize that the whimsical dimension can be used by literature teachers to help broaden the concepts students have about these writers of otherwise "serious" material.

Arranging composites of the various versions of the narrative ballads was a real adventure in folk history — and unearthing the variety of uses and abuses of good old Mother Goose opened a strange treasure chest of witticisms and oddities.

Sometimes we accept the familiar all too casually. There was real excitement for me in learning the evolution of the rhymes from the nursery to their designation as literature. I hope the material in this book will kindle the same flame for all those whose own curiosity leads them into its pages.

Gloria T. Delamar
Melrose Park, Pennsylvania
Fall 1987

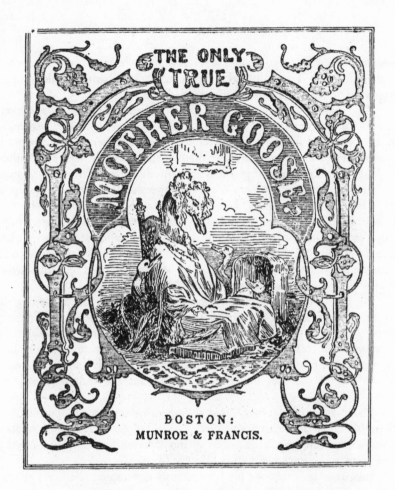

THE ONLY TRUE MOTHER GOOSE

BOSTON:
MUNROE & FRANCIS.

1. Goosey, Goosey, Gander, Whither Dost Thou Wander?

A General History of Mother Goose

The literature of Mother Goose has touched the life of virtually every person in the English-speaking world. Its era has spanned centuries, and its creations have been spawned by authors from the unknown to the well-known.

The very term *Mother Goose* evokes a whole body of work—with images of Mama goose, in apron and sunhat, waddling along with goslings close

1

behind. It brings forth memories of familiar verses learned from parents and teachers and shared with siblings and playmates. The chants of childhood are invariably linked to the Mother Goose tradition.

Who then, was this "Mother Goose"? Was she a real person? Was she *one* person? To the latter, the answer is *no*. She was many, and "she" was many "he's" as well. Tracing the origins of nomenclature and identification leads the scholar of children's literature along many paths. Some are clear, and others are fogged with the haze of poorly documented history. With many roots in the folklore tradition, the rhymes passed on by word of mouth, it's not surprising to find that the origins of some verses are simply not documentable. And despite the tradition of folklore that has preserved these rhymes, there is every reason to think that most were originally written by and for the gentry, and copied by the "folk" who worked for them, or observed them at their amusements. That some can be traced to serious writers is one clue. Other clues lie in their literary styles of composition.

But not all the early rhymes began in serious literary mien. Among the earliest preservations for the nursery were "infant amusements," which were simple games for parents or nurses to play with the young. But along with these were the numerous "riddles," which were adult amusements later adopted by the nursery, sometimes as rhymes with no indication of awareness on the part of the user that the verses were in fact riddles. (See Chapter 3.)

It's obvious that Mother Goose rhymes came from many sources. Even given the lack of documentation about the earliest pieces, ample information is available to offer a reliable history of the collected literature and lore that have come to be known simply as *Mother Goose*.

Language and its usage are continuously-developing sciences; certainly this is true of English. The so-called common-language of countries on two sides of the Atlantic Ocean has many uncommon areas. Among these is the designation of "Mother Goose" for a certain body of literature. It was an English publisher who borrowed the name "Mother Goose" from the French, yet until the twentieth century, in England the works were always known primarily as "nursery rhymes." The same works were adopted as "Mother Goose rhymes" in America. As twentieth century American publishers began to export more Mother Goose picture books to England, the division in terms became somewhat less pronounced, but remained discernible.

Nomenclature is only one of the issues that led to a great deal of current confusion as to what constitutes a "Mother Goose" rhyme. Some say it's the subject matter. Others say it's the patter of the verse. Some even say it's the length of the piece; no more than four lines, for instance. Some insist, rather unreasonably and in contradiction of actual practices, that the author must be unknown. These arguments are not applied to nursery rhymes in general—only to the traditional verses that common assent now classifies as

Mother Goose. What we have then, is that a nursery rhyme is not necessarily a "Mother Goose" rhyme, but a "Mother Goose" rhyme is a nursery rhyme. The maternal goose has undergone an interesting literary metamorphosis.

Her path through historical waters is fraught with eddies and falls plus calm and peaceful channels—information and misinformation—and a myriad of book titles and dates. She's come full circle from literature to nursery to literature.

The earliest traceable written reference to Mother Goose was discovered by the Scottish scholar and folklorist, Andrew Lang (1844–1912), in Loret's 1650 *La Muse Historique* (lettre v, 11 Juin) in which appeared the line, *Comme un conte de la Mère Oye* or "Like a Mother Goose story." Speculation of subsequent scholars suggested two possible origins for the story-teller referred to, both named Bertha.

One was the French Queen Bertha, the wife of Pepin (c714–768) and the mother of Charlemagne. This Bertha was known as "Queen Goose-foot" (*Reine Pédauque*) or "Goose-footed Bertha," possibly because of the size or shape of her foot which was said to be both large and webbed. Custom has shown her in illustrations as spinning, while surrounded by children, as she tells stories. From this sprung the French retort to a tall tale as being "from the time when Queen Bertha spun."

The other was Queen Bertha, wife of Robert II (Robert the Pious—c970–1031), also of France. This Bertha was a close blood-relation to her husband (Robert was excommunicated from the Catholic Church for this reason upon his marriage to her), and it was rumored that the close blood-tie had caused her to give birth to a child with the head of a goose.

The legends of the two Berthas have become intertwined, however, and certainly it is not clear that either was the reference in Loret's remarks. Some commentators have made the cryptic statement that the origin may be in the German *Fru Gosen* or *Fru Gode*. The more modern spelling here would convert this to *Frau* or *Mrs.*, which could be allied with *mother*, but the remainder appears to be more an English misinterpretation, for in fact, *goose* in German is *Gans*. Curiously, though mentioned by several writers, none offers any documentation, but only the one-sentence remark. And, indeed, there appears to be no reliable historical data.

The origins of the designation, therefore, must remain obscured by conjecture. The next step, however, can be traced with some accuracy. It began in 1697, when a French publisher, Charles Perrault, issued a book designating the contents to be from *Mother Goose*. This volume contained no rhymes. It contained eight fairy tales Perrault had contributed in 1696 and 1697 to a magazine printed at The Hague, *Moetjen's Recueil* (or, Moetjen's Anthology). The collection in book form was titled *Histoires ou contes du temps passé, avec des moralités* (Histories and Tales of Long Ago, with Morals). The frontispiece showed an old woman spinning and telling stories, with a placard on the page which bore the words *Contes de ma Mère l'Oye* (Tales of My Mother the Goose).

This book is important for several reasons. Of its eight stories, seven are still nursery favorites, "The Sleeping Beauty," "Little Red Riding Hood," "Blue Beard," "Puss in Boots," "The Sisters Who Dropped from Their Mouths Diamonds and Toads," "Cinderella or the Little Glass Slipper," and "Little Thumb," better known as "Tom Thumb." Only the tale of "Riquet with the Tuft" has not survived. (Perrault's use of names, however, was sexless. By deliberately mixing *apparent* forms [male or female] with the opposite [masculine or feminine] usage, the reader could interpret the hero/heroine or villain/villainess as being either male or female.) Perrault's book is also important in that the book was *for* children, and in that it introduced the name "Mother Goose" to the literary world. (In 1908, Maurice Ravel, 1875–1937, an outstanding figure in modern French music, composed *Ma Mère l'Oye*, known in English as *The Mother Goose Suite*, a suite of five pieces including the stories of "Sleeping Beauty" and "Tom Thumb.")

Charles Perrault was a serious scholar, author of numerous now forgotten works, and a member of the Académie Française. He said that the fairy stories were told as he had heard his son's nurse recite them. In fact, Perrault issued the book in the name of his ten-year-old son, Perrault d'Armancourt, the story being that he considered the book too trivial to bear his own name. Nevertheless, his publication of the volume, which is considered the first to be planned with children's pleasure in mind, is what has gained him a place in the annals of literature. And by presenting his tales as being from "Mother Goose," he set the stage for the name to become a household word.

The first English appearance of the name, "Mother Goose," is sometimes erroneously credited to Robert Powel, who presented puppet shows in England between 1709 and 1711. Powel wrote the scripts for the plays himself, although the stories themselves existed in story form. His offerings included *Robin Hood and Little John, Friar Bacon and Friar Bungay, The Children in the Wood, Whittington and His Cat, Dr. Faustus, Mother Shipton*, and one called *Mother Lowse*. In a *Punch and Judy* article of 1828 reference was made to a biography of Powel published in 1715, *A Second Tale of a Tub: or The History of Robert Powel the Puppet-Show-Man*. In the 1828 article *Mother Lowse* was incorrectly noted as being *Mother Goose*. This mistake was perpetuated by later authorities, eventually leading to the false assumption that Powel had presented one of the stories from Perrault's collection, one writer even speculating that he had gotten it from a sailor. That Powel's puppet shows were very popular is evident from comments by Joseph Addison (1672–1719) in *Spectator Papers* noting that when Powel set up his show in London opposite St. Paul's, the sexton rang his bell, but many churchgoers were enticed from piety to puppets. The sexton wrote to Addison to complain, "As things are now, Mr. Powel has a full Congregation, while we have a very thin House." His popularity notwithstanding, Powel's connection with Mother Goose is apocryphal.

Then, in 1729, J. Pote of Charing Cross published Perrault's volume of fairy tales, "Translated by Mr. Samber." To Robert Samber and Charles Perrault, therefore, belongs the credit for introducing the name of Mother Goose to the English-speaking world. But this was as the teller of "tales." Her name was not yet connected to the "rhymes" which would ensure her fame.

Those rhymes, however, began to appear in a few publications meant for children. In 1744, a London publisher, Mary Cooper, put out at least two, and perhaps three, tiny volumes under the title *Tommy Thumb's Pretty Song Book*. The exact number of volumes is not documented, and no copy of Volume I is to be found, but an original copy, now priceless, of Volume II is in the British Museum. The editor was listed as "N. Lovechild," believed to be a pseudonym, perhaps of Mary Cooper herself. It's interesting that the name Tommy Thumb appears in the title, and one has to wonder if there was a deliberate echo to the Perrault fairy tale of that name. The volume was very small, being only three inches tall and one and three-quarters inches wide. Illustrated with tiny crude woodcuts, it contained 38 nursery rhymes, some still remembered, and others long forgotten.

They included "Sing a Song of Sixpence," "Little Tom Tucker," "Hickere, Dickere, Dock" (sic), "Mistress Mary," "Bah, Bah, Black Sheep," "Little Robin Redbreast," "We Will Go to the Wood (says Robbin to Bobbin)," "There Was a Little Man," and a version of "Who Did Kill Cock Robbin?" As to other inclusions, most were of similar mien, but the following two examples indicate a rather liberal attitude as to what was suitable for children. It's not surprising that rhymes like these would be suppressed by the Victorian era that followed.

> Piss a Bed,
> Piss a Bed,
> Barley Butt—
> Your Bum is so heavy
> You can't get up.

> Blackamoor, Taunymoor,
> Suck a Bubby,
> Your Father's
> A Cuckold,
> Your Mother told me.

Although it's a fair assumption that some of the rhymes must have appeared in print before this edition, no copies are to be found. British scholars feel that the earlier printings were probably in the form of handbills, perhaps as early as 1600, and that it is possible collections of Mother Goose appeared in England as early as 1620, with reprints in 1648. Unfortunately, no copies of these supposed editions can be found.

In the same year as the above-mentioned book, 1744, John Newbery (1713–1767) opened his publishing shop in London and published his first volume for children, *A Little Pretty Pocket-Book*. A small book, similar to Mary Cooper's format, it was designed to both amuse and instruct children. It included advice for living as "letters" to the reader from "Jack, the Giant Killer," and most rhymes were followed by a "moral."

John Newbery was to gain recognition as the first publisher to devote a line to the publication of books expressly for children. Children's literature scholars often call Newbery the father of children's literature. In his honor, since 1922, the American Library Association has issued the Newbery medal, an award given to the year's "most distinguished contribution to American literature for children." Newbery, in his own day, was considered somewhat of a "character." He wrote, published, helped indigent authors, and maintained a flourishing business manufacturing and dispensing medicines. One of his publications, in line with his business interests, was a medical dictionary. He was interested in so many things that his friend, satirist Samuel Johnson (1709–1784), called him "Jack the Whirler." Johnson, as well as Oliver Goldsmith (c1730–1774), wrote for him.

Newbery issued *Nurse Truelove's New-Year's-Gift; or the Book of Books for Children* in 1755. (Note the similarity of his *Nurse Truelove* to Mary Cooper's *N. Lovechild*.) Among other pieces, it contained the cumulative tale, "The House That Jack Built." Two other publishers also issued books that contained some of the rhymes. *The Famous Tommy Thumb's Little Story-Book* was published by Stanley Crowder and Benjamin Collins, and *The Top Book of All, for Little Masters and Misses* was published by the same Crowder and Collins along with R. Baldwin. Both appeared around 1760, in a tiny format similar to that of Mary Cooper's little book.

But what about "Mother Goose"? Here, in 1760, she appears again; to remain firmly established as the mythical author of a host of nursery rhymes.

The single most important promoter of the designation of Mother Goose for children's rhymes was John Newbery. With his adoption of her name for a collection of mostly traditional rhymes, he usurped her former alliance with the fairy tales. The date for publication of this important edition is generally agreed to be about 1765 (anyway, some time between 1760 and 1766).

In 1960, however, Jacques Barchilon and Henry Pettit (*The Authentic Mother Goose Fairy Tales and Nursery Rhymes*; Denver: Swallow, 1960) postulated that the edition was not printed until 1780, claiming that there was no evidence of advertisements for the book until January 2, 1781, at which time Newbery's stepson, Thomas Carnan, advertised "The first publication of

Mother Goose's Melody." They contend, however, that the book was probably planned earlier, but not published. It is on record that Thomas Carnan entered the Newbery edition for copyright in 1780. Scholars who accept the 1765 *publication* date attribute the 1780 *copyright* date to legalities involved with the settlement of the concern's co-partnership.

So, *Mother Goose's Melody* may have been published circa 1765 or it may have been published 1780. Neither speculation is absolutely clear, although the earlier carries more weight in circumstantial evidence. No copy of the first edition is known to exist, but numerous reprints of it surfaced, in both England and America. Although the first reprints began to appear about 1785, *they* claim to be reprints of a Newbery edition of circa 1760. Oliver Goldsmith is supposed to have edited the volume, and also added witty "maxims" to the rhymes; Shakespearean lullabies comprise the second part of the little book. Goldsmith was known to have worked for Newbery, but he died in 1774—his editorship is not, however, obviated even if the book was not published until 1780, if, as contended, the book was planned long before.

The difference of fifteen years in the possible date of first publication will no doubt continue to engross the activities of scholars for many years. For the time being then, a literary reference must raise the issue for readers and then proceed. Iona and Peter Opie, the estimable editors of *The Oxford Dictionary of Nursery Rhymes* (1951) as well as of other highly-regarded volumes in the field, credit the circa 1765 date of publication, as do Ceil and William S. Baring-Gould, editors of *The Annotated Mother Goose* (1962). (As the present work requires numerous cross-references to the sourcebook, *The Melody*, only one date is given—that of "c1765.")

Whatever its actual date of publication, nothing else changes in analyzing the importance of *Mother Goose's Melody* to nursery lore. Even the fifteen year span changes nothing; no other publication predates it as the first collection of traditional nursery rhymes, or the first use of the term *Mother Goose*.

Mother Goose's Melody: or Sonnets for the Cradle is a landmark publication. It became an instant source of delight, continuing in circulation. It is so important to the literary history of Mother Goose that it is reprinted in its entirety herein as Chapter Four, with appropriate introductory remarks.

Originated by John Newbery, its success was further stimulated by Thomas Carnan. Carnan was the stepson and cosuccessor to the company, along with John's son, Francis Newbery. Francis, however, devoted most of his interests to the very profitable medicine side of the business, and it was primarily Carnan who continued the publishing company. It is generally accepted that it was the dissolution of the copartnership at Francis Newbery's death which prompted Carnan's copyright action. Another Francis Newbery, John's nephew, was also in the publishing business as a competitor, a fact which has caused errors in notation for careless researchers. When the nephew died in 1780, his business was passed to his widow, Elizabeth Newbery. Meanwhile, Thomas Carnan was responsible for the John Newbery firm until his death in 1788. For a few years, Francis Power, John Newbery's grandson, carried on the tradition, but sometime in the 1790s, Elizabeth Newbery acquired the old firm and incorporated it with hers. The firm stopped doing business as Newbery in about 1805, to be succeeded by John Harris, who had been Elizabeth Newbery's general manager. Although the Newbery imprint had disappeared from the world of children's books, the name lived on. The copyright to *Mother Goose's Melody* would have passed to the Harris firm.

Despite being copyrighted, this little book was reprinted and pirated numerous times. Isaiah Thomas, of Worcester, Massachusetts, issued a reprint circa 1785, and a second in 1794. Most subsequent reprintings are taken from Thomas's "Second Worcester Edition," although the cover pages of some indicate they were taken from the earlier edition. As apparently no complete copy of that edition exists, the second printing, of which a copy is in the American Antiquarian Society of Worcester, must be the one that was used. An English reprint was issued in 1796 by Simmons and Kirby of Canterbury. John Marshall of Aldermary Church Yard, who had issued *Nancy Cock's Pretty Song Book* circa 1780, issued reprints of *Mother Goose's Melody* in 1795, 1803, and 1816.

Isaiah Thomas, who had reissued *Mother Goose's Melody* in the United States, became known as "The American John Newbery." In 1788, he published *Tommy Thumb's Song Book for All Little Masters and Misses*. It was "To be sung to them by their Nurses, until they can sing themselves," and supposed to have been written "by Nurse Lovechild." Many of the pieces in it had appeared in Mary Cooper's 1744 "Volume II" of *Tommy Thumb's Pretty Song Book*," and the suspicion has been raised that it was actually a pirated reprint of the first (of which no copy seemed extant) and second volumes. This book, too, is represented by only one known original copy, which is at the American Antiquarian Society of Worcester.

In the meantime, Joseph Ritson, a literary scholar, bought a copy of the *Melody* in 1781 and became inspired to collect more. Another publication he drew on was a pamphlet of 1797 called *Infant Institutes*, a satire on Shakespearean commentators. It is primarily valuable because its undoubted author, the Rev. B.N. Turner, evidently recorded the rhymes purely from memory.

There were 79 pieces in Ritson's first edition of *Gammer Gurton's Garland, or, the Nursery Parnasus* which came out in 1784 (London: R. Christopher), and was reprinted, with some minor changes, in 1799. Seven years after Ritson's death, a third edition appeared in 1810 (London: R. Triphook), with extensive additions collected by Francis Douce, former keeper

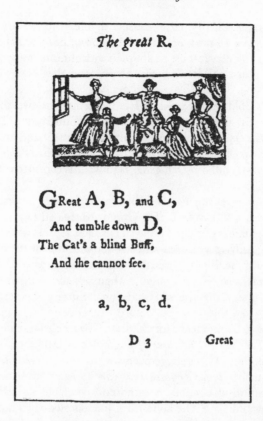

of manuscripts for the British Museum. It was in this book that a version of "Yankey Doodle" first appeared in print. (For more about this piece, see page 165.)

Benjamin Tabart of London printed *Songs for the Nursery Collected from the Works of the Most Renowned Poets* in 1805, a volume that became an important source for *Mother Goose's Quarto: or Melodies Complete* published by Munroe and Francis of Boston about 1825.

Newbery's successor, John Harris, did not reissue the *Melody*, but he did publish other books which contained a number of the rhymes. Among these were *Original Ditties for the Nursery* (1805), and single-rhyme editions like *The Comic Adventures of Old Mother Hubbard and Her Dog* (1805), *Cock Robin* (1819), and *Peter Piper's Practical Principles of Plain and Perfect Pronunciation* (1819).

Later pirated reprints of the *Melody*, with additional rhymes, were published in Boston and New York in the first quarter of the nineteenth century, establishing general usage, as well as the American adoption of the term *Mother Goose* in connection with the traditional nursery rhymes.

Many editions contributed to nursery rhyme history—but several stand out. Mary Cooper's *Tommy Thumb's Pretty Song Book* was the first *known* book of nursery rhymes. It must be coupled with *A Little Pretty Pocket-Book*, John Newbery's first children's book, however, as they both were issued in 1744.

Newbery's Goldsmith-edited *Mother Goose's Melody* was the first *important* collection. Tabart's *Songs for the Nursery* was the second. Ritson's *Gammer Gurton's Garland* was the third. Fourth was Munroe and Francis's *Mother Goose's Quarto: or Melodies Complete*. The fifth (actually consisting of two separate volumes), edited by James O. Halliwell, is considered the first *comprehensive* collection.

If anyone deserves the nickname of "Father Goose," bestowed on him in the twentieth century by the Baring-Goulds (discussed later), it would certainly have to be James Orchard Halliwell (1820–1889). He was a brilliant antiquarian, being only 18 years old when made a Fellow of the Royal Society. Later, he would be highly regarded for his work as a Spenserian and Shakespearean scholar. He was only 22 when he collected rhymes and traced their origins, presenting the old traditional nursery rhymes for scholarly study.

His were not books meant for children. They were (and are) for students of literature. *The Nursery Rhymes of England* was published in 1842, by T. Richards of London (with enlarged reprints in 1843, 1844, 1846, 1853, and c1860); its sequel, *Popular Rhymes and Nursery Tales*, was issued in 1849 by John Russell Smith of London. A hundred years later, the Opies (also discussed later) would say, "The collection, interspersed with notes about age and origins of the nursery rhymes, was the outcome of much random delving and is a treasure store of curious information. It was the first work to draw attention to the antiquity of the rhymes with any conviction, and the first collection which attempted to be comprehensive." While Halliwell's works have some errors corrected by later scholars, they have been, nevertheless, prime sources for every student of nursery rhymes since.

Halliwell professed that the rhymes were collected "principally from oral tradition," but it is obvious, from internal comments and contents, that he consulted, perhaps as follow-up, previous books (*Mother Goose's Melody, Songs for the Nursery, Gammer Gurton's Garland, Mother Goose's Quarto*, etc.) and did research among fifteenth-to-eighteenth century manuscripts. He deplored the lack of documentation available about many of the rhymes, but was resigned to it. He mentioned that in the short space of three years, he had collected considerably more than a thousand rhymes, selecting only a part for the first book. In the second volume, he drew comparisons of the English "trifles" with nearly identical pieces in the child lore of Europe.

The reverence Halliwell held for nursery literature is evident in the preface he wrote to the 1853 edition of *The Nursery Rhymes of England*.

The nursery rhyme is the novel and light reading of the infant scholar. It occupies, with respect to the A B C, the position of a romance which relieves the mind from the cares of a riper age.... The infants and children of the nineteenth century have not deserted the rhymes chanted so many ages since by the mothers of the north. This is a great nursery rhyme fact—proof that there is contained in some of these traditional nonsense rhymes a meaning and a romance, possibly intelligible only to the very young minds, that exercises an influence on the minds of children. It is obvious that there must exist something of this kind, for no modern competitors are found to supply altogether the place of ancient doggerel....

Those words are as applicable as the twentieth century nears its close as they were when written. Halliwell established nursery rhymes as a legitimate area of study in literature. His influence on subsequent studies is substantial. And though Halliwell dealt with "nursery rhymes" and never used the term *Mother Goose*, "Father Goose" seems an appropriate appellation for him.

Was "Mother Goose," then, acknowledged to be a made-up designation—from Loret—to Perrault—to Newbery—to common usage? From all accounts, yes, but legends die hard, and a new one appeared to cause later scholars considerable research and speculation.

Suddenly, on January 14, 1860, a claim that the "real Mother Goose" was a 1719 Boston grandmother, threw itself into the literary melee. Although readily discredited with the facts, the legend continues to be perpetuated. Writing under the pseudonym "Requiescat," John Fleet Eliot, a great-grandson of publisher Thomas Fleet, wrote a piece in *The Boston Transcript* setting forth his great-grandmother, Elizabeth Foster Goose, as the first—the real—Mother Goose.

The biography of the actual person who was the supposed inspiration for the name of Mother Goose shows that Elizabeth Foster, daughter of William and Ann Foster of Charleston, Massachusetts, was born on April 5, 1665. When she was 27, on July 5, 1692, she married a 57-year-old widower with ten children, Isaac Goose of Boston, Massachusetts. (The Goose surname may have evolved from Vergoose or Vertigoose.) Together, they had six more children. Isaac Goose died at the age of 73, on November 29, 1710.

In 1715, one of their daughters, Elizabeth, married Thomas Fleet, the ceremony being performed by the famous Cotton Mather. Young Fleet had immigrated to Boston from Bristol, England, in 1712, and set up a print shop in Pudding Lane (later Devonshire Street). Elizabeth and Thomas had six children. Their grandmother, Elizabeth Goose, lived with the family in rooms over the shop, where she told rhymes and tales to her grandchildren. Some were remembered from her childhood and some were original.

The legend then avers—alternately, depending on who is telling it—

either that Thomas Fleet was enchanted with the rhymes, which had become admired by the entire neighborhood — or that he had become sick of hearing them, but recognized their potential in the marketplace. In either case, he is said to have decided to put them in a book.

He is supposed to have published *Songs for the Nursery or Mother Goose's Melodies for Children* in 1719. No such edition has ever been found. In tracking the claim of John Fleet Eliot, it appears that he offered two "authorities," neither of which could be substantiated.

One of Eliot's "authorities" was a statement he said had been made to him in 1843 by Edward A. Crowinshield, a literary scholar, that in researching something else in the library of the American Antiquarian Society at Worcester, Massachusetts, Crowinshield had hurriedly examined a fragmentary copy of the Fleet book. Eliot evidently waited 17 years after hearing this to make his claim, but unfortunately (or perhaps fortunately, from Eliot's viewpoint) Crowinshield had died 11 months before Eliot's 1860 article. No searches or records at the Library indicate they ever possessed such a book as Fleet's *Mother Goose*.

As the other "authority," Eliot referred to the preface to the 1833 *Mother Goose's Melodies* in which appeared a comment on an edition of *Songs for the Nursery; or Mother Goose's Melody for Children* said to have been published by Thomas Fleet. It's likely that the author of the preface, not researching as carefully as he might, had confused two books and conjoined them into one title. Newbery's *Mother Goose's Melody: or Sonnets for the Cradle* (1760) and Tabart's *Songs for the Nursery Collected from the Works of the Most Renowned Poets* (1805) were both generally referred to in their shorter forms. The supposed title of the Fleet edition uses those abbreviations together.

As to dates, if Eliot's claim were true, Elizabeth Goose of Boston would have used the term "Mother Goose" ten years before Perrault's "Mother Goose" fairy tales were translated into English in 1729. That she or Fleet had heard of the French term and attached it to her rhymes, punning with her own name, seems merely a grasp at a wisp to try to give it substance.

More important are the dates of supposed publication and release of the assertion of authorship. Remember, Eliot's claim about the 1719 book was first heard in 1860, a hundred years after Newbery's Mother Goose edition had appeared, and 147 years after the "ghost volume's" supposed publication. It seems unlikely that knowledge of the earlier book could have been so long buried.

Several researchers have pointed out that Benjamin Franklin (1706–1790) possessed copies of everything published in the colonies, yet his library did not contain a copy of the "ghost volume." This is cited to support the denial of the "Boston Mother Goose" legend. As a counter-argument to this as somehow "proof" against the claim, it should perhaps be pointed out that

Halliwell's collections are still important, of course, but they have been replaced by the Opie volume as the dependable authority. Their book will continue to be a cornerstone of basic research to all who follow.

In fact, the only other study worth noting obviously drew freely on the Opie volume. In 1962, William S. Baring-Gould and Ceil Baring-Gould published *The Annotated Mother Goose* (New York: Bramhall House). The rhymes are presented with annotations that are formatted as sidenotes, giving the meanings for archaic words and offering pertinent historical remarks. The volume is handsome, but flawed by some basic errors, which probably only nursery-lore scholars would notice. Its poor indexing, though, would hamper anyone wanting to use the book for more than cursory reading.

The history of Mother Goose as literature has a number of other ramifications. There are political implications in many of the rhymes. Some are derived from ancient religious lore or folk legend. Some were written by well-known poets. They offer a rich lode of study to the scholar.

More importantly, they have been a source of endless delight to generations of children, for whom "Mother Goose" is a household word — the name of an almost real, literary friend.

Ding, dong, bell,
Pussy's in the well!
Who put her in?
Little Tommy Green,
Who pulled her out?
Little Johnny Stout,
What a naughty boy was that,
To try and drown poor Pussy-cat!

2. Potshots and Praise

Analysis and Relevance

When a body of work has the designation of classic literature, the material inevitably becomes the bailiwick and grist of reviewers, analysts, "kiddie lit" students, and scholars. Not to be dismissed are the responses of parents and of children themselves. And frequently, despite the onerous and sacrosanct designation of classic, there's a gap in critical agreement.

Opinions, even educated ones, tend to differ for many reasons. They are influenced and distinguished by whatever ethos prevails, whether that be of the era, of the locale, or of the individual's religious, cultural, or philosophical nature. Those varying, therefore dubious standards are nowhere so evident as in the potshots and praise heaped upon good old Mother Goose's literary works.

That they've been widely and warmly embraced by the public—by educators—by parents—by children—is a fact. This should be enough, but it isn't. A small minority of critics periodically insist on reissuing their arguments against a perceived "unwholesomeness" in the verses. Some even object to the "nonsense." But like the squeaky wheel that gets the oil, their attacks do attract at least a modicum of attention. In reaction, then, the upholders of the Mother Goose tradition must get on their soapboxes to defend the old dame. In addition to the large majority who embrace them out of familiarity and just plain "like," there are the literary scholars who bring forth the rhymes from their classification as classics, to reappraise them, and generally praise them anew.

It's a legitimate question to ask if a classic, Mother Goose in this case, is relevant today. Do the rhymes and doggerel spawned by an earlier day still have something of value in them for the contemporary child? Are they appropriate fodder for young minds?

Although the mores of what was thought fit for children were quite broad in Elizabethan days, the Victorian age brought a stricter note that forced a mold of "usefulness" and "morality" onto children's publishers. Adaptations in many of the familiar nursery rhymes show evidence of what influence the ages have had. Somewhere between the ribaldry thought fit for children in the Elizabethan era and the prudish stance of the Victorian, there's a compromise that's been inherited by the latter part of the twentieth century. In contemporary times, there has been a broad acceptance of, as well as an emphasis on, "real life" material. In "real life," people (thus, children) are happy and sad, kind and cruel, afraid and brave, and so on—in other words, all the actions, reactions, and emotions traditionally seen in Mother Goose rhymes.

Nevertheless, as far back as 1641, George Wither protested that many of the verses were unfit for children. This refrain was picked up by Sarah Trimmer at the beginning of the nineteenth century, and Samuel Goodrich shortly thereafter. Professor Allen Abbott agitated for the reform of nursery material in 1937, followed by Geoffrey Hall in 1949–50. One of the most detailed attempts to demote the beloved old Mother Goose works was offered in 1952 by Geoffrey Handley-Taylor of Manchester, England. Despite the conclusion of most nursery scholars that his efforts are misdirected, his comments and list offer the reader some insights into what motivates detractors of the rhymes. That he was sincere cannot be doubted. Sincerity, however, is not always enough.

There are some for whom the following list offers attractions for complete to qualified agreement with his premise. For others, it offers amusement. At the least, it shows how detractors interpret the rhymes. Caution: one person's interpretation of meaning is not necessarily another's, and the mind may well be strained to put examples to each item on the list. In any event, the list makes interesting reading. He wrote:

> The average collection of 200 traditional nursery rhymes contains approximately 100 rhymes which personify all that is glorious and ideal for the child. Unfortunately, the remaining 100 rhymes harbour unsavory elements. The incidents listed below occur in the average collection and may be accepted as a reasonably conservative estimate based on a general survey of this type of literature.

— 8 allusions to murder (unclassified),
— 2 cases of choking to death,
  1 case of death by devouring,
  1 case of cutting a human being in half,
— 1 case of decapitation,
  1 case of death by squeezing,
  1 case of death by shrivelling,
  1 case of death by starvation,
— 1 case of boiling to death,
  1 case of death by hanging,
  1 case of death by drowning,
  4 cases of killing domestic animals,
  1 case of body snatching,
  21 cases of death (unclassified),
— 7 cases relating to the severing of limbs,
  1 case of the desire to have a limb severed,
  2 cases of self-inflicted injury,
  4 cases relating to the breaking of limbs,
  1 allusion to a bleeding heart,
— 1 case of devouring human flesh,
  5 threats of death,
  1 case of kidnapping,
  12 cases of torment and cruelty to human beings and animals,
— 8 cases of whipping and lashing,
  3 allusions to blood,
  14 cases of stealing and general dishonesty,
  15 allusions to maimed human beings and animals,
  1 allusion to undertakers,
  2 allusions to graves,
  23 cases of physical violence (unclassified),
  1 case of lunacy,
  16 allusions to misery and sorrow,
  1 case of drunkenness,

4 cases of cursing,
1 allusion to marriage as a form of death,
1 case of scorning the blind,
1 case of scorning prayer,
9 cases of children being lost or abandoned,
2 cases of house burning,
9 allusions to poverty and want,
5 allusions to quarreling,
2 cases of unlawful imprisonment,
— 2 cases of racial discrimination.

Noted educator Bruno Bettelheim has quite the opposite attitude. In an essay on violence (see the Annotated Bibliography), he wrote:

> We try to satisfy other instinctual drives within acceptable limits or, if this doesn't seem feasible, to channel them into safe directions. . . . In regard to violence there seem to be no such reasonable efforts, but a covert denial of its existence as a drive. . . . Children's play is closely related to daydreams and dream fantasy. By inhibiting their aggressive fantasy play, we behave as if even thinking and dreaming about violence were evil. This attitude prevents children from forming a clear understanding about the world of difference that separates violent fantasies from acting violently in reality. If the child is not permitted to learn early what this difference consists of in respect to violence (to use Warshaw's terms, if he has not been given the chance to establish satisfactory modes of behavior in respect to violence) then, later on, he may not be able to draw a clear line between violent fantasies and violent action.
>
> By outlawing the child's violent fantasy we totally neglect what even Plato recognized: that the difference between the good and the bad man is that the first only dreams of evil deeds, while the latter engages in them. The ancient Greeks knew that the crucial difference between good and evil does not reside in a difference in fantasy content — and the children's play is nothing but the child's giving form and expression to his childish fantasies — but whether or not fantasy remains just that, or is acted out in reality with real consequences.

In another context, Bettelheim said:

> It is high time that both the myth of original sin and its opposite — the myth of original innocence — were dispatched to the land of the unicorns. Innocence is neither an inborn characteristic nor a useful protection or defense; most of the time it is little more than ignorance, too often clung to for (false) security.

Vita Sackville-West, in *Nursery Rhymes* (London: Michael Joseph, 1950), makes the point that "even though a tender atmosphere surrounds their incantations, sentimentality is noticeably absent from the nursery rhyme." She comments that the child's mind is "a very strange thing," which refuses to be frightened by things some adults consider frightening. "So perhaps Nanny in her sagacity was right in perpetuating the tales of terror and even bloodshed, sanctified by centuries."

In looking at the "violence" in Mother Goose, one also has to extend that view to consider whether or not there is any real harm done, traceable to exposure to the rhymes. How many children have tried to emulate the farmer's wife by cutting off the tails of mice? How many attempts have there been to cause death by shrivelling? — by boiling to death? — and how many children have gone out to devour human flesh after hearing Mother Goose?

One of the verses often pointed to as being violent and therefore culpable of teaching wrongful actions is:

> Ding Dong Bell,
> Pussy's in the well,
> Who put her in?
> Little Johnny Green.
> Who pulled her out?
> Little Tommy Stout.
> What a naughty boy was that
> To try to drown poor pussy cat.

Isn't there the same paradox here as exists between those who see a half *empty* glass of water where others see a half *full* one? Where detractors see Johnny Green's actions, they fail to note Tommy Stout's, or even the obvious moral in the last two lines of the verse. Then, there's

> Charley, Charley, stole the barley,
> Out of the baker's shop:
> The baker came out and gave him a clout,
> Which made poor Charley hop.

Why is it that some see only that the rhyme is about "stealing" and put it into a statistic as such, when indeed the crux of the verse is that Charley was caught and punished for taking the barley? As in so many cases, statistics are meaningful only if placed in context.

Many people have chuckled over Handley-Taylor's list, in wonderment that he deemed it so awful to even refer to undertakers, graves, misery and sorrow, poverty and want, etc. Are children to be protected from these realities? Or from any of those listed? Robert Franklin, editor and scholar, put it succinctly in 1984 when he said, "lots of pointy-domes have debated the 'less-than-desirable' behavior angle, but it's clear to me the behavior cataloged is not only desirable but crucial — to a Mother Goose rhyme!"

What limited views the detractors have. Here, in Mother Goose literature, is the world. Her works run the gamut from sense to nonsense. There's simple truth, humanity — good and bad, fact and fantasy. Oh, to see a cow *really* jump over the moon! If not to be seen in reality, what harm is there in seeing it in the imagination? In verses that tell about the commonplace things of life, children learn truth — and facts. After all, even the smallest children can relate to Humpty Dumpty's being an egg — and know what happens if an egg falls. Children who have been exposed to Mother Goose have learned not only the basics of life, but have had their minds stretched to outer limits.

Indeed, Mother Goose rhymes cover an enviably broad base of subject matter, style, and mood. May Hill Arbuthnot, in her classic study, *Children and Books* (Chicago: Scott, Foresman, 1947), noted, "It is a rewarding task to make a list of the different kinds of verses in *Mother Goose*." The following list (based on hers, but alphabetized and somewhat amended here), clearly shows what a wealth of material is to be found in these simple nursery ditties. An example is given with each category; it would be easy for most people to add more:

Accumulative stories: This is the house that Jack built...

Alphabets: A is an apple pie...

Animals: Three blind mice...

Birds and fowl: Jenny Wren; Higgledy, piggledy my black hen...

Counting: One, two, buckle my shoe...

Days of the week: Solomon Grundy, born on Monday.

Dialogue: Who killed Cock Robin?

Infant amusements —

   Fingerplays: Pat-a-cake...

   Games: Ring a-round a rosie...

   General: Dingle dingle doosey...

   Knee-trotting: To market, to market...

Imaginary creatures: Oh who is so merry ... light-hearted fairy...

Moral lessons: Ding, dong, bell...

Nature —

   Personified: Daffy-Down-Dilly...

   Real: The North wind doth blow...

Nonsense: Three wise men of Gotham...

People (a rich gallery of characters) —

   Children: Little Miss Muffet...

   Grown-ups: Old King Cole...

   Imaginary: Old Mother Goose when she wanted to wander...

   Grotesque: There was a crooked man...

Pranks: Georgie, Porgie, pudding and pie...

Proverbs: Early to bed, and early to rise...

Riddles: Little Nancy Etticoat...
Songs —
   Ballads: Frog he would a-wooing go...
   General: Mary had a little lamb...
   Lullabies: Rock-a-bye Baby...
Street cries: Hot-cross buns...
Superstitions: See a pin and pick it up...
Time verses: Thirty days hath September...
Tongue-twisters: Peter Piper picked a peck...
Verse stories: The Queen of Hearts she made some tarts...
Weather: Rain, rain, go away...

Coupled with the positive nature of the wide diversity found in nursery rhymes is the concomitant relationship of the bestower or sharer of the rhymes — parent, teacher, babysitter — to the child. Reading or hearing a nursery rhyme — teaching or learning a nursery rhyme — is a two-way communication. There's interaction. Children who know nursery rhymes are children someone has cared about. Tender loving care nurtures tender loving people.

Children who know nursery rhymes have a distinct advantage over those who do not. Early childhood educators—nursery, kindergarten, and first grade teachers—recognize the importance of these verses as part of early school training. An adjunct to the familiarity of the words is the richness revealed to the child when he or she sees different versions of the Mother Goose rhymes. Why here "Jack and Jill" are slender; and here they're chubby. Here the five little pigs are small and grubby; here they're all dressed up like grown-up humans. Here the colors are gentle and delicate; here they're bright primary hues. Here the pictures are big and full; here they're fine line drawings. It's important for both parents and teachers to expose children to various versions so their perceptions are enhanced.

There are a number of reasons why children should be exposed to the pleasure of Mother Goose while very young. The communication developed between reader and child has already been mentioned but can always stand reiteration.

Next, there's much to be gained from the language of the verses. May Hill Arbuthnot says, "Knowing dozens of the verses expands the imagination, increases the vocabulary, and develops an ear for the music of words. Enjoying *Mother Goose* predisposes children to other books. Poring over the illustrations is a liberal education in art appreciation. And meeting *Mother Goose* in the warm security of mother's or father's lap is a happy experience no child ever forgets."

Important, too, is that there is an immediate common bond from home to school when familiar material is introduced. Whether children leave home for the outside world first for day-care, nursery, kindergarten or first grade, there's usually a little apprehension in even the most eager youngster. Mother Goose brings back the warm familiarity of home and verses, making the new setting echo the known environment.

Also, as educators work with the words, the nursery verses help to reinforce speech patterns and vivid language. Some teachers have found that foreign-born children can learn English more quickly using the verses, as the rhymes help to convey the characteristic speech rhythms of the language. But they do it in a "fun" way, rather than as "lessons."

Edward Fenton, in a 1977 article wrote, "Another aspect of language which must be considered is the effect of its own literature upon it. A living language is like a palimpsest, layer upon layer, with meanings shining through it with curious iridescence. What would English be without, for instance, such all-pervading influences as the King James Bible, Mother Goose, Shakespeare, Lewis Carroll and Hemingway—to take a few names at random."

Finally, there is the realization that the rhymes form a legitimate basis upon which to build an appreciation of poetry. From the familiar patter of Mother Goose, it is an easy transition to Edward Lear's or Lewis Carroll's nonsense verses, to A.A. Milne's gentle humor, and to Christina Rossetti's, Dorothy Aldis's, or Eleanor Farjeon's poems of childhood. Even though the nursery rhyme is short and light-hearted — whatever the subject matter — it can build a bridge to other "words in tuneful order." Later, the appreciation of serious poetry is a natural step.

In fact, an appreciation for Mother Goose rhymes can also form a basis for the writing of one's own poetry. In an interesting October, 1984 edition of his poetry column in *Writer's Digest*, poet and teacher Judson Jerome made a solid point for "Nursery Versery." He began:

> Most serious poets are less concerned with reaching thousands of readers immediately than with reaching millions through the ages. By "serious," you understand, I don't mean grave or sententious. Serious poetry can be as daffy as "Little Miss Muffet." A serious poet is one who is serious about the art of poetry, whether it be tragic or whimsical, one who is serious about wanting to produce work of truly enduring value. We don't want much: just to be remembered by nearly everyone a few centuries from now.
>
> Whoever came up with those verses was doing something right. I think poets today would do well to study them carefully. . . . Whether you learn much about poetic technique or not, I'm sure you'll find yourself engrossed . . . the lessons they teach are applicable to even the most sophisticated poetry.

Jerome then recommends using the rhythm of a Mother Goose rhyme upon which to base original poetry. The poetic intent might be whimsical; it might be serious. But, pick a rhyme and simply follow the same *da DUM da DUM da DUM da* . . . *etc.*, even writing it down. Then write a poem using the same beat. This same "nursery versery" technique is recommended in a computer software program which is aimed at helping poets to spur creativity by converting the proven *poetic feet* and *meters* of Mother Goose rhymes to their own poetry.

Master poet Walter de la Mare (1873–1956), in his introduction to *Nursery Rhymes for Certain Times* (London: Faber & Faber, Ltd., 1956), spoke out for Mother Goose, saying her rhymes,

> free the fancy, charm tongue and ear, delight the inward eye, and many of them are tiny masterpieces of word craftsmanship — of the latest device in rhythm, indeed — the "sprung"! Last, but not least, they are not only crammed with vivid little scenes and objects and living creatures, but,

however fantastic and nonsensical they may be, they are a direct short cut into poetry itself. How any child who was ever delightedly dandled to their strains can have managed to grow up proof against their enchantment, and steadily and desperately more and more matter-of-fact and prosaic, is a question to which I can find no satisfactory answer.

The Russian poet, critic, translator, and scholar, Kornei Chukovsky, received an honorary degree from Oxford University on his eightieth birthday in 1962 for "services to British literature." He is known throughout the world for his lifetime record of the thought and language of children, published in a small book, *From Two to Five*. In it, he talks about the Russian child's rich inheritance of folklore, and compares it to "the great book that is called by the English *Mother Goose*." He notes that the English rhymes were "sifted through a thousand sieves . . . everything that is out of tune and incongruous with the psychology of the young child is gradually forgotten and becomes extinct."

Chukovsky points out that there is an "element of surprise," of "topsy-turvyness" in children's intellectual development. He maintains that in order for children to master an idea, they must first make it their "toy." This is done by turning it over, upside down, sideways, looking at it from all directions. He delights as a child would at words like "The children skated on the ice, / All on a summer's day. . . ." He gets indignant when he talks about a bowdlerized edition of *Mother Goose*:

> The famous "Hey, diddle, diddle" about the cow that jumped over the moon and the dog that laughed (like a human being) was redone by some sober "parson" as follows: the dog does not laugh, but barks; the cow does not jump over the moon but under the moon, that is, below, in the meadow. . . . Just a few words have been changed and the book has become quite sensible. In fact, it has only one fault: nothing would induce a child to love it or to sing its lines. And the "senseless" version, the "illegal" and banished one . . . will survive another thousand years because it represents the means by which the child confirms for himself the authentic and actual inter-relationship of objects and creatures.

Some contemporary educators say that folklore, fantasy, and realism are the best means of reaching the psyche of the child. If that is so, then Dame Gander surely deserves her high place on the list of what's appropriate for the young. Her works fulfill all three categories.

Children today are in reality not much different from children of the Elizabethan or Victorian periods. The humanity of people has a certain constancy. They may live in different times, they may eat and dress differently, their cultural settings may have little similarity, but the basic emotions, hungers, and drives of human beings have always been the same. As children mature, they have to learn to label their feelings — pleasure and anger, sadness and joy, love, hate, and pain. All these are to be found in nursery rhymes, showing the young that their feelings are not out of kilter with the rest of the world.

The bond that unites the generations has many facets. One of them is the link that communicates nursery rhymes from one age to the next. Whether that be on the scale of grown-up to child or on the larger scale of one culture or era to another, Mother Goose has justly earned her claim to relevance.

3. Antiquities for Lulling and Mulling

Lullabies, Infant Amusements, and Riddles

Among the first verses to make their way into the nursery were those accompanied by melodies—the lullabies. These were closely allied to "infant amusements." Along with the adult riddles that moved into the children's room, these form the trilogy on which the major portions of later collections were built. As such, they are valuable, and sometimes curious, subjects for the nursery-lore enthusiast.

What follows first here is a sampling of Mother Goose lullabies — there are also some in the landmark *Mother Goose's Melody*, which appears herein as Chapter 4. (An early lullaby by Thomas Dekker is on page 149.) The words of many of these songs intended to "lull" the infant are hardly soothing — an interesting phenomenon.

Lullabies are a natural outpouring between mother (or nurse) and child. "Lulling" was already an acknowledged term when John de Trevisa wrote in 1398, "Nouryces vse lullynges and other cradyl songes to pleyse the wyttes of the chylde."

Probably the most familiar lullaby in the English language, known both in America and in Britain, is "Rock-a-bye Baby," also known just as readily as "Hush-a-bye Baby."

Rock-a-bye Baby, in the tree top,
When the wind blows, the cradle will rock.
When the bough breaks,† the cradle will fall,
And down will come baby,† cradle and all.

†*Also, "when the wind ceases" and "down tumbles baby."*

Surely, the words to this, if they could be understood by an infant, would hardly be soothing to hear — "Down will come baby, cradle and all." The first written version was in *Mother Goose's Melody* (c1765) (see page 63). Legend has it, however, that the words were written by a Pilgrim youth who sailed to America on the *Mayflower* in 1620 and observed how the American Indian women hung birchbark cradles on tree branches where the wind could rock the cradles. It has been touted to be "the first poem produced on American soil" (*Book Lover*, 1904).

There are many lullabies, but only certain ones have been established in the "Mother Goose" realm. And though *Mother Goose's Melody* contained lullabies by Shakespeare (pages 70–75), the Bard's work has stayed primarily within its own milieu. Of the "Mother Goose" lullabies, only a few are given here. The first known printed dates are given for historical interest.

Bye, baby bunting,
Daddy's gone a-hunting,
Gone to get a rabbit skin
To wrap the baby bunting in.

— *Gammer Gurton's Garland 1784*

Bye, O my baby,
When I was a lady,
O then my baby didn't cry;

But my baby is weeping
For want of good keeping,
O I fear my poor baby will die.

— Gammer Gurton's Garland 1784

Hush thee, my babby
Lie still with thy daddy,
Thy mammy has gone to the mill,
To grind thee some wheat
To make thee some meat,
Oh, my dear babby, lie still.

— Songs for the Nursery 1805

Rock-a-bye, baby,
    Thy cradle is green,
Father's a nobleman,
    Mother's a queen;
And Betty's a lady,
    And wears a gold ring;
And Johnny's a drummer,
    And drums for the king.

— Songs for the Nursery 1805

Hush-a-bye a baa-lamb,
Hush-a-bye a milk cow,
You shall have a little stick
To beat the naughty bow-wow.

— Poetic Trifles c1840
— The Nursery Rhymes of England 1842

Bye, baby bumpkin,
Where's Tony Lumpkin?
My lady's on her death-bed,
With eating half a pumpkin.

— The Nursery Rhymes of England 1842

One might have expected that this would appear in the Goldsmith-edited circa 1765 *Mother Goose's Melody*. "Tony Lumpkin" is a character, a coarse but kind youth, in Goldsmith's 1773 *She Stoops to Conquer*. It first appeared, however, in Halliwell's 1842 collection.

Hush-a-bye-baby,
Daddy is near,

Mammy's a lady,
And that's very clear.

— Traditional Nursery Rhymes 1843

Baby, baby, naughty baby,
Hush, you squalling thing, I say.
Peace this moment, peace, or maybe
Bonaparte will pass this way.
   Baby, baby, he's a giant,
   Tall and black as Rouen steeple,
   And he breakfasts, dines, rely on't,
   Every day on naughty people.
Baby, baby, if he hears you,
As he gallops past the house,
Limb from limb at once he'll tear you,
Just as pussy tears a mouse.
   And he'll beat you, beat you, beat you,
   And he'll beat you all to pap,
   And he'll eat you, eat you, eat you,
   Every morsel snap, snap, snap.

—c1877

This curious "lullaby" has been said to be intended to intimidate the baby. More likely, as the baby could not understand the words, it had a cathartic effect for the parent or nurse. Certainly, if sung to a toddler, it would have to be conveyed in a teasing mode. As noted earlier, violence is not an unknown element in Mother Goose, and despite some querulous objections, it seems to do no harm.

Sleep, baby, sleep,
Thy father guards the sheep;
Thy mother shakes the dreamland tree
And from it fall sweet dreams for thee.
   Sleep, baby, sleep.

Sleep, baby, sleep,
Our cottage vale is deep;
The little lamb is on the green,
With wooly fleece so soft and clean.
   Sleep, baby, sleep.

Sleep, baby, sleep,
Down where the woodbines creep;
Be always like the lamb so mild,

A kind and sweet and gentle child.
　Sleep, baby, sleep.

Hush, little baby, don't say a word,
Papa's [Mama's] going to buy you a mocking-bird.

If that mocking-bird don't sing,
Papa's going to buy you a diamond ring.

If that diamond ring turns brass,
Papa's going to buy you a looking-glass.

If that looking-glass gets broke,
Papa's going to buy you a billy-goat.

If that billy-goat won't pull,
Papa's going to buy you a cart and bull.

If that cart and bull turn over,
Papa's going to buy you a dog named Rover.

If that dog named Rover won't bark,
Papa's going to buy you a horse and cart.

If that horse and cart fall down,
You'll still be the sweetest little baby in town.

—Nineteenth century American

In addition to singing their babies to sleep, mothers and nurses amused the little ones. Probably the oldest "infant amusement" is the game of "Peek-a-boo" wherein the adult covers her face, peeps through the fingers, and then spreads the hands apart to croon "Peek-a-boo." The earliest documented variation is a game mentioned as early as 1364, called "Bo-peep." In 1755 Dr. Samuel Johnson described it as, "The act of looking out and drawing back as if frightened, or with the purpose to fright some other." Halliwell, although suggesting it might be a form of hide-and-seek, said in 1842, "But, in even more ancient times the amusement appears to have been even simpler: a nurse would conceal the head of the infant for an instant and then remove the covering quickly, crying, 'Bo-Peep!'" He had collected a couplet for the hide-and-seek version:

Bo-peep, Bo-peep:
Now's the time for hide-and-seek.

Fingerplays were another "infant amusement," and a number were included in *Mother Goose's Melody* without being identified as such, but with

Goldsmith's maxims added. Among them are some of the best known, such as "Pat-a-cake" (page 65), and a version of "This little pig went to market" (page 66). The version known today differs a bit:

> This little piggy went to market,
> This little piggy stayed home,
> This little piggy had roast beef,
> This little piggy had none,
> And this little piggy cried,
> Wee, wee, wee,
> All the way home.†

†*Also, "I can't find my way home."*

This game for counting fingers or toes appears to have been known at least as early as 1728, if not earlier. It appeared in *The Famous Tommy Thumb's Little Story-Book* in about 1760. It is no doubt the best-known English-language fingerplay. Other popular rhymes for counting-off fingers are "John Brown had a little Indian..." (see page 90), and "Ten little Injuns..." (see page 200).

Many of these fingerplays and other infant amusements appear only as rhymes in Mother Goose books, with no indication that there are "games" attached to their recitation. Some are obviously games, but others give little inkling in the words. Among the most persistent inclusions in nursery rhyme collections are the following:

> Put your finger in foxy's hole,
>   Foxy's not at home:
> Foxy's at the back door,
>   Picking at a bone.

—1842

The game for this involves putting the first two fingers of one hand across the first two fingers of another, creating "foxy's hole." When the child places a finger in the hole, the fox (a thumb) nips at it.

> Here are mother's† knives and forks,
> Here is father's† table,
> Here is sister's† looking glass,
> And here is baby's cradle.

—1842

†*Also, "the lady's" each time.*

This involves some finger manipulation. With the backs of hands touching, slightly interlock fingers, but let them stand straight up to indicate knives and forks. Next, keeping fingers interlocked, turn hands over so that the backs of the hands are uppermost, with the fingertips inside the palms and the knuckles forming a table. Next, raise the index fingers from the table so that they form a triangle with the tips touching to indicate a looking glass. Last, raise the little fingers in the same positions as the index fingers and rock the hands to indicate a cradle rocking.

> Here's the church,
> And here's the steeple,
> Open the door
> And here are the people.
>
> Close the door
> While the people pray,
> Open the door
> And they all walk away.
>
> *—1883 or earlier*

Interlock hands with fingers pointing in toward the palms, backs of fingers to form a flat roof. Raise both index fingers, tips touching to form steeple. Thumbs represent church door; open them out. Show fingers inside for people. Close thumbs back up. Then, open thumbs again. People (fingers) walk to lap.

Two verses found in *Mother Goose's Melody* are "Shoe the Colt..." and "Is John Smith within..."; these are to be accompanied by patting the sole of the baby's foot.

And here are two "face-tapper" games:

Brow Bender,	TOUCH BABY'S FOREHEAD
Eye Peeper,	TOUCH EYES
Nose Dropper,	TOUCH NOSE
Mouth Eater,	TOUCH MOUTH
Chin Chopper,	TOUCH CHIN
Knock at the door,	TICKLE CHIN
Ring the bell,	PULL EAR
Lift up the latch,	RAISE NOSE
Walk in.	PUT FINGER IN MOUTH
Take a chair, sit by there,	
And how do you do this morning?	

—Tommy Thumb's Song Book 1788

Here sits the Lord Mayor,	TOUCH BABY'S FOREHEAD
Here sit his men,	TOUCH EYES
Here sits the cockadoodle,	TOUCH RIGHT CHEEK
Here sits the hen,	TOUCH LEFT CHEEK
Here sit the little chickens,	TOUCH TIP OF NOSE
Here they run in,	TOUCH MOUTH
Chin chopper, chin chopper,	CHUCK UNDER CHIN
Chin chopper, chin.	

— The Nursery Rhymes of England (rev.) 1846

My mother and your mother,
　Went over the way;
Said my mother to your mother,
　"It's chop-a-nose day."

— c1830

In this infant amusement, the child's nose is held between finger and thumb, then "chopped off" with the other hand; the hand is then held up with the thumb protruding between two fingers to look like the chopped-off nose.

My father was a Frenchman,
A Frenchman, a Frenchman,
My father was a Frenchman,
And he bought me a fiddle.
　He cut it here,
　He cut it here,
He cut it through the middle.

— 1844

One must be careful with this ditty, not to get too rough with little ones. The "reciter" holds out the child's arm. At the first "cut it here," the child's wrist is gently struck. At the second, the shoulder is struck. At "cut it through the middle," the inner muscle of the elbow joint is struck, bringing the arm to a snappy "fold."

The following are "dandling" or "knee-trotting" rhymes. Very small children are bounced in the arms; toddlers are usually sat upon a crossed-knee, facing the adult, and held by both hands. The rhythm of the rhyme's words indicates how fast the child should be bounced. It's easy to add the right motions to the words. In some of the pieces, the words signify that at the end, the child should be slid down the leg to land on the foot.

To market, to market,
　To buy a plum bun;
Home again, home again,
　Market is done.

—Worlde of Wordes 1598

To market, to market,
　To buy a fat pig;
Home again, home again,
　Jiggety, jig.

—Nineteenth century variation

This is the way the ladies ride,
　Nimble, nimble, nimble;
This is the way the gentlemen ride,
　A gallop, a trot, a gallop, a trot;
This is the way the farmers ride,
　Jiggety jog, jiggety jog;
And when they come to a hedge—they jump over!
And when they come to a slippery place—
　They scramble, scramble, scramble;
　　Tumble-down quick! [Dick!]

—The Nursery Rhymes of England 1842

A farmer went trotting upon his gray mare,
　Bumpety, bumpety, bump!
With his daughter behind him, so rosy and fair,
　Lumpety, lumpety, lump!
A raven cried, "Croak," and they all tumbled down,
　Bumpety, bumpety, bump!
The mare broke her knees, and the farmer his crown,
　Lumpety, lumpety, lump!
The mischievous raven flew laughing away,
　Bumpety, bumpety, bump!
And vowed he would serve them the same the next day,
　Lumpety, lumpety, lump!

—Original Ditties for the Nursery 1805

Tickling rhymes also found their way into Mother Goose lore:

A good child, a good child,†
As I suppose you be,
You'll neither laugh nor smile,
At the tickling of your knee.

—Mid-nineteenth century

†*Or, "If you are a gentleman."*

Round and round the garden,
Like a teddy bear;
One step, two step;
 Tickle you under there!

         — Twentieth century

  The child's palm is traced with circles, then the "reciter's" hand "walks" up the child's arm, to tickle the child in the armpit at the end.

Round about there,
Sat a little hare;
The bow-wows came and chased him
 Right up there!

         — Twentieth century

  Like the previous infant amusement, the palm is circled, and a hand "walks" up the arm; then the hand reaches up and tickles the child around the neck.

Tickle you, tickle you, in the hand,
 If you laugh, you are a man.
 If you cry, you are a baby,
 If you dance, you are a lady.
An old maid, an old maid,
 You will surely be,
 If you laugh or if you smile,
 While I tickle round your knee.

         — Twentieth century

  "O My Kitten a Kitten..." in *Mother Goose's Melody* (page 66) is a game for tossing the child in the air. A more involved tossing game follows:

American jump, American jump,
One — two — three;
Down at the bottom of the deep blue sea,
Catching fishes for my tea.
 — Dead?
 — Or alive?
 — Or around the world?

       — Late nineteenth century

  The adult holds the child by both hands and jumps it up and down. At the word "three," the child is brought up so that its legs can wrap around the adult's waist. Then, slowly, while the next two lines are said, the child slowly falls backward until hanging upside down. The child then chooses an answer. "Dead" means the child is slid to the floor. "Alive" means the child will be pulled upright. "Around the world" means the child will be whirled around.

| | NINETEENTH CENTURY |
| TRADITIONAL VERSION | VARIATION |

TRADITIONAL VERSION	NINETEENTH CENTURY VARIATION
Two little blackbirds,	Two little dicky birds,
Sitting on a hill.	Sitting on a wall.
One was named Jack	One named Peter,
One was named Jill.	The other named Paul.
Fly away Jack.	Fly away Peter.
Fly away Jill.	Fly away Paul.
Come back Jack.	Come back Peter.
Come back Jill.	Come back Paul.
Two little blackbirds	
Sitting on a hill.	

Another version of this, the first recorded, appears in *Mother Goose's Melody* (c1765), but without any indication that it is an infant amusement, with accompanying actions. Goldsmith knew this sleight-of-hand trick though, for it is recorded that he used to amuse Laetitia-Matilda Hawkins with it when she was little. It is played thus:

Slightly moisten two small pieces of paper and stick them to the nails of the index fingers. *Lines 1 & 2:* place the two index fingers on the edge of a table. *Line 3:* bob right index finger, to indicate Jack. *Line 4:* bob left finger, to indicate Jill. *Line 5:* swing right hand up over head and then bring back to table, this time placing the middle finger on the table edge and concealing the index finger with the little paper marking Jack. *Line 6:* repeat motions of line five with left hand. *Line 7:* swing right hand over head again, this time bringing back the index finger. *Line 8:* repeat motions of line seven with left hand. *Lines 9 & 10:* rest both index fingers on the table edge.

Dingle dingle doosey
    The cat's in the well,
The dog's away to Bellingen,
    To buy the bairn a bell.

— Gammer Gurton's Garland (rev.) 1805

The editors of the revised *Gammer Gurton's Garland* explained the infant amusement above, saying, "This is a Scottish ditty, on whirling round

a piece of lighted paper to the child. The paper is called the dingle doosey."
J. Mactaggart, in *Gallovidian Encyclopedia* (1824) wrote, "A dingle doosey (or
dousie) is a piece of wood burned red at one end as a toy for children. The
mother will whirl round the ignited stick very fast, when the eye, by following
it, seems to see a beautiful red circle. She accompanies this pleasant show to
her bairns with the following rhyme":

> Dingle dingle-dousie,
>   The cat's a' lousy:
> Dingle dingle-dousie,
>   The dog's a' fleas.
> Dingle dingle-dousie,
>   Be crouse ay, be crouse ay;
> Dingle dingle-dousie,
>   Yese hae a brose o' pease. . . .

Also performed to this rhyme:

> Ringle, ringle, Red Belt,
> Rides wi' the king.
> Nae a penny in 's purse,
> T' buy a gold ring.

—1898

Modern practice is perhaps less flamboyant, but infinitely safer—the end
of the stick is marked with red nail polish or paint.

"Ring" or "Circle" games are a frequent infant amusement. Whether the
circle is two people holding hands, or more, the first Mother Goose circle-
rhyme to come to most minds is "Ring-a-round a rosie. . . ." The "traditional"
words, here, however, are different on the two sides of the Atlantic:

AMERICAN VERSION	BRITISH VERSION
Ring-a-round a rosie,	Ring-a-ring o' roses,
A pocket full of posies,	A pocket full of posies,
Ashes! Ashes!	A-tishoo! A-tishoo!
We all fall down.	We all fall down.

VARIATION ON LAST TWO LINES

> Hush! Hush! Hush! Hush!
> We've all tumbled down.

A rather far-fetched interpretation of this piece has had would-be origin-
finders speculating that it is based on the Great Plague of London (1665), as

> *Ring-a-ring-a-roses,*
> *A pocket full of posies ;*
> *Hush! hush! hush! hush!*
> *We're all tumbled down.*

witness the rash ("roses"), herbs and spices to sweeten the air ("posies"), sneezing, and implicit dying ("all fall down"). But the time-lapse between the plague and the appearance of the game diminishes that theory. Also heard is the theory that children sang this during the catastrophic European Black Death (1347), the "ring" supposedly referring to the red spot that marked the onset of the disease, and the rest following the same allegations heard for the plague theory, which is the one most often repeated.

William Wells Newell, in *Games and Songs of American Children* (1883), cited a version of 1790 (sung to the melody known in the twentieth century), as well as another variation:

1790 VERSION	VARIATION
Ring a ring a rosie,	Round a ring of roses,
A bottle full of posie,	Pots full of posies,

All the little girls in our town,   The one who stoops last
Ring for little Josie. . . .   Shall tell whom she loves best.

This appears to be the original wording, as no earlier is found — and gives
no impression of being connected with the effects of the plague. The "tumble
down" version was in the first printing of "Ring-a-round a rosie. . ." in a book
for children, in 1881, in Kate Greenaway's *Mother Goose*, where the rhyme
was given as:

Ring-a-ring-a-roses,
A pocket full of Posies;
Hush! hush! hush! hush!
We're all tumbled down.

Even here, there were no sneezes. Other nineteenth century versions
show the "fall" as a bow, curtsey, or stoop. English and Irish additional stanzas
even get the children back up again:

The cows are in the meadow
Lying fast asleep,
    A-tishoo! A-tishoo!
We all get up again.

The early patterns of the words show no real resemblance to the Black
Death or the plague. The interpretations continue to surface, however, probably because people in some perverse way would like to believe that the inno-
cent rhyme has a grim history. There are numerous variations on the English
wording, and like so many other Mother Goose ditties, similar versions in the
European countries.

Riddles, in addition to the lullabies and infant amusements, form the
base of most early nursery collections. A version of "Pease Porridge Hot. . ."
that combines the familiar clapping-game with a riddle, appears in *Mother
Goose's Melody* (see Chapter 4). Books that followed leaned even more heavily on riddles as Mother Goose material.

The riddles found in nursery lore were originally intended for adult
amusement. As they've come down through numerous printings the words
vary but little. Many lost favor because their answers became obsolete whereas
those that survived tended to have more constant factors. Some didn't make
the transition to children's literature. But some have had remarkably long
lives. Legend has it that the Greek poet Homer died of shame as a result of
not being able to fathom the answer to, "All that we caught, we left behind,
and carried away all that we did not catch." (The answer is "fleas.")

Riddle collections which later were translated into English appeared in

Bruges, Belgium, in c1478 (see Riddle 1 below), and in Strasbourg, Alsace, in 1505 (Riddle 2).

Wynken de Worde printed *Demaundes Joyous* or *Amusing Questions* in England in 1511, it being based on a French text of the same title which had appeared in c1490. It included the unanswerable, "Whiche was fyrst, the henne or the egge?" (Also: Riddle 3, below.)

Riddles, however, had their adult heyday in the Elizabethan period, at which time many were transformed into verse form. And it is those forms which survive in Mother Goosery.

The Booke of Meery Riddles, (together with proper Questions and witty Proverbs to make pleasant pastime) existed in England in 1600 and probably 25 years earlier. It had 77 riddles, including several still current in Mother Goose (Riddles 4–9). It was reprinted a number of times throughout the seventeenth century, with some additional riddles of 1831 making their way into the nursery (Riddles 10–12). Even then, they were deemed of interest to children, being said to be "Very meete and delightful for Youth to try their wits" (1629) and "No lesse vseful then behoouefull for any yong man or child, to know if he be quick-witted, or no'" (1631).

Another important early collection is contained in the British Manuscript (Harley 1960) written out by Randle Holme (1627–1699) evidently while still a youth and long before he wrote *The Academy of Armory*. The spelling is very poor, and it appears that the riddles were collected in the oral tradition, but the collection contained many of those which had appeared in formal riddle books (Riddles 3 & 13–17).

Helping to firmly entrench riddles in Mother Goose literature was the later *A Choice Collection of Riddles, Charades, Rebuses, &c*, by Peter Puzzlewell, Esq. (probably a pseudonym, possibly for Elizabeth Newbery), published in London by Elizabeth Newbery in 1792.

Perhaps it is not so curious, when one considers the difficulty of many of the riddles, that many are regarded merely as rhymes. In fact, they frequently appear simply as such, and some children never have it pointed out to them (perhaps because the adults don't know) that Nancy Etticoat, for instance, isn't really just an odd little girl (Riddle 13).

The adult scholar might well think of the rhymes separate from their already-known answers to assess how incongruous it is that they are presented for children to mull over. Fortunately, most Mother Goose books put the answer immediately following the verse; the scholar, too, may prefer this to mulling over the cryptic semantics.

1.   Twelve pears hanging high,
       Twelve knights riding by;
       Each knight took a pear,
       And yet left eleven there.

("Eachknight" was the name of one knight, who took one pear.) Although Halliwell, when he collected this in 1843, refrained from attempting an answer, the answer, as given, correlates with that of the circa 1478 version.

2.   What God never sees;
        What the king seldom sees;
        What we see every day;
        Read my riddle, I pray.

   (An equal.)

3. 1511 version:
        What is it that is a wryte and is no man, and he dothe that
        no man can, and yet it serueth both god and man?

   c1645 version:
        There is a Bird of great renown, usefull in citty & in
        town, none work like unto him can doe: hes yellow black
        & green a very pretty Bird I mean, yet he is both firce
        & fell, I count hin wise that can this tell.

   Traditional version:
        Little bird of paradise,
        She works her work both neat and nice;
        She pleases God, she pleases man,
        She does the work that no man can.

   (A bee, that makes honey and wax.)

4.   Two legs sat upon three legs
        With one leg in his lap;
        In comes four legs
        And runs away with one leg;
        Up jumps two legs,
        Catches up three legs,
        Throws it after four legs,
        And makes him bring back one leg.

(Two legs = a man; three legs = sitting on a three-legged stool; one leg = with a leg of mutton on his lap; four legs = a dog comes in; the dog steals the mutton; the man catches up the stool; throws the stool at the dog; and makes the dog bring back the leg of mutton.)

5. **1600 version:**
>I came to a tree where were Apples;
>I eat no apples, I gaue away no apple;
>Nor I left no apples behinde me.
>And yet I eat, gaue away, and left behinde me.

Traditional version:
>There was a man who had no eyes,
>He went abroad to view the skies,
>He saw a tree with apples on it,
>He took no apples off, yet left no apples on it.

(The man had one eye — not the same as "no eyes"; there were two apples on the tree; he took one apple and left one — which is not the same as "no apples.") One clever illustrator solved the problem by nailing to the tree a board marked APPLES.

6.   I went to the wood and I got it;
>I sat me down, and I sought it;
>I kept it still against my will
>And so by force home I brought it.

("I" had a thorn in the foot; a similar American answer is, "a briar.")

7. **1600 version:**
>What is that as high as a hall, as bitter as gall,
>As soft as silke, as white as milke?

Traditional version:
>As soft as silk, as white as milk,
>As bitter as gall, a thick wall,
>And a green coat covers me all.

(A walnut on a tree.)

8. **1600 version:**
>What is it that is higher then a house, and yet
>seems much lesser than a mouse?

Traditional version:
>Higher than a house,
>Higher than a tree;
>Oh, whatever can that be?

(A star.)

9. **1600 version:**

What is it goes through thicke and thin and drawes his
guts after him?

Traditional version:

Old Mother Twitchet has but one eye,
And a long tail which she can let fly,
And every time she goes over a gap,
She leaves a bit of her tail in a trap.

(A needle and thread.)

10. **1600 version:**

What be they which be full all day, and empty at night?

Traditional version:

Two brothers we are, great burdens we bear,
On which we are bitterly pressed;
The truth is to say, we are full all the day,
And empty we go to rest.

(A pair of shoes.)

11. **1631 version:**

Hitty pitty within the wall,
And hitty pitty without the wall.
If you touch hitty my toy,
Hitty pitty will bite the boy.

Traditional version:

Hitty Pitty within the wall,
Hitty Pitty without the wall;
If you touch Hitty Pitty,
Hitty Pitty will bite you.

(A nettle.)

12. **1631 version:**

There dwels a shoomaker neere the hall that makes his
shooes without a nawle; though men of them doe not
were, yet they of them have many a paire.

Traditional version:

> A shoemaker makes shoes without leather,
> With all the four elements put together,
> Fire, Water, Earth, Air,
> And every customer takes two pair.

(A blacksmith.)

13. **1631 version:**

> I am cald by name of man, yet am as little as the mouse:
> When winter comes, I loue to be with my red gorget
> neere the house.

Traditional version:

> I'm called by the name of man,
> Yet am as little as a mouse;
> When winter comes I love to be
> With my red target near the house.

(A robin redbreast.)

14. **1645 version:**

> I have a little boy in a whit cote,
> The biger he is the leser he goes.

Traditional version:

> Little Nancy Etticoat
> With a white petticoat,
> And a red nose;
> She has no feet or hands,
> The longer she stands
> The shorter she grows.

(A lighted candle.) Other names have been Little Miss Hetty Cote, Old Nancy Netty Cote, Little nannie neetie coat, Hitty hetty coat, and Nanny Goat.

15.   There was a king met a king
>   In a narrow lane;
> Said the king to the king,
>   Where have you been?
> I have been a-hunting
>   The buck and the doe.

Will you lend me your dog?
   Yes, I will do so;
Call upon him, call upon him.
   What is his name?
I have told you twice,
   And won't tell you again.

(Both men's names were "King," and the dog's name was "Bin.")

16. 1645 version:

On yonder hill ther stand a Knight booted & spured &
stands upright gray-grisled is his horse, black is his
saddle, I have tould yu his name thrice what is it say
you?

Traditional version:

There was a man rode through our town,
   Gray Grizzle was his name;
His saddle-bow was gilt and gold,
   Three times I've named his name.

(The man's name was "His.") When Halliwell collected this in 1846, he
did not offer the answer.

17. 1645 version:

Four and twenty white Bulls
sate upon a stall,
forth came the red Bull
and licked them all.

Traditional version:

Thirty white horses
Upon a red hill,
Now they tramp,
Now they champ,
Now they stand still.

(One's teeth and tongue.)

18. 1645 version:

What is yt that is rond as a cup yet all my lord oxen
cannot draw it up?

Traditional version:
 As round as an apple,
 As deep as a cup,
 And all the king's horses
 Cannot pull it up.

(A well.)

19. Circa 1730 version (Harley MS, 7316):
 As I went to St. Ives I met Nine Wives,
 And every Wife had nine Sacs,
 And every Sac had nine Cats,
 And every Cat had Nine Kittens.
 How many Wives, Sacs, Cats and Kittens
 Went to St. Ives?

Traditional version:
 As I was going to St. Ives,
 I met a man with seven wives.
 Each wife had seven sacks,
 Each sack had seven cats,
 Each cat had seven kittens.
 Kits, cat, sacks, and wives;
 How many were going to St. Ives?

(The answer to the c1730 version is "none"; they were not going to St. Ives, they were coming from. The answer to the traditional version is "one"; "I" was going to St. Ives.)

20. Make three-fourths of a cross,
  And a circle complete,
  And let two semi-circles
   On a perpendicular meet;
  Next add a triangle
   That stands on two feet;
  Next two semi-circles,
  And a circle complete.

(T - O - B - A - C - C - O.)

21. A house full, a hole full,
  And you cannot gather a bowl full.

(Mist or smoke.)

22.   As white as milk, and not milk;
        As green as grass, and not grass;
        As red as blood, and not blood;
        As black as soot, and not soot.

(A blackberry—from blossom to full ripeness.)

23.   In Spring I look gay,
           Decked in comely array,
        In Summer more clothing I wear.
           When colder it grows,
           I fling off my clothes,
        And in Winter quite naked appear.

(A tree.)

24.   Four stiff-standers,
        Four dilly-danders,
        Two lookers, two crookers,
        And a wig-wag.

(A cow.) Frederick Tupper, a twentieth century American authority on riddles, called this a "world riddle," saying it was an enigma that could be "traced for thousands of years through the traditions of every people."

25. 1810 version:
        Humpty dumpty sate on a wall,
        Humpti dumpti had a great fall;
        Threescore mene and threescore more,
        Cannot place Humpty dumpty as he was before.

Traditional version:
        Humpty Dumpty sat on a wall,
        Humpty Dumpty had a great fall;
           All the king's horses
           And all the king's men,
        Couldn't put Humpty together again.

(An egg.) This is probably the best-known of Mother Goose's riddles, affording illustrators the obviousness of portraying Humpty as an egg. Henry Bett, twentieth century linguistics scholar, said its antiquity "is to be measured in thousands of years, or rather it is so great that it cannot be measured at all." It seems to have appeared in print in English first in *Gammer*

Gurton's Garland in 1810, although there is a manuscript addition of 1803 for *Mother Goose's Melody* (where the last line was "Could not set Humpty Dumpty up again"). The riddle has the same form throughout Europe — as *Boule, boule* in France, *Annebadadeli* in Switzerland, *Lille-Trille* in Denmark, *Thille Lille* in Sweden, *Hillerin-Lillerin* in Finland, and as *Trille-Trölle, Wirgele-Wargele, Gigele-Gagele, Rüntzelken-Püntzelken*, and *Hümpelken-Pümpelken* in different parts of Germany.

The *Oxford English Dictionary* describes *humpty dumpty* as the name of a late-seventeenth century boiled ale-and-brandy drink. The nursery definition, which according to the OED does not appear before 1785, is given as "a little humpty dumpty man or woman; a short clumsy person of either sex."

Lullabies created by adults to soothe children, "infant amusements" created to entertain them, and riddles created to test the wits of other adults and then handed down to the nursery in rhyme-form — these were the basics of children's literature — to which were added in time story rhymes, nature rhymes, nonsense verse, tongue-twisters, proverbs, game songs, and other rhythmical entertainments.

SE faw, *Margery Daw*,
 Jacky fhall have a new Mafter ;
Jacky muft have but a Penny a Day,
 Becaufe he can work no fafter.

It is a mean and fcandalous Practice in Authors to put Notes to Things that deferve no
Notice.

Grotius.

GREAT

GREAT A, little a,
 Bouncing B ;
The Cat's in the Cupboard,
 And fhe can't fee.

Yes fhe can fee that you are naughty, and
don't mind your Book.

SE

4. Newbery's *Mother Goose's Melody*
With Oliver Goldsmith's Maxims

Publisher John Newbery can be credited with giving the name *Mother Goose* to the body of works then known as "nursery rhymes." Among the writers employed by Newbery was Oliver Goldsmith (1728–1774). To put the significance of his contribution to nursery literature in context, a slight review of his career is in order.

Born in Ireland, Goldsmith became a popular English poet, dramatist, and novelist. Although trained as a physician, he found no success in that profession and turned to writing. Considered eccentric but lovable, he counted among his friends Sir Joshua Reynolds, the celebrated English portrait painter; Edmund Burke, British statesman and political writer; David Garrick, celebrated actor and manager of the Drury Lane Theatre; and Dr. Samuel Johnson, author, poet, and also occasional writer for Newbery. (For more about Johnson, see page 158.)

Goldsmith's major works include the poems *The Traveller* (1764) and *The Deserted Village* (1770); his sole and now classic novel *The Vicar of Wakefield* (1766); and popular comedies, of which *She Stoops to Conquer* (1773) is a prime example. In 1784, he published a rather detailed tongue-in-cheek account of Aesop's life, *Bewick's Select Fables*.

He is also credited by scholars with authorship of two anonymous juvenile works he did for John Newbery. This conclusion is supported by Sir James Prior in his biography, *The Life of Oliver Goldsmith, M.B., from a Variety of Original Sources* (London: J. Murray, 1837; Philadelphia: E.L. Carey & A. Hart, 1837), a work which has been greatly praised for its diligence.

The children's classic *Little Goody Two-Shoes; otherwise called Mrs. Margery Two-Shoes* (1765) is one. The other is *Mother Goose's Melody; or Sonnets for the Cradle*. Although his name does not appear in the book, every piece of circumstantial evidence validates the reasonable conclusion that Goldsmith was the author/editor of the volume. Its publication date is generally agreed to be about 1765 (no copy of a dated first edition is preserved). Goldsmith was a "hack writer" for Newbery between 1762 and 1767. He was known to have a fondness for and rapport with children, and had a knowledge of the rhymes. Laetitia-Matilda Hawkins, for instance, recorded in her memoirs, "I little thought what I should have to boast, when Goldsmith taught me to play *Jack and Jill*, by two bits of paper on his fingers." (See page 117.)

Most of the nursery rhymes in the collection are followed by "notes" and "maxims" which bear the clear stamp of Goldsmith's sense of humor and wit, as well as being consistent with his character. The facetious attributions given to these pithy comments are truly Goldsmithian. Especially amusing is the self-deprecating jibe in the comment following "Margery Daw...," which parodies the notes and maxims in the *Melody* itself by asserting, "It is a mean and scandalous Practice in Authors to put Notes to Things that deserve no Notice."

In Newbery's first book for the young, the 1744 *A Little Pretty Pocket-Book*, a similar format of "morals" was used, but those are far different in tone from the ones in the *Melody*. Goldsmith's witticisms are more droll than didactic. His hand also can be seen in occasional strange titles that disguise familiar verses. The 51 rhymes of *Mother Goose's Melody* are those that were already traditional in 1765, for the book was a collection of existing works, but the maxims and notes, as well as the tongue-in-cheek preface, bear the stamp of Goldsmith's art.

The preface bears the strong imprint of Goldsmith's cleverness, as well as evidences of his trademarks or idiosyncrasies. Goldsmith had a distinct attachment to the verse "There was an old woman, tossed in a blanket..." which is beaded into the text of the preface. The words are the same version he was known to recite frequently. On January 29, 1768, he even sang it at the Literary Club to pretend he didn't care that his play, *The Good Natur'd Man*, had just been hissed off the stage. This is recorded in *Anecdotes of the Late Samuel Johnson* by Hester Lynch Piozzi (1786), with Johnson's comment about Goldsmith, "to impress them still more with an idea of his magnanimity, he even sang his favourite song about 'An old Woman tossed in a Blanket seventeen times as high as the Moon.'" The elaborate narrative of the song, purported to be about the Hundred Years' War and Henry V, is not folklore, but new fiction written for the preface. It has been suggested that the entire editing of the *Melody* should be interpreted as a parody aimed at Bishop Percy's *Reliques* of 1765, a work Goldsmith decried as pretentious.

The rhymes in the *Melody* are interesting not only for the record of their age, but from the standpoint of what was considered appropriate for children in those days. The words to the nursery rhymes in Part I are enlightening. The same old "violence" and "nonsense" prevail, but so do certain vulgarities. Our forefathers and mothers were evidently not prudish regarding children's reading matter. Those familiar with the rhymes will readily remember the current "traditional" rewritings. Among others, "Little Robin Redbreast..." in its original form, and the note to "A Doleful Ditty," might be considered crude, but one must admit to their realism. The large number of verses having to do with adult courtship might seem of little interest to children, and the sometimes earthy words indicate these may not have been children's verses at all. Many of them, however, with altered lines, have remained in nursery folklore to the present day.

After Part I, the reader is treated to 16 "Lullabies by Shakespear" (sic). There has been some speculation about whether Shakespeare might have written some of the political satires that found their way into nursery lore, but the careless researchers who claim that Shakespeare "contributed" to the *Melody* have neglected to note that the Bard's life span was 1565–1623. The choice of Shakespeare's "lullabies" is fascinating. They provide further insight into what was considered appropriate for children in the mid–eighteenth century. Newbery and Goldsmith may have initiated their publication in this genre, but the numerous pirated reprints of the *Melody* indicate that the book, nursery rhymes, maxims and notes, and lullabies, had a unique appeal. In all respects, it is a landmark publication.

The *Melody* is such an important little volume that its inclusion here as a chapter needs no excuse. Its influence is apparent on almost all subsequent editions of nursery rhymes. Its importance, however, is almost overshadowed by its sheer delight. Here are many old and familiar rhymes; set alongside them are nursery pieces once traditional and popular which are never seen in contemporary Mother Goose books. Here also, are some verses and maxims that Victorian readers found shocking. And here are the burlesque comments of Oliver Goldsmith added to the rhymes.

The text of the *Melody* which follows in this chapter is shown on the title page as being the Joel Munsell's Sons' (Albany) 1889 reprint of the Isaiah Thomas, Worcester, Massachusetts, reprint of circa 1785. It must be further noted, then, that the Thomas edition is said to be a facsimile of the original 1765 Newbery edition. However, one point is clouded in this quagmire of reprintings. That issue concerns the verse "Se saw, sacaradown,/ This is the way to *Boston* Town...," which English publishers carry as "...This is the way to *London* Town...." To further complicate the issue, some records indicate that Thomas's 1785 edition has not survived intact, and that it *did* say *London*, but that in his second "reprint," in 1794, the word was changed to *Boston*. Most likely the Newbery edition said *London*, but the text as shown in the Munsell edition has been followed here. (Including *Se* for *See*.) Incidentally, the use of the words "Boston Town" in editions before 1822 is sometimes questioned as being incorrect, and somehow suspect, as Boston received her charter as a town in 1822. History records, however, that Boston was settled in 1630, so that argument is specious.

Thomas's facsimile of the Newbery edition was a little book, the cover itself being a mere two and a half inches wide by three and three-quarter inches high. Each verse (except the Shakespearean lullabies) was ornamented with a small woodcut, one and three-quarter inches wide by one inch high. (Both text and woodcuts are somewhat blurred.) Newbery's original publication was "strongly bound and gilt," so *Mother Goose* evidently made her debut glitteringly adorned.

In order to convey the true sense of the original, only the barely readable "f"-like "s" has been converted. The text is as in the original, but the inconsistent type styles of the editorial comments are here set in consistent italics. Rhyme-numbering replaces the original's page-numbering. Erratic capitalizations, sometimes odd punctuation, and varied spellings are left intact.

The end-pages of the *Melody* carry a list of advertised books, among them the *Melody* itself:

> *"Books for the Instruction and Amusement of Children, which will make them wise and happy...*
> "Mother GOOSE's MELODY; or Sonnets for the Cradle. In two Parts. Part 1st, contains the most celebrated Songs and Lullabies of the old British Nurses, calculated to amuse Children and excite them to Sleep. Part 2d, those of that sweet Songster and Nurse of Wit and Humour, Master William Shakespeare. Embellished with Cuts, and illustrated with Notes and Maxims, Historical, Philosophical, and Critical."

PREFACE.

PREFACE

By a very Great Writer of

very Little Books

Much might be said in favour of this collection, but as we have no room for critical disquisitions we shall only observe to our readers, that the custom of singing these songs and lullabies to children is of great antiquity: It is even as old as the time of the ancient *Druids*. *Charactotus*, King of the *Britons*, was rocked in his Cradle in the Isle of *Mona*, now called *Anglesea*, and tuned to sleep by some of these soporiferous sonnets. As the best things however, may be made an ill use of, so this kind of compositions has been employed in a satirical manner of which we have a remarkable instance so far back as the reign of King Henry the fifth. When that *great monarch* turned his arms against *France*, he composed the preceding march to lead his troops to Battle, well knowing that musick had often the power of inspiring courage, especially in the minds of good men. Of this his enemies took advantage, and, as our happy nation, even at that time, was never without a fraction, some of the malcontents adopted the following words to the king's own march, in order to ridicule his majesty, and to shew the folly and impossibility of his undertaking.

> *There was an old woman toss'd in a blanket,*
> *Seventeen times as high as the moon;*
> *But where she was going no mortal could tell,*
> *For under her arm she carried a broom.*
> *Old woman, old woman, old woman, said I*
> *Whither, ah whither, ah whither so high?*
> *To sweep the cobwebs from the sky,*
> *And I'll be with you by and by.*

Here the king is represented as an old woman, engaged in a pursuit the most absurd and extravagant imaginable; but when he had routed the whole *French* army at the battle of *Agincourt*, taking their kind and the flower of their nobility prisoners, and with ten thousand men only made himself master of their kingdom; the very men who had ridiculed him before, began to think nothing was too arduous for him to surmount, they therefore cancelled the former sonnet, which they were now ashamed of, and substituted this in its stead, which you will please to observe goes to the same tune.

> *So vast is the prowess of Harry the Great,*
> *He'll pluck a Hair from the pale fac'd moon;*
> *Or a lion familiarly take by the tooth,*
> *And lead him about as you lead a baboon.*
> *All Princes and potentates under the sun,*
> *Through fear into corners and holes away run*
> *While no dangers nor dread his swift progress retards,*
> *For he deals about kingdoms as we do our cards.*

When this was shewn to his majesty he smilingly said that folly always dealt in extravagancies, and that knaves sometimes put on the garb of fools to promote in that disguise their own wicked designs. "The flattery in the last (says he) is more insulting than the impudence of the first, and to weak minds might do more mischief; but we have the old proverb in our favour—*If we do not flatter ourselves, the flattery of others will never hurt us.*"

We cannot conclude without observing, the great probability there is that the custom of making *Nonsense Verses* in our schools was borrowed from this practice among the old *British* nurses; they have, indeed, been always the first preceptors of the youth of this kingdom, and from them the rudiments of taste and learning are naturally derived. Let none therefore speak irreverently of this ancient maternity, as they may be considered as the great grandmothers of science and knowledge.

Mother GOOSE's *Melody*

A LOVE SONG

I.

1.

THERE was a little man,
Who woo'd a little maid,
And he said, little Maid will you wed, wed, wed?
I have little more to say,
So will you aye or nay.
For the least said is soonest men-ded, ded, ded.

II.

Then replied the little Maid she said,
Little Sir, you've little said,
To induce a little Maid for to wed, wed, wed;
You must say a little more,
And produce a little ore,
E'er I make a little print in your Bed, Bed, Bed.

III.

Then the little Man reply'd,
If you'll be my little Bride,
I will raise my Love Notes a little higher, higher, higher;
Tho' my offers are not meet,
Yet you'll find my Heart is great,
With the little God of Love all on Fire, Fire, Fire.

IV.

Then the little Maid reply'd,
Should I be your little Bride,
Pray, what must we have for to eat, eat, eat?
Will the Flame that you're so rich in
Light a fire in the Kitchen,
Or the little God of Love turn the Spit, Spit, Spit?

V.

Then the little man he sigh'd,
And, some say, a little cry'd,

For his little Heart was big with Sorrow, Sorrow, Sorrow;
As I am your little Slave,
If the little that I have,
Be too little, little, we will borrow, borrow, borrow.

VI.

Then the little Man so gent,
Made the little Maid relent,
And set her little Heart a-thinking, king, king;
Tho' his offers were but small,
She took his little All,
She could but the cat and her Skin, Skin, Skin.

He who borrows is another Man's Slave, and pawns his Honour, his Liberty, and sometimes his Nose for the payment. Learn to live on a little, and be independent.

Patch on Prudence.

A DIRGE. 2.

LITTLE *Betty Winckle* she had a Pig,
It was a little Pig not very big;
When he was alive he liv'd in Clover,
But now he's dead, and that's all over;
Johnny Winckle, he
　　Sate down and cry'd,
Betty Winckle she
　　Laid down and dy'd.
So there was an End of One, two, and three,
Johnny Winckle He,
Betty Winckle She,
And *Piggy Wiggie.*

A Dirge is a Song made for the Dead; but whether this was made for Betty Winckle *or her Pig, is uncertain; no Notice being taken of it by* Cambden, *or any of the famous Antiquarians.*

Wall's System of Sense.

A *melancholy* SONG. 3.

TRIP upon Trenchers,
And dance upon Dishes,
My mother sent me for some Bawn, some Bawn:
She bid me tread lightly,
And come again quickly,

For fear the young Men should do me some Harm.
Yet didn't you see,
Yet didn't you see,
What naughty tricks they put up on me,
They broke my Pitcher,
And spilt the Water,
And huffed my Mother,
And chid her Daughter,
And kiss'd my Sister instead of me.

What a Succession of misfortunes befel this poor Girl! But the last Circumstance was the most affecting, and might have proved fatal.

Winslow's View of Bath.

CROSS Patch, draw the Latch,   4.
Set by the Fire and spin;
Take a cup and drink it up,
Then call your Neighbors in.

A common Case this, to call in our Neighbors to rejoice when all the good Liquor is gone.

Pany.

Amphion's SONG of Eurydice.   5.
I WON'T be my Father's Jack,
I won't be my Father's Gill,
I will be the Fiddler's Wife,
And have musick when I will.
    T'other little tune,
    T'other little Tune,
    Prithee, Love, play me
    T'other little Tune.

Maxim. Those arts are the most valuable which are of the greatest use.

THREE wise men of *Gotham*   6.
    They went to Sea in a Bowl.
And if the Bowl had been stronger
    My song had been longer.

It is long enough. Never lament the Loss of what is not worth having.

Boyle.

THERE was an old Man,   7.
And he had a Calf,
And that's Half;
He took him out of the Stall,

And put him on the Wall,
    And that's all.
Maxim. Those who are given to tell all they know generally tell more than they know.

THERE was an old Woman   **8.**
Liv'd under a Hill,
She put a mouse in a Bag,
And sent it to Mill:
The Miller did swear
By the point of his Knife,
He never took Toll
Of a Mouse in his Life.
The only Instance of a Miller refusing Toll, and for which the Cat has just Cause of Complaint against him.

                                             Cock upon *Littleton.*

THERE was an old Woman   **9.**
Liv'd under a Hill.
And if she isn't gone
She lives there still.
This is a self evident Proposition, which is the very Essence of Truth. "She lived under the Hill, and if she is not gone she lives there still." Nobody will presume to contradict this.

                                               Crausa.

PLATO's SONG.   **10.**

DING dong Bell,
The Cat is in the Well.
Who put her in?
Little *Johnny Green.*
What a naughty boy was that,
To drown Poor Pussy Cat,
Who never did any Harm,
And kill'd the Mice in his Father's Barn.
Maxim. He that injures one threatens an Hundred.

LITTLE *Tom Tucker*   **11.**
Sings for his Supper;
What shall he eat?
White Bread and Butter:
How will he cut it,
Without e'er a Knife?

PLATO's SONG.

DING dong Bell,
  The Cat is in the Well.
Who put her in ?
Little *Johnny Green.*
What a naughty Boy was that,
To drown Poor Puffy Cat,
Who never did any Harm,
And kill'd the Mice in his Father's
    Barn.

  Maxim. *He that injures one threatens an Hundred.*

               LITTLE

LITTLE *Tom Tucker*
  Sings for his Supper ;
What shall he eat ?
White Bread and Butter:
How will he cut it,
Without e're a Knife ?
How will he be married,
Without e'er a Wife ?

  To be married without a wife is a terrible
Thing, and to be married with a bad Wife is
something worse ; however, a good Wife that
sings well is the best musical Instrument in the
World.
             Puffendorff.
                SE

    How will he be married,
    Without e'er a Wife?
  To be married without a wife is a terrible Thing, and to be married with a bad Wife is something worse; however, a good Wife that sings well is the best musical Instrument in the World.

                            Puffendorff.

    SE Saw, *Margery Daw,*   12.
    Jacky shall have a new Master;
    Jacky must have but a Penny a Day,
    Because he can work no faster.
  It is a mean and scandalous Practice in Authors to put Notes to Things that deserve no Notice.

                               Grotius.

    GREAT A, little a,   13.
      Bouncing B;
    The Cat's in the Cupboard,
      And she can't see.
  Yes she can see that you are naughty, and don't mind your Book.

Se saw, sacaradown,   14.
Which is the way to *Boston* Town?
One Foot up the other Foot down,
That is the Way to *Boston* Town.
Or to any other Town upon the Face of the Earth.

                                        Wickliffe.

SHOE the Colt,   15.
Shoe the Colt,
   Shoe the wild Mare;
Here a nail,
There a Nail,
   Yet she goes bare.
*Ay, ay, drive the Nail when it will go: That's the Way of the World, and
is the Method pursued by all our Financiers, Politicians, and Necromancers.*

                                        Vattel.

IS *John Smith* within?   16.
Yes, that he is.
Can he set a Shoe?
Aye, marry two.
Here a Nail, and there a Nail,
Tick, tack, too.
Maxim. Knowledge is a Treasure, but Practice is the Key to it.

HIGH diddle, diddle,   17.
The Cat and the Fiddle,
The Cow jump'd over the Moon;
The little Dog laugh'd
To see such Craft,
And the Dish ran away with the Spoon.
*It must be a little Dog that laugh'd, for a great Dog would be ashamed
to laugh at such Nonsense.*

RIDE a Cock Horse   18.
To Banbury Cross,
To see what *Tommy* can buy;
A Penny white Loaf,
A penny white Cake,
And a Two penny Apple Pye.
*There's a good Boy, eat up your Pye and hold your tongue; for Silence is
the sign of Wisdom.*

COCK a doodle doo,   19.
My Dame has lost her Shoe;
My Master's lost his Fiddle Stick,
And knows not what to do.

The Cock crows us up early in the Morning, that we may work for our Bread, and not live upon Charity or upon Trust; for he who lives upon Charity shall be often affronted, and he that lives upon Trust shall pay double.

THERE was an old Man   20.
In a Velvet Coat,
He kiss'd a Maid
And gave her a Groat;
The Groat it was crackt,
And would not go,
Ah, old Man, d'you serve me so?

Maxim. If the Coat be ever so fine that a Fool wears, it is still but a Fool's Coat.

ROUND about, round about,   21.
    Magotty Pye;
My Father loves good Ale,
    And so do I.

Maxim. Evil company makes the Good bad and the Bad worse.

JACK and *Gill*   22.
Went up the Hill,
To fetch a Pail of Water;
Jack fell down
And broke his Crown,
And *Gill* came tumbling after.

Maxim. The more you think of dying, the better you will live.

Aristotle's STORY.   23.
THERE were two Birds sat on a Stone,
Fa, la, la, la, lal, de;
One flew away, and then there was one,
Fa, la, la, la, lal, de;
The other flew after,
And then there was none,
Fa, la, la, la, lal, de;
And so the poor Stone
Was lost all alone,
Fa, la, la, la, lal, de.

This may serve as a Chapter of Consequence in the next new Book of Logick.

HUSH a by Baby 24.
   On the Tree Top,
When the Wind blows
   The Cradle will rock.
When the Bough breaks
   The Cradle will fall,
Down tumbles baby,
   Cradle and all.

This may serve as a Warning to the Proud and Ambitious, who climb so high that they generally fall at last.
Maxim. Content turns all it touches into Gold.

LITTLE *Jack Horner* 25.
Sat in a Corner,
   Eating of *Christmas* Pye;
He put in his Thumb,
And pulled out a Plumb,
   And what a good Boy was I.

Jack was a Boy of excellent Taste, as should appear by his pulling out a Plumb; it is therefore supposed that his Father apprenticed him to a Mince Pye maker, that he might improve his Taste from Year to Year; no one standing in so much Need of good Taste as a Pastry Cook.
                    Benley on the Sublime and Beautiful.

PEASE Porridge hot, 26.
   Pease Porridge cold,
Pease Porridge in the Pot
   Nine Days old,
Spell me that in four Letters?
   I will, T H A T.

Maxim. The poor are seldomer sick for Want of Food, than the Rich are by the Excess of it.

WHO comes here? 27.
   A Grenadier.
What do you want?
   A Pot of Beer.
Where is your Money?
   I've forgot.

Get you gone
You drunken Sot.
*Maxim. Intemperance is attended with Diseases, and Idleness with
Poverty.*

JACK *Sprat*   28.
Could eat no Fat,
His Wife could eat no Lean;
And so, betwixzt them both,
They lick'd the Platter clean.
Maxim. Better go to Bed supperless, than rise in Debt.

WHAT Care I how Black I be,   29.
Twenty Pounds will marry me;
If Twenty won't, Forty shall,
I am my Mother's bouncing Girl.
*Maxim. If we do not flatter ourselves, the Flattery of others would have
no effect.*

TELL Tale Tit,   30.
    Your Tongue shall be slit,
And all the Dogs in our Town
    Shall have a Bit.
Maxim. Point not at the Faults of others with a foul Finger.

ONE, two, three,   31.
Four and Five,
I caught a Hare alive;
Six, seven, eight,
Nine and ten,
I let him go again.
Maxim. We may be as good as we please, if we please to be good.

A DOLEFUL DITTY.   32.
I.
THREE Children sliding on the Ice
    Upon a Summer's Day,
As it fell out they all fell in,
    The rest they ran away.

II.
Oh! had these Children been at School,
    Or sliding on dry Ground,

Ten Thousand Pounds to one Penny,
They had not then been drown'd.

III.

Ye Parents who have children dear,
   And eke ye that have none,
If you would keep them safe abroad
   Pray keep them all at home.

There is something so melancholy in this Song, that it has occasioned many People to make Water. It is almost as diuretick as the Tune which John *the Coachman whistles to his Horses.*

Trumpingion's Travels.

PATTY Cake, Patty Cake,   33.
Baker's Man;
That I will Master,
As fast as I can;
Prick it and prick it,
And mark it with a T,
And there will be enough
For *Jackey* and me.

Maxim. The surest Way to gain our Ends is to moderate our Desires.

D

WHEN I was a little Boy   34.
   I had but little Wit,
'Tis a long Time ago,
   And I have no more yet;
Nor ever, ever shall,
   Until that I die,
For the longer I love,
   The more Fool am I.

Maxim. He that will be his own Master, has often a Fool for his Scholar.

I.   35.

WHEN I was a little Boy
   I liv'd by myself,
And all the Bread
And Cheese I got
   I laid upon the Shelf;
The Rats and the Mice
   They made such a Strife,
That I was forc'd to go to Town
   And buy me a Wife.

II.

The Streets were so broad,
　The Lanes were so narrow,
I was forc'd to bring my Wife home
　In a Wheelbarrow;
The Wheelbarrow broke;
　And my Wife had a Fall.
　　Farewel
Wheelbarrow, Wife and all.
Maxim. Provide against the worst, and hope for the best.

O MY Kitten a Kitten,   36.
And oh! my Kitten, my Deary,
Such a sweet Pap as this
There is not far nor neary;
There we go up, up, up,
Here we go down, down, down,
Here we go backwards and forwards,
And here we go round, round, round.
Maxim. Idleness has no Advocate, but many Friends.

THIS Pig went to Market,   37.
That Pig staid at Home;
This Pig had roast Meat,
That Pig had none;
This Pig went to the Barn door,
And cry'd Week, Week, for more.
Maxim. If we do not govern our Passions our Passions will govern us.

ALEXANDER'S SONG.   38.

THERE was a Man of *Thessaly*,
　And he was wond'rous wise,
He jump'd into a Quick set Hedge,
　And scratch'd out both his Eyes:
And when he saw his Eyes were out,
　With all his Might and Main,
He jump'd into another Hedge,
　And scratched them in again.
　*How happy it was for the Man to scratch his Eyes in again, when they were
scratched out! But he was a Blockhead, or he would have kept himself out of
the Hedge, and not been scratch'd at all.*

Wiseman's new Way to Wisdom.

Mother GOOSE's Melody. 57

A LONG tail'd Pig, or a fhort
tail'd Pig,
Or a Pig without any Tail ;
A Sow Pig, or a Boar Pig,
Or a Pig with a curling Tail.
Take hold of the Tail and eat off
his Head ;
And then you'll be fure the Pig hog
is dead.

CÆSAR's

58 Mother GOOSE's Melody.

CÆSAR's SONG.

BOW, wow, wow,
Whofe Dog art thou ?
Little *Tom Tinker's* Dog,
Bow, wow, wow.

Tom Tinker's Dog is a very good Dog, and
an honefter Dog than his Mafter.

BAH,

A LONG tail'd Pig, or a short tail'd Pig,   39.
Or a Pig without any Tail;
A Sow Pig, or a Boar Pig,
Or a Pig with a curling Tail.
Take hold of the Tail and eat off his Head;
And then you'll be sure the Pig hog is dead.

CAESAR's SONG.   40.

BOW, wow, wow,
Whose Dog art thou?
Little *Tom Tinker's* Dog,
Bow, wow, wow.
Tom Tinker's *Dog is a very good Dog, and an honester Dog than his
Master.*

BAH, bah, black Sheep,
Have you any Wool?
Yes, marry have I,
Three Bags full;
One for my master,
One for my Dame,

But none for the little Boy
  Who cries in the Lane.
Maxim. Bad Habits are easier conquored Today than Tommorrow.

ROBIN and *Richard*   42.
  Were two pretty Men,
They lay in Bed
  'Till the Clock struck Ten:
Then up starts *Robin*
  And looks at the sky,
Oh! Brother *Richard*,
  The Sun's very high;
You go before
  With the Bottle and Bag,
And I will come after
  On little *Jack Nag.*
What lazy Rogues were these to lie in Bed so long, I dare say they have
no Clothes to their Backs; for Laziness clothes a man with Rags.

THERE was an old Woman,   43.
  And she sold Puddings and Pies,
She went to the Mill
  And the Dust flew into her Eyes:
Hot Pies
  And cold Pies to sell,
Wherever she goes
  You may follow her by the Smell.
Maxim. Either say nothing of the Absent, or speak like a friend.

THE Sow came in with a Saddle,   44.
The little Pig rock'd the Cradle,
The Dish jump'd a top of the Table,
To see the Pot wash the Ladle;
The Spit that stood behind a Bench
Call'd the Dishclout dirty Wench;
Ods plut, says the Gridiron,
  Can't ye agree,
I'm the Head Constable,
  Bring 'em to me.
Note. If he acts as a Constable in this Case, the Cook must surely be the
Justice of Peace.

WE'RE three Brethren out of *Spain*   45.
Come to court your Daughter *Jane:*

My Daughter *Jane* she is too young,
She has no skill in a flattering Tongue,
Be she young or be she old,
It's for her Gold she must be sold;
So fare you well, my Lady gay,
We must return another Day.
Maxim. Riches serve a wise Man, and govern a fool.

THERE were two Blackbirds   46.
  Sat upon a Hill,
The one was nam'd *Jack,*
  The other nam'd *Gill,*
Fly away *Jack,*
  Fly away *Gill,*
Come again *Jack,*
  Come again *Gill.*
Maxim. A Bird in the Hand is worth two in the Bush.

E.

BOYS and Girls come out to play,   47.
The Moon does shine as bright as day;
Come with a Hoop, and come with a Call,
Come with a good Will or not at all.
Loose your Supper, and loose your Sleep,
Come to your Play fellows in the Street,
Up the Ladder and down the Wall,
A Halfpenny Loaf will serve us all.
But when the Loaf is gone, what will you do?
Those who would eat must work—'tis true.
Maxim. All Work and no Play makes Jack *a dull Boy.*

A Logical SONG; *or the*   48.
Conjuror's *Reason for not getting Money.*
I WOU'D if I cou'd,
If I coud'nt how cou'd I?
I coud'nt, without I cou'd, cou'd I?
Cou'd you, without you cou'd, cou'd ye?
  Cou'd ye, cou'd ye?
Cou'd you, without you cou'd cou'd ye?
Note. This is a new Way of handling an old Argument, said to be in-
vented by a famous Senator; but it has something in it of Gothick
Construction.

Sanderson.

A LEARNED SONG.   49.

HERE'S A, B, and C,
D, E, F, and G,
H, I, K, L, M, N, O, P, Q,
  R, S, T, and U,
W, X, Y, and Z,
And here's the child's *Dad,*
Who is sagacious and discerning,
And knows this is the Fount of Learning.

Note. This is the most learned Ditty in the World; for indeed there is no Song can be made without the Aid of this, it being the Gamut *and Ground Work of them all.*

Mope's *Geography of the Mind.*

A SEASONABLE SONG.   50.

PIPING hot, smoaking hot,
What I've got,
You know not,
Hot hot pease, hot, hot, hot;
Hot are my Pease, hot.

There is more Musick in this Song, on a cold frosty Night, than ever the Syrens were possessed of, who captivated Ulysses; *and the Effects stick closer to the Ribs.*

Huggleford *on Hunger.*

DICKERY, Dickery Dock,   51.
The Mouse ran up the Clock;
The Clock struck one,
The Mouse ran down,
Dickery, Dickery, Dock.
Maxim. Time stays for no Man.

MOTHER GOOSE's
M E L O D Y .
PART II.
CONTAINING THE
LULLABIES of *Shakespear.*

WHERE the Bee sucks, there suck I,   1.
In a Cowslip's Bell I lie.
There I couch; when Owls do cry,
On a Bat's Back I do fly,
After Summer, merrily.

Merrily, merrily shall I live now,
Under Blossoms that hang on the Bough.

YOU spotted Snakes, with Double Tongue   2.
    Thorny Hedghogs, be not seen;
Newts and Blind worms, do no Wrong;
    Come not near our Fairy Queen.
Philomel, with Melody,
Sing in your sweet Lullaby;
Lulla, lulla, lulla, lullaby; lulla lulla lullaby.
Never, Harm, nor Spell, nor Charm,
Come our lovely Lady nigh;
So good Night, with lullaby.

TAKE, oh! take those Lips away,   3.
That so sweetly were foresworn;
And those Eyes, the Break of Day,
    Lights that do mislead the *Morn:*
But my Kisses bring again.
Seals of Love, but seal'd in vain.

SPRING   4.

WHEN Daisies pied, and Vilets blue.
And Lady smocks all Silver white;
And Cuckow buds of yellow Hue,
Do paint the Meadows with Delight:
The Cuckow then on every Tree,
Mock's married Men, for thus sings he;
Cuckow!
Cuckow! cuckow! O Word of Fear,
Unpleasing to a married Ear!
When Shepherd's pipe on oaten Straws,
And merry Larks are Ploughmen's Clocks:
When Turtles tread, and Rooks and Daws,
And Maiden's bleach their Summer smocks:
The Cuckow then on every Tree,
Mock's married Men, for thus sings he;
Cuckow!
Cuckow! cuckow! O Word of Fear,
Unpleasing to a married Ear.

WHEN Icicles hang on the Wall,   5.
And *Dick* the Shepherd blows his Nail;

And *Tom* bears logs into the Hall,
   And Milk comes frozen home in Pail:
When Blood is nipt, and ways be foul,
Then nightly sings the staring Owl,
Tu-whit! to-whoo;
   A merry Note,
   While greasy *Joan* doth keel the Pot.
When all around the wind doth blow,
   And coughing crowns the Parson's Sow;
And Birds sit brooding in the snow,
   And *Marian's* Nose looks red and raw;
When roasted Crabs hiss in the Bowl,
Then nightly sings the staring Owl,
Tu-whit! To-whoo;
   A merry Note,
   While greasy *Joan* doth keel the Pot.

TELL me where is Fancy bred,   6.
Or in the Heart, or in the Head?
How begot, how nourished?
Reply, reply.
It is engender'd in the Eyes,
With gazing fed, and Fancy dies
In the Cradle where it lies;
Let us all ring Fancy's knell,
Ding, dong, Bell;
Ding, dong, Bell.

UNDER the greenwood Tree,   7.
   Who loves to lie with me,
And tune his merry Note,
Unto the sweet Bird's Throat:
Come hither, come hither, come hither,
   Here shall he see
   No Enemy,
But Winter and rough Weather.

WHO doth Ambition shun,   8.
And loves to lie i' th' Sun
Seeking the food he eats,
And pleas'd with what he gets;
Come hither, come hither, come hither,
   Here shall he see

No Enemy,
But Winter and rough Weather.
If it do come to pass,
That any Man turn Ass;
Leaving his Wealth and Ease,
A stubborn Will to please,
Duc ad me, duc ad me, duc ad me;
   Here shall he see
   Gross Fools,
And many such there be.

BLOW, blow, thou Winter Wind, 9.
Thou art not so unkind
   As Man's Ingratitude;
Thy Tooth is not so keen,
Because thou art not seen,
   Altho' thy Breath be rude.
Heigh ho! sing, heigh ho! unto the green Holly;
Most Friendship is feigning; most loving mere folly.
   Then heigh ho, the Holly!
   This life is most jolly.
Freeze, freeze, thou bitter sky,
That dost not bite so nigh,
   As Benefits forgot:
Tho' thou the Waters warp,
Thy Sting is not so sharp
   As Friend remember'd not,
Heigh ho! sing &c.

O MISTRESS mine, where are you running? 10.
O stay here, your true Love's coming,
   That can sing both high and low.
Trip no farther, pretty Sweeting,
Journeys end in Lovers meeting,
   Every wise Man's Son doth know.
What is Love? 'tis not hereafter:
Present Mirth hath present Laughter.
What's to come, is still unsure:
In Decay there lies no Plenty;
Then come kiss me, sweet and twenty,
   Youth's a Stuff will not endure.

WHAT shall he have that kill'd the Deer? 11.
His leather skin and horns to wear;

Then sing him home: — take thou no Scorn
To wear the Horn, the Horn, the Horn:
It was a Crest ere tough wast born.
Thy Father's Father wore it,
And thy Father bore it.
The Horn, the Horn, the lusty Horn,
Is not a Thing to laugh to scorn.

WHEN Daffodils begin to 'pear,   12.
  With heigh! the Doxy over the Dale;
Why then comes in the Sweet o'th' Year,
  Fore the red Blood rains in the winter Pail,
The white Sheet bleaching on the Hedge,
  With heigh! the sweet Birds, O how they sing!
Doth set my progging Tooth an edge:
  For a Quart of Ale is a dish for a King.
The Lark, that tira lyra chants.
  With hey! with hey! the Thrush and the Jay:
Are summer Songs for me and my Aunts,
  While we lay tumbling in the Hay.

JOG on, jog on, the foot path Way,   13.
And merrily mend the Style a,
A merry Heart goes all the Day,
Your sad ties in a Mile a.

ORPHEUS with his Lute made Trees,   14.
And the Mountain Tops that freeze,
  Bow themselves when he did sing;
To his Musick, Plants and Flowers
Ever rose, as Sun and Showers
  There had made a lasting Spring.
Ev're Thing that heard him play,
Ev'n the Bellows of the Sea,
  Hung their Heads, and then lay by.
In sweet Musick is such Art,
Killing Care, and Grief of Heart,
  Fall asleep or hearing die.

HARK, hark! the Lark at Heav'n's Gate sings,   15.
  And *Phoebus'* gins arise,
His steeds to water at those Springs
  On chalic'd Flowers that lies,

And winking May buds begin
  To ope their golden Eyes,
With every thing that's pretty been;
  My Lady sweet, arise:
    Arise, arise.

THE poor Soul sat singing by a Sycamore tree,   16.
Her Hand on her Bosom, her Head on her Knee,
The fresh Streams ran by her, and murmur'd her Moans,
Her salt Tears fell from her, and soften'd the Stones;
  Sing, all a green Willow must be my Garland,
Let nobody blame him, his Scorn I approve,
I call'd my Love, false Love; but what said he then?
If I court more Women you'll think of more Men.

FINIS.

5. ABC's and 1, 2, 3's
Alphabets, Numbers, and Mnemonic Rhymes

Along with many of the traditional nursery rhymes, Mother Goose's ABC's have a long history in the classroom. Other alphabet devices have been based on Bible analogies or in primers using simple word lists printed alongside each letter of the alphabet, but the nursery versions have been the most-loved. Although intended to teach the alphabet to children, these compositions have been carried over onto the playground, and have a long tradition in picture books. Entire picture books have been devoted to the text and illustrations of only one alphabet rhyme.

As studies in children's literature, they show the changing alphabet, changing analogies thought pertinent to children, and varied patterns of rhythm. Many of the older alphabet-rhymes have been updated to include the complete set of 26 letters known in the contemporary alphabet.

In the eighteenth century, "I" served for "J"; "U" served for "V"; and "W" often appeared as "UU" or "Double U". These letters did not, therefore, appear in some of the nursery alphabets. Curiously, some omitted "U" and others omitted "V". In some alphabet rhymes, the letters "H" and "T" were also omitted, for whatever reason. (Also, "G" was often substituted for "J" in spelling, so that the older versions of nursery rhymes often refer to *Gill* rather than *Jill*—making *Iack* and *Gill*.)

Of particular note is a 1440 alphabet-rhyme collected from oral tradition and documented in 1849 by James O. Halliwell in *Popular Rhymes and Nursery Tales*: "Amongst the various devices to establish a royal road to infantine learning, none are more ancient or useful than the rhymes which serve to impress the letters of the alphabet upon the attention and memory of children. As early as the fifteenth century, 'Mayster Benet,' who was rector of Sandon, in Essex, in 1440, and afterwards a prebend of St. Paul's, composed or translated an alphabet rhyme, which not only professed to recall the memory of the letters, but at a time when the benefit of clergy was in vogue, held out the inducement of providing means for avoiding the punishment of death. The following copy is taken from two versions in MS. Harl. 541, compared with each other."

Who so wyll be wyse and worshyp to wynne, leern he on lettur and loke upon another of the A. B. C. of Arystotle. Noon argument agaynst that, ffor it is counselle for clerkes and knightes a thowsand; and also it myght amend a meane man fulle oft the lernyying of a lettur, and his lyf save. It shal not greve a good man, though gylt be amend. Rede on this ragment, and rule the theraftur, and whoso be grevid yn his goost governe the better. Herkyn and here every man and child how that I begynne:

A. to Amerous, to Aventurous, ne Angre the not to moche.
B. to Bold, to Besy, and Bourde not to large.
C. to Curtes, to Cruel, and Care not to sore.
D. to Dulle, to Dredefulle, and Drynk not to oft.
E. to Ellynge, to Excellent, ne to Ernstfulle neyther.
F. to Ferse, ne to flamilier, but Friendely of chere.
G. to Glad, to Gloryous, and Gelowsy thow hate.
H. to Hasty, to Hardy, ne to Hevy yn thyne herte.
J. to Jettyng, to Janglyng, and Jape not to oft.
K. to Keping, to Kynd, and ware Knaves tatches among.
L. to Lothe, to Lovying, to Lyberalle of goodes.
M. to Medlus, to Mery, but as Maner asketh.

N. to Noyous, to Nyce, nor yet to Newefangle.
O. to Orpyd, to Ovyrthwarte, and Othes thou hate.
P. to Preysyng, to Privy, with Prynces ne with dukes.
Q. to Queynt, to Querelous, to Quesytife of questions.
R. to Ryetous, to Revelying, ne Rage not to meche.
S. to Straunge, ne to Sterying, nor Stare not to brode.
T. to Taylous, to Talewyse, for Temperaunce ys best.
V. to Venemous, to Vengeable, and Wast not to Myche.
W. to Wyld, to Wrothfulle, and Wade not to depe,
   A mesurabulle meane Way is best for us alle.

The alphabet above is important to nursery literature in that it is the
earliest documented English-language alphabet-rhyme intended for the instruction of children. It does not, however, appear to have ever been
transliterated to modern English. Its laborious lines are probably the reason
it did not stay in vogue as child lore.

Following are some of the traditional alphabet verses found in Mother
Goose.

"The Tragical Death of A. Apple-pye, who was cut in pieces and eat by
twenty-five gentlemen, with whom all little people ought to be very well
acquainted."

A apple-pye [A was an apple pie],
B bit it,
C cut it,
D dealt it,
E eat it,
F fought for it,
G got it,
H had it,
J join'd for it [J jumped for it; later: I inspected it],
K kept it,
L long'd for it,
M mourn'd for it,
N nodded at it,
O open'd it,
P peep'd in it,
Q quarter'd it,
R ran for it,
S stole it,
T took it,

V viewed it, [later: U upset it]
W wanted it,
X. Y. Z. and Ampersy-and [later: ampersand]
They all wish'd for a piece in hand.†

At last they every one agreed
Upon the apple-pye to feed;
But as there seem'd to be so many,
Those who were last might not have any.
Unless some method there was taken,
That every one might save their bacon.
They all agreed to stand in order
Around the apple-pye's fine border.
Take turn as they in hornbook stand,
From great A down to &,
In equal parts the pye divide,
As you may see on t'other side.

(Halliwell here comments that a woodcut shows the pie surrounded by a square of letters, "though it is not very easy to perceive how the conditions of the problem are to be fulfilled.") The remainder of the book goes:

"A Curious Discourse that passed between the twenty-five letters at dinner-time."

Says A, give me a good large slice.
Says B, a little bit, but nice.
Says C, cut me a piece of crust.
Take it, says D, it's dry as dust.
Says E, I'll eat now fast, who will.
Says F, I vow I'll have my fill.
Says G, give it me good and great.
Says H, a little bit I hate.
Says I, I love the juice the best,
And K the very same confest.
Says L, there's nothing more I love,
Says M, it makes your teeth to move.
N noticed what the others said;
O other's plates with grief survey'd.
P praised the cook up to the life,
Q quarrel'd cause he'd a bad knife.
Says R, it runs short, I'm afraid.

†*Most versions end here.*

S silent sat, and nothing said.
T thought that talking might lose time;
U understood it at meals a crime.
W wish'd there had been a quince in'
Says X, those cooks there's no convincing.
Says Y, I'll eat, let others wish.
Z sat as mute as any fish,
While Amerpersy-and he licked the dish.

—1671 or earlier

This alphabet story has been dated back to at least 1671, by virtue of having been quoted then by the theologian, John Eachard. Halliwell collected and documented it as probably even older than the time of Charles II (1630–1685) as Eachard did not appear to have noted it as a novelty. Halliwell included the entire piece in his 1849 *Popular Rhymes and Nursery Tales.* Its omissions of "I" and "U" in the first part, but "J" and "V" in the second are curious, inasmuch as Halliwell indicates his version, although existing in oral tradition, is taken from a single small 32mo. book printed by Marshall of Aldermary Churchyard "some half-century since." The differing omission of letters and the difference in style of verse might indicate that the latter section was added to the first by another writer.

The first section, being the simplest also, is the one most frequently seen, untitled, with *pye* changed to the later *pie* and the contractions spelled out. Occasionally, some of the lines have varied from the traditional. "A was an Apple Pie" appeared in a 1743 spelling book, *The Child's New Plaything* published by Mary Cooper, in the 1761 *Tom Thumb's Play Book* published by A. Barclay in Boston, and since then, in numerous Mother Goose books. The last section, without the first and second, also has been included in various nursery books.

A was an Archer, and shot at a Frog;
B was a Blind man, and led by a dog;
C was a Cutpurse, and lived in disgrace;
D was a Drunkard, and had a red face;
E was an Eater, a Glutton was he;
F was a Fighter, and fought with a Flea;
G was a Gyant, and pulled down a House;
H was a Hunter, and hunted a Mouse;
I was an ill Man, and hated by all;
K was a Knave, and he robbed great and small;
L was a Liar, and told many Lies;
M was a Madman, and beat out his Eyes;
N was a Nobleman, nobly born;

O was an Ostler, and stole Horse's Corn;
P was a Pedlar, and sold many Pins;
Q was a Quarreller, and broke both his Shins;
R was a Rogue, and ran about Town;
S was a Sailor, a Man of Renown;
T was a Taylor, and Knavishly bent;
U was a Usurer took ten percent;
W was a Writer, and Money he earned;
X was one Xenophon, prudent and learned;
Y was a Yeoman, and worked for his Bread;
Z was one Zeno the Great, but he's dead.

—*Early eighteenth century*

This appeared in England around the turn of the century, and reappeared in Boston around 1761. Several alphabets of the nineteenth century began with "A was an Archer," the most famous of which is given further on.

Great A, B, and C,
And tumble down D.
The Cat's a blind Buff,
And she cannot see.

Great E, F, and G,
Come here follow me,
And we'll jump over
The Rosemary Tree.

Here's great H, and I
With the Christmas Pie;
Who will eat the Plums out?
I, H, and I.

Here's great K, and L,
Pray Dame can you tell,
Who put the Pig-Hog
Down into the Well?

Here's great M, and N,
Are come back again,
To bring the good Boy
A fine Golden Pen.

So great O, and P,
Pray what do you see?

A naughty boy whipt;
But that is not me.

Here's great Q, and R,
Are both come from far,
To bring you good news
About the French War [later: "late war"].

So S, T, and U,
Pray how do you do?
We thank you—the better
For seeing of you.

Here's W, and X,
Good Friends do not vex,
All Things will go well
Dear W, and X.

There's great Y, and Z,
On a Horse that is mad;
If you fall down, Farewel [sic]
Poor great Y and Z.

—*ca.1744*

This appeared in Newbery's first publication, *A Little Pretty Pocket-Book*, in 1744.

Great A, little a,
Bounceing B;
The Cats in ye Cupboard,
And She can't See.

—*ca.1744*

This first appeared in print in Cooper's 1744 *Tommy Thumb's Pretty Song Book*. It is said to be the origin of publishers of juvenile books displaying the device "AaB" in their signs. The London printer's shop of John Marshall became known colloquially as the "Great A and Bouncing B Toy Factory." (See also *Mother Goose's Melody*, page 60.)

Here's A, B, and C,
D, E, F, and G,
H, I, K, L, M, N, O, P, Q,
R, S, T, and U,
W, X, Y, and Z,
And here's the child's Dad,

Who is sagacious and discerning,
And knows this is the Fount of Learning.

—ca.1765

(For Oliver Goldsmith's maxim, see *Mother Goose's Melody*, page 70.)

Alternate words for the last three lines (reduced to two) appeared later in an American version:

And here's good Mama, who knows,
This is the font whence learning flows.

—ca.1825; Mother Goose's Quarto

Other concluding lines follow this version:

Here's A, B, C, D, E, F, and G,
H, I, J, K, L, M, N, O, P, Q, R, S, T, U, V,
W, X, Y, and Z—
And O, dear me,
When shall I learn
My A, B, C.

—1869 or earlier

William Wheeler collected the above version in 1869 in his edition of *Mother Goose's Melody*, noting that "O, dear me" "is thought to be a corruption of the Italian *O Dio mio*," meaning "O my God." Note that this version contains all 26 letters of the alphabet.

A for the ape, that we saw at the fair;
B for a blockhead, who ne'er shall go there;
C for a collyflower, white as a curd,
D for a duck, a very good bird;
E for an egg, good in puddings and pies;
F for a farmer, rich, honest, and wise;
G for a gentleman, void of all care;
H for the hound, that ran down the hare;
I for an Indian, sooty and dark;
K for the keeper, that looked in the park;
L for a lark, that soared in the air;
M for a mole, that ne'er could get there;
N for Sir Nobody, ever in fault;
O for an otter, that ne'er could be caught;
P for a pudding, stuck full of plums;

Q was for quartering it, see here he comes;
R for a rook, that croaked in the trees;
S for a sailor, that ploughed the deep seas;
T for a top, that doth prettily spin;
V for a virgin, of delicate mien;
W for wealth, in gold, silver, and pence;
X for old Xenophon, noted for sense;
Y for a year, which forever is green;
Z for the zebra, that belongs to the queen.

—Early nineteenth century

Great A was alarmed at B's behavior,
Because C, D, E, F, denied G a favor.
H had a husband, with I, J, K, and L.
M married Mary, and taught her scholars how to spell;
A, B, C, D, E, F, G, H, I, J, K, L, M, N,
O, P, Q, R, S, T, U, V, Double U, X, Y, Z.

—ca.1816

An 1856 comment in *Notes & Queries* indicated the above as having been known forty years previously. William Wheeler included this in the 1869 edition of *Mother Goose's Melody* which he edited. Note the absence of "W" and the presence of "Double U." Later versions tend to correct this.

A, B, C, and D,
Pray, playmates, agree.
E, F, G,†
Well so it shall be.
J, K, and L,
In peace we will dwell.
M, N, and O,
To play let us go.
P, Q, R, and S,†
W, X, and Y,
Will not quarrel or die.
Z, and amperse-and,
Go to School at command.

†*This version is missing five letters—H, I, T, U, V.*

The following three alphabet-rhymes exhibit words and patterns more in keeping with other later nineteenth century works for children. Also, they include all 26 letters of the alphabet. They are undated, but have appeared in

Mother Goose books for some time. They illustrate not only diverse approaches, but also diverse lengths. The third, with a verse to each letter, is much more child-oriented in subject matter than the second.

As A was sitting half Asleep,
    "It's time for Bed," said B;
C Crept into her little Cot,
    To Dreamland, off went D.
E closed his eyes, F fretful grew,
    "Good-night," G softly said,
H Hurried up the wooden Hill,
    I put Itself to bed.
J Jumped for Joy when bedtime came,
    K Kissed good-night all round,
L Lit the Lamp, M struck the Match,
    The land of Nod N found.
O Owned that he was Over-tired,
    to Pillowland P Pressed,
Q Queried why it was so Quiet,
    When R Retired to Rest.
S went in search of Slumberland,
    Too Tired was T To stay,
U went Upstairs, V Vanished too,
    And W led the Way.
When X eXclaimed, "How Y does Yawn,"
    With Zest responded Z,
"Dear me, it seems I'm last of all,"
    And tumbled into bed.

(The verse below is sometimes called "Tom Thumb's Alphabet.")

A was an archer, who shot at a frog,
B was a butcher, and had a great dog,
C was a captain, all covered with lace,
D was a drunkard, and had a red face,
E was an esquire, with pride on his brow,
F was a farmer, and followed the plough,
G was a gamester, who had but ill-luck,
H was a hunter, and hunted a duck,
I was an innkeeper, who loved to carouse,
J was a joiner, and built up a house,
K was King William, once governed this land,
L was a lady, who had a white hand,

M was a miser, and hoarded up gold,
N was a nobleman, gallant and bold,
O was an oyster girl, and went about town,
P was a parson, and wore a black gown,
Q was a queen, who wore a silk slip,
R was a robber, and wanted a whip,
S was a sailor, and spent all he got,
T was a tinker, and mended a pot,
U was a usurer, a miserable elf,
V was a vintner, who drank all himself,
W was a watchman, and guarded the door,
X was expensive, and so became poor,
Y was a youth, that did not love school,
Z was a zany, a poor harmless fool.

—Mid-nineteenth century

A was an angler,
    Went out in a fog,
    Who fished all the day,
    And caught only a frog.
B was cook Betty,
    A-baking a pie,
    With ten or twelve apples
    All piled up high.
C was a custard,
    In a glass dish,
    With as much cinnamon
    As you could wish.
D was fat Dick,
    Who did nothing but eat,
    He would leave book or play
    For a nice bit of meat.
E is an egg,
    In a basket with more,
    Which Peggy will sell
    For a shilling or more.
F is a fox,
    So cunning and sly,
    Who looks at the hen roost,
    I need not say why.
G was a greyhound,
    As fleet as the wind,
    In the race or the course,

Left all others behind.

H was a heron,
   Who lived near a pond,
   Of gobbling of fishes,
   He was wondrously fond.

I was the ice,
   On which Billy would skate,
   So up went his heels,
   And down went his pate.

J was Joe Jenkins,
   Who played on the fiddle,
   He began twenty times,
   But left off in the middle.

K was a kitten,
   Who jumped at a cork,
   And learned to eat mice,
   Without plate, knife, or fork.

L is a lark,
   Who sings us a song,
   And wakes us betimes,
   Lest we sleep too long.

M was Miss Molly,
   Who turned in her toes,
   And hung down her head,
   Till her knees touched her nose.

N was a nosegay,
   Sprinkled with dew,
   Pulled in the morning,
   And presented to you.

O is an owl,
   Who looks wondrously wise,
   But he's watching a mouse
   With his large round eyes.

P is a parrot,
   With feathers like gold,
   Who talks just as much,
   And now more than he's told.

Q is the Queen,
   Who governs the land,
   And sits on a throne,
   Very lofty and grand.

R is a raven,
   Perched on an oak,

Who with a gruff voice,
Cries "croak, croak, croak."
S is a stork,
With a very long bill,
Who swallows down fishes
And frogs to his fill.
T is a trumpeter,
Blowing his horn,
Who tells us the news
As we rise in the morn.
U is a unicorn,
Who, it is said,
Wears an ivory bodkin
On his forehead.
V is a vulture,
Who eats a great deal,
Devouring a dog
Or a cat at a meal.
W was a watchman,
Who guarded the street,
Lest robbers or thieves,
The good people should meet.
X was King Xerxes,
Who, if you don't know,
Reigned over Persia,
A great while ago.
Y is the year,
That is passing away,
And still growing shorter
Every day.
Z is a zebra,
Whom you've heard before,
So here ends my rhyme,
Till I find you some more.

Nobody ever said Mother Goose rhymes were perfect. This alphabet-rhyme has disconcerting switches from present to past tense which modern editors eschew. The occasional self-reference to the writer-rhymer is typical of many folk rhymes and songs of the era.

The old rhymes spawned many new alphabet picture books in the twentieth century. Unless their authors are very well-known in their own right, which is uncommon among poets for children, they, too, may find their works absorbed into the realms of Mother Goose land some day.

Numbers and counting were also natural subjects for instruction which could be made more palatable when put in verse rhyme. Whether this or pure fun was the intention of the creators, they have had long lives in the classroom and on the playground as well. Educators have long known that learning can be fun, and that fun-learning is more easily absorbed. And every teacher and parent knows that the child who has just learned to count is delighted with the knowledge and wont to repeat it ad infinitum.

The number-counting rhymes are frequently used as fingerplays, counting off the fingers in turn. The originators of the traditional Mother Goose rhymes are unsung writers, but their little works have lingered on. Among the traditional 1, 2, 3's are:

One, two, three, four, five,
Once I caught a fish alive,
Six, seven, eight, nine, ten,
Then I let him go again.
    Why did you let him go?
    Because he bit my finger so.
    Which finger did he bite?
    This little finger on the right.

—ca.1888

(A better known and earlier version, ca.1765, appears, with maxim, on page 64.)

One, two, buckle my shoe;
Three, four, shut the door;   open the door
Five, six, pick up sticks;
Seven, eight, lay them straight;
Nine, ten, a big fat hen;
Eleven, twelve, dig and delve;   I hope you're well
Thirteen, fourteen, draw the cur-   maid's a'courting
    tain;
Fifteen, sixteen, maids in the
    kitchen;
Seventeen, eighteen, maids in
    waiting;
Nineteen, twenty, my stomach's   my plate's empty.
    empty.
    (Sometimes added: *Please, Ma'am to give me some dinner*).
                            —Late eighteenth century

One, two, three, four,
Mary at the cottage door,

Five, six, seven, eight,
Eating cherries off a plate,†
Nine, ten, eleven, twelve,
Peasants oft in ditches delve.

—ca.1815

†*Frequently ends here.*

One potato, two potato,
Three potato, four.
Five potato, six potato,
Seven potato, more,
Eight potato, nine potato,
Ten potato, then,
Start all over and do it again.

John Brown had a little Indian,
John Brown had a little Indian,

John Brown had a little Indian,
  One little Indian boy.
One little, two little, three little Indians,
Four little, five little, six little Indians,
  Seven little, eight little, nine little Indians,
  Ten little Indian boys.
Ten little, nine little, eight little Indians,
Seven little, six little, five little Indians,
Four little, three little, two little Indians,
  One little Indian boy.

This is both a two-way fingerplay, and a technique for learning the numbers in reverse. (See also, "Ten Little Injuns...," page 200.)

When V and I together meet,
They make the number Six compleat [sic]
When I with V doth meet once more,
Then 'tis they Two can make but Four.
And when that V from I is gone,
Alas! poor I can make but One.

−1686

The roman numeral ditty above, before being adopted by Dame Goose, was originally a "catch" or round, which appeared in *The Pleasant Musical Companion* in 1686. In addition to the lesson in numerals, there is the pun involved if one remembers that V once served as both V and U (you).

X shall stand for playmates Ten;
V for Five stout stalwart men;
I for One, As I'm alive;
C for a Hundred, and D for Five;
M for a Thousand soldiers true;
And all these figures I've told to you.

−1886

This little piece of doggerel for learning Roman Numerals appeared in an edition of *Mother Goose Nursery Rhymes* in 1886.

One's none;
Two's some;
Three's many;
Four's a penny;
Five's a little hundred

−1842 or earlier

This little ditty was collected by Halliwell; there was at one time a custom of reciting it when presenting sweet-treats to another.

Traditional	1833 New England variant

One I love, two I love,
Three I love, I say.
Four I love with all my heart,
Five I cast away.
Six he loves, seven she loves,
   eight both love.
Nine he comes, ten he tarries,
Eleven he courts, twelve he
   marries.

Thirteen they quarrel,	Thirteen wishes,
Fourteen they part,	Fourteen kisses,
Fifteen he dies	All the rest,
Of a broken heart.	Little witches.

This is usually said as flower petals or apple seeds are counted. The custom is believed to go back at least as far as the end of the twelfth century, where it is referred to in other literature. Simpler versions, which omit the 1, 2, 3's, occur as:

He (she) loves me, he (she) loves me not, he loves me, he loves me not, etc.

He (she) loves me, he don't,
He'll have me, he won't,
He would if he could,
But he can't, so he don't.

Both ABC's and numbers have been incorporated into mnemonic devices. Among the best known and oldest of the rhymes designed to assist memory is the formula for knowing how many days there are in each month:

Thirty days hath September,
April, June, and November;
All the rest have thirty-one,
Excepting February alone,
And that has twenty-eight days clear,
And twenty-nine in each leap year.

By 1825, this had appeared in most nursery rhyme books, considered as traditional. It goes back several generations from that date.

A thirteenth century French poem, *De Compute* incorporates it. In 1577 William Harrison translated a Latin verse which may date to the same period as the French:

> Thirty dayes hath Nouember,
> Aprill, Iune and September;
> Twentie and eyght hath Febrary alone,
> And all the rest thirty and one,
> But in the leape you must adde one.

> Thirtie daies hath September,
> Aprill, June, and November;
> The rest haue thirty and one,
> Saue February alone,

Which moneth hath but eight and twenty meere,
Saue when it is a Bissextile or Leape-yeare.

—before 1612

The above version was quoted by Arthur Hopton in *A Concordancy of Yeares* in 1612, indicating it was taken already old from the Latin.

Other versions followed the pattern rather closely, although the following takes another approach:

Fourth, eleventh, ninth, sixth,
Thirty days to each affix;
Every other thirty-one,
Except the second month alone,
Which hath but twenty-eight in fine,
Till leap year give it twenty-nine.

—Late nineteenth century

Dirty days hath September,
April, June, and November;
From January up to May,
The rain it raineth every day.
February hath twenty-eight alone,
And all the rest have thirty-one.
If any of them had two and thirty,
they'd be just as wet and dirty.

—Parody by Thomas Hood (1799–1845)

For learning the days of the week there is:

Monday's child is fair of face.
Tuesday's child is full of grace.
Wednesday's child is full of woe.
Thursday's child has far to go.
Friday's child is loving and giving.
Saturday's child works hard for a living.
But the child that is born on the Sabbath Day,
Is blythe and bonny and good and gay.

—Early nineteenth century

This is the version traditional to American Mother Goose books. An interesting national controversy occurred in England in 1948, when a member of Parliament commented on the birth of a son to Princess Elizabeth as being on a Sunday, and quoted a version of the rhyme. Instantly, numerous versions were quoted throughout the country and its newspapers, offering variations for the lines. Among them were:

> Monday: fair in face; full in the face;
> Tuesday: full of God's grace; solemn and sad;
> Wednesday: merry and glad;
> Thursday: sour and sad; inclined to thieving;
> Friday: Godly given; free in giving; full of sin;
> Saturday: work for your living; pure within;
> Sunday: never shall we want; full of grace;
>   to heaven its steps shall tend alway;
> *(Some omit Sunday, or combine it with Christmas)*
> Christmas: is fair and wise and good and gay.

Whatever attributes were given to the other days, however, Sunday's child was always described in a desirable way.

Another mnemonic incorporates the days of the week into a "biography":

> Solomon Grundy,
> Born on Monday,
> Christened on Tuesday,
> Married on Wednesday,
> Took ill on Thursday,
> Worse on Friday,
> Died on Saturday,
> Buried on Sunday,
> This is the end
> Of Solomon Grundy.

The tale of Solomon Grundy has had a firm place in nursery literature ever since it was collected by Halliwell in 1842.

Other mnemonic verses dealt with historical matters:

No	Plan	Like	Yours	To	Study	History	Wisely.
o	l	a	o	u	t	a	i
r	a	n	r	d	u	n	n
m	n	c	k	o	a	o	d
a	t	a		r	r	v	s
n	a	s			t	e	o
	g	t				r	r
	e	e					
	n	r					
	e						
	t						

The Royal Houses could be remembered with the above sentence.

William the Conqueror, ten sixty-six,
Played on the Saxons oft-cruel tricks.
  Columbus sailed the ocean blue,
  In fourteen hundred and ninety-two.
The Spanish Armada met its fate,
In fifteen hundred and eighty-eight.
  In sixteen hundred and sixty-six,
  London burnt like rotten sticks.

The rhyme above is supposed to help recall certain historical dates.
Even the signs of the zodiac have been created mnemonically:

The Ram, the Bull, and the Heavenly Twins,
And next the Crab, the Lion shines,
The Virgin and the Scales,
The Scorpion, Archer, and He-Goat,
The Man that carries the Watering-Pot,
The Fish with the glittering tails.

There are many other verses that apply to what happens in various
months, such as when to wed, or what to plant; others tell what to do or eat
on specific days of the week. They do not, however, fall into the teaching
modes found in the mnemonic rhymes or in the more simple ABC's and 1,
2, 3's.

Numbers are frequently used at the beginning of counting-out rhymes.
These, too, are generally considered Mother Goose ditties, but, as they usually
have only a few numbers, are not employed as number-teaching tools.

Sometimes the 1, 2, 3's and ABC's of Mother Goose are used to accompany jumping a rope or bouncing a ball—when using the alphabet, the letter
on which one "misses" is supposed to be the first letter of one's sweetheart's
name.

However they are used—by children on the playground—or by parents
and teachers as first steps in teaching—Mother Goose's ABC's and 1, 2, 3's
have a long history, and will no doubt continue into the future as literary
accessories.

6. From Long Ago and Far Away
Sources in Religion, Legend, Antiquity

Many of the rhymes found in Mother Goose literature today have roots in times long past. Some cannot be traced, but others can be. These show interesting and sometimes curious derivations from other works of antiquity. Two verses are traced to the same multiple sources:

> If all the seas were one sea,
> What a *great* sea that would be!
> And if all the trees were one tree,

What a *great* tree that would be!
And if all the axes were one axe,
What a *great* axe that would be!
And if all the men were one man,
What a *great* man that would be!

And if the *great* man
Took the *great* axe,
And cut down the *great* tree,
And let it fall into the *great* sea,
What a *splish-splash* that would be!

Traditional   [1810 Variation]

If all the world were paper [. . . was apple-pie],
And all the sea were ink [. . . was ink],
If all the trees were bread and cheese,
What should we have to drink [. . . could we do for drink?]

These are deemed by some scholars to be parodies of the language used in ancient religious services. Others contend that they are the natural evolution and anglicization of these old words. The words have been rearranged in numerous ways, in numerous centuries, yet still convey the same basic sense—or in the doggerel versions, nonsense. To wit:

The Rabbi Jochanan ben Zacchai is said to have spoken of himself in the first century A.D. (with the Canticles *Schir ha Schrim Rabba* attributing similar comments to Rabbi Eliezer and Rabbi Joshua in the second century) in these words:
"If all the Heavens were parchment and all sons of men writers and all trees of the forest pens, they could not write what I have learned."

In the Koran, written in A.D. 651–652:
And were the trees that are in the earth pens, and the sea ink with seven more seas to swell its tide, the words of God would not be spent.

In the Bible, (John, 21:25) written in Greek and Latin in the fourth and fifth centuries:
But there are also many other things which Jesus did; were every one of them to be written, I suppose that the world itself could not contain the books that would be written.

In the Talmud, written in Palestine and Babylon in the first and sixth centuries:

If all the seas were ink and all rushes pens and all the whole Heaven parchment and all sons of men writers, they would not be enough to describe the depth of the Mind of the Lord.

From a Chaldean ode sung in synagogues on the first day of the Feast of Pentecost, translated by Rabbi Mayir ben Isaac in the eleventh or twelfth century.

Could we with ink the ocean fill. . .
And were the skies of parchment made. . .
To tell the love of God alone
Would drain the ocean dry.

In circa 1430, England's John Lydgate, evidently writing out of a bitter experience, gave a different twist to his conclusions, producing, "A balade warning men to beware of deceitful women":

In soth to saie, though all the yerth so wanne
Wer parchment smooth, white and scribabell,
And the gret se, that called is the Ocean,
Were tournid into ynke blackir than sabell,
Eche sticke a pen, eche man a scrivener abel,
Not coud thei writin woman's trechirie,
Beware therefore, the blind eteth many a flie.

A 1641 version has six stanzas, plus a manuscript stanza from about the same date. The first stanza of this version is evidently the source for the wording of the current nursery rhyme. (The rhyme, however, first appeared in a *nursery* book in 1810, in *Gammer Gurton's Garland*—and sometimes that version appears in Mother Goose books.) The following adult version appeared in *Witt's Recreations* a book of "ingenious conceites" and "merrie medecines":

If all the World were Paper,
And all the Sea were Ink;
If all the Trees were Bread and Cheese,
How should we doe for Drink?

If all the World were Sand'o,
Oh then what should we lack'o;
If as they say there were no Clay;
How should we take Tobacco?

If all our Vessels ran'a,
If none but had a crack'a;
If Spanish Apes eate all the Grapes,
How should we doe for a Sack'a?

If all the World were Men,
And Men lived all in Trenches,
And there were none but we alone
How should we doe for Wenches?†

If Fryers had no bald Pates,
Nor Nuns had no dark Cloysters;
If all the Seas were Beanes and Pease,
How should we doe for Oysters.

If there had beene no Projects,
Nor none that did great Wrongs;
If Fiddlers shall turne Players all,
How should we doe for Songs?

If all things were eternall,
And nothing their end bringing;
If this should be, then how should we,
Here make an end of singing.

†*The seventh verse: found in manuscript.*

A tune to the above was printed in Playford's *English Dancing Master* in 1651.

Folksongs of various European countries show the same general patter as the much earlier "religious" versions do. But, as in the 1641 version, it is earth, and not heaven, that is associated with paper. An Italian version goes:

I wish that the trees could speak, that the leaves on top were tongues, that the sea would turn to ink, the earth to paper.

An English version of Rabbi Mayir ben Isaac's ode was recorded at Cirencester in 1779, where it was evidently already traditional:

Cou'd we with Ink the Ocean Fill;
Was the whole Earth of Parchment made;
Was every single stick a Quill;
Was every Man a Scribe by Trade;
To write the Love of God alone
Would drain the Ocean dry;
Nor wou'd the Scroll contain the Whole,
Though stretched from Sky to Sky.

A game-version was recorded by G.F. Northall in 1892, in *English Folk-Rhymes*:

If all the food was paving-stones,
And all the seas were ink,
What should we poor mortals do
For victuals and for drink?
   It's enough to make a man like me,
   Scratch his head and think.

This was recited to the accompaniment of a handkerchief placed over the forefinger and thumb, draped to look like a gowned preacher bobbing as the words were spoken.

Whether parody or evolution, it is obvious that the two nursery rhymes cited have a long tradition gained from religion.

This is the house that Jack built.

   This is the malt,
That lay in the house that Jack built.

   This is the cat,
That killed the rat,
That ate the malt,
That lay in the house that Jack built.

   This is the dog,
That chased the cat,
That killed the rat,
That ate the malt,
That lay in the house that Jack built.

   This is the cow with the crumpled horn,
That tossed the dog,
That chased the cat,
That killed the rat,
That ate the malt,
That lay in the house that Jack built.

   This is the maiden all forlorn,
That milked the cow with the crumpled horn,
That tossed the dog,
That chased the cat,
That killed the rat,
That ate the malt,
That lay in the house that Jack built.

   This is the man all tattered and torn,
That kissed the maiden all forlorn,

That milked the cow with the crumpled horn,
That tossed the dog,
That chased the cat,
That killed the rat,
That ate the malt,
That lay in the house that Jack built.

This is the priest all shaven and shorn,
That married the man all tattered and torn,
That kissed the maiden all forlorn,
That milked the cow with the crumpled horn,
That tossed the dog,
That chased the cat,
That killed the rat,
That ate the malt,
That lay in the house that Jack built.

This is the cock that crowed in the morn,
That waked the priest all shaven and shorn,
That married the man all tattered and torn,
That kissed the maiden all forlorn,
That milked the cow with the crumpled horn,
That tossed the dog,
That chased the cat,
That killed the rat,
That ate the malt,
That lay in the house that Jack built.

This is the farmer that sowed his corn,
That kept the cock that crowed in the morn,
That waked the priest all shaven and shorn,
That married the man all tattered and torn,
That kissed the maiden all forlorn,
That milked the cow with the crumpled horn,
That tossed the dog,
That chased the cat,
That killed the rat,
That ate the malt,
That lay in the house that Jack built.

This is the end of a tale that was born,
About...the farmer that sowed his corn,
That kept the cock that crowed in the morn,
That waked the priest all shaven and shorn,
That married the man all tattered and torn,

That kissed the maiden all forlorn,
That milked the cow with the crumpled horn,
That tossed the dog,
That chased the cat,
That killed the rat,
That ate the malt,
That lay in the house that Jack built.

—1755 as a nursery rhyme

Scholars believe that the original of this cumulative rhyme is to be found in the Hebrew chant, "Had Gadyo," which first appeared in print in a 1590 Prague edition of the *Haggadah*, the poetical digressions of the *Talmud*. That chant bears even more resemblance to the folktale, "The Old Woman and Her Pig." Halliwell wrote that a historical interpretation was given at Leipsic in 1731, taken from the original in the Chaldean language. He felt the nursery version was "probably very old, as may be inferred from the mention of the priest all shaven and shorn." It was first printed as a nursery rhyme in *Nurse Truelove's New-Year's-Gift* (London: John Newbery, 1755).

Now I lay me down to sleep,†
I pray the Lord my soul to keep;
And if I should die before I wake,
I pray the Lord my soul to take.

—New England Primer Improved (Boston: John Green, 1750)

†*. . .down to take my sleep*
—New England Primer (Boston: Thomas Fleet, 1737)

First "nursery book" version

I lay me down to rest me,
I pray to God to bless me:
If I should sleep and never wake,
I pray the Lord my soul to take.

—ca.1840 London Jingles (J.G. Rusher)

This well-known children's prayer was first seen in print in the United States in the *New England Primer*, a publication widely circulated in the eighteenth century. In subsequent editions it was variously listed under the headings "Verses for Children" or "Prayer for Laying Down." It appeared in print in England in 1781. It wasn't until around 1840, though, that it was considered a nursery verse. Several different versions have appeared, but the 1750 version has remained the standard.

Early to bed
And early to rise,
Makes a man healthy,
And wealthy and wise.
> —1639 *Paroemiologia*, John Clarke;
> —1732–57 *Poor Richard's Almanack*, Benjamin Franklin

This ditty or proverb is popularly supposed to have been written by Benjamin Franklin, but history records otherwise. Sir Anthony Fitzherbert (born 1470) wrote, "At grammar scole I lerned a verse & that is this: *Sanat, sanctificat et ditat surgere mane.* That is to say: *'erly rysynge maketh a man hole in body, / holer in soule, & rycher in goodes.'*" Hugh Rhodes (ca.1545) wrote:

Ryse you earely in the morning,
   for it hath propertyes three:
Holyness, health, and happy welth,
   as my Father taught mee.

Although the proverb had appeared in Latin, its first printed appearance in English was in 1639, as noted above. It was in a number of seventeenth century Latin grammars and reading primers. It appeared in juvenile literature in two John Newbery books, *The Fairing: or a Golden Toy for Children* (1765) and in *The History of Goody Two-Shoes* (1767), which, according to best scholarly research, was written by Oliver Goldsmith. In the latter the lines are said to be written by Ralph the Raven, with the admonition it is a verse "which every little good Boy and Girl should get by Heart."

Another version seen in nursery books combines two proverbs to make the ditty:

The cock crows in the morn
To tell us to rise,
And he that lies late
Will never be wise;
For early to bed,
And early to rise,
Is the way to be healthy,
And wealthy and wise.
> —ca.1812 *Little Rhymes for Little Folks* (John Harris)

The proverb that makes up the first four lines appeared in similar versions in a number of collections, including Halliwell's of 1844.

For want of a nail, the shoe was lost;
For want of a shoe, the horse was lost;

For want of a horse, the rider was lost;
For want of a rider, the battle was lost;
For want of a battle, the kingdom was lost;
And all for the want of a horseshoe nail.
                          —1898 *The Nursery Rhyme Book* (Andrew Lang)

This proverb, now commonly found in nursery books, developed into its present form from several sources of similar mien. In about 1390, John Gower's *Confessio Amantis* contained:

For sparinge of a litel cost
Ful oftë time a man hath lost
The largë cotë for the hod.

In 1629, Thomas Adams in his *Sermons*, said, "The Frenchmen have a military proverb:

The loss of a nail, the loss of an army...
The want of a nail loseth the shoe,
    the loss of a shoe troubles the horse,
        the horse endangereth the rider,
            the rider breaking his rank molests the company
                so far as to hazard the whole army."

In 1640 George Herbert's *Outlandish Proverbs* used the first three lines but in the present tense ("the shoe is lost"). Benjamin Franklin used another form of the proverb in his *Poor Richard's Almanack* of 1758:

A little neglect may breed mischief...
For want of a nail the shoe was lost;
For want of a shoe the horse was lost;
And for want of a horse the rider was lost;
Being overtaken and slain by the enemy;
All for want of care about a horse-shoe nail.

Three blind mice, three blind mice,
See how they run, see how they run,
They all ran after the farmer's wife,
She cut off their tails with a carving knife,
Did you ever see such a sight in your life,
As three blind mice?
                          —After 1860 in this version

"Three blind mice..." was already a popular ditty before the words were revised into the form best known in the twentieth century. The round had made an appearance in Thomas Ravenscroft's *Deuteromelia or The Seconde part of Musick's melodie* in 1609. The version there, to a somewhat different tune, was:

Three blind mice, three blind mice,
Dame Iulian, Dame Iulian
the miller and his merry old wife,
She scrap'd her tripe, lick thou the knife.

Some time before 1860, an interim version appeared which was sung to the same tune as the 1609 version:

Three blind mice, three blind mice,
Ran around thrice, ran around thrice,
The miller and his merry old wife,
N'er laughed so much in all their life.

It was James Orchard Halliwell, however, who collected it as a nursery rhyme in 1842 in *The Nursery Rhymes of England*. His verse consisted of only the first, third, and fourth lines of the now traditional version.

Nose, nose, jolly red nose,
And what gave thee that jolly red nose?
Nutmeg and ginger, cinnamon and cloves,
That's what give me this jolly red nose.
                    —1609 *Deuteromelia* Thomas Ravenscroft

The original made a second appearance in 1609 in Beaumont and Fletcher's *The Knight of the Burning Pestle*. Although the nursery rhyme does not accent the *gin* of *ginger* the intent of the catch was to emphasize this syllable by drawing it out, creating a double entendre between the liquor versus the spices as being the cause of the red nose. This drinking song made its way into nursery lore in *Songs for the Nursery* (1805) and *Mother Goose's Quarto* (ca.1825).

Elsie Marley† is grown so fine,
She won't get up to feed the swine,
But lies in bed till eight or nine,
    Lazy Elsie Marley.†
                    —1842 Halliwell (as Nancy Dawson)
                    —1843 Halliwell (as Elsie Marley)

†*Nancy Dawson in the 1842 Halliwell.*

This "nursery" song is a very condensed version of two songs, similar to each other, about a dancer (Nancy) and tavern keeper (Elsie), both real people of the eighteenth century, who were, to put it delicately, of ill-repute.

I am a pretty wench,
And I come a great way hence,
And sweethearts I can get none:
But every dirty sow
Can get sweethearts enow
And I pretty wench can get none.
                    —1784 *Gammer Gurton's Garland*
                    —1788 *Tommy Thumb's Songbook*
                    —1842 *The Nursery Rhymes of England* (Halliwell)

This curious entry into children's literature has also appeared in longer versions in community songbooks of 1806 and 1906.

The cock's on the wood pile a-blowing his horn,
The bull's in the barn a-threshing of corn,
The maids in the meadows are making of hay,
The ducks in the river are swimming away.
                    —1810 *Gammer Gurton's Garland*

This is another example of a nursery ditty that has been "cleaned up." A 1740 manuscript of three lines, as well as the refrain of a game mentioned in 1894, has:

The bull in the barn, thrashing the corn,
The cock on the dunghill is blowing his horn.
I never saw such a sight since I was born.

Nursery	Mock Latin
In fir tar is,	Infir taris,
In oak none is,	Inoknonis
In mud ells are,	Inmudeelsis,
In clay none are.	In claynonis,
Goat eat ivy;	
Mare eat oats.	Canamaretots?
—1843 Halliwell	—1842 *Reliquae Antiquae*
	(Chambers)

This nursery rhyme is supposed to be recited very quickly and solemnly so it sounds like Latin. It goes back to words in a medical manuscript by William Wyrcestre ca.1450:

Is thy pott enty, Colelent?
Is gote eate yvy.

Mare eate ootys.
Is thy cocke lyke owrs?

This and the nursery version can be compared to a popular ditty of 1943, which purported to be original, written by Al Hoffman and Jerry Livingston:

Mairzy doats and dozy doats,
    And liddle lamzy divey.
A kiddley divey too, wouldn't you?
A kiddley divey too, wouldn't you?

Robin Hood, Robin Hood,
    Is in the mickle wood;
Little John, Little John,
    He to the town is gone.

Robin Hood, Robin Hood,
    Is telling his beads,
All in the green wood,
    Among the green weeds.

Little John, Little John,
    If he comes no more,
Robin Hood, Robin Hood,
    He will fret sore.

Little John was by Robin Hood's side from the beginning of the adventures of the legendary band who lived in Sherwood Forest and stole from the rich to give to the poor. Rhymes about Robin Hood were mentioned as early as 1377 by William Langland. Friar Tuck and Maid Marian appeared in the tales and ballads in the fifteenth century. This nursery lore version was collected by Halliwell in 1842.

Taffy was a Welshman, Taffy was a thief,
Taffy came to my house and stole a piece of beef;
I went to Taffy's house, Taffy wasn't in,
I jumped upon his Sunday hat, and poked it with a pin.

Taffy was a Welshman, Taffy was a sham,
Taffy came to my house and stole a leg of lamb;
I went to Taffy's house, Taffy was away,
I stuffed his socks with sawdust and filled his shoes with clay.

Taffy was a Welshman, Taffy was a cheat,
Taffy came to my house and stole a piece of meat;

I went to Taffy's house, Taffy was not there,
I hung his coat and trousers to roast before a fire.

Halliwell collected a version of this in 1842, indicating it was traditionally sung on the first of March, St. David's Day. The English evidently sang it at the Welsh borders and other parts of England in order to taunt the Welsh. It was printed in *Nancy Cock's Pretty Song Book*, circa 1780. (A ballad associated with St. David's Day is "There were three jovial Welshmen...," see page 223.)

Bobby Shafto's gone to sea,
  Silver buckles on his knee;
He'll come back and marry me,
  Bonny Bobby Shafto.

Bobby Shafto's fat and fair,
  Combing down his yellow hair;
He's my love forevermore,
  Bonny Bobby Shafto.

The original Bobby Shafto is said to have lived at Hollybrook, County Wicklow, and died in 1737. A third verse was added later:

Bobby Shafto's looking out,
All his ribbons flew about;
All the ladies gave a shout,
Hey for Bobby Shafto.

This verse was added for the benefit of Robert Shafto of Whitworth, who was a candidate for Parliament in 1761. It is said that Miss Bellasyse, the heiress of Brancepeth, died for love of him. The song was in *Songs for the Nursery* in 1805.

American	English
Ladybug, ladybug,	Ladybird, ladybird,
Fly away home.	
Your house is on fire	
And your children will burn.	And your children are gone.
All but one,	All except one
Her name is Ann,	And that's little Ann,
And she crept under	
The frying pan.	The warming pan.

This is a wishing rhyme. The ladybug is put on the back of the hand, the incantation is recited, a wish is made, and then the ladybug is blown softly so that she will fly away with the wish to make it come true. The verse seems to go back to antiquity, being known throughout the European countries and India. The ladybug has been compared to the Egytian scarab, and the invocation may have origins in beliefs associated with Isis or with the worship of Freya. A German theory is that it was a charm to speed the sun across the dangers of the fiery sunset. It was printed for the nursery in *Tommy Thumb's Pretty Song Book*, circa 1744.

> Snail, snail, come out of your hole,
> Or else I'll beat you as black as coal.
>> Snail, snail, put out your horns,
>> I'll give you bread and barley corns.

Like the chant to the Ladybug (or Ladybird), this incantation is believed to go back to antiquity. It is sometimes invoked as "Peer out, peer out, peer out of your hole...." Versions of it are known throughout Europe, Russia, and China. One custom is to hold a lighted candle near the snail in order to make it quit its shell. A Scottish belief is that if the snail shoots out its horns upon hearing the chant, it is predicting a "bonny day" for the morrow. Other beliefs are that a snail placed on ashes will trace the initial of a future lover, and that invocations to snails can cure warts and corns. Frazer, in *The Golden Bough*, relates that an old Saxon remedy for rupture in a child is to take a snail, thrust it at sunset into a hollow tree, and stop up the hole with clay. Then, as the snail perishes the child recovers. Chants were sung to snails to chase them out of the cornfields, and Dr. Buckland, at a meeting of the British Association of Geologists at Plymouth in 1841, remarked in reference to the damage done, that the rhyme had been created to invoke snails out of the crevices in limestone.

The evolution of nursery rhymes has seen rhymes change, be combined with others, and be confused with others. Two rhymes frequently confused with each other are those about "Tom, the piper's son." Beatrix Potter (1866–1943) made clever use of this intermingling by having *Pigling Bland* go off to market singing:

> Tom, Tom the piper's son,
>> stole a pig and away he ran!
> But all the tune that he could play, was,
>> "Over the hills and far away"!

It wouldn't be surprising to see this be absorbed into Mother Goose books as a traditional nursery rhyme some day. (Potter's correction of *run* to *ran* will no doubt be reversed to allow for the conventional rhyming with *son*.)

Incidentally, the "pig" referred to is not the farm animal as pictured in contemporary books; a "pig" was a sweetmeat—a little pastry-pie shaped like a pig, filled with raisins (currants) and spices, and with raisins for eyes. The street cry of the eighteenth century vendors, "A long tail'd pig or a short tail'd pig...," is included in *Mother Goose's Melody*. (See page 67.) This kind of "pig" is meant in the following rhyme:

Tom, Tom, the piper's son,
Stole a pig and away he run;
  The pig was eat,
  And Tom was beat,
And Tom went howling down the street.

                    —1805 *Songs for the Nursery*
                    —1810 *Gammer Gurton's Garland*

The cry dates back further than its nursery adoption. It may have been Walter Crane who first illustrated the pig as a real one, as it appears thus in his 1877 *The Baby's Opera*.

The other Tom was evidently quite a musician, as witness:

Tom, he was a piper's son,
He learnt to play when he was young,
And all the tune that he could play
Was "Over the hills and far away";
Over the hills and a great way off,
The wind shall blow my top-knot off.

Tom with his pipe made such a noise,
That he pleased both the girls and boys,
And they all stopped to hear him play,
"Over the hills and far away."

Tom with his pipe did play with such skill
That those who heard him could never keep still;
As soon as he played they began for to dance,
Even pigs on their hind legs would after him prance.

As Dolly was milking her cow one day,
Tom took his pipe and began for to play;
So Doll and the cow danced "The Cheshire Round,"
Till the pail was broken and the milk ran on the ground.

He met old Dame Trot with a basket of eggs,
He used his pipe and she used her legs;

She danced about till the eggs were all broke,
She began for to fret, but he laughed at the joke.

Tom saw a cross fellow was beating his ass,
Heavy laden with pots, pans, dishes, and glass;
He took out his pipe and he played them a tune,
And the donkey's load was lightened full soon.

Yet all the tune that he could play,
Was "Over the hills and far away";
Over the hills and a great way off,
The wind shall blow my top-knot off.

The refrain "Over the hills and far away" has been used by a number of English poets and songwriters. (See Chapter 10 re Burns.) One of the earliest recorded usages was in the 1670 broadside, *The Wind hath blown my Plaid away, or A discourse betwixt a young Woman and the Elphin Knight* (see Chapter 9). The refrain, alluded to as early as 1549, was:

> My plaid awa, my plaid awa,
> And ore the hill and far awa,
> And far awa to Norrowa,
> My plaid shall not be blown awa.

Another song was known in 1706, evidently written by P.A. Motteux for D'Urfey's comedy, *The Campaigners*, but not appearing in the published version of the play. It was printed as "The Distracted Jockey's Lamentation" in *Wit and Mirth: or Pills to Purge Melancholy*:

> Jockey was a Piper's Son,
> And fell in love when he was young;
> But all the Tune that he could play,
> Was, "oer the Hille and far away."
> And 'Tis o'er the Hills, and far away,
> 'Tis o'er the hills and far away,
> 'Tis o'er the hills and far away,
> The wind has blown my Plad away.

"Tom" has long been a nickname for a piper, as note Edmund Spenser's comment in 1579 that "Tom Piper makes us better melodie," and not many years later, Michael Drayton's "Tom Piper is gone out, and mirth bewails."

Yet, there is another nursery rhyme which recollects the patter of that in "Tom . . . all the tune that he could play. . . ," as well as that of "Jockey. . ." who may well have become "Jack" here:

> As I was going up the hill,
> I met with Jack the piper;
> And all the tune that he could play
> Was, "Tie up your petticoats tighter."
>
> I tied them once, I tied them twice,
> I tied them three times over;
> And all the song that he could sing
> Was, "Carry me safe to Dover."

—1853 Halliwell

Tweedledum and Tweedledee
  Agreed to fight a battle,
For Tweedledum said Tweedledee
  Had spoiled his nice new rattle.
Just then flew by a monstrous crow,
  As black as a tar-barrel,
Which frightened both the heroes so,
  They quite forgot their quarrel.
    — ca.1805 *Original Ditties for the Nursery* (John Harris)

Although the words "Tweedledum and Tweedledee" are sometimes attributed to Jonathan Swift or Alexander Pope, it's more probable they were coined by John Byrom, an eighteenth century hymn writer and shorthand teacher. In 1725 the rivalry between the German composer George Frederick Handel and Italian Composer Giovanni Battista Bononcini was noted in verse by Byrom:

Some say, compared to Bononcini
That Mynheer Handel's but a ninny;
Others aver that he to Handel
- Is scarcely fit to hold a candle;
Strange all this difference should be
Twixt tweedle-dum and tweedle-dee.

The nursery version did not appear until eighty years later, and the Byrom piece may have been known to the nursery-author, but it is equally possible that the term was in oral tradition earlier and both borrowed it. Its literary origins have no verifiable documentation. In Lewis Carroll's *Through the Looking Glass* (1865) Alice recalls the words of the nursery verse when she meets the identical characters marked "Dum" and "Dee," causing many readers to erroneously "remember" "*Tweedle*dum" and "*Tweedle*dee" as being in Carroll's book.

The Queen of Hearts
  She made some tarts,
All on a summer's day;
  The Knave of Hearts
  He stole the tarts,
And took them clean away.

The King of Hearts
Called for the tarts,
And beat the Knave full sore;
The Knave of Hearts
Brought back the tarts,
And vow'd he'd steal no more.

The King of Spades
He kissed the maids,
Which made the Queen full sore;
The Queen of Spades
She beat those maids,
And turned them out of door.

The Knave of Spades
Grieved for those jades,
And did for them implore;
The Queen so gent
She did relent
And vowed she'd ne'er strike more.

The King of Clubs
He often drubs
His loving Queen and wife;
The Queen of Clubs
Returns his snubs,
And all is noise and strife.

The Knave of Clubs
Gives winks and rubs,
And swears he'll take her part;
For when our kings
Will do such things,
They should be made to smart.

The Diamond King
I fain would sing,
And likewise his fair Queen;
But that the Knave
A haughty slave,
Must needs step in between.

Good Diamond King,
With hempen string,
The haughty Knave destroy!

Then may your Queen
With mind serene,
Your royal bed enjoy.

The entire suit of cards appeared in the version of this verse in *The European Magazine* for April 1782. There is some contention that the first stanza is far more story-like and simple than the other three and may have existed separately before this publication. Actually, the first two stanzas bear a resemblance to each other, while the third and fourth not only veer into present tense, but have the distinct imprint of "pointed satire." Peter and Iona Opie, in *The Oxford Dictionary of Nursery Rhymes* (1951), opine that Canning's use of the first set alone as the basis of a satire on poetic criticism in 1787 substantiates the probability that it was well-known, else the point of the satire would be lost on readers.

Only the first set—the Queen, Knave, and King of Hearts—have survived as nursery lore. Charles Lamb used it for his first nursery book in 1805, *King and Queen of Hearts: with the Rogueries of the Knave who stole the Queen's Pies*. Halliwell included it in his third edition of *The Nursery Rhymes of England* (1844) but in no other. As noted in Martin Gardner's *The Annotated Alice*, "This familiar nursery rhyme fit so neatly into Carroll's fantasy of living playing cards that he reprinted it without alteration." Actually, Carroll wrote "...stole *the* tarts, And took them *quite* away."

American traditional[†]

Jack and Jill went up the hill
To fetch a pail of water;
Jack fell down and broke his crown,
And Jill came tumbling after.

Up Jack got and home did trot,
As fast as he could caper;
He went to bed to mend his head[1]
With vinegar and brown paper.

When Jill came in, how she did grin[2]
To see Jack's paper plaster;
Mother vexed, did whip her next,[3]
For causing Jack's disaster[4]

[†]*British alternate lines:* [1]*To old Dame Dob, who patched his nob,* [2]*Then Jill came in, and she did grin,* [3]*Her mother whipt her, across the knee,* [4]*For laughing at Jack's disaster.*

"Jack and Jill (Gill)..." appeared around 1765 in *Mother Goose's Melody* as only one verse, with the woodcut showing two boys. (Kate Greenaway's

Jack and Jill
Went up the hill,
To fetch a pail of water :
Jack fell down
And broke his crown,
And Jill came tumbling after.

illustration in her 1881 *Mother Goose or the Old Nursery Rhymes* shows two girls.) The verse has been in most major collections of nursery verses since then, but the eighteenth century printings were generally of the first stanza only. Later editors usually used one, two, or three stanzas. With few exceptions, lines from either of those above have been used; occasionally *mother* or *Dame Dob* is seen as *Dame Gill*. There have also been elongated versions with as many as 15 verses.

Although some devotees of political satire in nursery rhymes see the verse as being about Cardinal Wolsey and his coadjutor, Bishop Tarbes, depicting their journey to France to arrange the marriage of Mary Tudor to the French Monarch, this is not generally accepted as being so. Another theory by the Rev. Sabine Baring-Gould appears in his *Curious Myths of the Middle Ages* (1866), putting it forth as having origins in a Scandinavian myth of great antiquity, wherein "Hjuki" and "Bil" were captured by the moon while drawing water, thus explaining markings on the full moon which look like two people with a bucket on a pole between them. Lewis Spence, in *Myth and Ritual* (1947), maintained that it derived from an ancient mystic ceremony, as "...no one in the folk-lore sense climbs to the top of a hill for water unless that water has special significance" (e.g., ritualistic morning dew).

A third theory points to the rhyming of *water* with *after* as indicating seventeenth century origins. Seventeenth century usage was that *Jack* and *Jill* were synonyms for *lad* and *lass*, as commonly seen in literature of the period.

And—isn't it possible that someone, long ago, just wrote a sing-song tale of two children at play?

Tracing origins is scholar's-play, and finding something no one else has unearthed is exhilarating; but sometimes efforts get convoluted. Trying to find implications and origins does create a lot of wordage that's fraught with conjecture.

Perhaps it's enough to enjoy the knowledge of the traditional nursery rhymes that do have connections to passages in antiquity.

A Pocketful of Rye;

Four-and-Twenty Blackbirds Baked in a Pie.

7. Skeleton Keys
to Dame Goose's Kingdom
Historical Allusions and Satires

There seems to be a casual and wide-spread belief that *all* the Mother Goose rhymes were originally political satires. That simply is not so. In fact, fewer than one might imagine fall into that category. And the ones that people mention as political satires often are not.

Some of the verses can be reasonably assumed to have certain implications. Despite some far-fetched claims for others, however, there is little to substantiate the interpretations. The continued belief that certain political allusions pertain to certain rhymes probably has three foundations. One, there have been a number of self-published books that have borrowed, and therefore perpetuated, the many unfounded conclusions drawn by Katherine Elwes Thomas, who wrote *The Real Personages of Mother Goose* in 1930. This volume was made into a film about the nursery "personages," a circumstance which thrust the theories into public appeal. Whatever limited circulation the self-published books and pamphlets had, they nevertheless repeated the colorful but erroneous conclusions. Second, few people bother to check on the scholastic credibility of something that seems on the surface to be a likely interpretation of something so insignificant (to them) as a nursery rhyme. And third, there is the human tendency to like the fact that there is something behind the seemingly simple words that reflect a deeper and adult interpretation.

In judging the viability of allusions hidden in the rhymes, there are two main criteria to invoke. First, there is the actual documentation of the times. Where papers, letters, and footnotes of the period refer to the verse as being about a certain political or royal exploit, there is proof. This is quite straightforward. The second is more circumstantial but nevertheless realistic. Satires are almost always written about situations current at the time. If the verse is about a reigning or recent monarch or other person of rank, a satire about the individual is immediately recognized by the general populace. Whether complimentary or derogatory, there are always citizens to take up the call. Few people are interested in mocking political periods long past, and even fewer are interested in furthering such doggerel. For a satire to work, it must be both understood and meaningful to those hearing it. Then, if it is catchy enough, it gains current popularity, and frequently, survives its period to move into lore and tradition. Then the irony frequently applicable is that the meaning behind the original satire is lost and only the words remain. That's what has happened to some of the ditties that moved from the street into the world of the nursery.

Making sense of historical satire and allusion gives the researcher a lot to think about. Many elements of the past have not been documented; their realities are clouded by passing time. And sometimes, where no proof is possible one way or another, one interpretation is as good as any, and there are times when the scholar has to forego proof and go with an informed guess.

We have then, several distinct phenomena. There are certain nursery rhymes that undoubtedly began life as satires on their times. Also, there are some which can reasonably be concluded to depict certain situations. We also have rhymes that people have put unfounded meanings to, sometimes stretching believability to a breaking point. There is not enough evidence to verify or even conclude within reason that many popular rhymes contain the political references attributed to them.

"Humpty Dumpty" is not really about Richard III, the Usurper of the throne in 1483, to be slain upon Bosworth Field the same year. (See page 48.)

"There was an old woman tossed in a blanket" is not about Henry V, this being a joke of Goldsmith's perpetrated in the preface to *Mother Goose's Melody* in ca.1765. (See page 55.)

"Three blind mice" cannot reasonably be interpreted to be about Queen Mary I of England (1516–1558), and Cranmer, Latimer, and Ridley, said by some to be the "three blind mice" who were burned at the stake. (See pages 105–07.)

"Jack and Jill" is not about Cardinal Wolsey and Bishop Tarbes. (See page 117.)

Neither "Little Boy Blue, come blow your horn" nor "Little Tom Tucker sings for his supper" can be reliably traced to Cardinal Thomas Wolsey (ca.1472–1530) as asserted by some writers. Even "Old Mother Hubbard," also unverifiably, is said to depict Wolsey. (See page 172.)

"Simple Simon" is not a satire on all seventeenth century Englishmen, they supposedly being at the mercy of the Scottish King, James I. (James, therefore, being "the pieman.") (See page 239.)

"Frog he would a-wooing go . . . Heigh! ho! says Anthony Rowley. . ." is very unlikely to be, as described by Katherine Elwes Thomas, a verse that "amusingly satirized the dramatic wooing of the elderly Elizabeth by the youthful Duke of Anjou [the French "frog"], the queen at that time forty-nine years of age, with the French prince telling off his youthful age at twenty-three." More scholarly interpreters do not make this connection. (See page 230.)

"Little Miss Muffet" is not about Mary, Queen of Scots (1542–1587), supposedly frightened by John Knox (1505–1572), Scottish religious reformer. (See page 202.)

"The Queen of Hearts" is not likely to be about Elizabeth, Queen of Bohemia (1596–1662), despite the fact that she was called "Queen of Hearts" because of her beauty. She was English, being the only daughter of James I of England, granddaughter of Mary, Queen of Scots, and later grandmother to George I. But, the verse does not appear until 1782, and if it does contain a lampoon, it more likely would be about contemporary figures. (See page 115.)

There is no reason to credit the allegation that "Yankee Doodle" is about Prince Rupert of Bohemia (1619–1682), one of thirteen children of the "King and Queen of Hearts." (See pages 115 and 165.)

"A carrion crow sat on an oak" is not about the plot of Lord Russell and Algernon Sydney to gain official recognition of the Duke of Monmouth, hoping that rather than James it would be Monmouth who would replace Charles I (1600–1649). (See page 222.)

"Hush-a-bye Baby, on the tree-top" cannot be credited as claimed by Katherine Elwes Thomas, who wrote, "Some happy wit has, in these four lines, crystallized the long and exciting history of James Stuart, the Pretender." She claims this is about the illegitimate James being smuggled into the protection of James II (1633–1701), his father. (For "Rock-a-bye" or "Hush-a-bye Baby" see page 28.)

"Wee Willie Winkie" does not refer to William III (1650–1702). (See pages 185–186.)

Some verses are quite straightforward, of course, incorporating the names of the intended subjects. These and Mother Goose rhymes with political allusions and other derivations that are reasonably traceable, follow:

> When good King Arthur ruled this land,
>   He was a goodly king;
> He stole three pecks of barley-meal
>   To make a bag-pudding.
>
> A bag-pudding the king did make,
>   And stuffed it well with plums;
> And in it put great lumps of fat,
>   As big as my two thumbs.
>
> The king and queen did eat thereof,
>   And noblemen beside;
> And what they could not eat that night,
>   The queen next morning fried.

The Arthurian legend dates back perhaps to A.D. 600, with most of the stories transmitted by the year 1000. The nursery rhyme, of course, dates from a much later period, and Halliwell, in 1842, thought it derived from a very old play.

Other versions have been about King Stephen, Good Queen Bess, Auld Prince Arthur, and King Henry, but Good King Arthur seems to have become firmly entrenched in the nursery verse. It first appeared thus in *Gammer Gurton's Garland* (ca.1799).

> Baa, baa, black sheep,
> Have you any wool?
> Yes sir, yes sir,
> Three bags full.
> One for my master,
> One for my dame,
> And one for the little boy
> Who lives in the lane.

Tradition assigns to this the import of a protest against the export tax imposed in Britain in 1275. The master is used as a symbol of the king; the dame as the nobility; and the little boy as the common people. It first appeared as a nursery rhyme in *Tommy Thumb's Pretty Song Book* (ca.1744), and with a different concluding line in *Mother Goose's Melody* (ca.1765). (See pages 67–68.) Rudyard Kipling used the opening lines for an 1888 short story, "Baa, Baa, Black Sheep."

> Dr. Foster went to Gloucester
> In a shower of rain;
> He stepped in a puddle
> Up to his middle,
> And never went there again.

It was not until 1920 that Boyd Smith suggested that this rhyme referred to a real incident involving Edward I (1239–1307), who as King (1272–1307), went to Gloucester where his horse was so deeply trapped in mud that planks had to be laid down to help the horse regain its footing. Edward vowed he would never return to the city. The rhyming of *puddle* with *middle* suggests that the old form of the word, *piddle*, may have been used originally. The rhyme, however, was first collected by Halliwell in 1844.

> Three wise men of Gotham,
> They went to sea in a bowl,
> And if the bowl had been stronger
> My song had been longer.

The delightful tale behind this doggerel is that King John (1340–1399) decided to pass through the town of Gotham, a village near Nottingham. The prevailing law was that any road the king travelled automatically became a public road thereafter. The villagers hatched a plan to divert the king. When his forerunners came to check out the passage, the townspeople acted like stupid fools, cavorting about, being silly, even attempting to trap a cuckoo by building a hedge around it, saying the purpose was to have a "perpetual summer." The king's men concluded that the village was populated by idiots, and the king was advised to take a different route. Thus, the tradition was created of the "fools of Gotham," which the Gothamites translate into the "wise men of Gotham" who saved the village from being divided by a public road. A manuscript of circa 1450 mentions the "foles of gotyam," and there is a story "Of the iii wyse men of gotham" in *C Mery Talys* of 1526. It first appeared as a nursery rhyme in *Mother Goose's Melody*. (See page 58.)

The tradition of being known as fools evidently was not disturbing (in that the tale indicates this was a subterfuge) and historians of the Sussex area have been known to claim the Gotham as being the one near Pevensey. Early

in the 1800s, the American writer Washington Irving dubbed New York City as "Gotham," a nickname that stuck, further promoted by the twentieth century use of the designation in the popular comic book and television series of "Bat Man and Robin."

> I had a little nut tree,
>   Nothing would it bear,
> But a silver nutmeg
>   And a golden pear.
> The King of Spain's daughter
>   Came to visit me,
> And all for the sake
>   Of my little nut tree.

John Orchard Halliwell believed that this song was about the visit of Juana of Castile, the mad daughter of the King of Spain, to the court of Henry VII in 1506. Although there is no documentation, popular tradition has clung to this as the meaning of the verse. Halliwell collected it in 1843.

The King of France went up the hill,
With forty thousand men;
The King of France came down the hill,
And ne'er went up again.

This ditty is about Henry IV (1553–1610), the event being referred to in a letter from James Howell, dated Paris, 12 May, 1620, written to his friend Sir James Crofts, "France as all Christendom besides was in a profound peace ... when Henry the fourth fell upon some great Martiall designe, the bottom whereof is not known to this day; ... he levied a huge army of 40,000 men, whence came the Song, *The King of France with fourty thousand men....*" This had happened in 1610. The Henry IV theory is generally accepted, as Howell had credence as a historiographer.

James O. Halliwell collected this as a nursery rhyme in 1842, indicating he had found reference to the verse in a tract of 1642 called *Pigges Corantoe, or Newes from the North*, where it was called "Old Tarleton's Song." As the jester, Ned Tarleton, had died in 1588, he concluded the song must predate that time. As it was common in those days for jests to be arbitrarily attributed to Tarleton, this is not conclusive evidence. (Similar to the attribution of all spoonerisms to W.A. Spooner, and all old jokes to Joe Miller.)

The routing of the French King by the English Edward, the Black Prince, sings to England's glory, and one would have thought it would be retained intact, but nevertheless, the song also is seen in nursery versions as "The Duke of York went up the hill...." But then, anyone who ever led an army would be subject to the same words.

Little Jack Horner
Sat in the corner,
Eating his Christmas Pie;
He put in his thumb,
And pulled out a plum,
And said, "What a good boy am I."

There seems little doubt that this verse is about one Thomas Horner, steward to Richard Whiting, last of the abbots of the wealthy Glastonbury Cathedral, in 1539 the only untouched religious house in Somerset. The story behind it is that Whiting sent Horner to London during that time of the Dissolution, when Henry VIII was laying hold to all church properties. Horner was to carry a Christmas gift to the monarch: a pie in which were concealed the title deeds to 12 wealthy manors. Horner is said to have opened the pie and taken out the deed to a real plum, the manor of Mells. Later, he told the abbot that the king had given the title to him. As further proof, he offered the fact that the king had knighted him Sir John. This would not have been an unlikely dubbing in exchange for the deliverance of the (11?) titles, as the honor meant little else than an exemption from certain taxes. History records that Thomas Horner took up residence at Mells soon after the Dissolution. (Surprises in pies were not unknown; see the next verse.)

The rest of Thomas Horner's history shows that he served on the so-called "jury" when Abbot Whiting was found guilty of "having secreted from the profane touch of Henry VIII the gold sacramental cups used for ages in Holy communion. . ." (*Letters Relating to the Suppression of Monasteries*; Oxford: Camden Society, 1843)," whereupon Whiting was hanged, beheaded, and quartered. A popular couplet known in the next century was:

> Hopton, Horner, Smyth, and Thynne,
> When abbots went out, they came in.

Horner's descendants deny, of course, that he was the original "Jack Horner" and insist that Thomas bought the deed from the King. They further point out that his name was *Thomas*, and not *Jack*—but *Jack* was a common term for *knave*, so the rhyme-makers were not necessarily amiss. In addition, the Horner clan mentions an old tale from around 1340, *Tale of a Basyn*, which is the precursor to a 1764 chapbook, *The History of Jack Horner* (this Jack being only 13 inches high). However, the latter is a long ballad, which *may* be based on the earlier piece, but brings in the Christmas pie/thumb/plum incident awkwardly. Reference to the nursery rhyme also appears in Henry Carey's *Namby Pamby* in 1725.

Curiously, the Horner family does subscribe to the theory that "The House that Jack Built" is based on their estate holdings. (Here they evidently have no objection to the use of *Jack*.) The connection is not endorsed by documentation or the findings of scholars. (See pages 101–103.)

A version of "Little Jack Horner. . ." appeared in *Mother Goose's Melody*. (See page 63.)

> Sing a song of sixpence,
>   A pocket full of rye,
> Four and twenty blackbirds
>   Baked in a pie;
> When the pie was opened,
>   The birds began to sing;
> Wasn't that a dainty dish
>   To set before the king?
>
>> The king was in the counting-house,
>>   Counting out his money,
>> The Queen was in the parlor,

Eating bread and honey;
The maid was in the garden,
Hanging out the clothes,
Along came a blackbird,
And snipped off her nose.

Several interpretations are given to this rhyme, all at variance to each other—obviously the rhyme cannot be ascribed to all of them. Indeed, tracing it to any specific allegation is impossible given the lack of documentation, yet none are easily disproved, either.

The simplest explanation is that the song is merely about a custom of the day—for instance, an Italian cookbook, *Epulario, or, the Italian Banquet* (1549, translated into English in 1598), has a recipe "to make pies so that birds may be alive in them and flie out when it is cut up." In 1723, the Duke of Bolton's cook, John Nott, referred to a practice of former days whereby the birds from such a pie were supposed to put out the candles, thus causing the guests to be thrown into darkness and a "diverting Hurley-Burley."

Another interpretation puts a mythological origin to the verse. The blackbirds are seen as the twenty-four hours of the day; the king is the sun; the queen is the moon; and the maid is the earth; the earth's day is "snipped" by a "blackbird of time."

Another theory says the song is about the first printing of the English Bible, the blackbirds being the letters of the alphabet (perhaps combining I/J and U/V?) who had been "baked in a pie," that is, "set in pica type." The first English setting was the New Testament printed by William Tyndale in 1525–26. The first complete Bible in English translation was printed in 1539, and the popular King James version appeared in English in 1611.

The political allusions assigned to "Sing a song of sixpence" by some scholars indicate that the blackbirds are doubly symbolic of twenty-four manorial deeds concealed in a pie by about-to-be-dissolved monasteries (the blackbirds also being symbolic of the monks) trying to sway Henry VIII (1491–1547). The rye is supposed to be an additional tribute.

Others say it is about Henry VIII; the queen is Catherine of Aragon blithely unaware that she was about to be usurped; the maid is Anne Boleyn in her pretty clothes from France—Anne, who married the king and was subsequently "snipped" (in some versions "snapped") by the grimmest "blackbird," the headsman with the axe.

In 1790, Shakespearean commentator George Steevens (1736–1800) made reference to the rhyme in a quip about Poet Laureate Henry James Pye, saying about Pye's first flowery poetic tribute to the king, "And when the Pye was opened the birds began to sing. Was not that a dainty dish to set before the king?" This incident caused a persistent supposition that Steevens had authored the rhyme. "Sixpence" had already appeared in print, however, as one verse in *Tommy Thumb's Pretty Song Book* (ca.1744, when Steevens was eight years old), as two verses in *Nancy Cock's Pretty Song Book* in about 1780, and also in *Gammer Gurton's Garland* of 1784, followed by numerous reappearances. Halliwell collected it in 1842. The use of "pocketful of rye," in essence a specific sack-measure of grain, and the reference to the "counting house" by inference put the rhyme in the sixteenth century, as do other references to it in literature of that period. From all counts, Steevens could hardly have been the author.

> Flour of England, fruit of Spain,
> Met together in a shower of rain;
> Put in a bag, tied round with a string;
> If you'll tell me this riddle,
> I'll give you a ring.

The riddle-answer to this is generally accepted as being "a plumpudding." There is reasonable conjecture, however, that it was a satire on Queen Mary of England as the flour and Philip II as the fruit of Spain. The couple did meet in a downpour of rain in 1554, and Mary publicly gave Philip a ring, symbolic of marriage. "Put in a bag, etc." is said to refer to the tight hold that Mary kept on Philip. The verse comes from the period, so may have some viability as a satire. It was collected as a nursery verse by Halliwell in 1844.

Some nursery rhyme commentators have attributed any rhyme about a "little man" to be the husband of Mary I, Philip II of Spain, as he was very short and thin in physique. He was not popular with the English people, but there is not sufficient reason to think these rhymes are all about him. One, however, is so apropos, that it might be given some consideration:

> I had a little husband, no bigger than my thumb;
> I put him in a pint pot, and there I bid him drum.
> I bought a little horse, that galloped up and down;
> I bridled him, and saddled him,
> And sent him out of town.
> I gave him some garters, to garter his hose,
> And a little silk handkerchief, to wipe his pretty nose.

Mary had showered Philip with gifts, including a horse and several honors, e.g. that of the Garter. Philip, however, left her before the year was out, yet later, she raised money from the "pint pot," a term then applied to church-funds accruing from fines imposed by the confessors, to give him aid in his fight with France. The last line is also given in some older texts, as "to wipe his snotty nose." The rhyme entered nursery lore and was included in

Nancy Cock's Pretty Song Book, as well as subsequent collections, including Halliwell's of 1842.

Ride a cock-horse to Banbury Cross,
To see a fine lady upon a white horse;
Rings on her fingers and bells on her toes,
She shall have music wherever she goes.

The fine lady is usually identified as Queen Elizabeth I (1533–1603) who was known to be very fond of rings and proud of her beautiful hands, and whose royal pageants were frequently accompanied by the herald of guns, drums, flutes, and trumpets.

Some commentators have thought it was about Lady Godiva, famous wife of the Earl of Mercia. Other interpretations carry even less credibility.

Variations on the words have included reference to "an old woman," to a "black" horse, and to "Coventry Cross." The lady first appeared in a nursery rhyme collection in *Gammer Gurton's Garland*, 1784, and in many since then.

Hey diddle diddle, the cat and the fiddle,
The cow jumped over the moon;
The little dog laughed to see such sport,
And the dish ran away with the spoon.

This is a somewhat controversial ditty as far as accepted allusions go. Elizabeth I (1533–1603), according to some commentators, is the "cat" of other rhymes, as well. The editors of *The Oxford Dictionary of Nursery Rhymes*, Peter and Iona Opie say, "Probably the best-known nonsense verse in the language, a considerable amount of nonsense has been written about it." Nevertheless, there is good reason why belief in the satire of this verse persists. How delicious to think about the possibilities:

Line 1. There's documentation of a fidle (*sic*) dance called "Hey didle didle" (*sic*) current in 1569, and possibly existing earlier. Elizabeth was known to love dancing alone in her rooms to the accompaniment of the fiddle. And she was frequently called "the cat" because of the way she played with her cabinet as though the ministers were so many mice.

Line 2. This too might well depict Elizabeth—"the cow jumped over the moon"—for she revelled in conducting elaborate charades at Whitehall and Hampton Court.

Line 3. Here, possibly, is a reference to Robert Dudley, Earl of Leicester (ca.1532–1588) whom Elizabeth considered marrying, saying, "He is like my little lap-dog...."

Line 4. The courtier who was honored with carrying certain golden dishes into the state dining room was referred to as "the dish," and the Queen's premeal "taster of the royal meals," always a beautiful young woman of court who made sure the dishes were not poisoned, was called "the spoon." A particular "dish," Edward, Earl of Hertford, and "spoon," Lady Katherine Grey, sister of the famous Lady Jane Grey, were secretly married. When Elizabeth discovered this, she had them confined to the Tower of London where they lived their remaining seven years, having two children born to them there.

Other connections some scholars have suggested to the rhyme are that it is reminiscent of the worship of Hathor, the Egyptian goddess of love, who is sometimes pictured as having a cow's head; that it refers to heavenly constellations—i.e., Taurus the Bull, and Canis Minor, the little dog; and that it describes the periodic flight of the Egyptians from the rising floods of the waters of the Nile.

"Hey diddle diddle" is a perfect example of researchers and scholars going various ways in interpretation. Lacking either proof or disproof, one can only take all the available information and process it for one's self. As for the ditty's entry into nursery collections, where it certainly has a strong foothold, it was in *Mother Goose's Melody* (ca.1765), with one slightly different line. (See page 61.)

Good Queen Bess was a glorious dame,
When bonny King Jemmy from Scotland came;
We'll pepper their bodies,

Their peacable noddies,
And give them a crack of the crown.

Elizabeth I of England (1533–1603), daughter of Henry VIII and Anne
Boleyn, was known as Harry's Daughter Gloriana; the Virgin Queen; and
Good Queen Bess. She was much loved, desiring to rule by love rather than
compulsion. When she was 70, she agreed that upon her death the crown
could be passed to James V, son of Mary, Queen of Scots. As the rhyme indicates, "Jemmy" was not popular with the English.

Mistress Mary, quite contrary,
How does your garden grow?
With silver bells and cockle shells,
And pretty maids all in a row.

Tradition says this is about Mary, Queen of Scots (1542–1587), and that
the silver bells reflect her Popish leanings and the cockle-shells refer to the
designs on an actual dress she was given by the French Dauphin. The "pretty
maids," in this case, would be the celebrated ladies-in-waiting, the "Four
Marys": Mary Beaton, Mary Seaton, Mary Fleming, and Mary Livingston.
   It is also possible that the rhyme stemmed from religious satire, explana-
tions given being that the reference is to "Our Lady's Convent," the bells being the sanctus bells, the cockleshells being the badges of the pilgrims, and
the pretty maids, the nuns.
   Two other interpretations show it as a lament by Catholics about the
persecution of the Roman Church, or conversely, one by Protestants about the
reinstatement of the Roman Church.
   The nursery version was in *Tommy Thumb's Pretty Song Book* (ca.1744).
The version in *Nancy Cock's Pretty Song Book* (ca.1780) had the last line as
"Sing cuckolds all on a row," a curious line indeed for a supposed children's
collection. This last line reflected a song called "Cuckolds all a row" that appeared in Playford's *Dancing Master* in 1651. Other last lines have had in a
row such items as lady-bells, columbines, cowslips, or muscles.

Jack Sprat could eat no fat,
His wife could eat no lean;
And so betwixt them both, you see,
They licked the platter clean.

"Jack Sprat and his wife" are generally interpreted to be King Charles I
(1600–1649) and his wife Henrietta Maria (1609–1666) who was the daughter
of France's Henry VI, and sister of Louis XIII. Henrietta Maria, a Roman
Catholic, was disliked by the Puritan English. That she "ate the fat" (no lean)

refers to her inclinations toward spoil and plunder. Charles, having inherited the Spanish War along with the throne from James I, demanded large supplies from his first Parliament, mainly Puritans who objected to his having taken a French Catholic spouse. They responded with a meager £140,000, whereupon Charles, in a rage, dissolved the Parliament, or "licked the platter clean." To finance the war, he revived the hated system of "benevolences" and the quartering of soldiers in private homes. Charles thus refilled his platter and could continue to benefit through the imposition of these sanctions and repeatedly "lick the platter clean."

The verse evidently first saw print in 1639 in John Clarke's *Paroemiologia Anglo-Latina*. In both 1659 and 1670, it was published as an old English proverb. It appeared in *Mother Goose's Melody* ca.1765.

There was a crooked man and he walked a crooked mile,
He found a crooked sixpence against a crooked stile;
He bought a crooked cat, which caught a crooked mouse,
And they all lived together in a little crooked house.

The history books of Scotland describe General Sir Alexander Leslie as "the little old crooked man with the keen eyes." This verse is said to be about his exploits with "the crooked sixpence," Charles I of England (1600–1649). The "crooked stile" would be the border between the countries. They reached a pact and "lived together." (The Scottish General, however, had kept his best officers on half pay, a wily precaution that proved prudent when in 1640 the "crooked sixpence" tried to cross the "crooked stile" again. Eventually, they reached a more permanent treaty.) Halliwell collected the first eight lines in 1842.

In 1926, in *Less Familiar Nursery Rhymes*, Robert Graves gave an additional verse:

...He brought it crooked back,
   To his crooked wife Joan,
And cut a crooked snippet
   From the crooked ham-bone.

Purple, yellow, red, and green,
The King cannot reach it, nor the Queen;
   Nor can Old Nol whose power's so great;
   Tell me this riddle while I count eight.

The King referred to here is Charles I. The date of the rhyme can be surmised to be 1648 by the reference to Old Nol, which was the Royalist's nickname for Oliver Cromwell. Cromwell, lord protector of England, did not come into power until June 1647. As the King is spoken of as alive in the rhyme, the riddle must have been created before Charles' execution in January 1649.

The riddle was collected by Halliwell in 1842, with the accompanying interpretation. (The answer to the riddle is "a rainbow.")

> As I was going by Charing Cross,
> I saw a black man upon a black horse;
> They told me it was King Charles the First —
> Oh dear, my heart was ready to burst!

Charles I of England was executed in 1649, and the last two lines of this lament were found in a 1660 manuscript of a ballad, appearing there as:

> But because I cood not a vine Charles the furste
> By my troth my hart was readdy to burst.

"Black" as used in the seventeenth century vernacular, refers to the color of the hair. It is more likely here that it refers to the blackness of the brass of Charles' statue, which was moved from King Street to Charing Cross in 1675. (And later to Whitehall.) A subsequent street cry was:

> I cry my matches at Charing Cross,
> Where sits a black man upon a black horse.

The nursery version appears to be a combination of the lines from the ballad and the street cry. It appeared in *Pretty Tales* in 1808, and was collected by Halliwell in 1843.

> High ding a ding, did you hear the bells ring?†
> The parliament soldiers are gone to the king.
> Some they did laugh, and some they did cry,
> To see the parliament soldiers go by.
>
> High ding a ding, and ho ding a ding,
> The parliament soldiers are go to the king.
> Some with new beavers, some with new bands,
> The parliament soldiers are all to be hang'd.*
>
> *Also:* †*I heard a bird sing;* **Are gone to the king.*

Curiously enough, some nursery commentators disagree as to whether this is about Charles I because of the first stanza, or Charles II because of the second. It would appear that the rhyme is about them both, as the parliament soldiers first went to execute Charles I, and then went to Charles II to offer him the crown. It made its appearance as a nursery rhyme in 1798 in volume II of *Christmas Box*.

Curly Locks, Curly Locks, wilt thou be mine?
Thou shalt not wash dishes, nor yet feed the swine;
But sit on a cushion and sew a fine seam,
And feed upon strawberries, sugar, and cream.

Although there's no documentation, tradition assigns this to Charles II (1630–1685) who was dubbed "Curly Locks" after introducing the peruke in which he is always pictured. His flight into exile in Holland was said to have had him at times relegated to washing dishes and feeding swine. Upon his return, the verse promises, he will lead a fittingly royal life. A version of the ditty appeared in the 1797 satire, *Infant Institutes*, and the nursery version appeared in *Gammer Gurton's Garland* in 1810. It was not collected by Halliwell until 1853.

Lucy Locket lost her pocket,
Kitty Fisher found it;
Not a penny was there in it,
But the binding round it.†

†*Also: Nothing in it, nothing in it, / Only ribbon round it.*

Halliwell collected a version of this in 1842, identifying Lucy Locket and Kitty Fisher as synonyms for two famous courtesans in favor with Charles II.

Although there was a Kitty Fisher around 1759 about whom several songs were written, there seems little reason to associate this ditty with her. There is a "Lucy Lockit" in John Gay's *The Beggars's Opera* of 1728. "Lucy Locket" is sung to the same tune as "Yankee Doodle."

See saw, sack a day;
Monmouth is a pretty boy,
Richmond is another,
Grafton is my only joy,
And why should I these three destroy,
To please a pious brother?

King Charles II had a number of illegitimate children to whom he was genuinely devoted. The Duke of Monmouth, said to be his favorite, was the son of Lucy Waters; the Duke of Richmond was the son of Frances Theresa

Stewart, Duchess of Richmond; and the Duke of Grafton was one of the king's several sons by Barbara, Duchess of Cleveland, Lady Castlemain. The "pious brother" was Charles's brother, the future James II, who disliked the handsome, but troublesome Monmouth, even more so when Charles talked of having Monmouth legitimatized and declared his successor.

> Little General Monk
> Sat upon a trunk,
> Eating a crust of bread;
> There fell a hot coal
> And burnt in his clothes a hole,
> Now little General Monk is dead.
>> Keep always from the fire:
>> If it catch your attire,
>> You, too, like Monk, will be dead.

With his name clearly a part, this pointed doggerel obviously refers to the great Cromwellian soldier, General George Monck, Duke of Albemarle (1608–1669). Its first appearance in print seems to have been in about 1795, in *History of Master Friendly*. When Halliwell collected it in 1842, the last three lines were included, they being typical of the moralizing tacked on to nursery ditties.

> Hark, hark, the dogs do bark;
> The beggars are coming to town;
> Some in rags and some in tags,
> And some in velvet gowns [And one in a velvet gown].

Although there is historical reference to the "beggars coming to town" in Tudor days, to the distress of those living in isolated outskirts, the rhyme is traditionally assigned to the Dutchmen in league with William III (1650–1702), as "beggars" was a common nickname in England for the Dutch. The "one in a velvet gown" may refer to William himself. The rhyme is evidently derived from a song in *Westminster Drollery* (1672), the first verse of which was:

> Hark, hark, the Doggs do bark,
>> My Wife is coming in
> With Rogues and Jades,
>> And roaring blades,
> They make a devilish din.

The ditty was in *Gammer Gurton's Garland* in 1784, and *Tommy Thumb's Pretty Song Book* in 1788.

What is the rhyme for porringer?
What is the rhyme for porringer?
The king he had a daughter fair
And gave the Prince of Orange her.

This derives from a Jacobite song of around 1689 whose other verses hinted at threatening the life of William, Prince of Orange (1650–1702), later William III. The nursery snippet refers to his marriage to Mary, later Mary II, the daughter of James II. This couple is also lampooned in the following verse. "Porringer" appeared in Jacobite collections in 1819 and 1829, and was collected by Halliwell as a nursery rhyme in 1842. (As a riddle, it answers itself.)

William and Mary, George and Anne,
Four such children had never a man;
They put their father to flight and shame,
And called their brother a shocking bad name.

This taunting, disrespectful rhyme is about the daughters and sons-in-law of James II, concluding with a jab about their attitudes toward their brother, James Francis Edward Stuart, the "Old Pretender." The "shocking bad name" they called their brother was *bastard*.

Over the water and over the lea,
    And over the water to Charley.
Charley loves good ale and wine,
    And Charley loves good brandy,
And Charley loves a pretty girl
    As sweet as sugar candy.

Over the water and over the lea,
    And over the water to Charley.
I'll have none of your nasty beef,
    Nor I'll have none of your barley,
But I'll have some of your very best flour
    To make a white cake for my Charley.

Everything in this rhyme describes the life of Charles Edward Stuart (1720–1788), the daring "Bonnie Prince Charlie," eldest son of the Old Pretender. Afflicted with a lifelong love of ale and wine, sweets, and pretty girls, Bonnie Prince Charlie briefly showed his military courage, then spent the last years of his life in Rome and Florence, under the title of the Duke of Albany. He was also dubbed the "Young Pretender." Bonnie Prince

Charlie was the subject of much English and Scottish poetry. The nursery ditty was itself a parody of a Jacobite song of 1748. It was in *Songs for the Nursery* in 1805, *Mother Goose's Quarto* in ca.1825, and collected by Halliwell in 1842.

> Lady Queen Anne [Queen Anne, Queen Anne],
> She sits in the sun [You sit in the sun],
> As fair as a lily
> As brown as a bun [As white as a swan].

This pokes fun at Queen Anne (1665–1714), last Stuart ruler of England, who loved to sit in the gardens of Kensington palace with her tambour frame or light books of verse. When Halliwell collected it in 1849, he presented it as a game in which a ball was hidden on one player:

> Queen Anne, Queen Anne, who sits on her throne,
> As fair as a lily, as white as a swan;
> The king sends you three letters,
> And begs you'll read one.
>   I cannot read one unless I read all,
>   So pray, _____, deliver the ball.

> Georgie Porgie [Rowley Powley], pudding and pie
> Kissed the girls and made them cry;
> When the boys came out to play [girls began to cry]
> Georgie Porgie [Rowley Powley] ran away.

The usual connection of this verse is with George I (1660–1727), but some commentators have suggested that it could be about either George Villiers, the Duke of Buckingham or Charles II. The verse was collected by Halliwell in 1844 as "Rowley Powley...."

English royalty, as can be seen, has been the main butt of the satires to be found in the sometimes nonsensical wordings of Mother Goose rhymes. In the twentieth century, rhymes written for the purposes of satire are frequently rewritten from either the nursery or other classic works. Perhaps original and rewritten contemporary jabs and jibes will some day be contained in nursery lore, and researchers still to come will try to trace their meanings.

HEAR WHAT MA'AM GOOSE SAYS!

MY dear little Blossoms, there are now in this world, and always will be, a great many grannies besides myself, both in petticoats and pantaloons, some a deal younger to be sure; but all monstrous wise, and of my own family name. These old women, who never had chick nor child of their own, but who always know how to bring up other people's children, will tell you with very long faces, that my enchanting, quieting, soothing volume, my all-sufficient anodyne for cross, peevish, won't-be-comforted little bairns, ought to be laid aside for more learned books, such as *they* could select and publish. Fudge! I tell you that all their batterings can't deface my beauties, nor their wise pratings equal my wiser prattlings; and all imitators of my refreshing songs might as well write a new Billy Shakespeare as another Mother Goose — we two great poets were born together, and we shall go out of the world together.

No, no, my Melodies will never die,
While nurses sing, or babies cry.

8. The Bard Evokes the Nursery
Tracking Shakespearean References

Probably no literary pursuits are more marked by close attention to details than those of Shakespearean scholars. Everything noted by the Bard of Avon has some import. That William Shakespeare, who wrote for the masses and was embraced by the literati, should be associated with nursery rhymes is no surprise. Living from 1564 to 1616 and considered the greatest of English poets and dramatists, he was well-versed in the lore of his day. About a quarter of the Mother Goose rhymes current today were known during Shakespeare's youth. (See chart on page 14.)

Of course, assessing his intentions and allusions from this distance leaves a possible gap in interpretation. While some nursery scholars insist that references in his plays are to certain verses, others suggest they may not be. But the possibility that they are requires that the nursery scholar, as well as the Shakespearean, take a look at the phrases.

Here then, are lines from Shakespeare that evoke lines or phrases from nursery lore. Dates given for the plays are those most traditionally cited; most of the nursery rhymes may be found in full elsewhere in this volume; if not, they are given here.

- From *Merry Wives of Windsor* (1597–1601)
  I.i. ...*Slender*. I had rather than forty shillings I had my Book of Songs and Sonnets here. (Enter *Simple*)
  How now, Simple! where have you been? I must wait on myself, must I? You have not the Book of Riddles about you, have you?
  Simple. Book of Riddles! why did you not lend it to Alice Shortcake upon All-hallowmas last, a fortnight afore Michaelmas?...

The book referred to is thought by Shakespearean scholars to be *The Booke of Meery Riddles*, which was in copy in 1600, and probably, by other references as well as by internal evidence, as early as 1575, as *The book of Riddels*. It contained some of the riddles still known in the nursery today. (See Chapter 3.)

  IV.ii. *Mistress Page* (describing how Mr. Ford thinks himself a cuckold)
  ...and so buffets himself on the forehead, crying, "Peer out, Peer out...."

"Snail, snail, come out of your hole..." has also been invoked as "Peer out...." Mr. Ford, of course, is referring to his cuckold's "horns."

- From *Twelfth Night or, What You Will* (1599–1600)
  V. *Clown.* (song ending the play)
  When that I was a little tiny boy,
    With a hey, ho, the wind and the rain.
  ...But when I came to man's estate,
    With hey, ho, etc....

These lines have been compared to "When I was a little boy..." (see page 65).

- From *King Lear* (1605–1606)
  III.ii. *Fool* (singing)
  He that has and a little tiny wit, —
    With hey, ho, the wind and the rain, —

Must make content with his fortunes fit,
 For the rain it raineth every day.

These lines have been compared to "When I was a little boy..." (see page 65).

> III.iv. *Lear.* ...Judicious punishment! 'twas this flesh begot
>   Those pelican daughters.
> *Edgar.* Pillycock sat on Pillicock-hill:
>   Halloo, halloo, loo, loo!

The 1810 edition of *Gammer Gurton's Garland* contained the couplet:

Pillycock, pillycock, sate on a hill,
If he's not gone—he sits there still.

(The verse resembles "There was an old woman, liv'd under a hill..." which is on page 59.)

The reference to the "pelican daughters" is to the belief that young pelicans fed on the flesh of their mothers' breasts. Although some interpretations ally *pillycock* to *pelican*, others suggest it is an old vulgarism which has since been suppressed.

> III.vi. *Edgar* (in his character of Mad Tom, speaking to Lear)
> *Edgar.* Sleepest or wakest thou, jolly shepherd?
>   Thy sheep be in the corn;
>   And for one blast of thy minikin mouth,
>   Thy sheep shall take no harm.

This is clearly a parallel to:

Little Boy Blue, come blow your horn,
The sheep's in the meadow, the cow's in the corn.
Where's the little boy who looks after the sheep?
Under the haystack [haycock], fast asleep.
 Will you wake him, no, not I,
 For if I do, he's sure to cry.

(The last two lines are not always seen with the verse.) It was collected for the nursery in *The Famous Tommy Thumb's Little Story-Book*, ca.1760. Boy Blue is also seen in A.A. Milne's *When We Were Very Young*, 1924. The "Little Boy Blue" of Eugene Field's poem is not connected to the nursery rhyme.

• From *The Two Noble Kinsmen* (written with John Fletcher, 1613)
  III.v. (The jailor's daughter sings.)
  There were three fools, fell out about an howlet
    The one said it was an owl,
    The other he said nay,
    The third he said it was a hawk, and her bells were cut away.

The similarity to "There were three jovial Welshmen. . ." is obvious (see page 223).

Less traceable references are those to "Ding, dong, bell, pussy's in the well. . . ." There was also current a round that was later printed in Ravenscroft's *Pammelia, Musicks Miscellanie* in 1609:

  Jacke boy, ho boy newes,
    The cat is in the well,
  Let us ring now for her Knell,
  Ding dong ding dong Bell.

It should be noted, too, that the practice of ringing bells as a "knell" or "toll" was very common. The following two references, therefore, may or may not harken back to the nursery rhyme.

• From *The Merchant of Venice* (1596–1597)
  III.ii. (Music while *Bassanio* comments on the caskets to himself.)
  . . . Let us all ring fancy's knell:
  I'll begin it, — Ding, dong, bell.

• From *The Tempest* (1611–1612):
  I.ii. *Ariel* (singing about Ferdinand's father)
  . . . Sea nymphs hourly ring his knell:
  Burthen. Ding-dong.
  Ariel. Hark! now I hear them, — Ding-dong, bell.

Some nursery commentators have pointed out that "Jack and Jill" (or Gill) appears in Shakespeare's works. In *Midsummer Night's Dream*, III.ii. *Puck* says, "Jack shall have Jill, Naught shall go ill. . ." and in *Love's Labour's Lost*, V.ii., *Berowne* says, "Our wooing doth not end like an old play; Jack hath not Jill." It is not likely, however, that these are references to the nursery verse; most scholars hold to the theory that Shakespeare used the terms *Jack* and *Jill* in their vernacular as *lad* and *lass*.

Numerous other writers have also made references to nursery rhymes, of course. Among those who made liberal use of these were Henry Carey (ca.1690–1743), Charles Lamb (1775–1834), Lewis Carroll (1832–1898), Rudyard Kipling (1865–1934), and Beatrix Potter (1866–1943). Writers who alluded to Mother Goose in passing are legion — and hardly of sufficient interest to note.

9. Nursery Versery from Erudite Pens
Identifying Some Authors

In the proliferation of child-lore anthologies, there are a number of rhymes whose authors are not deserving of the fate of the anonymous "Mother Goose" or "traditional nursery" designation. Some of these writers can be traced accurately, others with less certainty. There are also some works by writers whose names have always been firmly attached to their material, which nevertheless have been published in children's literature as "Mother Goose" rhymes.

There's more than one reason why certain verses, with or without author credits attached, have been absorbed into the Mother Goose milieu. In the early days of printed literature, it was not uncommon for pieces to appear without author bylines. Even where author credits were given in one publication, this might not hold true throughout a piece's republications. Thus, it was inevitable that many writers' names became dissociated from their works. In addition, authors have always, naturally, liked to see their works in print. If a publisher wanted to issue a "Mother Goose" book, with mostly anonymous rhymes, but also with such pieces as "Old Mother Hubbard," "Three Little Kittens," or "Wynken, Blynken, and Nod," few authors would refuse to be included.

Other questions arise also. Is a piece automatically a "Mother Goose" rhyme if it appeared in a collection so titled? Is it a "Mother Goose" rhyme if it is *perceived* to be so by users? There's the matter of semantics again — in the United States, "Mother Goose" is the accepted terminology for a certain group of children's rhymes. In England, the term "nursery rhymes" covers the same material, although the influx of American publications has made some conversion in nomenclature. But the extension of semantics reaches to the fine line where one must try to differentiate between these "traditional" nursery rhymes and the "literary" ones, the latter usually referring to verses written for children by known authors. But the muddy waters of academia are, and probably always will be, subject to the stirrings of "the folk" — by oral and written tradition that defies academic labels and makes what it will of literary output.

We have then, several categories. There are the ancient pieces of child-lore originally preserved through oral tradition, and, since the eighteenth century, in various written forms. There are a few whose authorship is credited without finite documentation, but deemed reliably certain from the general evidence available, by common assent of authorities in the field. There are the authorships which were once known, but became relegated to anonymity. There are also those anonymous by the author's choice, but revealed or discovered later. And finally, there are pieces which have always been credited to their authors, yet have been accepted into that child-lore aura that separates the "Mother Goose" or traditional nursery rhyme from other literary works for children.

Most of the children's verses by Edward Lear, Christina Rossetti, Lewis Carroll, and Eugene Field, for instance, have appeared as a body of work not designated as Mother Goose. Thus, we tend to think of them as literary nursery rhymes. Yet, the pieces of theirs which appear below have been included in editions of Mother Goose. As bylines have frequently been ignored with public domain works, sometimes their names have not appeared. For the most part, unless people are children's literature scholars, or perhaps writers with a professional interest in author creditation, they are content to enjoy the work without undue concern for who wrote it. Children certainly do not care, nor is there any reason they should. As maturity develops, however, the appreciation of the talents that created the material brings with it an interest in the creator.

Publishing practices are responsible for much of the confusion about Mother Goose authorship. As the nineteenth century was ending, fewer of these nebulous instances were perpetrated on then-contemporary works, but the old prejudices remained in effect. Without concern for new research that identified authors, the works continued to appear anonymously in nursery editions. Indeed, even with the facts available, they will no doubt continue to endure anonymity. The antiquity of much of "Mother Goose" material contributes, as does the sincere albeit erroneous belief that all these pieces are somehow "folklore."

There does seem to be a greater concern among late twentieth century writers and publishers to properly document known writers of works. It is with that imperative in mind that this chapter identifies known authors of so-called "Mother Goose" rhymes. One can imagine the surprise many of them would feel to know these pieces had survived as nursery lore.

As nearly as possible, the following verses are in the chronological order of their authors' births. In a few cases, only the author's name and initial year of publication of the rhyme are known, as obscure authors' birth and death dates are not recorded for posterity in encyclopedias. As one may assume that in general the verses were created by writers in adulthood, birth dates used in conjunction with "best known" dates essentially keep the chronological appearance of the rhymes close to fact. It is fascinating to the nursery lore scholar interested in tracing origins to examine the backgrounds and other literary works of these authors, thereby to gain some insights into the evolution of these pieces into Mother Goose literature.

Fragment of original:

The Wind hath blown my Plaid away, or, A Discourse betwixt a young Woman and the Elphin Knight.

(The Knight)
...Married with me if thou wouldst be,
A courtesie thou must do me.

For thou must shape a sark to me,
Without any cut or heme, quoth he.

Thou must shape it knife-and-sheerlesse,
And also sue it needle-threedlesse....

(The young woman)
If that piece of courtesie I do to thee,
Another thou must do to me.

I have an aiker of good ley-land,
Which lyeth low by yon sea-strand.

For thou must eare it with thy horn,
So thou must sow it with thy corn.

And bigg a cart of stone and lyme,
Robin Redbreast he must trail it hame.

Thou must barn it in a mouse-holl,
And thrash it into thy shoes soll.

And thou must winnow it in thy looff,
And also seck it in thy glove.

For thou must bring it over the sea,
And thou must bring it dry home to me.

When thou hast gotten thy turns well done,
Then come to me and get thy sark then. . . .

The two following traditional nursery rhymes are *separately* derived from the above.

Traditional derivation I:

Can you make me a cambric shirt,
  Parsley, sage, rosemary, and thyme,
Without any seam or needle work?
  And you shall be a true lover of mine.

Can you wash it in yonder well,
  Parsley, sage, rosemary, and thyme,
Where never spring water, nor rain ever fell?
  And you shall be a true lover of mine.

Can you dry it on yonder thorn,
  Parsley, sage, rosemary, and thyme,
Which never bore blossom since Adam was born?
  And you shall be a true lover of mine.

Now you have asked me questions three,
  Parsley, sage, rosemary, and thyme,
I hope you'll answer as many for me;
  And you shall be a true lover of mine.

Can you find me an acre of land,
  Parsley, sage, rosemary, and thyme,
Between the salt water and the sea sand?
  And you shall be a true lover of mine.

Can you plow it with a ram's horn,
  Parsley, sage, rosemary, and thyme,
And sow it all over with one peppercorn?
  And you shall be a true lover of mine.

Can you reap it with sickle of leather,
  Parsley, sage, rosemary, and thyme,
And bind it up with a peacock's feather?
  And you shall be a true lover of mine.

When you have done and finished your work,
  Parsley, sage, rosemary, and thyme,
Then come to me for your cambric shirt;
  And you shall be a true lover of mine.

Traditional derivation II:

My father left me three acres of land,
  Sing ivy, sing ivy;
My father left me three acres of land,
  Sing holly, go whistle and ivy!

I plowed it with a ram's horn,
  Sing ivy, sing ivy;
And sowed it all with one peppercorn,
  Sing holly, go whistle and ivy!

I harrowed it with brambles five,
  Sing ivy, sing ivy;
And reaped it with my pocketknife,
  Sing holly, go whistle and ivy!

I tied it up with purple yarn,
  Sing ivy, sing ivy;
And got the mice to carry it to the barn,
  Sing holly, go whistle and ivy!

I thrashed it with a goose's quill,
  Sing ivy, sing ivy;
And got the cat to carry it to the mill,
  Sing holly, go whistle and ivy!

The miller he swore he would have her paw,
  Sing ivy, sing ivy;
And the cat she swore she would scratch his face,
  Sing holly, go whistle and ivy!

My father left me three acres of land,
Sing ivy, sing ivy;
My father left me three acres of land,
Sing holly, go whistle and ivy!

The original of the above is attributed to James I of Scotland (1394–1437): James was sent to France for asylum in 1406, but captured by the British, who educated him and treated him well, finally releasing him in 1424, whereupon he took the throne of Scotland. He brought peace to Scotland by ruthless methods. His popularity was lessened by his vindictiveness and quick temper.

Despite his violent side, he was known to be a writer of poetry and ballads. A broadside ballad attributed to him, *The Wind has blown my Plaid away, or, The Discourse betwixt a young Woman and the Elphin Knight*, was printed in about 1670, more than 200 years after he died. The ballad may well have been inspired by a *tale* traced to the fourteenth century (contemporary to James I) which appeared in *Gesta Romanorum*. This was retold in 1812, in German, by the brothers Grimm in their fairy tale collection — the story of a king who vows to marry any maid who can make him a shirt from three square inches of linen. The American folklorist, author of the five-volume *English and Scottish Popular Ballads*, Professor F.J. Child (1825–1896) said, "A man asking a maid to sew him a shirt is equivalent to asking for her love, and her consent to sew the shirt is equivalent to an acceptance of the suitor."

The "adapters" who "modernized" the early ballad are unknown, but as nursery lore, "Can you make me a cambric shirt..." appeared in the 1810 *Gammer Gurton's Garland*, and in Halliwell's 1843 collection, and remained in nursery literature ever since. Halliwell did not collect "My father gave me three acres of land..." until 1853, but it, too, became a traditional children's verse. The refrains, mentioning plants frequently thought to have magical powers, may well be derived from earlier incantations.

Thomas Dekker (sometimes spelled Decker) (ca.1572–1632), an English dramatist and poet who also wrote pamphlets and satirical pieces, wrote the following verses. Among his dramas are *The Shoemaker's Holiday* (1600) and *Old Fortunatus* (1600).

Golden slumbers kiss your eyes,
Smiles awake you when you rise.
Sleep, pretty wanton; do not cry,
And I will sing you a lullaby:
Rock them, rock them, lullaby.

Care is heavy, therefore sleep you;
You are care, and care must keep you.

Sleep, pretty wanton; do not cry,
And I will sing you a lullaby:
Rock them, rock them, lullaby.

Ben Jonson (1573–1637):

I went to the toad that lives under the wall,
I charmed him out, and he came at my call;
I scratched out the eyes of the owl before,
I tore the bat's wing: what would you have more?

Buzz, quoth the blue fly,
Hum, quoth the bee,
Buzz and hum they cry,
And so do we;
In his ear, in his nose,
Thus do you see,
He ate the dormouse,
Else it was thee.

Jonson was an English dramatist (both comedies and tragedies), lyric poet, and actor, whose life and works bridged the Elizabethan and Jacobean periods. He was a friend of Shakespeare and other greats of his day. His tomb in Westminster Abbey is inscribed, "O rare Ben Jonson." (He is the only person ever entombed in the Abbey in a vertical position, with his head to the sky, a situation brought about because King Charles I had promised him burial in any nave of his choice, but at his death, it was found that the chosen spot had only "eighteen inches of square ground," a circumstance that seems itself appropriate for a Mother Goose rhyme, but even Goldsmith and Shakespeare passed it by. A contemporary ditty does satirize the circumstance — in an appropriately Mother Goose–like manner: "Ben Jonson's dead; How shall we bury him? On his head? No, he was a merry man; On his feet — It's the best we can — Rare Ben Jonson, The Vertical man." — *Eve Stedman, 1985.*

"I went to the toad that lives under the wall..." is the song of the eleventh hag in Jonson's *The Masque of Queens* (1609). Jonson himself explained the toads, owls' eyes, and bats' wings for Queen Elizabeth I, saying, "These also, both by the confessions of Witches, and testemonye of writers, are of principal vse in theyr witchcraft." It first appeared as a nursery rhyme in Halliwell's collection of 1842.

"Buzz, quoth the blue fly..." is from Jonson's *The Masque of Oberon* (1616). It first appeared as a nursery rhyme in *Songs for the Nursery* (1805) and reappeared again in Halliwell's 1842 collection, wherein it was described as "a most common nursery song at the present time," without creditation, Halliwell evidently being unaware that it was by Jonson.

Will you lend me your mare to ride?
No, she is lame leaping over a stile.
Alack! and I must go to the fair,
I'll give you good money for lending your mare.
Oh, oh! say you so?
Money will make the mare to go.

This is from Edmund Nelham (ca.1609), a seventeenth century English "Gentleman of the Chapel Royal" by 1617. This catch appeared as early as 1609, with numerous publications, eventually moving into the nursery, causing the rhyme to be included in Halliwell's collection of 1846. The last line, as "Money will make the gray mare to go," was included in Halliwell's proverb collection of 1659.

By John Wallis (1616–1703):

When a Twister a-twisting will twist him a twist,
For the twisting of his twist, he three twines doth intwist;
But if one of the twines of the twist do untwist,
The twine that untwisteth, untwisteth the twist.

Untwirling the twine that untwisteth between,
He twirls, with his twister, the two in a twine;
Then, twice having twisted the twines of the twine,
He twitcheth, the twice he had twined, in twain.

The twain that, in twining, before in the twine,
As twines were intwisted; he now doth untwine;
Twixt the twain inter-twisting a twine more between,
He, twirling his twister, makes a twist of the twine.

Dr. Wallis is a hybrid entry into Mother Goose lore, having been an English grammarian and mathematician who systematized the use of formulas, and introduced the use of the symbol ∞ for *infinity*.

This marvelously twisted tongue-twister appeared in his *Grammatica Linguae Anglicanae* (1674), evidently translated and enlarged from a four-line French version he had heard in 1653. It first appeared for children around 1825 in *Mother Goose's Quarto*, and has remained (usually anonymously) in juvenile literature ever since.

There was a little man,
And he woo'd a little maid,

And he said, Little maid will you wed [you wed, wed, wed]?
  I have little more to say,
  Than will you, yea or nay?
For the least is soonest mended [soonest mended, ded, ded].

  Then this little maid she said,
  Little sir, you've little said,
To induce a little maid for to wed [to wed, wed, wed];
  You must say a little more,
  And produce a little ore,
E'er I make a little print in your bed [Ere I to the church will led, led, led].

  Then the little man replied,
  If you'll be my little bride,
I will raise my love notes a little higher [little higher, higher, higher];
  Though I little live to prate
  Yet you'll find my heart is great,
With the little God of Love all on fire [on fire, fire, fire].

  Then the little Maid she said [maid replied],
  Your fire may warm the bed [If I should be your bride],
Pray, what must what must we have for to eat [to eat, eat, eat]?
  Will the flames that you're so rich in
  Make a fire in the kitchen,
And little God of Love turn the spit [the spit, spit, spit]?

  Then the little man he sighed,
  And some say a little cried,
And his little heart was big with sorrow [with sorrow, sorrow, sorrow];
  I'll be your little slave,
  And if the little that I have,
Be too little, little dear, I will borrow [will borrow, borrow, borrow].

  Then the little man so gent,
  Made the little maid relent,
And set her little soul a-thinking [a-thinking, king, king];
  Though his little was but small,
  Yet she had his little all,
And could have of a cat but her skin [her skin, skin, skin].

The above are by Sir Charles Sedley (aka Sidley) (ca.1639–1701) or (less likely) Sir Charles Sedley (1721–1778). In 1764, Horace Walpole recorded in his Printing Office journal, "Printed some copies of a ballad by Sir Charles Sidley, beginning 'There was a little man.'" The elder was a Restoration wit and song-writer; the younger was his great-grandson, a contemporary and friend of Walpole's. Most scholarly conclusions lean toward the elder as being the author; it is likely that his great-grandson had possession of the piece and passed it over to Walpole for printing on a broadside.

The broadside version, as above, differs here and there from the 1765 version published in *Mother Goose's Melody* (see page 56). As the broadside appeared the year before, one must assume that the changes were incorporated by the editor of *Mother Goose's Melody*, who also added a maxim to the verse.

	Alternative lines
Patty Cake, Patty Cake,	Pat-a-cake, pat-a-cake,
Baker's Man:	
That I will Master,	Make me a cake
As fast as I can.	As fast as you can.
Prick it and prick it,	Prick it, and pat it,
And mark it with a T,	And mark it with a B,
And there will be enough	And put it in the oven
For Jackey and Me.	For Baby and me.

The first column above is by Thomas d'Urfey (1653–1723); the first version of this old favorite appeared as an infant's chant in d'Urfey's comedy, *The Campaigners* (1698). The second version appears more traditionally in most Mother Goose collections. It is a hand-clapping game for small children, often accompanied with additional fingerplay motions to act out the verse.

The following is probably by Jonathan Swift (1667–1745):

Oh my kitten a kitten
And oh my kitten my deary.
Such a sweet pap is this [sweet pet as this]
There is not a far nor neary.

Here we go up, up, up,
Here we go down, down, down.
Here we go backwards and backwards,
And here we go roundroundround.

Swift, British clergyman, author, poet, and satirist, is best known for his brilliant satire on humankind, *Gulliver's Travels* (1726). His last years were lost in insanity. Although some Swift scholars have doubted his authorship of the rhyme, others cite early notes referring to it, and point to the publication, probably in 1728, of a parody which used the pattern to deride Swift himself:

O my sweet Jonathan, Jonathan,
O my sweet Jonathan Swifty...

This would indicate that the original must have circulated before 1728. It appeared in 1740 as "The Nurse's Song" in the fourth volume of Allan Ramsay's *Tea-Table Miscellany*. It was evidently meant to be a chant to accompany swinging a child. It made further appearances in the 1744 *Tommy Thumb's Pretty Song Book*, and in Newbery's circa 1765 *Mother Goose's Melody* (see page 66).

Probably by John Lookes (1675):

There was an old woman
  Sold puddings and pies;
She went to the mill
  And dust blew in her eyes.
She has hot pies
  And cold pies to sell;
Wherever she goes
  You may follow her smell.

Lookes was an English ballad-writer, composer of "The Ragman" which closely resembles the broadside ballad "The Old Pudding Pye Woman" (registered in 1675), of which the above is the first verse. Ninety years later, a version appeared in *Mother Goose's Melody*, with a maxim. (See page 68.) Additional verses of the broadside described the old woman's disgusting personal habits and concluded with a warning not to buy her pies. Thus, while the nursery version (the first verse) might indicate that one would know the woman by the delicious smell of her pies, the original intent was quite different.

Original lines

Nauty Pauty, Jack-a-Dandy,†
Stole a piece of Sugar-Candy,
From the Grocer's Shoppy-shop,
And away did hoppy-hop.

†*Traditional line: Namby-Pamby, Jack-a-Dandy,*

Alternate traditional lines

Handy-spandy, Jack-a-Dandy,
Loves plum cake and sugar candy,
He bought some at a grocer's shop,
And out he came, hop, hop, hop, hop.

The original version of the above is by Henry Carey (ca.1690–1743). Carey was an English poet and musician, author-composer of "Sally in Our Alley." In 1725 he published *Namby Pamby or a Panegyric on the New Versification*. The headpiece was "Nauty-Pauty, Jack-a-Dandy. . . ." As Carey introduced other nursery rhymes into his treatise, it is thought that the theme, at least, of "Nauty-Pauty. . ." was based on existing child-lore, possibly the same referred to in the anonymous poem "The Heaven-Drivers," which dates back to 1701, in the lines, ". . . You Saucy Jack a dandy / Nurs'd up with tea and sugar candy. . . ." Such a tracing back to a possibly original theme, however, is burdened with conjecture.

It is interesting that the first line became, in the traditional version, "Namby-Pamby, Jack-a-Dandy. . ." because that was the nickname Carey and Alexander Pope bestowed on Ambrose Philips, whose sentimental, sweetly sickening style was being parodied in the original Carey version. Some subsequent editor no doubt decided to make the allusion even less subtle by using Carey's nickname for Philips in the first line. And that edited version is what became the traditional verse.

Richard Brown (ca.1701) wrote the following original version (I):

'Tis pitty poor Barnet a Vigilant, Vigilant Curr,
That us'd for to bark, if a mouse, if a mouse did but stir,
Should being grown old, and unable, unable to bark,
Be doom'd by a Priest, be doom'd by a Priest, to be hanged by his clark,
I pray good Sir therefore, weigh right well, right well his Case,
And save us poor Barnet, Hang cleric, hang cleric, hang cleric in's place.

Traditional version (I):

Barnaby Bright he was a sharp cur,
He always would bark if a mouse did not stir,
But now he's grown old, and can no longer bark,
He's condemned by the parson to be hanged by the clerk.

Traditional version (II):

Peter White will ne'er go right;
Would you know the reason why?
He follows his nose wherever he goes,
And that stands all awry.

Brown was an English composer of rounds (also then called catches) and other witty songs. Both of the above were originally meant for three voices entering at one-third intervals from each other.

Traditional version:

    Old King Cole
      Was a merry old soul,
   And a merry old soul was he;
      He called for his pipe
      And he called for his bowl,
  And he called for his fiddlers three.

Every fiddler, he had a fiddle,
And a very fine fiddle had he;
Twee tweedle dee, tweedle dee, went the fiddlers.
Oh there's none so rare
As can compare
With King Cole and his fiddlers three.

Original version:

Good King Cole,
And he call'd for his Bowle,
And he call'd for Fidler's three;
And there was a Fiddle, Fiddle,
And twice Fiddle, Fiddle,
For 'twas my Lady's Birth-day,
Therefore we keep Holy-day
And come to be merry.

The original is possibly by William King (1708). It is not certain if King actually wrote "Old King Cole . . ." but there is no evidence of its existence before its appearance in his satire, *Useful Transactions in Philosophy*. King purported to speculate on the subject of the rhyme, mentioning the Prince that Built Colchester, and a Reading clothier named Cole-Brook, then concluding that it was the former. Quite possibly he wrote the rhyme himself, then used it as a stepping stone for his thesis.

There were three English kings named Cole, but the one written about in the ditty, which underwent some changes and made its way firmly into Mother Goose domain, is believed to be the popular and courageous Cole of the third century, who ascended to the throne following Asclepiod. In Colchester, England, the vestige of a legendary Roman amphitheatre is known as "King Cole's Kitchen."

By Dr. Samuel Johnson (1709–1784):

I put my hat upon my head
And walked into the Strand,
And there I met another man
Whose hat was in his hand.

If a man who turnips cries,
Cry not when his father dies,
It is proof that he would rather
Have a turnip than his father.

Johnson wrote many acclaimed works, among them *A Dictionary of the English Language* (1755) and *Lives of the Poets* (1779–81). His prose has been called ponderous, but acknowledged to be incisive and distinguished, with shrewd and interesting, though prejudiced, critical judgments. Johnson was the dictator of literary taste in London, and the predominant literary figure of his age. The other well-known writers of the day are frequently spoken of as "being one of Dr. Johnson's circle."

The above two are the only nonsense verses known to have been written by Johnson. History records that after hearing a silly piece by Lope de Vega which he declared was "a mere play on words," he immediately created "If a man who turnips cries" which he said made as much sense.

The following long work is by William Cowper (1731–1800) and is called "The Diverting History of John Gilpin 'showing how he went farther than he intended and came safe home again'":

John Gilpin was a citizen
   Of credit and renown,
A train-band captain eke was he
   Of famous London town.

John Gilpin's spouse said to her
      dear,
   "Though wedded we have been
These twice ten tedious years, yet
      we
   No holiday have seen.

"Tomorrow is our wedding-day,
   And we will then repair
Unto the Bell at Edmonton,
   All in a chaise and pair.

"My sister, and my sister's child,
   Myself, and children three,
Will fill the chaise; so you must
      ride
   On horseback after we."

He soon replied, "I do admire
   Of womankind but one,
And you are she, my dearest dear,
   Therefore it shall be done.

"I am a linen-draper bold,
   As all the world doth know,

And my good friend the calender
   Will lend his horse to go."

Quoth Mrs. Gilpin, "That's well
      said;
   And for that wine is dear,
We will be furnished with our
      own,
   Which is both bright and
      clear."

John Gilpin kissed his loving wife;
   O'erjoyed was he to find,
That though on pleasure she was
      bent,
   She had a frugal mind.

The morning came, the chaise
      was brought,
   But yet was not allowed
To drive up to the door, lest all
   Should say that she was proud.

So three doors off the chaise was
      stayed,
   Where they did all get in;
Six precious souls, and all agog
   To dash through thick and
      thin.

Smack went the whip, round
    went the wheels,
  Were never folks so glad,
The stones did rattle underneath,
  As if Cheapside were mad.

John Gilpin at his horse's side
  Seized fast the flowing mane,
And up he got, in haste to ride,
  But soon came down again;

For saddle-tree scarce reached had
    he,
  His journey to begin,
When, turning round his head,
    he saw
  Three customers come in.

So down he came; for loss of
    time
  Although it grieved him sore,
Yet loss of pence, full well he
    knew,
  Would trouble him much
    more.

"Twas long before the customers
  Were suited to their mind,
When Betty screaming came
    downstairs,
  "The wine is left behind!"

"Good lack!" quoth he—"yet
    bring it me,
  My leathern belt likewise,
In which I bear my trusty sword,
  When I do exercise."

Now Mistress Gilpin (careful
    soul!)
  Had two stone bottles found,
To hold the liquor that she
    loved,
  And keep it safe and sound.

Each bottle had a curling ear,
  Through which the belt he
    drew,
And hung a bottle on each side,
  To make his balance true.

Then over all, that he might be
  Equipped from top to toe,
His long red cloak, well brushed
    and neat,
  He manfully did throw.

Now see him mounted once
    again
  Upon his nimble steed,
Full slowly pacing o'er the stones,
  With caution and good heed.

But finding soon a smoother road
  Beneath his well-shod feet,
The snorting beast began to trot,
  Which galled him in his seat.

So, "Fair and softly," John he
    cried,
  But John he cried in vain;
That trot became a gallop soon,
  In spite of curb and rein.

So stooping down, as needs he
    must
  Who cannot sit upright,
He grasped the mane with both
    his hands,
  And eke with all his might.

His horse, who never in that sort
  Had handled been before,
What thing upon his back had
    got
  Did wonder more and more.

Away went Gilpin, neck or
    naught;
  Away went hat and wig:

He little dreamt, when he set out,
  Of running such a rig.

The wind did blow, the cloak did
  fly,
Like streamer long and gay,
Till, loop and button failing
  both,
  At last it flew away.

Then might all people well
  discern
The bottles he had slung;
A bottle swinging at each side,
  As hath been said or sung.

The dogs did bark, the children
  screamed,
Up flew the windows all;
And every soul cried out, "Well
  done!"
  As loud as he could bawl.

Away went Gilpin—who but he?
  His fame soon spread around;
"He carries weight!" "He rides a
  race!"
  "'Tis for a thousand pound!"

And still, as fast as he drew near,
  'Twas wonderful to view
How in a trice the turnpike-men
  Their gates wide open threw.

And now, as he went bowing
  down
His reeking head full low,
The bottles twain behind his back
  Were shattered at a blow.

Down ran the wine into the road,
  Most piteous to be seen,
Which made his horse's flanks to
  smoke
  As they had basted been.

But still he seemed to carry
  weight,

With leathern girdle braced;
For all might see the bottle-necks
  Still dangling at his waist.

Thus all through merry Islington
  These gambols he did play,
Until he came unto the Wash
  Of Edmonton so gay;

And there he threw the Wash
  about
On both sides of the way,
Just like unto a trundling mop,
  Or a wild goose at play.

At Edmonton his loving wife
  From the balcony spied
Her tender husband, wondering
  much
  To see how he did ride.

"Stop, stop, John Gilpin!—Here's
  the house!"
They all at once did cry:
"The dinner waits, and we are
  tired;"—
  Said Gilpin—"So am I."

But yet his horse was not a whit
  Inclined to tarry there!
For why?—his owner had a house
  Full ten miles off, at Ware.

So like an arrow swift he flew,
  Shot by an archer strong;
So did he fly—which brings me to
  The middle of my song.

Away went Gilpin, out of breath,
  And sore against his will,
Till at his friend the calender's
  His horse at last stood still.

The calender, amazed to see
  His neighbor in such trim,
Laid down his pipe, flew to the
  gate,
  And thus accosted him:

"What news? what news? Your
    tidings tell;
    Tell me you must and shall—
Say why bareheaded you are
    come,
    Or why you come at all?"

Now Gilpin had a pleasant wit
    And loved a timely joke;
And thus unto the calender
    In merry guise he spoke:

"I came because your horse
    would come,
    And, if I well forebode,
My hat and wig will soon be
    here.—
    They are upon the road."

The calender, right glad to find
    His friend in merry pin,
Returned him not a single word
    But to the house went in;

Whence straight he came with
    hat and wig;
    A wig that flowed behind,
A hat not much the worse for
    wear,
    Each comely in its kind.

He held them up, and in his turn
    Thus showed his ready wit,
"My head is twice as big as yours,
    They therefore needs must fit.

But let me scrape the dirt away
    That hangs upon your face;
And stop and eat, for well you
    may
    Be in a hungry case."

Said John, "It is my wedding-day,
    And all the world would stare,
If wife should dine at Edmonton,
    And I should dine at Ware."

So turning to his horse, he said,
    "I am in haste to dine;
"Twas for your pleasure you came
    here,
    You shall go back for mine."

Ah, luckless speech, and bootless
    boast!
    For which he paid full dear;
For, while he spake, a braying ass
    Did sing most loud and clear;

Whereat his horse did snort, as he
    Had heard a lion roar,
And galloped off with all his
    might
    As he had done before.

Away went Gilpin, and away
    Went Gilpin's hat and wig;
He lost them sooner than at first;
    For why?—they were too big.

Now Mistress Gilpin, when she
    saw
    Her husband posting down
Into the country far away,
    She pulled out half-a-crown;

And thus unto the youth she said
    That drove them to the Bell,
"This shall be yours, when you
    bring back
    My husband safe and well."

The youth did ride, and soon did
    meet
    John coming back amain:
Whom in a trice he tried to stop,
    By catching at his rein;

But not performing what he
    meant,
    And gladly would have done,
The frighted steed he frighted
    more,
    And made him faster run.

Away went Gilpin, and away
  Went postboy at his heels,
The postboy's horse right glad to
    miss
  The lumbering of the wheels.

Six gentlemen upon the road,
  Thus seeing Gilpin fly,
With postboy scampering in the
    rear,
  They raised the hue and cry:

"Stop thief! stop thief! — a high-
    wayman!"
  Not one of them was mute;
And all and each that passed that
    way
  Did join in the pursuit.

And now the turnpike gates
    again
  Flew open in short space;
The toll-men thinking, as before,
  That Gilpin rode a race.

And so he did, and won it too,
  For he got first to town;
Nor stopped till where he had
    got up
  He did again get down.

Now let us sing, Long live the
    king!
  And Gilpin, long live he!
And when he next doth ride
    abroad
  May I be there to see!

The English poet William Cowper, a man subject to melancholy all his life, wrote serious, solemn pieces, including the intensely religious *Olney Hymns*, which are still Sunday familiars. His poetic pictures of rural life foreshadow romanticism.

"John Gilpin" is an isolated example of Cowper at play. Despite the unnatural inverted phrases, cliches, and occasional strains in scansion, the narrative is carried by its adventure and humor. It is unusually long to have ever been included in Mother Goose collections, but was nevertheless so published. There are also juvenile editions with "John Gilpin" comprising the entire book, drawn with the chubby, colorful characters so typical of nursery rhyme illustrations. Cowper scholars deplore this "doggerel," which Cowper is said to have "jotted down during a sleepness night." It is, however, an interesting example of a serious poet's attempt at light verse, as well as of the diverse work that has been published as "Mother Goose."

Formed long ago, yet made today,
Employed while others sleep;
What few would like to give away,
Nor any wish to keep.

This verse is attributed to Charles James Fox (1749–1806), an English Whig statesman and orator who urged the abolition of slave trade and the political freedom for assenters. The second line of the riddle was originally, "I'm most enjoyed while others sleep." The riddle appeared in 1792 in *A Choice Collection of Riddles, Charades, Rebuses, Etc.* by Peter Puzzlewell (London: E. Newbery). (The answer to the riddle is "a bed.")

A delightful extended verse is "The Butterfly's Ball" by William P. Roscoe (1753–1831):

"Come, take up your hats, and away let us haste
To the Butterfly's Ball and the Grasshopper's Feast,
The Trumpeter, Gadfly, has summon'd the crew,
And the Revels are now only waiting for you."
So said little Robert, and pacing along,
His merry Companions came forth in a throng,
And on the smooth Grass by the side of a Wood,
Beneath a broad oak that for ages had stood,
Saw the Children of Earth and the Tenants of Air
For an Evening's Amusement together repair.

And there came the Beetle, so blind and so black,
Who carried the Emmet, his friend, on his back,
And there was the Gnat and the Dragonfly too,
With all their Relations, green, orange, and blue.
And there came the Moth, with his plumage of down,
And the Hornet in jacket of yellow and brown;
Who with him the Wasp, his companion, did bring,
But they promised that evening to lay by their sting.
And the sly little Dormouse crept out of his hole,
And brought to the Feast his blind Brother, the Mole;
And the Snail, with his horns peeping out of his shell,
Came from a great distance, and length of an ell.

A Mushroom, their Table, and on it was laid
A water-dock leaf, which a table-cloth made.
The Viands were various, to each of their taste,
And the Bee brought her honey to crown the Repast.
Then close on his haunches, so solemn and wise,
The Frog from a corner look'd up to the skies;
And the Squirrel, well pleased such a diversion to see,
Mounted high overhead and look'd down from a tree.

Then out came the Spider, with finger so fine,
To show his dexterity on the tight-line,
From one branch to another his cobwebs he slung,
Then quick as an arrow he darted along,
But just in the middle — oh! shocking to tell,
From his rope, in an instant, poor Harlequin fell.
Yet he touch'd not the ground, but with talons outspread
Hung suspended in air, at the end of a thread.

Then the Grasshopper came with a jerk and a spring,
Very long was his Leg, though but short was his Wing;
He took but three leaps, and was soon out of sight,
Then chirp'd his own praises the rest of the night.
With step so majestic the Snail did advance,
And promised the Gazers a Minuet to dance;
But they all laughed so loud that he pulled in his head,
And went in his own little chamber to bed.

Then as Evening gave way to the shadows of Night,
Their Watchman, the Glowworm, came out with a light.
"Then Home let us hasten while yet we can see,
For no Watchman is waiting for you and for me."
So said little Robert, and pacing along,
His merry Companions return'd in a throng.

Roscoe, English lawyer, member of Parliament, historian, botanist, poet, and early abolitionist, wrote *The Butterfly's Ball* in 1807 for his small son's birthday. It was one of the earliest pieces for children with no moral attached. Its immediate popularity opened a new era of fairyland poetry, and produced many imitators.

The Scottish folk scholar, king of fairy-tale collections, Andrew Lang (1844–1912), included *The Butterfly's Ball* in an 1898 English volume, catapulting it into Mother Goose lore.

Original Lines	Nursery Rhyme
I do not love you, Dr. Fell,	I do not like thee, Doctor Fell,
But why I cannot tell,	The reason why I cannot tell;
But this I know full well	But this I know, and know full well,
I do not love you, Dr. Fell.	I do not like thee, Doctor Fell.

Tradition says that Thomas Brown (1760) wrote this about Dr. Fell, dean of Christ Church, Oxford, upon being threatened with expulsion if he did not offer an immediate translation of Martial's "Non amo te, Sabidi, nec possum dicere quare;/ Hoc tantum possum dicere, Non amo te." Brown, evidently the possessor of a certain amount of fool's courage, offered the above parody as the "translation." It is possible that he was familiar with *Faenestra in Pectore* (1660), wherein Thomas Forde paraphrased Martial's epigram as: "I love thee not Nel, but why I can't tell:/ But this I can tell, I love thee not Nel."

At any rate, Brown was allowed to stay at Oxford, and the so-called translation appeared in his *Works* in 1760 and in *Beauties of Tom Brown* in 1808. It is not known how the verse, with revised scansion, found its way into the realm of the nursery, but it appeared in Robert Graves' *Less Familiar Nursery Rhymes* in 1926, then in several additional American collections — by 1947 being mentioned as lines that every child learns (*Home Chat*, 8 November 1947), although this statement might be debatable.

Yankee Doodle

1. Yankee Doodle went to town, riding on a pony,
    Stuck a feather in his hat, and called it macaroni.
    Yankee Doodle, keep it up, Yankee Doodle dandy,
    Mind the music and the step, and with the girls be handy.

2. Yankee Doodle came to town, how d'you think they serve him,
    One took his bag, another his scrip, the quicker for to starve him.
    Yankee Doodle, keep it up, Yankee Doodle dandy,
    Mind the music and the step, and with the girls be handy.

3. Yankee Doodle came to town, put on his strip-ed trousers,
    And vowed he couldn't see the place, there were so many houses. etc.

4. Father and I went down to camp, along with Captain Goodin,
    And there we saw the men and boys as thick as hasty pudding. etc.

5. And there we saw a thousand men, as rich as Squire David,
    And what they wasted every day, I wish it could be sav-ed. etc.

6. The 'lasses they eat every day, would keep a house a winter,
    They have so much that I'll be bound, they eat it when they're a mind to.
    etc.

7. And there was Captain Washington, upon a slapping stallion,
    A-giving orders to his men, I guess there was a million. etc.

8. And then the feathers in his hat, they looked so very fine, ah,
    I wanted peskily to get, to give to my Jemima. etc.

9. And there we saw a swamping gun, large as a log of maple,
    Upon a deuc-ed little cart, a load for father's cattle. etc.

10. And every time they fired it off, it took a horn of powder,
    It made a noise like father's gun, only a nation louder. etc.

11. I went as near to it myself, as Jacob's underpinning,
    And father went as nigh again, I thought the deuce was in him. etc.

12. Cousin Simon grew so bold, I thought he would have cocked it,
    It scared me so, I streak-ed off, and hung by father's pocket. etc.

13. But Captain Davis had a gun, he kind of clapped his hand on't,
    He stuck a crooked stabbing iron, upon the little end on't. etc.

14. And there I see a pumpkin shell, as big as mother's basin,
    And every time they touched it off, they scampered like the nation. etc.

15. The troopers, too, would gallop up, and fire right in our faces,
    It scared me almost half to death, to see them run such races. etc.

16. And there was a little keg, its heads were made of leather,
    They knocked upon't with little clubs, and called the folks together. etc.

17. And then they'd fife away like fun, and play on cornstalk fiddles,
    And some had ribbons red as blood, all wound about their middles. etc.

18. And there was Captain Washington, and gentlefolks about him,
    They say he's grown so tarnal proud, he will not ride without 'em. etc.

19. He got him on his meeting clothes, upon a slapping stallion,
    He set the world along in rows, in hundreds and in millions. etc.

20. Old Uncle Sam came then to change, some pancakes and some onions,
    For 'lasses cake, to carry home, to give his wife and young ones. etc.

21. I saw another snarl of men, a digging graves, they told me,
    So tarnal long, so tarnal deep, they 'tended they should hold me. etc.

22. It scared me so I hooked it off, nor stopped, as I remember,
    Nor turned about till I got home, locked up in mother's chamber.

The most persistent theory of the origin of this ditty is that it was composed by Dr. Richard Shuckburgh (ca.1760), an English surgeon who evidently served in the Colonies with the British General Edward Braddock during the French and Indian War (1754–1760), and after Braddock's death in 1755, attached to Lord Jeffrey Amherst's army at Albany in 1758. He is said to have written it as a lampoon on the elaborate uniforms of the colonial troops. Over a hundred years later, there was so much controversy about the origin that in 1909 Dr. O.G. Sonneck attempted to fathom it in a report made for the Library of Congress. His only conclusion was that the tune might well have originated elsewhere, but the words undoubtedly originated in America. It is curious, though, that the tradition of Schuckburgh's authorship existed during his lifetime and survived for well over a hundred years before the veracity of the claim was questioned—and especially frustrating to later researchers not to be able to find any valid reasons as to *why* Schuckburgh's claim to authorship was suddenly in jeopardy. One can only report the controversy.

There are a number of other theories about the origins of this popular ditty. Frank Kidson (*Musical Quarterly*, 1917) thought the tune existed originally without words, pointing to *doodle* as also being used as *deedle* and meaning to sing or hum a melody. He suggested it was a dance tune, as witness the later words of the chorus, and thought that "The Yankee Tootle" (or "Doodle") was a reference to the tune as played on a flute or fife. (Eighteenth century music tutors had pupils pronounce *tootle* when "double-tonguing" the flute.) Some researchers feel that the music-only theory is somewhat supported by a report in the Boston *Journal of the Times* (29 September 1768) which referred to "the Yankee Doodle Song ... the capital piece in the band of music." *The Pennsylvania Evening Post* (22 July 1775) reported that "General Gage's troops are much dispirited ... and ... disposed to leave off dancing any more to the tune of Yankey Doodle...." This seems a specious argument, given that any number of pieces of music that have words are played as dance tunes by a band, sometimes having the words sung along, and other times not.

Other theories include the idea that it was derived from a mediaeval church service, that it was an anti–Cromwellian parody, and that it was originated from an old Dutch folk song, the latter presented by Duyckink's *Encyclopedia of American Literature* and also mentioned by Mary Mapes Dodge in *Hans Brinker*. (It should be noted, perhaps, that although *Hans Brinker* was highly regarded as authentic, Dodge had never been to Holland.) The old Dutch refrain was:

Yankee didee doodle down
   Didee dudel lawnter;
Yankee viver, voover, vown,
   Botermeik and Tawnter.

The origin of the word *Yankee* itself, is clouded with speculation. Some say it is variation of *yenghees* which itself was a corruption by the Canadian Indians for the French *anglais*. An officer in General Burgoyne's army said it was derived from the Cherokee word *eankke*, meaning a coward or slave, and was bestowed upon New Englanders by Virginians annoyed because the New Englanders had not assisted them in a war with the Cherokees. As seen, the Dutch used the word *yankee* as above, but the Dutch *Janke* is the diminutive for *John*. There is also a Scottish word *yankie*. William Gordon, in his 1788 *Independence of United States* claimed *yankee* "was a . . . favorite word with farmer Jonathan Hastings of Cambridge about 1713. . . . The inventor used it to express excellency. A *Yankee* good horse, or *Yankee* cider and the like. . . . The students at Harvard used to hire horses of him; their intercourse with him and his use of the term on all occasions, led them to adopt it." A final theory, proffered by Edward Everett Hale, is that it originated around 1775 with Edward Bangs, who graduated from Harvard in 1777. (Might this be a legacy from Farmer Hastings?) Hale also attributed the current chorus, "Yankee doodle keep it up . . ." to Bangs.

Although the term *Yankees* referred to all colonials (or colonists) at the time of the Revolutionary War (called by the British the War of Independence), during and after the Civil War (called by the Southerners the War between the States), Southerners (called Rebels by Northerners) used Yankees as a derogatory term for Northerners, all of which only proves that terminology is a living, growing, changing phenomenon. Northerners carry the designation proudly, as did the early colonists who turned the tables of usage upon the English.

The most curious history clinging to the song is that it was originally intended to parody the colonials, but became almost an anthem they brandished at the British. *The Oxford Dictionary of Nursery Rhymes* (1951) reported a letter written by a British soldier, in 1777, who wrote of the Boston events, ". . . but after . . . the affair at Bunker's Hill, the Americans gloried in it. Yankee Doodle is now their paean, a favourite of favourites, played in their army, esteemed as warlike as the Grenadiers' March — it is the lover's spell, the nurse's lullaby. After our rapid successes, we held the Yankees in great contempt, but it was not a little mortifying to hear them play this tune, when their army marched down to our surrender."

English nursery book editors, understandably perhaps, are not as fond of "Yankee Doodle . . ." as Americans, and the single stanza, the first two lines (without chorus) of number one above, are usually all that are presented. The first two lines (without chorus) of stanza two, incidentally, were the first appearance of the rhyme in children's literature, when they appeared (set up as four lines) in *Gammer Gurton's Garland* in 1810. Halliwell collected it in 1842 as:

Yankee Doodle came to town,
Upon a Kentish poney,
Stuck a feather in his hat,
And called him Macaroni.

The term *macaroni*, incidentally, means a *fop* or *dandy*.

Although there were a number of politically-oriented verses during the Revolutionary War, the narrative stanzas as given above follow rather closely the traditional texts of the picture books, *Yankee Doodle*, illustrated by F.O.C. Darley (New York: Trent, Filmer, 1865), and *Yankee Doodle; An Old Friend in a New Dress*, illustrated by Howard Pyle (New York: Dodd, Mead, 1881.)

Dance, little baby, dance up high:
Never mind, baby, mother is by;
Crow and caper, caper and crow,
There, little baby, there you go;
Up to the ceiling, down to the ground,
Backwards and forwards, round and round:
Dance, little baby, and mother shall sing,
With the merry gay coral, ding, ding-a-ding, ding.†

†*Nineteenth-century baby-rattles were frequently decorated with a sprig of coral.*

I like little Pussy [I love...],
    Her coat is so warm;
And if I don't hurt her
    She'll do me no harm.
So I'll not pull her tail,
    Nor drive her away,
But Pussy and I
    Very gently will play;
She shall sit by my side,
    And I'll give her some food;
And she'll love me because
    I am gentle and good.

I'll pat little Pussy,
    And then she will purr,
And thus show her thanks
    For my kindness to her;

I'll not pinch her ears,
   Nor tread on her paw,
Lest I should provoke her
   To use her sharp claw;
I never will vex her,
   Nor make her displeased,
For Pussy don't like
   To be worried or teased.

Twinkle, twinkle, little star,
How I wonder what you are!
Up above the world so high,
Like a diamond in the sky.

When the blazing sun is gone,
When he nothing shines upon,
Then you show your little light,
Twinkle, twinkle, all the night.

Then the traveller in the dark,
Thanks you for your tiny spark!
He could not see which way to go,
If you did not twinkle so.

In the dark blue sky you keep,
And often through my curtains peep,
For you never shut your eye
Till the sun is in the sky.

As your bright and tiny spark
Lights the traveller in the dark,
Though I know not what you are,
Twinkle, twinkle, little star.

These are by Jane Taylor (1783–1824). The sisters Jane and Ann (1782–1866) Taylor are credited with being the first English authors to write exclusively for children. Trained to follow in their father's footsteps as engravers, they nevertheless devoted much of their time to writing poetry for children and began to sell it to periodicals.

In 1804, they published *Original Poems for Infant Minds: By Several Young Persons.* The three "young persons" were Jane and Ann, with minor contributions from their friend Adelaide O'Keefe. The book was successful enough to be translated into Dutch, German, and Russian. In 1806, Jane and Ann published *Rhymes for the Nursery,* which included "Twinkle, twinkle, little star...." "Dance little baby..." was also in this book, probably written by Jane, although this cannot be documented. The volume was hugely successful, having a 27th edition in 1835. *Hymns for Infant Minds* came out in 1808. The Taylor sisters, unlike so many other poets, actually made money from their collections of verses.

Their styles were so much alike that it was virtually impossible to tell their work apart, except for the "A" or "J" that occasionally followed a verse. Much of the work was didactic and moralistic, which explains why it eventually fell out of favor. Some of the other less lesson-filled nature lyrics have also survived.

"I like little Pussy. . ." has been anthologized by numerous scholars with attribution to Jane Taylor. Yet, though it is in her style, it does not appear in any of the Taylor books, nor in records of the family or publisher. Here, as in many other instances, the dilemma of documentation clouds the byline. The first two verses seem to have appeared first in the Boston *Only True Mother Goose* around 1843, with another appearance, plus the third verse, in the London *Verses and Hymns for Children* (ca.1845). The fourth verse was tacked on at some later date, in true Mother Goose tradition. As heavy moralizing in children's literature has become less popular, it is obvious why only the first verse has survived as a Mother Goose rhyme.

While Jane Taylor's authorship of "Dance, little baby. . ." and "I like little Pussy. . ." is clouded, "Twinkle, twinkle, little star. . ." is an outstanding example of a so-called "Mother Goose" rhyme whose real authorship faded from view. There is no question that it was written by Jane Taylor, who titled it "The Star." The first verse remains one of the most popular children's rhymes ever written, chanted by children and adults alike as they gaze up into the sky. It is frequently followed by the "wish" verse which many people mistakenly think *is* the real second verse of the poem:

> Star light, Star Bright,
> First star I've seen tonight.
> I wish I may, I wish I might,
> Have the wish I wish tonight.

"The Star," like many other Mother Goose rhymes, has been widely parodied, but that by Lewis Carroll deserves special note (see page 194).

> Violante [Hannah Bantry],
>   In the pantry,
> Gnawing at a mutton bone,
>   How she gnawed it,
>   How she clawed it;
> When she found herself alone.

By Maria Edgeworth (1767–1849): The Irish Edgeworth wrote realistic novels of Ireland, notably *Castle Rackrent* (1800), *Belinda* (1801), *The Absentee* (1812), and *Ormond* (1817). In addition she wrote children's stories. "Violante" (as it was in the original version) appeared as a song sung by Frederick in her story *The Mimic* (1796). In Halliwell's 1846 revision and enlargement of *The Nursery Rhymes of England* a similar ditty appeared, with no author attribution:

Hie, hie, says Anthony,
Puss in the pantry
Gnawing gnawing
A mutton mutton-bone;
See now she tumbles it,
See now she mumbles it,
See how she tosses
The mutton mutton-bone.

Sarah Catherine Martin (1768–1826) wrote this famous verse:

Old Mother Hubbard
Went to the cupboard,
   To fetch her poor dog a bone;
But when she got there
The cupboard was bare,
   And so the poor dog had none.

She went to the baker's
   To buy him some bread;
But when she came back
   The poor dog was dead.

She went to the joiner's
   To buy him a coffin;
But when she came back
   The poor dog was laughing.

She took a clean dish
   To get him some tripe;
But when she came back
   He was smoking a pipe.

She went to the fish-house
   To buy him some fish;
But when she came back
   He was licking the dish.

She went to the ale-house
   To get him some beer;
But when she came back
   The dog sat in a chair.

She went to the tavern
   For white wine and red;
But when she came back
   The dog stood on his head.

She went to the fruiterer's
   To buy him some fruit;
But when she came back
   He was playing the flute.

She went to the hatter's
   To buy him a hat;
But when she came back
   He was feeding the cat.

She went to the barber's
   To buy him a wig;
But when she came back
   He was dancing a jig.

She went to the tailor's
   to buy him a coat;

But when she came back
  He was riding a goat.

She went to the cobbler's
  To buy him some shoes;
But when she came back
  He was reading the news.

She went to the seamstress
  To buy him some linen;
But when she came back
  The dog was a-spinning.

She went to the hosier's
  To buy him some hose;
But when she came back
  He was dressed in his clothes.

The dame made a curtsey,
  The dog made a bow;
The dame said "Your servant,"
  The dog said, "Bow-wow."

This wonderful dog
  Was Dame Hubbard's delight;
He could sing, he could dance,
  He could read, he could write.

She gave him rich dainties
  Whenever he fed,
And erected a monument
  When he was dead.

Sarah Catherine was the daughter of Sir Henry Martin and an early love of Prince William Henry (later William IV, 1765–1837). In 1804, at the age of 36, she was visiting her future brother-in-law, John Pollexfen Bastard, M.P. of Kitley, Devon. As he tried to write a letter, he was distracted by her chattering and cavalierly suggested that she run away and write "one of your stupid little rhymes."

She did, and the result was *The Comic Adventures of Old Mother Hubbard and Her Dog*. It was built upon an old nursery rhyme character known since at least the sixteenth century. The archaic rhyming of *laughing* (as in Shakespeare's *loffing*) with *coffin* suggests that this verse may have been part of the original. The patter of the verse and structure, and even the title, follow closely that of a narrative that appeared first in 1706 in *Pills to Purge Melancholy* and were published again—just a year before Martin's efforts—as T. Evans' 1803 *Old Dame Trot, and Her Comical Cat*. The similarity suggests that Martin must have been familiar with the cat's tale. (Which did not survive as nursery lore.) Some of T. Evans' verses, for instance, are:

Old Dame Trot, some cold fish had got,
Which for pussy, she kept in store,
When she looked there was none
The cold fish was gone,
For puss had been there before.

She went to the butcher's
To buy her some meat,
When she came back
She lay dead at her feet.

She went to the undertaker's
For a coffin and shroud,
When she came back,
Puss sat up and meowed.

The tale of Mother Hubbard was published in 1805 by John Harris, selling over 10,000 copies in a few months. Subsequent printings contained continuations of the tale, the last two verses, for instance, not having been included in the original. As shown here, it contains the verses as they have come down through the years. Various publications sometimes alter the order of the verses, but they have remained remarkably standard. The original title, however, is rarely attached to the tale.

The Pibroch of Donuil Dhu†

Pibroch of Donuil Dhu,
   Pibroch of Donuil,
Wake thy wild voice anew,
   Summon Clan Conuil.
Come away, come away,
   Hark to the summons!
Come in your war array,
   Gentles and commons.

Come from deep glen and
   From mountains so rocky,
The war-pipe and pennon
   Are at Inverlochy.
Come every hill-plaid and
   True heart that wears one,
Come every steel blade and
   Strong hand that bears one.

Leave untended the herd,
   The clock without shelter;
Leave the corpse uninterred,
   The bride at the altar;
Leave the deer, leave the ster,
   Leave nets and barges:
Come with your fighting gear,
   Broadswords and targes.

†*Also seen as Donnel Dhu and Donald Dhu; the reference is to Donald the Black.*

Come as the winds come when
  Forest are rended;
Come as the waves come when
  Navies are stranded:
Faster come, faster come,
  Faster and faster,
Chief, vassal, page and groom,
  Tenant and master.

Fast they come, fast they come;
  See how they gather!
Wide waves the eagle plume,
  Blended with heather.
Cast your plaids, draw your blades,
  Forward each man set!
Pubroch of Donuil Dhu,
  Knell for the onset!

Born in Edinburgh, Scotland, Sir Walter Scott (1771–1832), the versifier of the above effort, is nevertheless considered a British novelist and poet, as well as lawyer, public official, and publisher. His early work included *Lay of the Last Minstrel* (1805) and *The Lady of the Lake* (1810). Later, he turned to writing prose romances, among them *The Heart of Midlothian* (1818) and *Ivanhoe* (1820). Though lame from childhood, he took long walks, using them to satisfy his avid interest in collecting Border ballads and legends, and in the process becoming quite knowledgeable about nursery lore.

His work, however, was never intended for the very young. The clearly inappropriate appearance of *The Pibroch of Donuil Dhu* (first publication: 1816) in subsequent Mother Goose collections shows the lengths to which some publishers would go to pad their books. Surely no child of nursery age would find much of amusement or interest therein, and the ballad no longer appears in contemporary children's collections. Its earlier status is primarily of scholarly interest.

W hat are little babies made of, made of?
What are little babies made of?
  Diapers and crumbs and sucking their thumbs;
That's what little babies are made of?

What are little boys made of, made of?   [Robert Southey]
What are little boys made of?
  Snips and snails and puppy-dog tails;
That's what little boys are made of   [And such are . . .].

What are little girls made of, made of?
What are little girls made of?
  Sugar and spice and everything nice;
That's what little girls are made of.

What are young men made of, made of?
What are young men made of?
  Sighs and leers and crocodile tears;
That's what young men are made of.

What are young women made of, made of?   [Robert Southey]
What are young women made of?
  Rings and jings and other fine things;†
That's what young women are made of   [And such are . . .].

What are our sailors made of, made of?
What are our sailors made of?
  Pitch and tar, pig-tail and scar;
That's what our sailors are made of.

What are our soldiers made of, made of?
What are our soldiers made of?
  Pipeclay and drill, the foeman to kill;
That's what our soldiers are made of.

What are our nurses made of, made of?
What are our nurses made of?
  Bushes and thorns and old cow's horns;
That's what our nurses are made of.

What are our fathers made of, made of?
What are our fathers made of?
  Pipes and smoke and collars choke;
That's what our fathers are made of.

What are our mothers made of, made of?
What are our mothers made of?
  Ribbons and laces and sweet pretty faces;
That's what our mothers are made of.

What are old men made of, made of?
What are old men made of?
  Slippers that flop and a bald-headed top;
That's what old men are made of.

†*Original: Sugar and spice and all things nice.*

What are old women made of, made of?
What are old women made of?
Reels, and jeels, and old spinning wheels;
That's what old women are made of.

What are all folks made of, made of?
What are all folks made of?
Fighting a spot and loving a lot,
That's what all folks are made of.

Two stanzas of this popular rhyme (as marked) are attributed to Robert Southey (1774–1843). Southey, English poet and historian, became poet laureate in 1813. He wrote prose (history, biography) and long epic poems, but is more popularly remembered for his short poems, for instance "The Battle of Blenheim" and "Inchcape Rock." Many academics, however, agreed with Lord Byron, who was one of the sharpest critics of Southey's poetry, that "Southey's prose is perfect." Among these works are the *Common-Place Book, The Doctor*, collected *Letters*, and biographies of Cowper, Wesley, and Nelson.

Although the rhyme above cannot be absolutely verified as Southey's, it is generally thought to be by him and dated at about 1820. It was included in Burton Stevenson's *Dictionary of Proverbs* with the title "What all the world is made of." (It is sometimes seen as "What Folks are Made of....") Its omission in Southey's collected works and in his comments on nursery rhymes in *The Doctor* do not necessarily preclude his authorship of the verse. He may well have considered it a "throw-away" ditty. After all, he wrote an enormous amount—his collected verses, with explanatory notes, fill ten volumes, and his prose occupies forty. The ditty is certainly in keeping with the light touch of other pieces of his such as "Ode to a Pig while his Nose was being Bored" and "To a Goose," neither of which drifted into Mother Goose territory. "What are ... made of..." was a favorite of Henry W. Longfellow's, who recited it frequently.

A version of "What are little boys made of..." appeared in Halliwell's 1842 collection. In the familiar folk tradition, the popular ditty inevitably acquired additional verses, written by authors unknown, until it became a ballad of some length.

Three little kittens lost their mittens;
  And they began to cry,
"Oh, mother dear, we very much fear
  That we have lost our mittens."
"What! Lost your mittens, you naughty kittens!
  Then you shall have no pie!"

"Mee-ow, mee-ow, mee-ow."
  "No, you shall have no pie."

The three little kittens found their mittens;
  And they began to cry,
"Oh, mother dear, see here, see here!
  See, we have found our mittens!"
"What! Found your mittens, you silly kittens,
  And you may have some pie."
"Purr-r, purr-r, purr-r,
  Oh, let us have some pie."

The three little kittens put on their mittens,
　　And soon ate up the pie;
"Oh, mother dear, we greatly fear
　　That we have soiled our mittens!"
"What! Soiled your mittens, you naughty kittens!"
　　Then they began to sigh.
"Mee-ow, mee-ow, mee-ow."
　　Then they began to sigh.

The three little kittens washed their mittens
　　And hung them out to dry;
"Oh, mother dear, do you not hear
　　That we have washed our mittens?"
"What! Washed your mittens, then you're good kittens.
　　But I smell a rat close by."
"Mee-ow, mee-ow, mee-ow.
　　We smell a rat close by."

This is most likely by Eliza Follen (1787–1860). Eliza Lee (Cabot) Follen was an influential writer in the New England Unitarian movement, with an involvement in antislavery and feminist causes. This and other verses were published in her collection, *New Nursery Songs for All Good Children*, circa 1843. Although the title indicated these were "new" nursery songs, for reasons unknown she also described them as "traditional." Perhaps it was modesty. Perhaps it was to give them an air of continuity. However, as there are no traces of "Three little kittens..." in previous folk sources, with its first appearance in her collection scholars deem it reasonable to assume that this was an original tale written for the book by Eliza Follen. It appeared in 1843 in *Only True Mother Goose Melodies* and from that date made its way into Mother Goose lore, usually found not credited to Follen or to her early book.

Mary had a little lamb,
　　Its fleece was white as snow;
And everywhere that Mary went
　　The lamb was sure to go.

He followed her to school one day;
　　That was against the rule;
It made the children laugh and play
　　To see a lamb at school.

And so the teacher turned him out,
　　But still he lingered near,

And waited patiently about
    Till Mary did appear.

Then he ran to her and laid
    His head upon her arm,
As if he said, "I'm not afraid—
    You'll keep me from all harm."

"What makes the lamb love Mary so?"
    The eager children cry.
"Oh, Mary loves the lamb, you know,"
    The teacher did reply.

And you each gentle animal
    In confidence may bind,
And make them follow at your call
    If you are always kind.

Sarah Josepha Hale (1788–1879) created the famous little lamb. After being widowed in 1822, Sarah J. (Buell) Hale, with five children to support, turned to writing as a career. Against great odds, she managed not only to support her family, but to establish herself, in 1828, as the editor of *Ladies Magazine* in Boston, the first periodical in America solely for women. In 1837, the magazine consolidated with *Godey's Lady's Book* and she left New England for Philadelphia, to become both well known and influential as its editor. For seventeen years she waged a campaign, using the magazine's editorials and letters to each successive president, to have Thanksgiving established as a national holiday, finally succeeding when Lincoln issued such a proclamation in 1863. (Annual proclamations were invoked until 1941, when Thanksgiving became an official annual national holiday.)

Earlier in her career she had edited a magazine for children called *Juvenile Miscellany*, where "Mary had a little lamb. . ." had appeared for the first time, over her initials, in the September–October 1830 issue. The magazine carried an ad announcing the publication of Hale's *Poems for Our Children*, which was published later that year, and which included "Mary. . .lamb." Curiously, she may have been responsible herself for the subsequent question of authorship. In her anthology, as was common practice, she used her own poems as well as those of others, all without author attribution. In later poetry and songbooks on which she collaborated with the renowned Boston school musician, Dr. Lowell Mason, her name appeared as the author. By 1855, however, all of her own books which contained the verse were out of print.

Although she was a very popular writer in her day, and some of her poems showed great depth, "Mary had a little lamb. . ." is now the only one

The following well-known moralistic poem is by Mary Howitt (1799–1888):

The Spider and the Fly

"Will you walk into my parlor?" said the spider to the fly —
"'Tis the prettiest little parlor that ever you did spy.
The way into my parlor is up a winding stair;
And I have many curious things to show you when you're there."
"Oh, no, no," said the little fly; "to ask me is in vain;
For who goes up your winding stair can ne'er come down again."

"I'm sure you must be weary dear, with soaring up so high;
Will you not rest upon my little bed?" said the spider to the fly.
"There are pretty curtains drawn around; the sheets are fine and thin;
And if you like to rest a while, I'll snugly tuck you in!"
"Oh, no, no," said the little fly; "for I've often heard it said,
They never, never wake again, who sleep upon your bed!"

Said the cunning spider to the fly —
"Dear friend, what can I do
To prove the warm affection I've always felt for you?"
"I thank you, gentle sir," she said, "for what you're pleased to say,
And bidding you good-morning now, I'll call another day."
The spider turned him round about, and went into his den,
For well he knew the silly fly would soon come back again;
So he wove a subtle web in a little corner sly,
And set his table ready, to dine upon the fly.
Then he came out to his door again, and merrily did sing —
"Come hither, hither, pretty fly, with pearl and silver wing;
Your robes are green and purple — there's a crest upon your head!
Your eyes are like the diamond bright but mine are dull as lead!"

Alas! alas! how very soon this silly little fly,
Hearing his wily, flattering words, came slowly flitting by.
With buzzing wings she hung aloft, then near and nearer drew;
Thinking only of her brilliant eyes, her green and purple hue —
Thinking only of her crested head — poor foolish thing! At last,
Up jumped the cunning spider, and firmly held her fast!
He dragged her up his winding stair, into his dismal den,
Within his little parlor — but she ne'er came out again!
And now dear little children, who may this story read,
To idle, silly, flattering words, I pray you ne'er give heed;
Unto an evil counselor close heart, and ear and eye,
And take a lesson from this tale of the Spider and the Fly.

Howitt (nee Mary Botham) was the daughter of English Quakers. When she married the Quaker Howitt, they espoused liberal causes like the anti-slavery movement, women's property tax rights, and at one time, even spiritualism. The two collaborated in trying to produce wholesome literature for children.

The quality of Mary Howitt's work is uneven. "Buttercups and Daisies," for instance, is a pedestrian ode to nature which ends on a cloying pious note. In contrast, there is the delightful fantasy of "The Fairies of the Caldon Low." Even "the Spider and the Fly" is marred by uneven scansion, and the heavy moralizing at the end—although its not untypical of what many considered proper reading for children of that time.

The phrase "Come into my parlor, said the spider to the fly" is often nowadays invoked to indicate the need to be wary of someone who may have ulterior motives.

There was a little girl, and she had a little curl
Right in the middle of her forehead;
When she was good, she was very, very good,
But when she was bad she was horrid.

One day she went upstairs, while her parents, unawares,
In the kitchen down below were occupied with meals;
And she stood upon her head, on her little truckle bed,
And then began hurraying with her heels.

Her mother heard the noise, and thought it was the boys
A-playing at a combat in the attic;
But when she climbed the stair, and saw Jemima there,
She took and did whip her most emphatic.

The first stanza above is credited to Henry Wadsworth Longfellow (1807–1882), New England poet and professor of modern languages and belles lettres, who is best known for his sentimental and inspirational verses, longtime classics of American literature. The widespread acceptance of his simple, natural work led to his being credited with the popularization of poetry. He wrote "Day Is Done," *The Village Blacksmith, Evangeline, Hiawatha,* and many others. He was called both "The Poet of the Commonplace" and "The Children's Poet." Among his creations are a number of verses *about*, but not *for*, children, of which the best known is "The Children's Hour." It was common in his day, however, for poems to appear without author credits, and the "little girl with the curl" found its way into Mother Goose legend.

For many years, scholars disagreed about whether this verse was American or British, and it was even once speculated that Thomas Bailey Aldrich was the author. But most authorities now agree that the first stanza, at least, was written one day by Longfellow about his daughter Edith when she refused to have her hair curled.

The Home Life of Henry W. Longfellow, by Blanche Roosevelt Tucker Macchetta, 1882, was published only two months after the poet's death. In it the biographer reported that Longfellow would acknowledge authorship of the rhyme when sufficiently taxed with it. She gave as his version:

> There was a little durl,
> And she had a little curl,
> That hung in the middle of her forehead.
> When she was dood,
> She was very dood indeed,
> But when she was bad she was horrid.

There is good reason to believe that the poet was not especially interested in perpetuating this piece of doggerel along with his more serious poetry. Longfellow himself reported, in *Table Talk*, "When I recall my juvenile poems and prose sketches, I wish that they were forgotten entirely. They, however, cling to one's skirt with a terrible grasp." Longfellow's son, Ernest Wadsworth Longfellow, confirmed the comments made in the Macchetta biography when he wrote his own *Random Memories* in 1922.

Early (anonymous) publications of the verse were in Longfellow's local papers. A baby-talk version appeared in the December 21, 1870, *Reveille* (Salem, Massachusetts, near Longfellow's country home), and a musical version appeared in the *Balloon Post* of April 11, 1871, published at Boston (near the suburb of Cambridge where the poet lived most of his adult life). It first appeared as a "traditional" nursery rhyme in *Sugar and Spice, And All That's Nice*, published in 1885, three years after Longfellow's death. That version had the three stanzas given above. The author of the additional two stanzas remains unknown to this day, but there is no reason to speculate that they were by Longfellow, too. The first stanza remains the best known and most published. In the twentieth century, the little poem, as either the first stanza, or the complete piece, has appeared in anthologies with Longfellow actually given credit for it.

Traditional English-language Version

Wee Willie Winkie runs through the town,
Upstairs and downstairs in his nightgown,
Rapping at the window, crying through the lock,
"Are the children all in bed? For now it's eight o'clock."

Original Version

Wee Willie Winkie rins through the town,
Up stairs and doon stairs, in his nicht-gown,
Tirlin' at the window, cryin' at the lock,
"Are the weans in their bed? — for it's noo ten o'clock."

Hey Willie Winkie, are ye comin' ben?
The cat's singin' gay thrums to the sleepin' hen,
The doug's spelder'd on the floor, and disna gie a cheep,
But here's a waukrife laddie! that winna fa' asleep.

Onything but sleep, ye rogue! — glowrin' like the moon,
Rattlin' in an airn jug wi' an airn spoon,
Rumblin' tumblin' roun' about, crawin' like a cock,
Skirlin' like a kenna-what — wauknin' sleepin' folk.

Hey, Willie Winkie! — the wean's in a creel!
Waumblin' off a bodie's knee like a vera eel,
Ruggin' at the cat's lug, and ravellin' a' her thrums —
Hey, Willie Winkie! — See, there he comes!

Wearied is the mither that has a stoorie wean,
A wee stumpie stoussie, that canna rin his lane,
That has a battle aye wi' sleep before he'll close an ee —
But a kiss frae aff his rosy lips gies strength anew to me.

"Willie Winkie" is by William Miller (1810–1872). At one time called "The Laureate of the Nursery," the Scottish poet Miller's work is virtually unknown today. Even "Wee Willie Winkie . . ." has been reduced to Mother Goose attribution. Its first appearance was in 1841, in *Whistle-Binkie; a Collection of Songs for the Social Circle*, published by David Robertson. It reappeared, without Miller's byline, circa 1843 in *The Only True Mother Goose Melodies* (implying a long tradition behind them), published in Boston by Munroe and Francis. The first verse, in its more Anglicized version, was subsequently published in other collections in 1843, 1844, and 1846, and been a part of Mother Goose lore ever since.

Although "Wee Willie Winkie" was the Jacobite nickname for William Prince of Orange, later William III (1650–1702), it is not likely that, 140 years later, Miller intended the verse to have any political implications.

Traditional Nursery Version	Alternate lines
If I had a donkey that wouldn't go,	and he wouldn't go,
Would I beat him?	Do you think I would whip him?

Oh, no, no,
I'd put him in the barn
And give him some corn,
The best little donkey
That ever was born.

I'd give him a carrot,
And cry, "Gee whoa,
Gee up, Neddy."

Original version

If I had a donkey wot wouldn't go,
I never would wollop him—no, no, no;
I'd give him some hay and cry gee O!
And come up Neddy.

The original version of the donkey verse is by Jacob Beuler (ca.1822). Beuler was an English composer of broadside songs. The original version, as shown, was the chorus of a six-verse music-hall ballad written in mocking response to the Prevention of Cruelty to Animals Act of 1822, sponsored by Richard "Humanity" Martin, founder of the R.S.P.C.A. Beuler, however, said he did not originate the first two lines, saying, "These two lines were given to me, to work upon by a friend, for which I return thanks; for the song has proved one of the most popular I have ever written." Although some interpreters conjecture that this meant the two lines were already traditional, there seems to be no documentation thereto; it is more likely that the friend referred to was the originator.

The song was mentioned by Dickens in *The Old Curiousity Shop* (1841). In September 1885, a version appeared in *Harper's Young People* with the comment that it was thought to be from "that wonderful old woman Mother Goose."

There was an old woman of Leeds
Who spent all her time in good deeds;
  She worked for the poor
  Till her fingers were sore,
This pious old woman of Leeds.

There was an old woman of Norwich,
Who lived upon nothing but porridge;
  Parading the town,
  She turned cloak into gown,
The thrifty old woman of Norwich.

There was an old woman of Surrey,
Who was morn, noon, and night in a hurry;

Called her husband a fool,
Drove her children to school,
The worrying old woman of Surrey.

As a little fat man of Bombay
Was smoking one very hot day,
    A bird called a snipe
    Flew away with his pipe,
Which vexed the fat man of Bombay.

There was a poor man of Jamaica,
He opened a shop as a baker:
    The nice biscuits he made
    Procured him much trade
With the little black boys of Jamaica.

A tailor who sailed from Quebec,
In a storm ventured once upon deck;
    But the waves of the sea
    Were as strong as could be,
And he tumbled in up to his neck.

There was an old man of Tobago,
Who lived on rice, gruel, and sago;
    Till, much to his bliss,
    His physician said this—
To a leg, sir, of mutton, you may go.

The last four rhymes were in all likelihood written by R.S. Sharpe (ca.1822). Sharpe was a grocer who dabbled in poetry and wrote several books for children. These four limericks are the ones which survived in nursery lore from *Anecdotes and Adventures of Fifteen Gentlemen* published by John Marshall circa 1822, and attributed by scholars to Sharpe. With the enlightened attitudes in the mid- and later twentieth century about possibly racial slurs, "There was a poor man of Jamaica" fell out of favor.

The first three limericks above have survived from *The History of Sixteen Wonderful Old Women* published by John Harris in 1821. The similarity of the titles, almost appearing as though *Gentlemen* was a sequel to *Wonderful Old Women*, has led to speculation as to whether Sharpe may have contributed to the earlier edition. Both are shown here for the scrutiny of those interested in comparison and documentation. An examination of the examples shows a markedly different style of presentation in the two pieces. The third and fourth lines in *Old Women* show a cruder relationship to their "set-up" lines than the third and fourth lines of *Gentlemen* show to the exposition of their little tales. In addition, the fifth lines in *Old Women* are echoes of the first lines. The last lines of *Gentlemen* are utilized to conclude the tale. Even where the subject is brought back in, as in "There was an old man of Bombay," the last line is inherent to a conclusion.

Edward Lear, of course, is indubitably associated with the limerick form, and many people erroneously assume that the nursery rhymes above are by Lear. Actually, they appeared 25 years before Lear published his. One, however, had a profound effect on Lear (1812–1888), whose work follows.

Fragment from *"Calico Pie"*

Calico Pie,
The little birds fly
Down to the Calico Tree.
　　Their wings were blue
　　And they sang "Tilly-loo"
　　Till away they all flew,
And they never came back to me,
　　They never came back,
　　They never came back,
They never came back to me.

Refrain from *"The Jumblies"*

Far and few, far and few,
　　Are the lands where the Jumblies live;
Their heads are green, and their hands are blue;
　　And they went to sea in a Sieve.

There was an old man with a beard,
Who said, "It is just as I feared! —
　　Two Owls and a Hen,
　　Four Larks and a Wren,
Have all built their nests in my beard!"

The English Edward Lear is chronologically the first poet whose name is surely attached to juvenile poetry that could conjure laughter. One of 21 children, most of whom died in infancy, his life was one of wealth and protection until the age of 13. Even before his father's imprisonment for debt and his mother's subsequent poverty and anxiety, his sister, Ann, 26 years older than he, had cared for him, and she continued in this role. He was cheerful and lively, although suffering from a mild form of epilepsy which he referred to all his life as "The Terrible Demon."

By the time he was 15, his drawings had begun to earn money. In London, he drew scientific drawings for doctors, and in the country began to perfect his skill at birds, butterflies, and animals. This all came to fruition when he became friends with the earls of Derby (in all, four), and amused the children of their families.

The artist became a writer with the publication of *The Book of Nonsense*, entirely a work of limericks, in 1846. In the introduction to *More Nonsense*, in 1872, he wrote, "Long years ago, in the days when much of my time was passed in a country house where children and mirth abounded, the lines beginning 'There was an old man of Tobago' were suggested to me by a valued friend as a form of verse lending itself to limitless variety for Rhymes and Pictures; and thenceforth the greater part of the original drawings and verses for the first *Book of Nonsense* were struck off with a pen, no assistance ever having been given me in any way but that of uproarious delight and welcome at the appearance of every new absurdity."

In 1871, he published *Nonsense Songs and Stories*, primarily pseudo-serious narrative poems. Of these, the best known is probably "The Owl and the Pussycat."

It should be noted that Lear called his five-line work *verses* and that the term *limerick* is dated by the *Oxford English Dictionary* as being 1898, ten years after Lear's death and 77 years after the first published "limericks" (not then called that).

There is a curious interrelationship between Edward Lear and Mother Goosery. For one thing, his works are identified. The body of his material for children is recognized as true children's literature, and "kiddie-lit" scholars have little trouble separating Lear's work from unidentified Mother Goose rhymes. The average reader, however, accepts the fragments of "Calico Pie" and "The Jumblies" as common Mother Goose material. Conversely, because Lear is so closely associated with limericks, he is incorrectly given credit for such limericks as those on pages 187–188. Of all his own limericks, the one perceived as being Mother Goose material is "There was an old man with a beard," probably the best known of all Lear's limericks.

Another paradox is that although Lear's name is firmly attached to his work today, initially he had trouble establishing his authorship. Because of his association with an Earl of Derby, there were those who ascribed the work to that nobleman. One anecdote tells of the time Lear overheard this argument while in a railway carriage. The proponent was insisting that there was no such person as Edward Lear and that *The Book of Nonsense* was written by the Earl of Derby, whose first name was Edward, and that *Lear* was simply *Earl* with transposed letters. According to Lear's own account, he presented the gentleman his hat, handkerchief, and stick, all labeled with his name, and also with letters addressed to himself which he had in his pocket, and "flashing all these articles at once on my would-be extinguisher's attention, I speedily reduced him to silence." His cartoons of himself put a final close to speculations about the authenticity of his authorship, for they were unmistakable.

The Fairies

Up the airy mountain,
  Down the rushy glen,
We daren't go a-hunting
  For fear of little men;
Wee folk, good folk,
  Trooping all together;
Green jacket, red cap,
  And white owl's feather!

Down along the rocky shore
  Some make their home;
They live on crispy pancakes
  Of yellow tide-foam;
Some in the reeds
  Of the black mountain-lake,
With frogs for their watch-dogs,
  All night awake.

High on the hilltop
  The old King sits;
He is now so old and gray
  He's nigh lost his wits.
With a bridge of white mist
  Columbkill he crosses,
On his stately journeys
  From Slieveleague to Rosses;
Or going up with music
  On cold starry nights,
To sup with the Queen
  Of the gay Northern Lights.

They stole little Bridget
  For seven years long;
When she came down again
  Her friends were all gone.
They took her lightly back
  Between the night and morrow;
They thought that she was fast
    asleep,
  But she was dead with sorrow.
They have kept her ever since
  Deep within the lake,
On a bed of flag-leaves,
  Watching till she wake.

By the craggy hillside,
  Through the mosses bare,
They have planted thorn-trees
  For pleasure here and there.
Is any man so daring
  As dig them up in spite,
He shall find their sharpest thorns
  In his bed at night.

Up the airy mountain,
  Down the rushy glen,
We daren't go a hunting
  For fear of little men;
Wee folk, good folk,
  Trooping all together;
Green jacket, red cap,
  And white owl's feather!

The above verses are by William Allingham (1824–1889), an Irish man-of-letters who held civil clerical posts until becoming an editor of the well-known *Fraser's Magazine* at the age of 46. He published his own poems, and also collections of stories, ballads, and songs, and a book on ballads, *The Ballad Book*. In the twentieth century a collection of his verses was reprinted as *Robin Redbreast and Other Verse*.

Children's literature scholar May Hill Arbuthnot (1947) called *The Fairies*, "as fine a lyric poem as you can give children. They like it first because it sings, and second because it contains the vital statistics they have always wished to know about 'the good people.' What do they wear? Where do they live? What do they eat? What tricks do they play? Allingham's poem supplies all the answers. You must, of course, read it aloud to catch the dancing, tripping rhythm of the trooping fairies, and the sudden change to the grave, sober narrative of little Bridget."

The Fairies is another of those dubious entries into Mother Goose collections. It is somewhat long, and Allingham has always been known to be the author. One has to assess then, whether publishers dubbed it Mother Goose in order to pad their books, or because they simply felt it was too delightful not to be included in their editions. Sometimes only the first stanza (which is the same as the last) appears as an eight-line entry, which gives more of a Mother Goose aura.

Little Things

Little drops of water,
    Little grains of sand,
Make the mighty ocean
    And the pleasant land.

So the little moments,
    Humble though they be,
Make the mighty ages
    Of eternity.

So our little errors
    Lead the soul away
From the paths of virtue,
    Far in sin to stray.

Little deeds of kindness,
    Little words of love,
Help to make earth happy
    Like the heaven above.

The first four lines of "Little Things" are all that contemporary readers know of the American Julia Fletcher Carney (1825–1908). This pious homily is representative of much of the turn-of-the-century material aimed at instruction and moralization, rather than entertainment, for young readers. The first stanza, however, contains a subtle philosophy that is not only palatable, but beautiful, when separated from the rest of the verse. (Note the strong similarity of that stanza to the verses of Robert Louis Stevenson.) One can understand why it, and only it, was garnered for Mother Goose use.

Mix a pancake
Stir a pancake
    Pop it in the pan;
Fry the pancake,
Toss the pancake, —
    Catch it if you can.

If a pig wore a wig,
What could we say?
Treat him as a gentleman,
    And say, "Good day."
If his tail chanced to fail,
What could we do?
Send him to the tailoress
    To get one new.

Seldom "can't,"
    Seldom "don't";
Never "shan't,"
    Never won't."

Who has seen the wind?
    Neither I nor you:
But when the leaves hang trembling
    The wind is passing thro'.

Who has seen the wind?
    Neither you nor I:
But when the trees bow down their heads
    The wind is passing by.

By Christina Georgina Rossetti (1830–1894): Rossetti was the daughter of Italian exiles in London. Her parents and siblings were all scholars, painters, and writers, living in genteel poverty. She, too, painted as well as wrote. The gay child, who doted on small "beasties" and was not averse to handling frogs and caterpillars, grew into a melancholy, deeply religious young woman. After two unhappy love affairs, she became a recluse, indifferent to what kind of clothes she wore. Nevertheless, her poems for children are gay and light-hearted. Her books include *Goblin Market and Other Poems* (1862) and the classic *Sing Song* (1872).

The poems above, of all her work, are curiously perceived to be of longer tradition in nursery lore. They are frequently judged to be "Mother Goose" rather than Rossetti. There is, though, a subtle poetic cadence to her work.

This difference is more obvious in a poem she based on a traditional folk verse, all the more interesting for that reason. Notice the quick, broad strokes of the Mother Goose rhyme, as compared to the fragility and lyricism of Rossetti's verse.

Traditional Mother Goose rhyme

(The term *daffy-down-dilly* for *daffodil* was used by Thomas Tusser [ca.1524–1580] as far back as 1573.)

Daffadowndilly
    Has come up to town,
In a yellow petticoat
    And a yellow gown.

Rossetti:
Growing up the vale
    By the uplands hilly,
Growing straight and frail,
    Lady Daffadowndilly.

In a golden crown,
And a scant green gown
    while the spring blows chilly,
Lady Daffadown,
    Sweet Daffadowndilly.

The short and snappy "Seldom 'can't'. . ." is a rare instance of moralizing on Rossetti's part—also a rare instance of unpoetic style—a style much more in keeping with the Mother Goose tradition it is perceived to be.

For many, of course, the work of Lewis Carroll—pseudonym of Charles Lutwidge Dodgson (1832–1898)—is unmistakable:

Twinkle, twinkle, little bat!
How I wonder what you're at!
Up above the world you fly,
Like a teatray in the sky.

The Walrus and the Carpenter

The sun was shining on the sea,
  Shining with all his might;
He did his very best to make
  The billows smooth and
    bright—
And this was odd, because it was
  The middle of the night.

The moon was shining sulkily,
  Because she thought the sun
Had got no business to be there
  After the day was done—
"It's very rude of him," she said,
  "To come and spoil the fun!"

The sea was wet as wet could be,
  The sands were dry as dry.
You could not see a cloud, be-
    cause
  No cloud was in the sky;
No birds were flying overhead—
  There were no birds to fly.

The Walrus and the Carpenter
  Were walking close at hand;
They wept like anything to see
  Such quantities of sand—
"If this were only cleared away,"
  They said, "it would be grand!"

"If seven maids with seven mops
  Swept it for half a year,
Do you suppose," the Walrus
    said,
  "That they could get it clear?"
"I doubt it," said the Carpenter,
  And shed a bitter tear.

"O Oysters, come and walk with
    us!"
  The Walrus did beseech.
"A pleasant walk, a pleasant talk,
  along the briny beach;
We cannot do with more than

four,
  To give a hand to each."

The eldest Oyster looked at him,
  But never a word he said;
The eldest Oyster winked his eye,
  And shook his heavy head—
Meaning to say he did not choose
  To leave the oyster-bed.

But four young Oysters hurried
    up,
  All eager for the treat;
Their coats were brushed, their
    faces washed,
  Their shoes were clean and
    neat—
And this was odd, because, you
    know,
  They hadn't any feet.

Four other Oysters followed them,
  And yet another four;
And thick and fast they came at
    last,
  And more, and more, and
    more—
All hopping through the frothy
    waves,
  And scrambling to the shore.

The Walrus and the Carpenter
  Walked on a mile or so,
And then they rested on a rock
  Conveniently low—
And all the little Oysters stood
  And waited in a row.

"The time has come," the Walrus
    said,
  "To talk of many things:
Of shoes—and ships—and seal-
    ing-wax—
  And cabbages—and kings—

And why the sea is boiling hot—
  And whether pigs have wings."

"But wait a bit," the Oysters
  cried,
  Before we have our chat;
For some of us are out of breath,
  And all of us are fat!"
"No hurry!" said the Carpenter.
  They thanked him much for
  that.

"A loaf of bread," the Walrus
  said,
  "Is what we chiefly need;
Pepper and vinegar besides
  Are very good indeed—
Now, if you're ready Oysters
  dear,
  We can begin to feed."

"But not on us!" the Oysters
  cried,
  Turning a little blue.
"After such kindness, that would
  be
  A dismal thing to do!"
"The night is fine," the Walrus
  said.
  "Do you admire the view?"

"It was so kind of you to come!
  And you are very nice!"
The Carpenter said nothing but,
  "Cut us another slice.
I wish you were not quite so
  deaf—
  I've had to ask you twice!"

"It seems a shame," the Walrus
  said,
  "To play them such a trick.
After we've brought them out so
  far,
  And made them trot so quick!"
The Carpenter said nothing but,
  "The butter's spread too thick!"

"I weep for you," the Walrus said;
  I deeply sympathize."
With sobs and tears he sorted out
  Those of the largest size,
Holding his pocket-handkerchief
  Before his streaming eyes.

"O Oysters," said the Carpenter,
  "You've had a pleasant run!
Shall we be trotting home again!"
  But answer came there none—
And this was scarcely odd, be-
  cause
  They'd eaten every one.

Dodgson was an Oxford don and mathematician, a writer of learned treatises on mathematics, a bachelor who began to write nonsense verses to amuse the three daughters of his friend, Dr. Liddell of Christ Church, where Dodgson lectured.

At a picnic in 1862, he told the girls the first version of the book which appeared three years later, under the pseudonym of Lewis Carroll, *Alice's Adventures in Wonderland* (1865). In 1871 he published *Through the Looking Glass*. Suddenly, his real name was discovered, and the shy, sensitive man was disconcerted to find that he was famous and sought-after. He refused to acknowledge his fame, and when Queen Victoria asked for copies of his works, he sent her the treatises on mathematics and nothing more. And despite the academic knowledge that the author's real name was Dodgson, it is the persona of Lewis Carroll that remains attached to the material.

The parody of "Twinkle, twinkle, little star..."—"Twinkle, twinkle, little bat..." was chanted by the Mad Hatter in *Alice's Adventures in Wonderland*. Carroll's piece, however, is more than mere parody. It is itself a parody of a different order. In *The Annotated Alice*, Martin Gardner wrote, "Carroll's burlesque may contain what professional comics call an 'inside joke.' Bartholomew Price, a distinguished professor of mathematics at Oxford and a good friend of Carroll's, was known among his students by the nickname 'The Bat.' His lectures no doubt had a way of soaring high above the heads of his listeners." Among the curiosities that befall nursery rhymes, this, and one section from "The Walrus and the Carpenter" are isolated instances of the perception by some that the pieces are "Mother Goose" rather than "Lewis Carroll."

"The Walrus and the Carpenter" is from *Through the Looking Glass*. Although the narrative in its entirety is not confused as being anything but Carroll's work, the four lines "'The time has come,' the Walrus Said, / 'To talk of many things; / Of shoes—and ships—and sealing-wax—/ And cabbages—and Kings—'" is thought by many to be from the Mother Goose tradition. Carroll himself may have inadvertently triggered the confusion, as it was he who gave permission for "The Walrus and the Carpenter" to be included in several "Mother Goose" books.

Carroll was obviously fond of nursery rhymes, as evidenced by the many nursery-rhyme characters who inhabit his narrative verses.

The following famous verse is by Eugene Field (1850–1895):

Wynken, Blynken, and Nod

Wynken, Blynken, and Nod one night
   Sailed off in a wooden shoe—
Sailed on a river of crystal light,
   Into a sea of dew.
"Where are you going, and what do you wish?"
   The old moon asked the three.
"We have come to fish for the herring fish
   That live in this beautiful sea.
Nets of silver and gold have we!"
   Said Wynken,
   Blynken,
   And Nod.

The old moon laughed and sang a song,
   As they rocked in the wooden shoe,
And the wind that sped them all night long
   Ruffled the waves of dew.
The little stars were the herring fish

That lived in that beautiful sea —
"Now cast your nets wherever you wish —
    Never afeared are we";
So cried the stars to the fishermen three:
    Wynken,
    Blynken,
    And Nod.

All night long their nets they threw
    To the stars in the twinkling foam —
Then down from the skies came the wooden shoe,
    Bringing the fishermen home;
'Twas all so pretty a sail it seemed
    As if it could not be,
And some folks thought 'twas a dream they'd dreamed
    Of sailing that beautiful sea —
But I shall name you the fishermen three:
    Wynken,
    Blynken,
    And Nod.

Wynken and Blynken are two little eyes,
    And Nod is a little head,
And the wooden shoe that sailed the skies
    Is the wee one's trundle bed;
So shut your eyes while mother sings
    Of wonderful sights that be,
And you shall see the beautiful things
    As you rock in the misty sea
Where the old shoe rocked the fishermen three: —
    Wynken,
    Blynken,
    And Nod.

Field was an American midwestern newspaper journalist whose column "Sharps and Flats" for the *Chicago Daily News* (later the *Record*) helped establish him. His poetry for children is generally not humorous, and some of it is clearly more *about* children than *for* them. Nevertheless, his sentimental "newspaper verse" earned him a permanent place in literature. Among the best known of these are "The Sugar-Plum Tree," "The Duel" (a rare entry into nonsense verse for Field), "The Rock-a-bye Lady," the adult-nostalgic "Little Boy Blue," and, of course, "Wynken, Blynken, and Nod."

Of all his work, only "Wynken, Blynken, and Nod" was adopted for Mother Goose collections, where it appeared so often without attribution that it was considered a "traditional" nursery rhyme, although it is included, with attribution, in even the shortest sections of representative Field work in other anthologies.

Mother Goose version

Oh where, oh where has my little dog gone?
  Oh where, oh where can he be?
With his ears cut short and his tail cut long,
  Oh where, oh where is he?

Original version: *Der Deitcher's Dog*

Oh where, oh where ish mine lit-tle dog gone;
Oh where, oh where can he be...
His ears cut short and his tail cut long:
Oh where, oh where ish he?

I loves mine la-ger' tish ve-re goot beer,
Oh where, oh where can he be...
But mit no mon-ey I can-not drink here,
Oh where, oh where ish he?

A-cross the o-cean in Gar-ma-nie
Oh where, oh where can he be...
Der deitcher's dog ish der best com-pan-ie
Oh where, oh where ish he?

Un sas-age ish goot, bo-lo-nie of course,
Oh where, oh where can he be...
Dey makes un mit dog und dey makes em mit horse,
I guess dey makes em mit he.

By Septimus Winner—pseudonyms: Alice Hawthorne, Percy Guyer, Mark Masen, Paul Stenton—(1827–1902): Winner was a Philadelphia music publisher and critic, who wrote and edited over 200 volumes of music for more than 20 instrument. He is credited with being the arranger and composer of more than 2000 songs. Most are now forgotten; many were Civil War songs: "Our Nation Calls for Peace Again" and "What Is Home Without a Mother" are two. Some of his prodigious output survived, though. He composed the hymn "Whispering Hope." In 1854, under the pseudonym of Alice Hawthorne, he wrote "Listen to the Mocking Bird," which spawned a genre known as "Hawthorne Ballads."

The "comic ballad" *Der Deitcher's Dog* was published in 1864, and after huge success in music halls was adopted for the nursery. The first verse went into Mother Goose books in the Anglicized version shown above.

Septimus Winner was also the author of another song that became, without its chorus, a "traditional" Mother Goose rhyme, and with occasional variations in the lines. "Ten little Injuns..." (*Indians* in some versions) was originally written in 1868, for American minstrel shows. It had many imitators, including another that went into nursery literature.

Ten little Injuns standin' in a line,
One toddled home and then there were nine;
Nine little Injuns swingin' on a gate,
One tumbled off and then there were eight.

Chorus:
One little, two little, three little, four little, five little Injun boys,
Six little, seven little, eight little, nine little, ten little Injun boys.

Eight little Injuns gayest under heav'n,
One went to sleep and then there were seven;
Seven little Injuns cutting up their tricks,
One broke his neck and then there were six. (Chorus)

Six little Injuns kicken' all alive,
One kick'd the bucket and then there were five;
Five little Injuns on a cellar door,
One tumbled in and then there were four. (Chorus)

Four little Injuns up on a spree,
One he got fuddled and then there were three;
Three little Injuns out in a canoe,
One tumbled overboard and then there were two. (Chorus)

Two little Injuns foolin' with a gun,
One shot t'other and then there was one;
One little Injun livin' all alone,
He got married and then there were none. (Chorus)

—*Septimus Winner*

Only one year after Winner's "Ten Little Injuns" appeared in America, English ballad-writer Frank Green wrote the "Ten little nigger boys..." version (1869) for use in England's minstrel shows:

Ten little nigger boys went out to dine;
One choked his little self, and then there were nine.

Nine little nigger boys sat up very late;
One overslept himself, and then there were eight.

Eight little nigger boys travelling to Devon;
One said he'd stay there, and then there were seven.

Seven little nigger boys chopping up sticks;
One chopped himself in half, and then there were six.

Six little nigger boys playing with a hive;
A bumble-bee stung one, and then there were five.

Five little nigger boys going in for law;
One got in chancery, and then there were four.

Four little nigger boys going out to sea;
A red herring swallowed one, and then there were three.

Three little nigger boys walking in the Zoo;
A big bear hugged one, and then there were two.

Two little nigger boys sitting in the sun;
One got frizzled up, and then there was one.

One little nigger boy living all alone;
He got married, and then there were none.

Variations and more imitations of "Ten Little Injuns," as the piece remained popular, ranged from the use of *Negroes* and *Darkies* to *Youthful Africans*. The tragedies that befell these ten unfortunate boys also varied from version to version, but they readily became part of nursery tradition. Twentieth century America became sensitive to pieces using the term *nigger*, which enlightened anthologizers no longer included in their collections, so Green's version began to disappear from the western side of the Atlantic.

An interesting side-note is that England's Agatha Christie got the theme for one of her best known mystery-detective stories from what was by then a nursery favorite. She took the storyline from Green's version. Her book became a classic, and had 1945 and 1974 films based on it, which in America were titled *And Then There Were None*. In England, however, early editions of the book and the earlier film were called *Ten Little Niggers*. The stage play was called *Ten Little Indians*. All ended, in imitation of the nursery rhyme, with the implied marriage of the hero and heroine survivors.

Jeremiah, blow the fire,
Puff, puff, puff!
First you blow it gently,
Then you blow it rough.

By John Stamford: These lines are the chorus of a music-hall song by English composer Stamford, first published in 1877. Its first recorded use for children was in L.E. Walter's 1924 *Mother Goose's Nursery Rhymes*, but it has appeared in a number of nursery books since then.

L ittle Miss Muffet sat on a tuffet,†
Eating her curds and whey;
Along came a spider, who sat down beside her [There came a big spider]
And frightened Miss Muffet away.

†*three-legged stool or grassy knoll.*

Dr. Thomas Muffet (Moffett? Moufet?), an entomologist who died in 1604, wrote *The Silkwormes and their flies "lively described in verse."* Miss Muffet is said to depict his daughter, Patience. Accreditation is deemed shaky by some, as the first extant version is dated 1805 in *Songs for the Nursery,* whose 1812 edition read "Little Mary Ester sat upon a tester...." Halliwell's 1842 collection read "Little Miss Mopsey sat in a shopsey...."

The identified authors of "Mother Goose rhymes" present an odd array of backgrounds and life-works. Some were serious poets or writers of adult literature whose contributions to the world of the nursery are generally not known. Some wrote for children, but their works have not survived in the juvenile field except for a piece or two that made it into Mother Goose literature. Others wrote for children and entered the nursery double-fold — as a body of work, as well as being represented in Mother Goose. Others stayed firmly in the juvenile field, with none of their pieces being designated as Mother Goosery.

Their chronologies may be somewhat relevant in determining these placements. Of the more renowned juvenile writers, Sarah Josepha Hale (1788–1879), Edward Lear (1812–1888), Christina Rossetti (1830–1894), Lewis Carroll (1832–1898), and Eugene Field (1850–1895) crossed over the line, but the bulk of their works remained outside of the Mother Goose realm. Robert Louis Stevenson (1850–1894), although of the same time span, had no works dubbed as "Mother Goose," despite the fact that his *A Child's Garden of Verses* (1885) echoed the patter and patterns found in typical Mother Goose material.

Writers who lived into the twentieth century have had their works clearly identified with them as the authors. Laura E. Richards (1850–1943), Emilie Poulsson (1853–1939), Rudyard Kipling (1865–1936), Beatrix Potter (1866–1943), Walter de la Mare (1873–1956), Eleanor Farjeon (1881–1965), A.A. Milne (1882–1956), and Rachel Field (1894–1942) are simply not found in Mother Goose books. This can probably be attributed to a generally greater concern and respect for identification of authors of works, as well as to the acknowledgment of children's literature as an important and separate area of scholarly study.

10. Paralleling Childlore
to Create Literature

Nursery Rhymes and Robert Burns

Robert Burns (1759–1796), Scottish poet and ballad-writer, had a uniquely healthy attitude toward basing much of his work on existing folk material. Where many folklorists designate only adaptations by isolated cultures (mountain folk or ethnic conclaves of one kind or another) as "true" folklore, Burns took the attitude that he was as much "folk" as anyone else — with as much right to adapt or amplify known works.

Thus, in many of his verses and songs he used fragments of folk material common to his era. Inevitably, some of those lines were from the same sources as Mother Goose material. Scholars of children's literature like to point this out, but usually omit showing the comparisons. These parallels are as important to Mother Goose scholars as they are to Burns scholars.

This is not to say that Burns lacked originality. The former ploughman was acknowledged, even in his own time, to have a "native genius," and high intellect. His peers lionized him as "Caledonia's Bard." Rather, he was inspired by the songs that were a part of his culture to new expressions of their themes.

His works depicted lovingly the rural life he knew, much of it sparked with his gift of humor. Simplicity, spontaneity, and genuine emotion marked his poetry. Unsuccessful at farming, he accepted the patronage of several women, but his tendency toward dissolute living led to his death at the age of 37. Probably his best known songs are "Auld Lang Syne," and "Comin' Through the Rye." Among longer poems are "Tam O'Shanter" and "The Cotter's Saturday Night."

The work Burns did on the six volumes of *Scot's Musical Museum* for publisher James Johnson, from 1787 to 1796, was that of editor, adapter, arranger, and creator. The last two volumes were published after his death. During his lifetime, most were shown as anonymous, as he had a passion to collect (and adapt) the Scottish songs. A rough system of codes (songs marked 'R,' 'B,' 'X,' or 'Z') indicated the extent of his work on the pieces. The key was so rough, however, that 'Z' seems to have meant anything from total composition, to various degrees of patching or remodelling, to the slightest editorial handling. He said, "There is no reason for telling everybody this piece of intelligence," although he admitted that in "a good many . . . little more than the chorus is ancient."

Robert Burns did not write for children. When Burns borrowed from folk or nursery verses, he transformed the themes to clearly adult poetry. (Many of the Mother Goose rhymes themselves were not intended for children.) As few collections intended for children's use were printed at that time, he was borrowing primarily from oral tradition. And although many pieces did not make the transition from oral tradition to print until years after Burns' time, it should be remembered that they existed earlier, and that Burns himself admitted to drawing upon them, using sometimes only one, but usually more than one line or stanza. Written in his own compromise language of English sprinkled with Scots, his works transcended their folk origins to earn a place in classic literature.

Following are examples of Mother Goose rhymes, with the dates when they were first printed for children, plus the parallel poetry by Robert Burns. Each of these was intended by Burns as a song, which is evident in the lilt of the words. The borrowed fragments (some more, some less) show how the poet "worked over" folklore.

A cow and a calf,
An ox and a half,
　Forty good shillings and three;
Is that not enough tocher†
For a shoemaker's daughter,
　A bonny lass with a black e'e?†

—Songs for the Nursery 1805

†*Tocher means dowry; e'e is eye.*

　The above is one of two verses of a humorous ballad called "Jumpin' John; or Joan's Placket" which was printed in Playford's *Dancing Master* in 1698, and is believed to be the same referred to by Samuel Pepys in a diary entry of 22 June 1667.

Burns:　　　　　　　　　　Her Daddie Forbad

Her daddie forbad, her minnie† forbad;
　Forbidden she wadna be:
She wadna trow't† the browst† she brew'd
　Wad taste sae bitterlie.
　　　The lang† lad they ca' Jumpin John
　　　　Beguiled the bonnie lassie,
　　　The lang lad they ca' Jumpin John
　　　　Beguiled the bonnie lassie.

†*Mother; believe; malt liquor; long.*

A cow and a cauf,† a yowe† and a hauf†
　And thretty gude shillin's and three;
A very gude tocher,† a cotter-man's dochter,†
　The lass with the bonnie black ee.†
　　　The lang lad they ca' Jumpin John
　　　　Beguiled the bonnie lassie,
　　　The lang lad they ca' Jumpin John
　　　　Beguiled the bonnie lassie.

—Robert Burns 1788

†*Calf; ewe; half; dowry; daughter; eye.*

Over the water and over the lea,
　And over the water to Charlie.†

†*"Bonnie" Prince Charlie*

Charlie loves good ale and wine,
  And Charlie loves good brandy,
And Charlie loves a pretty girl,
  As sweet as sugar candy.

Over the water and over the lea,
  And over the water to Charlie.
I'll have none of your nasty beef,
  Nor I'll have none of your barley;
But I'll have some of your very best flour,
  To make a white cake for my Charlie.

—Songs for the Nursery 1805

Andrew Lang identified the above as a parody of a Jacobite song from 1748. A similar one was known in 1779.

Burns: Come Boat Me O'er to Charlie

Come boat me o'er, come row me o'er,
  Come boat me o'er to Charlie;
I'll gie John Ross another bawbee,
  To boat me o'er to Charlie.

We'll o'er the water and o'er the sea,
  We'll o'er the water to Charlie;
Come weal, come woe, we'll gather and go,
  And live or die wi' Charlie.

I lo'e weel my Charlie's name,
  Tho' some there be abhor him:
But O, to see auld Nick gaun hame,
  And Charlie's faes before him!

I swear and vow by moon and stars,
  And sun that shines so early,
If I had twenty thousand lives,
  I'd die as aft for Charlie.

We'll o'er the water and o'er the sea,
  We'll o'er the water to Charlie;
Come weal, come woe, we'll gather and go,
  And live or die with Charlie!

—Robert Burns (date unknown)

There was a piper had a cow,
  And he had nought to give her.

He pulled out his pipes and played her a tune,
  And bade the cow consider.

The cow considered very well
  And gave the piper a penny,
And bade him play the other tune,
  "Corn rigs are bonny."
                              — *Songs for the Nursery 1805*

In the 1693 *An Answer to the Scotch Presbyterian Eloquence*, the song "Corn Rigs Are Bonny" is mentioned as being popular several years previously. A ditty called "The Tune the Old Cow Died Of," was very popular in the 1830s. More than one wit has declared that what the cow probably died of was "the tune played on the bag-pipe."

Burns: The Rigs of Barley

This poem, with four stanzas of eight lines each, is the tale of a moonlight tryst, with the refrain:

Corn rigs, an' barley rigs [ridges],
  An' corn rigs are bonnie:
I'll ne'er forget that happy night,
  Amang the rigs wi' Annie.
                              — *Robert Burns 1783*

We're all a dry with drinking on't;
We're all a dry with drinking on't;
The Piper kissed the Fidler's Wife,
And I can't sleep for thinking on't.
                  — *Tommy Thumb's Pretty Song Book 1744*

This ditty was popular in both England and Scotland, where it was apparently already traditional when it appeared around 1740 in *Caledonian Country Dances* (London: John Walsh).

Burns: My Love She's But a Lassie Yet

My love she's but a lassie yet;
  My love she's but a lassie yet;
We'll let her stand a year or twa,
  She'll no be half sae saucy yet.
I rue the day I sought her, O,
  I rue the day I sought her, O;
Wha gets her needs na say she's woo'd,
  But he may say he's bought her, O!

Come, draw a drap o' the best o't yet;
  Come, draw a drap o' the best o't yet;
Gae seek for pleasure where ye will,
  But here I never miss'd it yet.
We're a dry wi' drinking o't,
  We're a dry wi' drinking o't;
The minister kiss'd the fiddler's wife,
  An' could na preach for thinkin' o't.

—Robert Burns 1788

I: O the little rusty, dusty, rusty miller.
       I'll not change my wife for either gold or siller.

— Gammer Gurton's Garland 1810

II: Traditional nursery
    Hey, the dusty miller!
    Ho, the dusty miller!
    Dusty was his coat,
    Dusty was his color,
    Dusty was the kiss
    I got from the miller!
    O, the dusty miller
    With the dusty coat,
    He will spend a shilling†
    Ere he win a groat.†

— The Nursery Rhymes of England (rev.) 1844

†Halliwell's version: He'll earn a shilling/ Or he'll spend a groat.

The song "Dusty Miller" is in the 1708 *Compleat Country Dancing Master* (London: John Walsh). Burns is said to have based his version on a manuscript fragment dated at 1766.

Burns: Hey, the Dusty Miller

    Hey, the dusty miller,
      And his dusty coat;
    He will win a shilling,
      Or† he spend a groat.
        Dusty was the coat,
          Dusty was the colour,
        Dusty was the kiss
          That I got frae the miller.

   †Ere.

Hey, the dusty miller,
   And his dusty sack;
Leeze me† on the calling
   Fills the dusty peck.
     Fills the dusty peck,
       Brings the dusty siller;
     I wad gie my coatie
       For the dusty miller.

—Robert Burns 1788

†*Dear to me.*

I.   John, come sell thy fiddle,
   And buy thy wife a gown.
   No, I'll not sell my fiddle,
   For ne'er a wife in town.

—Gammer Gurton's Garland 1784

II.   Jacky, come give me thy fiddle,
     If ever you mean to thrive.
   Nay, I'll not give my fiddle
     To any man alive.
   If I should give my fiddle,
     They'll think that I'm gone mad,
   For many a joyful day
     My fiddle and I have had.

—Songs for the Nursery 1805

The original from which the nursery rhymes and Burns's ballad are derived was known in 1694 and was popular into the next two centuries.

Burns: Rattlin', Roarin' Willie

O rattlin', roarin' Willie,
   O, he held to the fair,
An' for to sell his fiddle,
   An' buy some other ware;
But parting wi' his fiddle,
   The saut tear blin't his ee;
And rattlin', roarin' Willie,
   Ye're welcome hame to me!

O Willie, come sell your fiddle,
   O sell your fiddle sae fine;
O Willie, come sell your fiddle,

And buy a pint o' wine!
If I should sell my fiddle,
  The warl' would think I was mad;
For mony a rantin' day
  My fiddle and I hae had.

As I cam by Crochallan,
  I cannily keekit ben—†
Rattlin', roarin' Willie
  Was sitting at yon boord en';
Sitting at yon boord en',
  Amang guid companie;
Rattlin', roarin' Willie,
  Ye're welcome hame to me!

—Robert Burns 1787

†*I quietly looked in.*

Burns said that the last stanza was "composed out of compliment to one of the worthiest fellows in the world, William Dunbar, Esq."

There was a jolly miller once,
  Lived on the river Dee;
He worked and sang from morn till night,
  No lark more blithe than he.
And this the burden of his song
  Forever used to be,
I care for nobody, no!, not I,
  If nobody cares for me.

—The Tom Tit's Song Book ca.1790

The Scottish ballad from which this is no doubt derived dates to the early 1700s.

Burns: I Hae a Wife

I hae a wife o' my ain,
  I'll partake wi' naebody;
I'll tak cuckold frae nane,
  I'll gie cuckold to naebody.

I hae a penny to spend,
  There—thanks to naebody;
I hae nothing to lend,
  I'll borrow frae naebody.

I am naebody's lord,
   I'll be slave to naebody;
I hae a guid braid sword,
   I'll tak dunts† frae naebody.

I'll be merry and free,
   I'll be sad for naebody;
Naebody cares for me,
   I care for naebody.

                                —Robert Burns 1788

†*Blows.*

It is said that Burns wrote the above a few days after his marriage to Jean Armour.

Little Blue Betty lived in a den,
She sold good ale to gentlemen;
Gentlemen came every day,
And little Blue Betty hopped away.
She hopped up stairs to make her bed,
And she tumbled down and broke her head.
                     —Gammer Gurton's Garland 1810

Though the nursery rhyme and Burns's ballad appear to take different directions, they share one line, and may be less diverse than appears at first. "Little Blue Betty" was evidently a reference to a woman who offered more than good ale to the gentlemen of the day, with the record indicating she presided at the sign of "The Golden Can."

An earlier song than Burns's bridges the two:

There wonned a wife in Whistle-cockpen—
Will ye no, can ye no, let me be!
She brewed guid ale for gentlemen,
And ay she waggit it wantonly.

Burns: Scroggam

There was a wife wonn'd† in Cockpen,
      Scroggam;
She brewed gude ale for gentlemen,
Sing auld Cowl, lay you down by me,
Scroggam, my dearie, ruffum.

†*Dwelled.*

The gudewife's dochter fell in a fever,
    Scroggam;
The priest o' the parish fell in anither,
Sing auld Cowl, lay you down by me,
Scroggam, my dearie, ruffum.

They laid the twa i' the bed thegither,
    Scroggam;
That the heat o' the tane might cool the tither,
Sing auld Cowl, lay you down by me,
Scroggam, my dearie, ruffum.

                            —Robert Burns (date unknown)

This, too, was included in the 1803 *Scot's Musical Museum*.

In 1792 Burns contributed the juvenile song "Where have you been to-day, Billy, my son?..." to the *Scot's Musical Museum*. It was allied to the precursor "Lord Randal..." and to "Where have you been, Billy boy?..." (see pages 236–239). He had already written his own version of the theme, however, in 1788, acknowledging that the chorus was old:

I'm Owre [O'er] Young to Marry Yet

I am my mammie's ae bairn,†
    Wi' unco† folk I weary, Sir;
And lying in a man's bed,
    I'm fley'd† wad mak me eerie, Sir.

†*only child; strange; scared.*

      Chorus: I'm owre† young, I'm owre young,
            I'm owre young to marry yet;
            I'm owre young, 'twad be a sin
              To tak me frae my mammie yet.

†*Too. Alternate form: o'er.*

My mammie coft† me a new gown,
    The kirk maun† hae the gracing o't;
Were I to lie wi' you, kind Sir,
    I'm fear'd ye'd spoil the lacing o't.

†*Bought; the church must.*

Hallowmas is come and gane,
    The nights are lang in winter, Sir;

And you an' I in ae bed,
   In troth I dare na venture, Sir.

Fu'† loud and shrill the frosty wind
   Blaws thro' the leafless timmer,†, Sir;
But if ye come this gate again,
   I'll aulder be gin simmer,† Sir.

                              —Robert Burns 1788

†*Full; woods (timber); I'll older be by summer.*

Scholars have been intrigued with the use by various poets of the line "Over the hills and far away..." which also appears in "Tom, he was a piper's son..." (see page 112). Included here is the version by Burns, using a marine variation of the line in one verse:

On the Seas and Far Away

This has four eight-line stanzas, telling the woes of a maid who misses her sailor who is off to fight the foe.

Chorus: On the seas and far away,
   On the stormy seas and far away;
   Nightly dreams and thoughts by day
   Are aye with him that's far away.

Here, then, is the poem in which he uses the "poet's phrase":

The Bonnie Lad That's Far Away

O how can I be blithe and glad,
   Or how can I gang† brisk and braw,†
When the bonnie lad that i lo'e best
   Is o'er the hills and far awa'?

It's no frosty winter wind,
   It's no the driving drift and snaw;
But aye the tear comes in my ee,†
   To think on him that's far awa'.

My father pat me frae his door,
   My friends they hae disown'd me a':
But I hae ane will tak my part,
   The bonnie lad that's far awa'.

†*Go; fine; eye.*

A pair o' glooves he bought to me,
   And silken snoods he gae me twa;
And I will wear them for his sake,
   The bonnie lad that's far awa'.

O weary winter soon will pass,
   And spring will cleed† the birken shaw:†
And my young babie will be born,
   And he'll be hame that's far awa'.

                        —Robert Burns 1788

†*Clothe; birchwoods.*

I: Wee Totum Fogg,
Sits upon a creepie;†
Half an ell† o' gray
Wad be his coat and breekie.†

                       —Very old Scottish verse

†*Stool; a yard; breeches.*

II: Little Tommy Tacket
Sits upon his cracket;†
Half a yard of cloth
Will make him coat and jacket;
Make him coat and jacket,
Breeches to the knee,
And if you will not have him,
You may let him be.

           —The Nursery Rhymes of England 1852

†*Three-legged stool.*

Burns: Wee Willie

Wee Willie Gray, and his leather wallet;
Peel a willow-wand, to be him boots and jacket:
The rose upon the briar will be him trews† and doublet,
The rose upon the briar will be him trews and doublet!
Wee Willie Gray, and his leather wallet;
Twice a lily flower will be him sark† and cravat;
Feathers of a flee wad feather up his bonnet,
Feathers of a flee wad feather up his bonnet.

          —Robert Burns (date unknown)

†*Trousers; shirt.*

Burns's "Wee Willie" appeared in a volume of the *Scot's Musical Museum* (1803) that was not printed until seven years after his death.

And so, here, the bard who created literary poetry that paralleled nursery rhymes, retained child-lore, for Burns intended "Wee Willie Gray" as a nursery song.

11. Sit and Spin a Spell
Narrative Ballads

Not all of old Dame Gander's works are short and snappy. Despite the assertion of a few nursery-lorists that a piece can only be considered a Mother Goose rhyme if it is short — some actually say only four lines! — the fact is that there are a number of long ballads in her traditional repertoire. Most tell a tale. The oldest has been a popular childlore game since the fourteenth century. Others date from the fifteenth through the nineteenth centuries.

These ballads, however, are one area where there has been a lack of standardization of the words. They have been part of the folk tradition of adding

216

verses from time to time, here and there. Ballads are intrinsically different from other poetry. They frequently do not rhyme in certain lines, and they often do not scan properly. They are a composite of two sources, mutually dependent on each other, the initial author and the subsequent process of collective authorship. It is this process which makes it hard to say any particular version of a ballad is the authoritative or definitive one. Words, phrases, lines, and refrains or choruses have changed, are changing, and will no doubt continue to change.

For his monumental study, *English and Scottish Ballads* (1883–1898), Professor F.J. Child sifted and preserved every version of every traditional ballad then known to exist in the two tongues. He presented, for instance, 15 versions of "Lord Randal," along with references to continental versions. This is not to say that there were no repetitious stanzas offered. Modern folksong-book editors usually choose one version they like and let it go at that.

Though the ballads have grown, the tendency of many publishers has been arbitrarily to cut the versions to suit a particular pagination scheme. Scholars who look in more than one source are usually treated to both similar verses and a number of different ones. Certain stanzas have a way of appearing over and over again.

Rather than abridged versions, what are presented in this chapter are actually amplifications—composites of the stanzas found extant, put together to create the narrative ballad at its best. These composites combine stanzas linked with natural transitions that maintain the basic narrative structure and theme. Like Mother Goose's ducklings "all in a row," they are presented in full regalia—but cognizant of other stanzas lurking in the mill pond.

The stanzas have been formatted for easy scanning. The melodies to most are so well known that they can be sung without musical notation. And some are traditionally spoken, being ballads mainly in the sense that they are narrative poems told in a rhythmic pattern. There are, of course, many other ballads in folklore, but only those which are traditionally found in Mother Goose books are included here, along with pertinent notes.

The choruses and refrains are characteristic of ballads. Simply, the chorus is sung after each stanza, and the refrain is a line sung after certain lines in every stanza. While the choruses and refrains may be enjoyed for their own sakes, the "reading eye" has little patience with the repetition. Thus, the ballads are presented here with the choruses and refrains introduced, but not unnecessarily repeated. This common practice, incidentally, has also caused some ballads to eventually lose their choruses and refrains, much to the distress of purist balladeers.

The following presentation is generally in chronological order, but this has been violated where it seemed more important to group certain ballads by subject. Ballads that are related to or derived from each other are placed together in order to permit easier comparison, and those about Christmastime are also together.

1.   London Bridge is falling down, falling down, falling down,
      London Bridge is falling down, my fair lady.
2.   London Bridge is broken down, broken down, broken down,
      London Bridge is broken down, my fair lady.
3.   How shall we build it up again, etc.
4.   Build it up with penny loaves, etc.
5.   Penny loaves will crumble so, etc.
6.   Build it up with needles and pins, etc.
7.   Needles and pins will bend and break, etc.
8.   Build it up with building-blocks, etc.
9.   Building-blocks will tumble down, etc.
10.   Build it up with wooden sticks, etc.
11.   Wooden sticks will fall away, etc.
12.   Build it up with stones and clay, etc.
13.   Stones and clay will wash away, etc.
14.   Build it up with bricks and mortar, etc.
15.   Bricks and mortar will not stay, etc.
16.   Build it up with iron bars, etc.
17.   Iron bars will rust away, etc.
18.   Build it up with ropes of steel, etc.
19.   Ropes of steel will bend and bow, etc.
20.   Build it up silver and gold, etc.
21.   Silver and gold will be stolen away, etc.
22.   We will set a man to watch, etc.
23.   Suppose the man should fall asleep, etc.
24.   Give him a pipe to smoke all night, etc.
25.   Suppose the pipe should fall and break, etc.
26.   We'll get a cock to crow all night, etc.
27.   Suppose the cock should run away, etc.
28.   We'll get a dog to make him stay, etc.
29.   Suppose the dog should catch a thief, etc.
30.   Here's the prisoner we have caught, etc.
31.   What's the prisoner done to you, etc.
32.   Stole my watch and broke my chain, etc.
33.   What will you take to set him free, etc.
34.   One hundred pounds will set him free, etc.
35.   One hundred pounds he has not got, etc.
36.   Then off to prison he must go, etc.
37.   To which prison should he go, etc.
38.   Take him over London Bridge, etc.

39a. London Bridge is falling down, etc. (again through the cycle)
39b. London Bridge has now been sold, etc.
40. Arizona's where it is, etc.
41. Yankee Doodle keep it up, etc.

The favorite old game-ballad is known throughout the European countries, and has been traced to a game, *Coda Romano*, played by Florentine
children in 1328 (William Wells Newell, *Games and Songs of American
Children*, 1883, 1903). In Rabelais' *Gargantua*, written in 1534, "the fallen
bridges" is one of the games played. The stanzas about the "prisoner" date
from the late 1800s. The last three stanzas are relatively new, prompted by the
mid-twentieth century sale of the bridge.

The bridge which is constantly falling down and impossible to repair is
linked to rites of antiquity. Myths prevailed that unless a living human, in particular, a child, was built into the foundations of a bridge, the evil gods of
the river would not be placated and the bridge would continually fall down—
many old bridges in Europe and the Orient have had human skeletons found
in them when they were taken down.

The first London Bridge was engineered by a monk of England, Peter of
Colebrook. The building of it took from 1176 to 1209, but Peter died before
its completion and was buried in a chapel on the bridge. Not a sacrifice, but
nevertheless symbolic. Above the bridge's gate were seen the heads of
criminals, and the bridge itself, a masonry structure of 19 arches weighted
down by shops and dwellings, was the center of London life for 600 years. It
was replaced with another bridge 60 yards up-river, built by the architect
John Rennie, with his son Sir John Rennie, from 1825–1831. Upon being
replaced and dismantled in 1967, the Rennie masonry facade was sold to
an American private developer and re-erected at Lake Havasu City, Arizona.

To play the game, two players are chosen to join hands and raise them
high to form the arch of the bridge. The rest sing and march in a circle, moving under the arch. At the words "my fair lady" the arch falls down to trap
a player. The two players who form the bridge have already privately decided
which of them is "silver" and which is "gold." The prisoner is asked his choice,
which he or she whispers so that the other players will not hear. He or she then
takes a place behind the player whose word was chosen, usually holding on
at the waist. (An additional capture occurs at the words "here's the prisoner
we have caught.") The song is sung until all players have been caught. At the
end, the gold and silver teams have a tug-of-war until one side is pulled down
by the other. (The tug-of-war does not seem to be as prevalent in England as
in America.)

In 1725, Henry Carey referred to the game of "London-Bridge" in *Namby
Pamby*, his nursery satire. A rather condensed version appeared in the first

collection of nursery rhymes for children, *Tommy Thumb's Pretty Song Book*, circa 1744. The lines and refrain had a different pattern therein:

London Bridge is broken down, Dance over my Lady Lee,
London Bridge is broken down, With a gay lady.

It has been suggested that "my Lady Lee (also Lea)" is a reference to the Lea River, which loses its identity where it runs into the Thames.

Bird's Courting Song

1.   Hi! said the little leather-winged bat,
I'll tell you the reason that,
The reason that I fly by night,
Is because I've lost my heart's delight.
     Howdy, dowdy, diddle-um-day,
     Howdy, dowdy, diddle-um-day,
     Howdy, dowdy, diddle-um-day,
     And a hey-lee-lee, lye-lye-lo.

2.   Hi! said the blackbird sitting on a chair,
Once I courted a lady fair,
She proved fickle and turned her back,
And ever since then I've dressed in black. etc.

3.   Hi! said the little mourning dove,
I'll tell you how to regain her love,
Court her night and court her day,
Never give her time to say, oh nay. etc.

4.   Hi! said the bluebird as he flew,
Once I loved a young gal, too,
But she got saucy and wanted to go,
So I bought a new string for my bow. etc.

5.   Hi! said the woodpecker sitting on a fence,
Once I courted a handsome wench,
She proved fickle and from me fled,
And ever since then my head's been red. etc.

6.   Hi! said the swallow sitting on a barn,
Courting, I think, it is no harm,
I pick my feathers and sit up straight,
And hope everyone will choose a mate. etc.

7.   Hi! said the cuckoo as he flew,
When I was a young man, I chose two,

If one didn't love me, the other one would,
And don't you think my notion's good? etc.

8. Hoot! said the owl with her head of white,
A lonesome day and a lonesome night,
Thought I heard some pretty girl say,
She'd court all night and sleep all day. etc.

9. No, oh, no! said the turtle-dove,
That's no gain to his love,
If you want to gain your heart's delight,
Keep him awake both day and night. etc.

10. Hi! said the robin with a squirm,
I wish I had a great big worm,
I'd fly away into my nest,
I have a wife I think is the best. etc.

Twentieth century folklorists John A. Lomax and Alan Lomax (*Best Loved American Folk Songs*, New York: Grosset & Dunlap, 1947) suggest that this song is derived from Geoffrey Chaucer's *Parliament of Fowls* (ca.1380), which itself was based on an ancient folktale theme. "As Chaucer tells it . . . Dame Nature summons the fowls together in convention on St. Valentine's Day to contest in compliments for the favors of a charming young lady eagle. The falcon and the other predatory birds behave like knights and make courtly speeches, but commoners of the barnyard express coarse and cynical sentiments." The ballad has long been a nursery favorite.

1. I have a four sisters (brothers) beyond the sea,
    Perrie, Merrie, Dixie, Dominie,
And they each sent a present to me,
    Petrum, Partrum, Paradisi, Temporie,
    Perrie, Merrie, Dixie, Dominie.

2. The first sent a goose (chicken), without a bone,
    Perrie, Merrie, Dixie, Dominie,
The second a cherry, without a stone,
    Petrum, Partrum, Paradisi, Temporie,
    Perrie, Merrie, Dixie, Dominie.

3. The third sent a book which no one can read, etc.
The fourth sent a blanket, without e'er a thread, etc.

4. How can there be a goose (chicken) without e'er a bone? Etc.
How can there be a cherry without e'er a stone? Etc.

5. How can there be a book which no one can read? Etc.
How can there be blanket without e'er a thread? Etc.

6.   When the goose is (chicken's) in the egg-shell there is no bone, etc.
      When the cherry's in the bud, there is no stone, etc.
7.   When the book's in the press, no one it can read, etc.
      When the blanket's in the fleece there is no thread, etc.

This was found written in a manuscript around 1440, but does not seem to have otherwise been printed until 1838 when W. Dauney included it in *Ancient Scottish Melodies*. Halliwell collected it in 1849. Other first lines have been, "My true love lives far from me," "I have a true love over the sea," and "I have four cousins. . . ." The content is very like the American "Riddle Song" in which the chicken and cherry are mentioned along with the "baby with no crying . . . when it's sleeping."

Dauney thought the refrain was a relic of the times when Romish hymns were adapted for secular purposes. When the Church of England banned the use of Latin in church services, popular flaunting songs were developed in what became known as *macaronic* verse—verses in English and Latin. It has also been suggested that the refrain here may be a corruption of a Latin exorcism.

1.   A carrion crow sat on an oak,
      Watching a tailor shape his cloak,
            With a heigh ho, the carrion crow,
            Sing tol de rol, de riddle row.
2.   The carrion crow began to rave,
      And called the tailor a lousy knave,
            With a heigh ho, the carrion crow,
            Sing tol de rol, de riddle row.
3.   "Wife," cried tailor, "bring my bow,
      That I may shoot yon carrion crow," etc.
4.   The tailor shot and missed his mark,
      And shot his own sow through the heart, etc.
5.   "Wife, bring treacle in a spoon,
      For our poor sow is in a swoon," etc.
6.   The old sow died, and the bells did toll,
      And the little pigs pray'd for the old sow's soul, etc.
7.   "Zooks," quoth the tailor, "I care not a louse,
      For we shall have black puddings, chitterlings, and souse," etc.
8.   The carrion crow cried out "caw" and "pork,"
      The carrion crow still upon the oak, etc.

This is frequently seen in nursery rhyme books with the lines from stanzas 1, 3, 4, 5, and no refrain. It has been dated in a manuscript of 1489 and was in *Grandmamma's Nursery Rhymes*, circa 1825.

(The last phrase of each stanza, in refrain fashion, may be repeated if one wishes.)

1. There were three jovial Welshmen, as I have heard men say,
    And they would go a-hunting, upon St. David's Day.

2. All the day they hunted, and nothing could they find,
    But a ship a-sailing, a-sailing with the wind.

3. One said it was a ship, the other he said, "nay,"
    The third said it was a house, with the chimney blown away.

4. And all the night they hunted, and nothing could they find,
    But the moon a-gliding, a-gliding with the wind.

5. One said it was the moon, the other he said, "nay,"
    The third said it was a cheese, and half of it cut away.

6. And all the day they hunted, and nothing could they find,
    But a hedgehog in a bramble bush, and that they left behind.

7. The first said it was a hedgehog, the second he said, "nay,"
    The third said it was a pincushion, and the pins stuck in wrong way.

8. And all the night they hunted, and nothing could they find,
    But a hare in a turnip field, and that they left behind.

9. The first said it was a hare, the second he said, "nay,"
    The third said it was a calf, and the cow had run away.

10. And all the day they hunted, and nothing could they find,
    But an owl in a holly tree, and that they left behind.

11. One said it was an owl, the other he said, "nay,"
    The third said 'twas an old man, and his beard was going grey.

This song was evidently known earlier than 1613, for a portion of it appears in Shakespeare and Fletcher's *Two Noble Kinsmen*. (See page 142.) It was also part of a black-letter broadside ballad, *Choice of Inventions, Or Severall sorts of the figure of three*, recorded in the Stationer's register January 2, 1632, where the three men were from *Gotam*, which may be a corruption of *Gotham*.

St. David's Day, March 1, is also connected with the taunting rhyme, "Taffy was a Welshman..." (see pages 109–10).

The first five verses were printed in *The Top Book of All* in 1760. Later, Halliwell collected the entire tale.

1. Lavender's blue, dilly dilly, lavender's green,
    When I am King, dilly dilly, you shall be queen;
    Who told me so, dilly dilly, who told me so?
    "Twas my own heart, dilly dilly, that told me so.

2. If you'll have me, dilly dilly, I will have you,
    I'll love you so, dilly dilly, and will be true;

Call up the maids, dilly dilly, at four o'clock,
Some to the wheel, dilly dilly, some at the rock.

3.   Call up your men, dilly dilly, set them to work,
Some with a plough, dilly dilly, some with a fork;
Some to make hay, dilly dilly, some to thresh corn,
While you and I, dilly dilly, keep ourselves warm.

4.   Let the birds sing, dilly dilly, and the lambs play,
We shall be safe, dilly dilly, out of harm's way;
Let the rain come, dilly dilly, and the sun shine,
I will be yours, dilly dilly, you will be mine.

5.   You shall but dance, dilly dilly, we shall but dine,
You shall not work, dilly dilly, nor feed the swine;
You shall but sit, dilly dilly, sew a fine seam,
Strawberries eat, dilly dilly, sugar and cream.

6.   You shall have rings, dilly dilly, silver and gold,
I'll love you young, dilly dilly, I'll love you old;
I'll give you stars, dilly dilly, I'll give you the moon,
Then you and I, dilly dilly, shall sing love's tune.

7.   Roses are red, dilly dilly, violets are blue,
If you love me, dilly dilly, I will love you.
Lavender's blue, dilly dilly, lavender's green,
I'll be your King, dilly dilly, you'll be my Queen.

This stems from a black-letter broadside printed between 1672 and 1685, named *Diddle Diddle, Or, The Kind Country Lovers*. A version was included in *Songs for the Nursery* in 1805. The internal refrain, *dilly dilly*, replaced the original *diddle diddle* when it appeared in *Gammer Gurton's Garland* in 1810. In 1948 the song "Lavender Blue" by Larry Morey and Eliot Daniel, based on the old nursery rhyme, with quite similar words, became popular in both America and England.

The Derby Ram

1. As I was going to Derby,
Upon a market day,
I saw the biggest ram, sir,
That ever was fed with hay,
That ever was fed with hay.

2. And if you think "not so," sir,
If you should think I lie,

Oh you go down to Derby, sir,
And you'll see same as I,
And you'll see same as I.

3. The ram that was in Derby,
As all have heard it said,
He was the biggest ram, sir,

That ever wore a head,
That ever wore a head.

4. The ram was fat behind, sir,
The ram was fat before,
He measured ten yards round, sir,
I think it was no more,
I think it was no more.

5. The ram he had four feet, sir,
He had four feet to stand,
And every track he made, sir,
It covered an acre of land,
It covered an acre of land.

6. The wool grew on his back, sir,
It reach-ed to the sky,
And there the eagles built their
    nests,
I heard the young one's cry,
I heard the young one's cry.

7. The wool grew on his belly,
    sir,
It reach-ed to the ground,
It was sold in Derby Town, sir,
For forty thousand pound,
For forty thousand pound.

8. The wool on this ram's flanks,
    sir,
It drag-ged on the ground,
The Devil cut it off, sir,
To make himself a gown,
To make himself a gown.

9. The wool upon his tail, sir,
Filled more than fifty bags,
You'd better keep away, sir,
When that tail shakes and wags,
When that tail shakes and wags.

10. The wool upon his tail, sir,
Was very fine and thin,
Took all the girls of Derby Town,
Full seven years to spin,
Full seven years to spin.

11. The ram it had a horn, sir,
That reach-ed to the moon,
A man went up in December,
And never came down till June,
And never came down till June.

12. The space between his horns,
    sir,
'Twas more than a man could
    reach,
And there they built a pulpit, sir,
The parson there to preach,
The parson there to preach.

13. The ram it had a tail, sir,
Most wonderful to tell,
It reached across to Ireland, sir,
And rang St. Patrick's bell,
And rang St. Patrick's bell.

14. And when they fed this ram,
    sir,
They fed him twice a day,
And every time they fed him, sir,
He ate a ton of hay,
He ate a ton of hay.

15. And when they watered this
    ram, sir,
They watered him twice a day,
And every time they watered him,
    sir,
He drank the creek away,
He drank the creek away.

16. And he who killed the ram,
    sir,
Was drown-ed in the blood,
And he who held the dish, sir,
Was carried away in the flood,
Was carried away in the flood.

17. The blood flowed from the
    ram, sir,
It flowed for many a mile,
It turned the wheel of a mill, sir,

That hadn't been turned in a
 while,
That hadn't been turned in a
 while.

18. The blood ran forty miles, sir,
They say it was no more,
The water-wheels turned fast, sir,
It made the mill-stones roar,
It made the mill-stones roar.

19. And all the boys in Derby,
 sir,
Came begging for his eyes,
To kick about the street, sir,
As any good football flies,
As any good football flies.

20. The first tooth in his head,
 sir,
It made a hunter's horn,
The next tooth in his head, sir,
It held a bushel of corn,
It held a bushel of corn.

21. The mutton from the ram, sir,

It gave the whole army meat,
And what was left I'm told, sir,
Was served up to the fleet,
Was served up to the fleet.

22. Indeed, it is the truth, sir,
I never was taught to lie,
And if you go to Derby, sir,
You may eat a bit of the pie,
You may eat a bit of the pie.

23. And if you don't believe me,
 sir,
And think I do not know,
Then you go down to Derby, sir,
And see if it isn't so,
And see if it isn't so.

24. The man that owned this
 ram, sir,
Was counted very rich,
But the one that made this song,
 sir,
Was a lying son of a witch,
Was a lying son of a witch.

"The Derby Ram" has been known since at least the beginning of the eighteenth century; the ram has even been incorporated into the coat-of-arms of Derby. This ballad about one of the most elaborate lies ever told is said to have been the favorite song of "he who never lied"—George Washington. A variation on the last lines was noted in *Notes and Queries* in 1904 as sung by a Cape Cod sailor, who sang it as "lying son of a bitch." The ballad made its debut in child-lore in *The Only True Mother Goose Melodies*, about 1843, and has been repeated in nursery books many times since then.

Animal, insect, and bird weddings are the subject of several popular Mother Goose ballads. They show a fair resemblance to each other, and the general stance is contained in a separate nursery ditty:

A cat came fiddling out of a barn,
With a pair of bagpipes under her arm;
She could sing nothing but, Fiddle cum fee,
The mouse has married the humble-bee.
Pipe; cat; dance; mouse;
We'll have a wedding at our good house.

This rhyme is known with a number of minor variations, the earliest of which is recorded in a Wiltshire manuscript dated 1740. Its first appearance in nursery books was in two J.G. Rusher books, *Nursery Songs* and *London Jingles*, both published in about 1840. Its reference to the wedding of the mouse and the "humble-bee" is curious in light of the fact that the ballads known are either about the frog and mouse or about the fly and the humble-bee (or bumble-bee).

1.   Frog, he would a-wooing go, Mm-hm, Mm-hm.
    Frog, he would a-wooing go,
    And he dressed himself from head to toe, Mm-hm, Mm-hm.
2.   Frog, he went a courting he did ride, Mm-hm, Mm-hm,
    Frog, he went a courting he did ride,
    A sword and pistol by his side, Mm-hm, Mm-hm.

3.   He rode up to Miss Mousie's door, etc.
      Where he had been many times before, etc.

4.   He did knock at Miss Mousie's den, etc.
      He said, "Miss Mousie, are you within?" etc.

5.   "Yes, Mister Frog, I set and spin," etc.
      "Just lift the latch and please come in," etc.

6.   He took Miss Mousie on his knee, etc.
      He said, "Miss Mousie will you marry me?" etc.

7.   "First I must ask my Uncle Rat," etc.
      And see what he will say to that," etc.

8.   "Without my Uncle Rat's consent," etc.
      "I wouldn't marry the president," etc.

9.   "Uncle Rat has gone to town," etc.
      "And I can't say when he'll be home," etc.

10.   Late that night when the rat came home, etc.
      "Who's been here since I've been gone?" etc.

11.   "A very fine gentleman has been here," etc.
      "Who wishes me to be his dear," etc.

12.   Uncle Rat laughed and shook his fat sides, etc.
      To think his niece would be a bride, etc.

13.   Then Uncle Rat he went to town, etc.
      To buy his niece a wedding gown, etc.

14.   When Uncle Rat gave his consent, etc.
      The weasel wrote the publishment, etc.

15.   Solemnly walked in Parson Rook, etc.
      Under his arm a wedding book, etc.

16.   Mister Frog was dressed in green, etc.
      Miss Mousie she looked just like a queen, etc.

17.   Now, say what was the groom dressed in? etc.
      Grass-green britches with silver stitches, etc.

18.   Now, say what was the bride dressed in? etc.
      A sky-blue veil and a gold breast pin, etc.

19.   The owls did hoot and the birds they sang, etc.
      And through the woods the music rang, etc.

20.   Where will the wedding supper be? etc.
      Away down yonder in hollow tree, etc.

21.   What will the wedding supper be? etc.
      Two green beans and a black-eyed pea, etc.

22.   What will the guests all have to drink? etc.
      Persimmon beer and a bottle of ink, etc.

23.   The first to come was the little moth, etc.
      For to lay the table cloth, etc.

24. Next to come was a little fly, etc.
    And he fetched in an apple pie, etc.
25. Next to come was a lady-bug, etc.
    She had molasses in a jug, etc.
26. Next to come was a little brown bug, etc.
    He went swimming in the lady-bug's jug, etc.
27. Next to come was Mister Tick, etc.
    He ate so much it made him sick, etc.
28. Next to come was Doctor Fly,
    Said Mister Tick would surely die, etc.
29. Next to come was Miss Butterfly, etc.
    She ate so much she almost died, etc.
30. Next to come was the little green snake, etc.
    He coiled himself on the wedding cake, etc.
31. Next to come was a bumble-bee, etc.
    With a big bass fiddle on his knee, etc.
32. Next to come was a little black cricket, etc.
    He tuned up his banjo and he started to pick it, etc.
33. Next to come was a creeping snail, etc.
    A big guitar upon his tail, etc.
34. Up then jumped the bumble-bee, etc.
    And danced a jig with old Miss Flea, etc.
35. The little red ant, she said, "I can't," etc.
    When she tried for to do the dance, etc.
36. Last to come was the mocking-bird, etc.
    He said, "This wedding is absurd," etc.
37. They all went sailing upon the lake, etc.
    And got swallowed up by a big black snake, etc.
38. Now there's the end of one, two, three, etc.
    The Rat, the Frog, and Miss Mousie, etc.
    Hm, Hm, Hm.

This ballad goes back at least four centuries, having been rendered in 1549 in *The Complaynt of Scotlande*. The ballad "A moste Strange wedding of the ffrogge and the mowse" was licensed by the Stationers to Edward White 21 November 1580. In 1611, Thomas Ravenscroft included "The Marriage of the Frogge and the Mouse" in *Melismata*, where it began as:

It was the Frogge in the well,
    Humble-dum, humble-dum.
And the merrie Mouse in the Mill,
    Tweedle, tweedle, twino.

Alternate refrains to "Mm-hm, Mm-hm" are "ah-hah"; "uhn-huhn"; "eh-heh"; "ee-hee"; or "gunk gunk" or "och-kungh" (like a frog).

Two frequently seen variations of the storyline end either with the Mouse's refusal to answer or with the wedding, in both instances followed by the Frog being swallowed up by the Drake. A version appeared in *Gammer Gurton's Garland* in 1784 and another was collected by Halliwell in 1842. The following is representative:

1. A Frog he would a-wooing go,
    Heigh ho, says Rowley.
    Whether his mother would let him or no,
    With a rowley, powley, gammon, and spinach,
    Heigh ho, says Anthony Rowley.

2. So off he set with his opera hat,
    Heigh ho, says Rowley.
    And on the road he met with a rat,
    With a rowley, powley, gammon, and spinach,
    Heigh ho, says Anthony Rowley.

3. Pray, Mr. Rat, will you go with me, etc.
    Kind Mrs. Mousey for to see? etc.

4. They came to the door of Mousey's hall, etc.
    They gave a loud knock and they gave a loud call, etc.

5. Pray, Mrs. Mouse are you within? etc.
    Oh, yes, kind sirs, I'm sitting to spin, etc.

6. Pray, Mrs. Mouse will you give us some beer? etc.
    For Froggy and I are fond of good cheer, etc.

7. Pray, Mr. Frog, will you give us a song? etc.
    But let it be something that's not very long, etc.

8. Indeed, Mrs. Mouse, replied the frog, etc.
    A cold has made me as hoarse as a dog, etc.

9. Since you have caught cold, Mr. Frog, Mousey said, etc.
    I'll sing you a song that I have just made, etc.

10. But while they were all a merry-making, etc.
    A cat and her kittens came tumbling in, etc.

11. The cat she seized the rat by the crown, etc.
    The kittens they pulled the little mouse down, etc.

12. This put Mr. Frog in a terrible fright, etc.
    He took up his hat, and he wished them good night, etc.

13. But as Froggy was crossing over a brook, etc.
    A lily-white duck came and gobbled him up, etc.

14. So there was the end of one, two, and three, etc.
    The Rat, the Mouse, and the little Frog-ee, etc.

The comparison to "Frog he would a-wooing go, Mm-hm..." is obvious, despite the differences in narrative. This "rowley powley" version did not appear until the nineteenth century, and today is seen almost always with the narrative as shown above. A correspondent to *Notes and Queries* gave *rowley powley* as the name for a plump fowl, with the succinct comment that "both gammon and spinach are posthumous connections."

In some versions the refrain is "Kitty alone, Kitty alone, Kitty alone and I! Cock me cary, Kitty alone, Kitty alone and I." Also seen are "Crocka-my-daisy, Kitty alone, Kitty alone and I"; "Cuddle alone and I"; "Heigh ho! says Brittle! With a namby pamby, Manniken, panniken, Heigh! says Barnaby Brittle"; "Fa, la, linkum, leerie! And a mousie in a mill, Linkum-a-leerie, linkum-a-leerie, cow-dow"; "Heigho, crowdie! with a howdie crowdie"; and the macaronic "With a rigdum bonum duo coino, Coi min ero giltee caro coi minero coino, Stim stam pammediddle lara bona ringcan, Ringcan bonum dur coino."

1. Fiddle-dee-dee, fiddle-dee-dee,
   The fly has married the bumblebee.†

2. Said the fly, said he, "Will you marry me,
   And live with me, sweet bumblebee:" etc.

3. Said the bee, said she, "I'll live under your wing,
   And you'll never know I carry a sting." etc.

4. And the bees did buzz and the flies did sing,
   Did you ever hear so merry a thing? etc.

5. And then to think that of all the flies,
   The bumblebee should carry the prize, etc.

6. But where now shall this wedding be?
   For a hey nonny no, in an old ivy tree, etc.

7. And there was bid to this wedding,
   All flies in the field and worms creeping, etc.

8. The snail she came crawling all over the plain,
   With her jolly trinkets at her train, etc.

9. Ten bees there came all clad in gold,
   And all the rest did them behold, etc.

10. But the thornbug refused this sight to see,
    And to a cow-plot away flew she, etc.

11. All went to the church and married was he,
    The fly was married to the bumblebee, etc.

12. When Parson Beetle had married the pair,
    They both went out to take the air, etc.

†*These opening lines are repeated as a chorus.*

13.   And now where shall we our dinner make?
        For a hey nonny no, down by the lake, etc.
14.   And what will the wedding dinner be?
        Some dogwood soup and catwood tea, etc.
15.   And there we shall have good company,
        With humbling and bumbling and much melody, etc.
16.   When ended was their wedding day,
        The fly he took his sweet bee away, etc.
17.   He took her to live beside the marsh,
        'Tween one cat-tail and one long grass, etc.
18.   And there came a son, young Master gnat,
        They made him the heir of all—that's that, etc.

If, as seems likely, this ballad was the one referred to in "The cat came fiddling out of the barn...," its origins must predate 1740. Tracing the dates of various stanzas is almost impossible, for they have been added in the folk tradition. The editors of *The Oxford Dictionary of Nursery Rhymes* have speculated that stanzas 1, 2, 3, 12, 4, 5 (in that order) may have been written by Walter Crane and his wife when he illustrated the verses for *Baby's Bouquet* in 1879. (The first line of stanza 12 read "So when the parson had joined the pair.")

Halliwell collected one stanza in 1842, as:

Fiddle-dee-dee, fiddle-dee-dee,
The fly shall marry the humble-bee.
They went to the church, and married was she:
The fly has married the humble-bee.

The following two ballads, together, tell a tale, but it should be noted that the first was written *after* the second. Publisher John Harris commissioned the writing of the wedding of Cock Robin and Jenny Wren to precede the already-popular "The Death and Burial of Cock Robin," publishing it in 1806 as *The Happy Courtship, Merry Marriage and Pic-nic Dinner, of Cock Robin and Jenny Wren. To Which is added, Alas! The Doleful Death of the Bridegroom.*

1.   'Twas on a merry time, when Jenny Wren was young,
        So neatly as she danced, and so sweetly as she sung, —
2.   Robin Redbreast lost his heart—he was a gallant bird;
        He doffed his hat to Jenny, and thus to her he said: —
3.   "My dearest Jenny Wren, if you will but be mine,
        You shall dine on cherry-pie, and drink nice currant-wine.

4. "I'll dress you like a Goldfinch, or like a Peacock gay;
So if you'll have me, Jenny, let us appoint the day."

5. Jenny blushed behind her fan, and thus declared her mind,
"Then let it be tomorrow, Bob; I take your offer kind.

6. "Cherry-pie is very good; so is currant-wine;
But I will wear my brown gown, and never dress too fine."

7. Robin rose up early, at the break of day;
He flew to Jenny Wren's house, to sing a roundelay.

8. He met the Cock and Hen, and bade the Cock declare,
This was the wedding-day with Jenny Wren the fair.

9. The Cock then blew his horn, to let the neighbors know
This was Robin's wedding-day, and they might see the show.

10. And first came Parson Rook, with his spectacles and band;
And one of Mother Goose's books he held within his hand.

11. Then followed him the Lark, for he could sweetly sing;
And he was to be clerk at Cock Robin's wedding.

12. He sung of Robin's love for little Jenny Wren;
And when he came unto the end, then he began again.

13. The Bulfinch walked by Robin, and thus to him did say,
"Pray, mark, friend Robin Redbreast, that Goldfinch dressed so gay; —

14. "What though her gay apparel becomes her very well;
Yet Jenny's modest dress and look must bear away the bell!"

15. Then came the bride and bridegroom; quite plainly was she dressed;
And blushed so much, her cheeks were as red as Robin's breast.

16. But Robin cheered her up; "My pretty Jen," said he,
"We're going to be married, and happy we shall be."

17. The Goldfinch came on next, to give away the bride;
The Linnet, being bridesmaid, walked by Jenny's side.

18. And as she was a-walking, said, "Upon my word,
I think that your Cock Robin is a very pretty bird."

19. "And will you have him, Jenny, your husband now to be?"
"Yes, I will," says Jenny, "and love him heartily."

20. The Blackbird and the Thrush and charming Nightingale,
Whose sweet "jug" sweetly echoes through every grove and dale; —

21. The Sparrow and Tomtit, and many more were there;
All came to see the wedding of Jenny Wren the fair.

22. "O, then," says Parson Rook, "who gives this maid away?"

23. "I do," says the Goldfinch, "and her fortune I will pay; —

24. "Here's a bag of grain of many sorts, and other things beside;
Now happy be the bridegroom, and happy be the bride!"

25. Then on her finger fair, Cock Robin put the ring;
"You're married now," says Parson Rook; while the Lark aloud did sing, —

26. "Happy be the bridegroom, and happy be the bride!

27.   And may not man, nor bird, nor beast, this happy pair divide."
      The birds were asked to dine; not Jenny's friends alone,
      But every pretty songster that had Cock Robin known.

28.   They had a cherry-pie, besides some currant-wine,
      And every guest brought something, that sumptuous they might dine.

29.   Now they all took a bumper, and drank to the pair;
      Cock Robin the bridegroom, and Jenny Wren the fair.

30.   The dinner things removed, they all began to sing;
      And soon they made the place near a mile around to ring.

31.   The concert it was fine; and every bird tried
      Who best should sing for Robin, and Jenny Wren the bride.

32.   When in came the Cuckoo, and made a great rout;
      He caught hold of Jenny, and pulled her about.

33.   Cock Robin was angry, and so was the Sparrow,
      Who fetched in a hurry his bow and his arrow.

34.   His aim then he took, but he took it not right;
      His skill was not good, or he shot in a fright;

35.   For the Cuckoo he missed, — but Cock Robin he killed!
      And all the birds mourned that his blood was so spilled.

Although the entire ballad above has been published as part of Mother Goose in the twentieth century, lines also seen are stanzas seven and twelve combined as one verse, standing alone.

1.   Who killed Cock Robin?
     "I," said the Sparrow,
     "With my bow and arrow,
     And I killed Cock Robin."

2.   Who saw him die?
     "I," said the Fly,
     "With my little eye,
     And I saw him die."

3.   Who caught his blood?
     "I," said the Fish,
     "With my little dish,
     And I caught his blood."

4.   Who made his shroud?
     "I," said the Beadle,
     "With my little needle,
     And I made his shroud."

5.   Who shall dig his grave?
     "I," said the Owl,

"With my pick and shovel,
And I'll dig his grave."

6. Who'll be the parson?
"I," said the Rook,
"With my little book,
And I'll be the parson."

7. Who'll be the clerk?
"I," said the Lark,
"If it's not in the dark,
And I'll be the clerk."

8. Who'll carry the link [torch]?
"I," said the Linnet,
"I'll fetch it in a minute,
And I'll carry the link."

9. Who'll be the chief mourner?
"I," said the Dove,
"I'll mourn for my love,
And I'll be chief mourner."

10. Who'll carry the coffin?
"I," said the Kite,
"If it's not through the night,
And I'll carry the coffin."

11. Who'll bear the pall?
"We," said the Wren,
"Both the cock and the hen,
And we'll carry the pall."

12. Who'll sing the psalm?
"I," said the Thrush,
As she sat on a bush.
"And I'll sing a psalm."

13. And who'll toll the bell?
"I," said the Bull [finch],
Because I can pull,
And I'll toll the bell."

14. All the birds of the air
Fell a-singing and a-sobbing,
When they heard the bell toll
For poor Cock Robin.

"Cock Robin..." is believed by some scholars to be derived from the early Norse myth about the death of Balder, god of summer sunlight and the incarnation of the life principle, who was slain by Hoder at Loki's instigation. There are also sixteenth century references to similar tales. Then, the ballad evidently had renewed life as an allegory of the intrigues around the 1742 downfall of Sir Robert Walpole, First Earl of Oxford (1676–1745), whose ministry was known as the Robinocracy. Its first appearance in a nursery book coincided with this time period; the first four verses were in *Tommy Thumb's Pretty Song Book* of approximately 1744. After about 1770 the entire verse was a favorite and was printed in numerous editions as chapbooks and toy books, and was included in collections. Some of the versions included animal mourners such as a deer, fox, toad, ass, lamb, goat, and a human appearing as a beadle. Halliwell collected "Cock Robin..." in 1849. The rhyme is also known in European countries. Between 1844 and 1851, a Walter Potter made a set-piece of 100 stuffed birds, displayed at the Bramber Museum, Sussex, as "The Death and Burial of Cock Robin."

The following two ballads, "Lord Randal" and "Billy Boy," clearly show their relationship. The narrative is known throughout Europe and the Scandinavian countries, and recorded in the seventeenth century, possibly concerning either the death by poisoning of King John in 1216, or the 1332 poisoning of Thomas Randolph, or Randal, Earl of Murray, Governor of Scotland, and nephew of Robert Bruce. Shakespeare included the incident in the final scenes of *King John* (1596–1597).

There is, in addition, a nursery rhyme which carries the same theme:

Where have you been today, Billy, my son?
Where have you been today, my only man?
I've been a wooing, mother, make my bed soon,
For I'm sick at heart, and fain would lie down.

What have you ate today, Billy, my son?
What have you ate today, my only man?
I've ate eel-pie, mother, make my bed soon,
For I'm sick at heart, and shall die before noon.

Lord Randal

1. Where have you been, Lord Randal, my son?
   Where have you been, my handsome young man?
   I've been out a-courting, Go make my bed soon,
   Mother, I'm sick at the heart and I want to lie down.
2. Where had you your supper, Lord Randal, my son?
   Where had you your supper, my handsome young man?
   I dined with my true love, Go make my bed soon,
   Mother, I'm sick at the heart and I want to lie down.
3. What had you for supper, etc.
   Some eels fried in butter, etc.

4.   What color was it, etc.
     It was brown and brown-speckled, etc.
5.   What's become of your warden, etc.
     He died in the muirlands, etc.
6.   What's become of your stag-hounds, etc.
     They swelled and they died, etc.
7.   What'll you will to your father, etc.
     My mules and my wagons, etc.
8.   What'll you will to your mother, etc.
     My house and my lands, etc.
9.   What'll you will to your brother, etc.
     My hounds and my musket, etc.
10. What'll you will to your sister, etc.
     My rings off my fingers, etc.
11. What'll you will to your true love, etc.
     A cup of strong poison, etc.
12. Why such for your true love, etc.
     She gave me the poison that I did drink down, etc.
13. And when you are dead, etc.
     Go dig me a grave, side my grandfather's son, etc.

Balladeer John Jacob Niles reported in 1960 that he had "investigated 52 American versions of 'Lord Randal,' and found that 40 of them indicated poisoning by way of cooked eels. The remaining 12 mention cold poison, snake heads, parsnips, and other less interesting dishes. To increase their indigestibility, the eels are nearly always fried, and the frying compound varies all the way from butter to soap grease."

"Lord Randal" is the name usually referred to by scholars as the original name for this ballad, but other names have been used, too: Johnny Randal; Jimmy Randal; Johnny Randolph; Johnny Ramsey; Johnny Reeler; Johnny Reelsey; John Willow; Johnny Elzie; McDonald; Tiranti, my son; Charley Harley, my son; Sweet Nelson, my boy; Laird Rowlands; My own purtee boy; Bonnie Tammy; My bonny wee croodin doo; Fair Andrew, my son; Henery, my son; King Henry; Willie, oh Willie; and Oh Billy, my boy. There has been some speculation that the "King Henry" version may well have been created to parody the death of Henry I (1068–1135) from eating a dish of lampreys.

Billy Boy

1.   Oh, where have you been, Billy Boy, Billy Boy?
     Oh, where have you been, charming Billy?
     I have been to seek a wife, she's the joy of my life,
     She's a young thing and cannot leave her mother.

2.   Is she fit to be your love, Billy Boy, Billy Boy?
      Is she fit to be your love, charming Billy?
      She's as fit to be my love, as my hand is for my glove,
      She's a young thing and cannot leave her mother.
3.   Is she fit to be your wife, etc.
      She's as fit to be my wife, as my blade is for my knife, etc.
4.   Did she ask you to come in, etc.
      Yes, she asked me to come in, with a dimple in her chin, etc.
5.   Did she set you in a chair, etc.
      Yes, she set me in a chair, she had wrinkles in her ear, etc.
6.   Did she ask you for to eat, etc.
      Yes, she asked me for to eat, she had plenty bread and meat, etc.
7.   Can she make a pot roast well, etc.
      Yes, she can make a pot roast well, I can tell it by the smell, etc.
8.   Can she make a cherry pie, etc.
      Yes, she can make a cherry pie, in the twinkling of an eye, etc.
9.   Can she brew and can she bake, etc.
      Yes, she can brew and she can bake, she can make our wedding-cake,
          etc.
10.   Can she sew a button on, etc.
      Yes, she can sew a button on, and it never will be gone, etc.
11.   Can she hem and can she fell [seam], etc.
      Yes, she can hem and she can fell, she can use her needle well, etc.
12.   Can she card and can she spin, etc.
      Yes, she can card and she can spin, she can make it thick or thin, etc.
13.   Can she make-up her own bed, etc.
      Yes, she can make-up her own bed, with the pillows at the head, etc.
14.   Can she tend a flower-bed, etc.
      Yes, she can tend a flower-bed, full of roses, glory-red, etc.
15.   Can she read and can she write, etc.
      Yes, she can read and she can write, and look pretty day and night, etc.
16.   Can she dance and can she sing, etc.
      Yes, she can dance and she can sing, she can do most anything, etc.
17.   How tall is she, etc.
      She's just tall enough to kiss, and to hug her is pure bliss, etc.
18.   How old is she, etc.
      She's three times six, four times seven, twenty-eight and eleven, etc.
      She's a young thing and cannot leave her mother [last line sung slowly].

"Billy Boy. . ." was known early in the eighteenth century, and a version
was recorded in a manuscript of 1776. Although there are variations, including different sets of numbers for the last stanza, the narrative is essentially
the same. Robert Burns used the theme in "I am my mammie's ae bairn" (see

page 212). Halliwell collected the ballad in 1844, and it has had a long life in both folklore and nursery books.

1. Simple Simon met a pieman, going to the fair;
    Said Simple Simon to the pieman, let me taste your ware.

2. Says the pieman to Simple Simon, show me first your penny;
    Says Simple Simon to the pieman, indeed I have not any.

3. Simple Simon went a-fishing, for to catch a whale;
    But all the water he had got was in his mother's pail.

4. Simple Simon went to look, if plums grew on a thistle;
    He pricked his finger very much, which made poor Simon whistle.

5. Then Simple Simon went a-hunting, for to catch a hare;
    He rode a goat into the street, but could not find one there.

6. He went to shoot a fine wild duck, but the wild duck flew away;
    Says Simple Simon, I can't hit him, because he will not stay.

7. He went to catch a dickey-bird, and thought he could not fail;
    Because he had got a little salt, to put upon its tail.

8. He went to take a birdie's nest, was built upon a bough;
    A branch gave way, and Simon fell, into a dirty slough [swamp].

9. He went to ride a spotted cow, that had a spotted calf;
    She threw him on the ground, though, which made the people laugh.

10. He went to slide upon the ice, before the ice would bear;
    Then he plunged in to his knees, which made poor Simon stare.

11. Once Simon made a great snowball, and brought it in to roast;
    He laid it out before the fire, and soon the ball was lost.

12. Simple Simon went for honey, in the mustard pot;
    He bit his tongue until he cried, that was the good he got.

13. Simple Simon went to town, to buy a piece of meat;
    He tied it to his horse's tail, to keep it clean and sweet.

14. He washed himself with a blackening-ball, because he had no soap;
    Then smiling told his mother, I'm a beauty now, I hope.

15. He went for water in a sieve, but soon it all ran through;
    And now poor Simple Simon, bids you all adieu.

There is some question as to whether *Simple Simon* became the term for "a natural, a silly fellow" from the nursery rhyme, or if the term existed long before and was used for such in the rhyme. Tales of the simple fellow appear to have been known in the Elizabethan period. A ballad first known as *Dead and Alive* and later as *Simple Simon's Misfortunes and his Wife Margery's Cruelty* dates to at least 1685, and the melody "Simple Simon" is in Playford's *The Dancing Master* of 1665. A chapbook, *Simple Simon*, was advertised by Cluer Dicey and Richard Marshall in 1764. The first four stanzas are the best known, especially the first two.

The following two pieces are from the same source, but have survived separately as a folk/nursery ballad and as a nursery rhyme:

1.   Oh dear, what can the matter be?
      Dear, dear, what can the matter be?
      Oh, dear, what can the matter be?
      Johnny's so long at the fair.†

2.   He promised he'd buy me a fairing should please me,
      And then for a kiss, oh! he vowed he would tease me,
      He promised he'd bring me a bunch of blue ribbons,
      To tie up my bonny brown hair. etc.

3.   He promised to buy me a pair of sleeve buttons,
      A pair of new garters that cost him but two pence,
      He promised he'd bring me a bunch of blue ribbons,
      To tie up my bonny brown hair. etc.

4.   He promised he'd bring me a basket of posies,
      A garland of lilies, a garland of roses,
      A little straw hat, to set off the blue ribbons
      That tie up my bonny brown hair.

      †First stanza repeated as a chorus.

A version of this popular old song was found in a manuscript dating from around 1775; in about 1792 it was printed as "O! dear what can the matter be?" The ballad was included as a nursery song in Walter de la Mare's *Come Hither* in 1923, and in L.E. Walter's *Mother Goose's Nursery Rhymes* in 1924, among other collections.

Johnny shall have a new bonnet,
    And Johnny shall go to the fair,
And Johnny shall have a blue ribbon
    To tie up his bonny brown hair.

And why may not I love Johnny?
    And why may not Johnny love me?
And why may not I love Johnny,
    As well as another body?

And here's a leg for a stocking,
    And here's a leg for a shoe,
And here's a kiss for his daddy,
    And two for his mammy, I trow.

And why may not I love Johnny?
  And why may not Johnny love me?
And why may not I love Johnny
  As well as another body?

This nursery verse, obviously derived from the earlier ballad, was first printed in *Songs for the Nursery* in 1805, reappeared in *Mother Goose's Quarto* circa 1825, and was collected by Halliwell in 1853.

1.   A fox jumped up one winter's night,
    And begged the moon to give him light,
    For he'd many miles to trot that night
    Before he reached his den O!
        Den O! Den O!
    For he'd many miles to trot that night
    Before he reached his den O!

2.   The fox and his wife, they never had strife,
    They never ate mustard in all their whole life,
    They ate their meat without fork or knife,
    And loved to be picking a bone O!
        Bone O! Bone O!
    They ate their meat without fork or knife,
    And loved to be picking a bone O!

3.   The fox when he came to yonder stile,
    He lifted his lugs and he listened a while;
    O ho, said the fox, it's but a short mile,
    From this unto yonder wee town O!
        Town O! Town O!
    O ho, said the fox, it's but a short mile,
    From this unto yonder wee town O!

4.   The fox, when got to the farmer's gate,
    Who should he see but the farmer's drake;
    I love you well for your master's sake,
    And long to be picking your bone O!
        Bone O! Bone O!
    I love you well for your master's sake,
    And long to be picking your bone O!

5.   The gray goose she ran round the hay-stack,
    O ho, said the fox, you are very fat,
    You'll grease my beard and ride on my back
    From this unto yonder wee town O!

          Town O! Town O!
   You'll grease my beard and ride on my back
   From this unto yonder wee town O!

6.   The first place he came to was a farmer's yard,
       Where the ducks and the geese declared it hard
       That their nerves should be shaken and their rest so marred
       By a visit from Mr. Fox O!

Fox O! Fox O!
That their nerves should be shaken and their rest so marred
By a visit from Mr. Fox O!

7. He took the grey goose by the neck,
And swing him right across his back;
The grey goose cried out, Quack, quack, quack,
With his legs hanging dangling down O!
            Down O! Down O!
The grey goose cried out, Quack, quack, quack,
With his legs hanging dangling down O!

8. Old Gammer Widdle Waddle jumped out of bed,
And out of the window she popped her head;
Oh! John, John, John, the grey goose is gone,
And the fox is off to his den O!
            Den O! Den O!
Oh! John, John, John, the grey goose is gone,
And the fox is off to his den O!

9. John ran up to the top of the hill,
And blew his whistle loud and shrill,
Said the fox, that is very pretty music; still,
I'd rather be in my den O!
            Den O! Den O!
Said the fox, that is very pretty music; still,
I'd rather be in my den O!

10. Then the old man got up in his red cap,
And swore he would catch the fox in a trap,
But the fox was too cunning, and gave him the slip,
And ran through yonder wee town O!
            Town O! Town O!
But the fox was too cunning, and gave him the slip,
And ran through yonder wee town O!

11. The fox went back to his hungry den,
And his little foxes, eight, nine, ten;
Quoth they, Good Daddy, you must go there again,
If you bring such good cheer from the farm O!
            Farm O! Farm O!
Quoth they, Good Daddy, you must go there again,
If you bring such good cheer from the farm O!

12. They all gathered around him then,
His wife and the little foxes, ten;

Said he, we shall have the fat goose then,
With his legs hanging dangling down O!
       Down O! Down O!
Said he, we shall have the fat goose then,
With his legs hanging dangling down O!

13.   The fox and his wife, without any strife,
Said they never ate better goose in their life;
They did very well without fork or knife,
And the little ones picked the bones O!
       Bones O! Bones O!
They did very well without fork or knife,
And the little ones picked the bones O!

This old ballad is popular in both America and England, dating to at least early in the nineteenth century. "Old Gammer Widdle Waddle" is variously known as either "Gammer" or "Mother" with the name "Slipper Slopper"; "Hipple-hopple"; "Snipper Snapper"; "Flipper Flapper"; "Chittle Chattle"; or "Wig Wag." A version of stanza eight is frequently found alone in nursery rhyme books, it being the first printed in children's literature in *Gammer Gurton's Garland* 1810, where it appeared as:

Old Mother Widdle Waddle jumpt out of bed,
And out at the casement she popt her head:
Crying the house is on fire, the grey goose is dead,
And the fox is come to the town, oh!

Aiken Drum

1.   There was a man lived in the moon,
    Lived in the moon, lived in the moon,
There was a man lived in the moon,
    And his name was Aiken Drum.
2.   And he played upon a ladle,
    Upon a ladle, upon a ladle,
And he played upon a ladle,
    And his name was Aiken Drum.
3.   And his hat was made of good cream cheese, etc.
4.   And his coat was made of good roast beef, etc.
5.   And his buttons were made of penny loaves, etc.
6.   And his waistcoat was made of crust of pies, etc.
7.   And his breeches were made of haggis bags, etc.
8.   There was another man in another town,
    Another town, another town,

There was a man in another town,
And his name was Willy Wood.

9. And he played upon a razor,
A razor, a razor,
And he played upon a razor,
And his name was Willy Wood.

10. And he ate up all the good cream cheese, etc.

11. And he ate up all the good roast beef, etc.

12. And he ate up all the penny loaves, etc.

13. And he ate up all the good pie crust, etc.

14. But he choked upon the haggis bags,
Haggis bags, haggis bags,
But he choked upon the haggis bags,
And that ended Willy Wood.

The *haggis bag* is the stomach in which the heart, liver and lungs of a sheep or calf are seasoned and boiled to produce *haggis*. This song was known in Scotland in 1821, but the name *Aikendrum* appears in an earlier ballad which indicates he may have been a soldier in the army opposing the Whigs in the battle of Sheriffmuir (1715). *Aikendrum* also appears as a strange little Brownie in a poem in *The Dumfries Magazine* (October 1825).

The version collected by Halliwell in 1842 appears corrupted, as it crisscrosses the stanzas with Billy Pod and Edrim Drum, each having some of the actions ascribed to the other in the now traditional version. The version, as above, was printed in *Baby's Bouquet* in 1879.

Twelve Days of Christmas

(This is a cumulative song; after each day is added, the rest are sung in reverse.)

1. On the first day of Christmas, my true love gave to me,
A partridge in a pear tree.

2. On the second day of Christmas, my true love gave to me,
Two turtle doves,
And a partridge in a pear tree.

3. ...third day, etc.
Three French hens, etc.

4. ...fourth day, etc.
Four calling birds [colly birds], etc.

5. ...fifth day, etc.
five gold rings, etc.

6. ...sixth day, etc.
Six geese a-laying, etc.

7.　　...seventh day, etc.
　　　Seven swans a-swimming, etc.
8.　　...eighth day, etc.
　　　Eight maids a-milking, etc.
9.　　...ninth day, etc.
　　　Nine pipers piping, etc.
10.　　...tenth day, etc.
　　　Ten drummers drumming, etc.
11.　　...eleventh day, etc.
　　　Eleven ladies dancing, etc.
12.　　On the twelfth day of Christmas, my true love gave to me,
　　　Twelve lords a-leaping,
　　　Eleven ladies dancing,
　　　Ten drummers drumming,
　　　Nine pipers piping,
　　　Eight maids a-milking,
　　　Seven swans a-swimming,
　　　Six geese a-laying,
　　　Five gold rings.
　　　Four calling birds,
　　　Three French hens,
　　　Two turtledoves,
　　　And a partridge in a pear tree.

This is so traditional, in France, as well as in England, Canada, and America that most people would not think of it as a Mother Goose ballad. It dates to sacred chants of the fifteenth century which were secularized by the 18th century. It appeared as given above (except for "colly" instead of "calling" birds) in a little children's book, *Mirth without Mischief* (London: C. Sheppard, ca.1780). Halliwell collected a version as a nursery verse in 1842, where there were "...four canary birds...eight ladies dancing...nine lords a leaping...ten ships a sailing...eleven ladies spinning...and twelve bells ringing."

The English text is quite well standardized now, although in earlier days a variety of items were named for the successive twelve days. This carol, or ballad, narrative verse, or cumulative tale, with its delightful picture possibilities, has been the sole subject of a number of picture books for children.

1.　　We will go the wood, says Robin to Bobbin,
　　　We will go to the wood, says Richard to Robin,
　　　We will go to the wood, says John all alone,
　　　We will go to the wood, says everyone.

2.   What to do there? says Robin to Bobbin,
       What to do there? says Richard to Robin,
       What to do there? says John all alone,
       What to do there? says everyone.
3.   We'll shoot at a wren, etc.
4.   She's down, she's down, etc.
5.   Then pounce, then pounce, etc.
6.   She is dead, she is dead, etc.
7.   How get her home? etc.
8.   In a cart with six horses, etc.
9.   Then hoist, boys, hoist, etc.
10.   How shall we dress her? etc.
11.   We'll hire seven cooks, etc.
12.   How shall we boil her, etc.
13.   In a brewer's big pan, etc.

The hunting of the wren is a custom of antiquity that down to the eighteenth century was conducted on the morning of Christmas Day, and later transferred to the morning of St. Stephen's Day, December 26. ("Morning" translates to "starting after midnight.") In 1696, folklore writer John Aubrey described "...a whole Parish running like madmen from Hedg to Hedg a Wren-hunting." Frazer, in *The Golden Bough* (1890) described how the wren was attached to the top of a long pole, with its wings extended, then carried from house to house while the captors chanted:

We hunted the wren for Robin the Bobbin,
We hunted the wren for Jack of the Can,
We hunted the wren for Robin the Bobbin,
We hunted the wren for everyone.

The captors collected money at the houses, then carried her to the churchyard and dug a grave and buried her, "with the utmost solemnity, singing dirges over her." From the ancient Greeks to modern Europeans, the wren was always considered the king of birds, and it was considered unlucky to kill one. This custom, therefore, is somewhat of a dichotomy, but it has been suggested that it stems from the first Christian missionaries to Britain, who resented the honor in which the wren was held by the pagan Druids, and so ordered the wren-hunting.

A version of the nursery rhyme appeared in *Tommy Thumb's Pretty Song Book*, circa 1744, after which it became a nursery favorite. Halliwell collected both English and Manx versions of it in 1842.

It has been suggested that the following verse is related to "We will go to the wood...." Not only does the name Robin/Bobbin reappear, but the

contention is that certainly a large stomach capacity would be needed for consuming a wren so large it would take a cart with six horses to carry it
home.

> Robin the Bobbin, the big-bellied Ben,
> He ate more meat than fourscore men;
> He ate a cow, he ate a calf,
> He ate a butcher and a half,
> He ate a church, he ate the steeple,
> He ate the priest and all the people!
>   A cow and a calf,
>   An ox and a half,
>   A church and a steeple,
>   And all the good people,
> And then complained that his stomach wasn't full yet.

Although some nursery commentators have speculated that "Robin the
Bobbin..." may refer to Henry VIII (1491–1547) because of his voracious appetite for both food and the gobbling up of church estates, this hypothesis
is not generally accepted by scholars. In the first nursery version, in *Tommy
Thumb's Pretty Song Book*, the verse mentions two people, "Robin and Bobbin." Halliwell collected a version. Alternative characters to whom the rhyme
alludes are "Robert the Parbet" and "Benjamin Benjamin, Big-Bellied-
Ben."

1. Dame, get up and bake your pies,
      Bake your pies, bake your pies;
    Dame get up and bake your pies,
      On Christmas day in the morning.
2. Dame, what makes your maidens lie,
      Maidens lie, maidens lie;
    Dame what makes your maidens lie,
      On Christmas day in the morning.
3. Dame, what makes your ducks to die, etc.
4. Their wings are cut and they cannot fly, etc.

This song was known early in the seventeenth century and by the eighteenth existed in several versions. It did not appear as a nursery ditty until
Halliwell designated it as such in 1842; it was in *Baby's Opera* in 1877.

The following verse was given as the second part of "Dame get up..."
in *Bishoprick Garland* by Sir Cuthbert Sharpe, in 1834. It is more familiar today as a separate ballad or carol. It also was in *Baby's Opera* in 1877.

1.   I saw three ships come sailing by,
        Come sailing by, come sailing by,
     I saw three ships come sailing by,
        On New Year's† day in the morning.

2.   And what do you think was in them then,
        Was in them then, was in them then,
     And what do you think was in them then,
        On New Year's day in the morning.

3.   Three pretty girls were in them then,
        Were in them then, were in them then,
     Three pretty girls were in them then,
        On New Year's day in the morning.

     †*Also: Christmas.*

4.   See the ships all sailing by,
            All sailing by, all sailing by,
        See the ships all sailing by,
            On New Year's day in the morning.

And what about old Dame Gander herself? Were any ballads written
about her? What about shorter verses? — curiously, only a few short verses, and
it may require some stretch of the imagination to interpret some of those as
being about *Mother* Goose, rather than some anonymous "Goosey
Gander"—and only one ballad—although one might include the Preface to
Father Gander's Rhymes About the Animals (see pages 260–261).

Traditional	Original
Goosey, goosey gander,	Goose-a, goose-a, gander,
Whither shall I wander?	Where shall I wander?
Upstairs and downstairs,	Up stairs, down stairs,
And in my lady's chamber.	In my lady's chamber;
There I met an old man	There you'll find a cup of sack
Who would not say his prayers.	And a race of ginger.
I took him by the left leg	
And threw him down the stairs.	
—The Tom Tit's Song Book *ca.1790*	*—Gammer Gurton's Garland* *1784*

Goosey, goosey gander,
Who stands yonder,
Little Jenny Baker;
Take her up and shake her.

This little ditty first appeared in J.G. Rusher's *London Jingles* of about
1840; it was collected by Halliwell in 1853, with the name "Betsy Baker." A
version that added two more lines has also been known, "Give her a bit of
bread and cheese, / And throw her over the water."

Gray goose and gander,
    Waft your wings together,
And carry the good king's daughter
    Over the one-strand river.

The *Oxford Dictionary of Nursery Rhymes* (1951) reported: "There was
some correspondence about this beautiful fragment in *The Times Literary
Supplement*, October 1947. It was surmised that the 'one-strand river' is the

sea, a metaphor 'suggestive of early Anglo-Saxon imagery.'" Halliwell collected this in 1844, but gave no indication where he had obtained it, beyond the usual suggestion that it was orally collected. It has been reprinted a number of times since then.

> Cackle, cackle, Mother Goose,
> Have you any feathers loose?
> Truly have I, pretty fellow,
> Half enough to fill a pillow.
> Here are quills, take one or two,
> And down to make a bed for you.

Although this was very likely known earlier, it did not appear in print until 1924 in L.E. Walter's *Mother Goose's Nursery Rhymes*, where the last two lines were, "And here are quills, take one or ten, / And make from each, pop-gun or pen."

1. Old Mother Goose, when she wanted to wander,
   Would ride through the air on a very fine gander.
2. Mother Goose had a house, 'twas built in a wood,
   Where an owl at the door, for a sentinel stood.
3. She had a son Jack, a plain-looking lad,
   He was not very good, nor yet very bad.
4. She sent him to market, a live goose he bought,
   Here, mother, says he, it will not go for nought.
5. Jack's goose and the gander, grew very fond;
   They'd both eat together, or swim in one pond.
6. Jack found one morning, as I have been told,
   His goose had laid him, an egg of pure gold.
7. Jack rode to his mother, the news for to tell,
   She called him good boy, and said it was well.
8. Jack sold his gold egg, to a merchant untrue,
   Who cheated him out of, the half of his due.
9. Then Jack went a-courting, a lady so gay,
   As fair as the lily, and sweet as the May.
10. The merchant and squire, soon came at his back,
    And began to belabor, the sides of poor Jack.
11. The squire got the goose, which he vowed he would kill,
    Resolving at once, his pockets to fill.
12. And then the gold egg, was thrown in the sea,
    And Jack tried to jump in, to get it you see.
13. Then old Mother Goose, that instant came in,
    And turned her son Jack, into famed Harlequin.

14.   She then with her wand, touched the lady so fine,
       And turned her at once, into sweet Columbine.
15.   The gold egg in the sea, was still thrown away then,
       When Jack jumped in, and got it again.
16.   And Old Mother Goose, the goose saddled soon,
       And mounting its back, flew up to the moon.

This was first recorded in a chapbook of about 1815, where it was called *Old Mother Goose or, The Golden Egg* (by T. Batchelar). Sometimes only the first stanza is given as a nursery verse.

Additional ballads are included in other chapters for one reason or another: "Hush, little baby, don't say a word..." (Chapter 3), and "Can you make me a cambric shirt...," "My father left me three acres of land...," "What are little babies made of...," and "Yankee Doodle..." (all Chapter 9).

12. Cooking the Goose
That Laid the Golden Egg

Uses and Abuses of Mother Goose Rhymes

Any body of literature as popular as the rhymes that comprise nursery or
Mother Goose lore, could expect to be copied, parodied, and twisted. If "imitation is the sincerest form of flattery," then a great many of the old children's
verses have had much praise indeed. The forms of that flattery have encom-
passed literary parodies, updated parodies, foreign-sound mimicry, cultural
revisions, religious revisions, primers based on nursery themes, spoofs, and

"censored" versions. The quality of that praise-by-imitation, in many cases, leaves much to be desired. A large number have nothing to offer to the field of literature except the fact that they are drawing upon the recognition factor of the originals. On the other hand, sometimes the reuse of a theme has been inspired, or at the least, poetic in itself.

In parody treatment, the range is from almost straight line-for-line comparison, to far reaching wordy renderings of the basic themes. Some are ingenious. Lewis Carroll's "Twinkle, Twinkle, little bat" (see page 194), for instance, transcends mere parody of Jane Taylor's "Star" (see page 170) and has earned its own place in anthologies.

A particularly clever parody combines a jab at both "Yankee Doodle..." and "Sing a Song of Sixpence..." in addition to incorporating two opposing nationalistic songs. It is recorded in *The Memoirs of the Duke of Windsor*, written in 1951. It concerned, however, a parody he had heard during his American Tour of 1919. The Duke told how entranced George V was with the parody Windsor took back to England—something he had heard in a Canadian border town:

Four and twenty Yankees, feeling very dry,
Went across the border to get a drink of Rye.
When the Rye was opened, the Yanks began to sing,
"God Bless America, but God save the King!"

In 1842, when James O. Halliwell had published *The Nursery Rhymes of England*, his friend James Robinson Planché wrote:

Halliwell, Halliwell, my pretty man,
Make me a book as fast as you can;
Write it and print it, and mark it with a P.,
And send it by Parcels Deliverye.

Another 1842 parody was a ballad on the reception after the christening of the Prince of Wales, called *The Christening Cake* (John Lea) which began:

When great Victoria ruled the land,
She ruled it like a Queen,
She had a Princess and a Prince,
Not very far between.

Other versifiers inserted "modern" modes to old favorites to create updated-parodies. "Modern" does become an anachronistic usage itself—as the next generation uses the same term. Modern was as modern may no longer be. But at any rate, noting the dates when the pieces were written, we have:

Early to bed and early to rise,
Will make you miss all the regular guys.

> — *George Ade ca.1900*

Early to bed and you will wish you were dead,
Bed before eleven, nuts before seven.

> — *Dorothy Parker ca.1936*

Early to rise and early to bed
Makes a male healthy and wealthy and dead.

> — *James Thurber 1939*

Rhyme for Astronomical Baby

Bye Baby Bunting,
Father's gone star-hunting;
Mother's at the telescope
Casting baby's horoscope.
Bye Baby Buntoid,
Father's found an asteroid;
Mother takes by calculation
The angle of its inclination.

> — *Rev. Joseph Cook ca.1904*

Old Mother Hubbard went to the cupboard,
For something to quench her thirst,
But when she went there, the cupboard was bare:
Mr. Hubbard had been there first.

> — *recited by Clement Atlee*
> *in election speech, February 16, 1950.*

Clement Atlee (1883–1967) became British prime minister in 1945.

Scientific Three Blind Mice

Three rodents with defective visual perception,
Three rodents with defective visual perception,
Observe how they perambulate, observe how they perambulate.
They perambulated after the agriculturist's spouse,
She severed their hind appendages with a kitchen utensil.
Have you ever seen such a spectacle in your existence,
As three rodents with defective visual perception?

> — *Scouts? Mid to Late Twentieth Century*

The Anthropologist

Sing a song of mores! Tell us of taboo!
Sort out sexy stories! Watch how menfolks woo!
Study twenty slatterns clad in wool and tweed!
Call them culture patterns!
         —Words by Margaret Mead.
         From Faculty Club, *by Howard Mumford Jones,*
         The Atlantic, *January 1959*

Mary had a little lamb,
His foot was full of soot,
And everywhere that Mary went,
His sooty foot he put.

         — Twentieth century American

Many of the nursery rhymes so well known in the English language have their counterparts in European countries. Including these in their various languages is outside the scope of this study. But one or two curious foreign-sound mimicries bear notice. On the faked-foreign side, we see a humorous rendering of one kind:

Nursery Song in Pidgin English

Singee a songee sick a pence,
  Pockee muchee lye;
Dozen two time blackee bird
  Cookee in e pie.
When him cutee topside
  Birdee bobbery sing;
Himee tinkee nicey dish
  Setee foree King!
Kingee in a talkee loom
  Countee muchee money;
Queeney in e kitchee,
  Chew-chee breadee honey.
Servant galo shakee,
  Hangee washee clothes;
Cho-chop comee blackie bird,
  Nipee off her nose!

         —Anonymous ca.1904

Another kind of foreign-sound-mimicry uses the foreign language itself to effect an English-language Mother Goose rhyme. When read aloud in

French, in just the right cadence, one can see how the following French ditty cleverly sounds like the English "Humpty Dumpty."

Un petit d'un petit
S'étonne aux Halles
Un petit d'un petit
Ah! degrés te fallent
Indolent qui ne sort cesse
Indolent qui ne se mène
Qu'importe un petit d'un petit
Tout Gai de Reguennes.
— Mots d'Heures: Gousses, Rames; The d'Antin Manuscript,
by Luis d'Antin Van Rooten (New York: Grossman, 1967)

Among foreign nursery verses are *Chinese Mother Goose Rhymes* published in translation by Isaac T. Headland in 1900. These are not the familiar English verses in another tongue; they are Chinese originals. Interestingly, they illustrate that cultures as diverse as the Orient and Occident nevertheless feed their children on similar literary food. From the innocuous to the implications of violence, they offer the same patterns seen in the annals of English-language children's rhymes. For example:

Lady-bug, lady-bug, fly away do,
Fly to the mountain, and feed upon dew,
Feed upon dew, and sleep on a rug,
And then run away, like a good little bug.

Pat a cake, pat a cake, little girl fair,
There's a priest in the temple without any hair.
You take a tile, and I'll take a brick,
And we'll hit the priest in the back of the neck.

Sometimes versions of the old nursery rhymes were changed in folk fashion to suit new locales and ways of looking at life. Most of the so-called traditional verses appear in both English and American collections. Ray Wood purported to have collected rhymes "of pure American invention" in *The American Mother Goose* (1938), and in *Fun in American Folk Rhymes* (1952). A bare mention is made that it is "possible" some of the verses came to America with English colonists (a number of them did). Although Wood's books are perhaps satisfactory as collections of American playground lore, Carl Withers' *A Rocket in My Pocket: The Rhymes and Chants of Young Americans* (1948) seems better researched to be presented as American lore. One of many examples of Wood's lax attitude is his inclusion of the following without noting that it is a paraphrase or parody of the original (but American-authored) verse:

Mary had a little lamb,
Its fleece was white as cotton,
And everywhere that Mary went
The lamb it went a-trottin'.

A few of Wood's rhymes bear special mention as American revisions of traditional pieces. Wood seems to have been unaware of the fact that these were revisions. (Only the first date of collection is shown.)

Hickety-pickety, my black hen,
She lays eggs for gentlemen,
Sometimes one, and sometimes ten,
Hickety-pickety, my black hen.

—collected by Halliwell 1849

American:
Hickety-pickety, my black hen,
She lays eggs for the railroad men;
Sometimes one, and sometimes two,
Sometimes enough for the whole blame crew.

I.   I had a little bonny nagg
          His name was Dapple Gray;
        And he would bring me to an ale-house
          A mile out of my way.

—ca.1650 manuscript, according
to Halliwell 1842, 1849

The next version most likely evolved from the one above.

II.   I had a little pony,
          His name was Dapple-Gray;
        I lent him to a lady
        To ride a mile away.
        She whipped him she lashed him,
        She rode him through the mire
        I would not lend my pony now,
        For all the lady's hire.

—ca.1825 Poetical Alphabet
(Henry Mozeley & Sons, Pub.)
—collected by Halliwell 1842, 1849

American:
I had a little horse,†
His name was Dapple Gray,
I sent him to the barn,
To get himself some hay.
First he walked,
Then he trotted,
Then he loped,
Then he galloped.

†*Like the above, this is intended as a "bouncing-knee" game; the accelerating pattern for bouncing is more evident here.*

I had a little husband,
No bigger than my thumb;
I put him in a pint-pot
And there I bid him drum.
I bought a little horse
That galloped up and down;
I bridled him, and saddled him
And sent him out of town.
I gave him a pair of garters
To garter up his hose,
And a little silk handkerchief,
To wipe his pretty nose [snotty nose].
— *ca.1780; Nancy Cock's Pretty Song Book (Marshall)*

American:
I had a little sweetheart no bigger than my thumb,
I put her in a coffeepot battered like a drum,
I took it by the handle and threw it in the river,
Saying: "Goodbye, my sweetheart, goodbye, my honey,
If it hadn't been for you I might have had a little money."

When I was a little boy I lived by myself,
And all the bread and cheese I got I laid upon a shelf;
The rats and the mice they made such a strife,
I had to go to London-town to buy me a wife.
The streets were so broad and the lanes were so narrow,
I was forced to bring my wife home in a wheelbarrow.
The wheelbarrow broke and my wife had a fall,
Farewell wheelbarrow, little wife and all.
— *ca.1744; Tommy Thumb's Pretty Song Book (Cooper)*

American:
There was an old bachelor who lived all alone,
He was starved to almost skin and bone;
When he grew tired of such a life
He went to Boston to get a wife.
The roads were muddy, the streets were narrow;
To bring his wife home he bought a wheelbarrow.
But the wheelbarrow broke and down she did fall;
'Twas the last he saw of wheelbarrow, wife and all.

In 1870, Christopher Pearse Cranch (1813–1892) wrote a delightful but curious combination of tribute and "we've outgrown you—so farewell" to Mother Goose. *Father Gander's Rhymes About the Animals* (for middle-sized children) were verse stories. "The Bear and the Squirrel," for instance, was intended to be sung to the tune of "Heigh Ho, says Anthony Rowley." The book's verse preface, however, was a paean of praise to Mother Goose's works—concluding with the notion that it was time to replace her with Father Gander:

Father Gander's Rhymes About the Animals: Preface

Old Mother Goose has had her say,
  Some simple things she taught you,—
Light baby-rhymes for Christmas times,—
  Such were the themes she brought you.

Good Mother Goose, she sang her songs,
  More than you now can number;
Oft did they make young tears and ache
  Turn into golden slumber.

It was a pretty thing to see
  How oft you stopped and listened,
And checked your cries and wiped your eyes,
  That opened wide and glistened.

While your dear mother o'er and o'er
  Beguiled you with her singing,—
How Jack and Jill went up the hill,
  How Banbury bells went ringing.

How Horner ate his Christmas pie,
  Cock Robin was assaulted,
How young Bo-peep lost all her sheep,
  How moonstruck Mooley vaulted.

How in a huge shoe sat the dame,
  By countless children worried,
While breadless broth and blows, when wroth,
  She gave them, bedward hurried.

How piper's sons stole countless pigs,
  How blackbirds sang while baking, —
Such were the rhymes, in those young times,
  Heard between sleep and waking.

Good Mother Goose a helper was,
  Whom we will never slander;
But now you care no more for her,
  Listen to Father Gander,

You left the nursery long ago,
  You need good books — not nurses.
So may our pages suit your ages,
  And may you like our verses.

Cranch's book is fine — but he certainly didn't succeed in replacing Mother Goose with Father Gander. Father Gander's book is held in rare book rooms today, but Mother Goose continues to be reprinted in numerous sizes, colors, and versions.

The old rhymes contained a number of political allusions. In modern times, the old rhymes have been rewritten, or their titles have been invoked, to create new political jibes on old themes. An 1871 political satire was labeled *The Old Woman who lived in a shoe; and how she fared with her many children, etc.* Franklin Roosevelt and his administration were lampooned in *Mother Goose in Washington: A Story of Old King Dole and His Humpty Dumpty Court* issued in 1936 by the Telegraph Press of New York. When Robert Penn Warren wrote his 1947 Pulitzer Prize novel about the corrupt political career and subsequent downfall of Louisiana's Huey Long, he titled it *All the King's Men*, taking the line from "Humpty Dumpty."

In 1947's England, the economic times spawned the following ditty:

The Queen was in the parlour,
  Polishing the grate;
The King was in the kitchen,
  Washing up a plate;
The maid was in the garden,
  Eating bread and honey,
Listening to the neighbors
  Offering her more money.

The English government took out space in newspapers to spread the message:

W HO'LL KILL JOHN BULL?
I says John Bull,
I speak for the nation—
We'll work with a will
And we'll thus kill inflation.

—March 28, 1948

And the English National Savings Committee issued:

S olomon Grundy,
Rich on Monday,
Spent some on Tuesday,
More on Wednesday,
Poor on Thursday,
Worse on Friday,
Broke on Saturday,
Where will he end
Old Solomon Grundy?

When advertisers pattern their promotions on some other work, you can be sure that work is deemed to be so familiar that the public will have no trouble making the connection. Nursery rhymes are natural media for commercial enterprises to usurp. One of the first, as well as the largest advertising uses of Mother Goose occurred in the United States, between 1915 and 1917, when William Wrigley, chewing-gum magnate, distributed 14,000,000 "Mother Goose" books over a period of two years, with the verses rewritten to include chewing gum. These combinations of rhyme and illustration were featured individually in magazines and newspapers, on billboards, and in other advertisements, as well as in the booklet form. Together, their "Wrigley's Mother Goose—Introducing the Sprightly Spearmen," proved to be one of the company's most popular and successful advertising campaigns. It is gratifying to note that some of the verses also had footnotes that made sure the company was not making outrageous nutritional claims.

The following two examples are copyrighted 1915 Wm. Wrigley Jr. Company, and used with permission of Wm. Wrigley Jr. Company:

M other Spear Hubbard,
Found a bare cupboard,
Said she "there isn't a crumb!
But, it's not so bad—

For which I am glad—
I still have my ⟨doublemint⟩ gum!"

> (Mother Hubbard's meals were irregular, it seems, but she had a good appetite for them anyhow. Wrigley's is *not* food, but it helps your food do you the most good! [—Wrigley].)

Little Miss Muffet-Spear
Sat on a tuffet-queer
Eating her curds and whey,
And when I espied her
With WRIGLEY'S beside her
I knew she was happy that day!

At around the middle of the twentieth century, the English people were treated to such as the following:

There was a little man,
And he felt a little glum,
He thought that a Guinness was due, due, due.
So he went to 'The Plough'. . .
And he's feeling better now,
For a Guinness is good for you, you, you.

Mary, Mary, quite contrary,
How does your romance go?
A boy, a girl, a Bravington ring,
And bridesmaids all in a row.

Reformers, zealots, and misguided do-gooders of various ilks have rewritten the rhymes to promote their views. Though their intentions may have been sincere, and even worthy, the distortions of Dame Gander's rhymes are almost without exception an abomination to advocates of good literature for the nursery. One need not be a literary purist to decry these travesties. Tampering with the soul of these rhymes has created few works of merit—most are affectations that the world can easily live without.

In 1931, G.F. Hill wrote *The Truth About Old King Cole*, purporting that the good king's girth (traditionally illustrated as rather rotund) was due to overeating, overdrinking, and oversmoking, wherefore the monarch was advised to practice self-control. Though the intention may have been to suggest good eating habits, the diatribe falls short.

C.M. Bartug published two books intended to promote other good habits, *Mother Goose Safety Rhymes* (1940) and *Mother Goose Health Rhymes* (1942). For example, "Little Tommy Tucker" is manipulated so that he must go to the corner store before having his bread and butter, "but he Stops—Looks—Listens,/ When he goes for more." "Jack Horner" is exhorted to clean his hands before eating his Christmas pie.

Douglas W. Larche, in *Father Gander's Nursery Rhymes* (1985), claimed to "take the delights of the old Mother Goose and apply them to the ideals we all want our children to have—equality, love, responsibility, an appreciation of life and all living things, good nutrition and conservation of resources." Few would argue with the principles concerned. The execution of the lessons, however, leaves much to be desired. The book is filled with such nonsense as changing the mulberry bush to a "miracle" bush, and lecturing Jack Horner (in a third stanza):

Though it is sweet, an occasional treat
Won't make your parents say "Whoops!"
If you try every day to choose foods the right way
From the basic nutritional groups.

Larch's worst offense, however, is his arbitrary "pairing" of the traditional nursery characters. He is evidently of the opinion that no one can live alone, so solitude is unknown in his converted versions. No character, child or adult, has solitary experiences, and widowhood and single parenthood are simply wiped out. Jack Horner has acquired Nell Horner; Georgie Porgie has Margie Wargie (the name is a cloying deviation in itself); Wee Willie Winkie is coupled with Wendy Winkie; Old Mother Hubbard has Father Hubbard to keep her company; Little Boy Blue shares his haystack with Little Girl Green; and even Bo-Peep has been matched with Joe Peep. To top off the pairings, the Old Woman Who Lived in a Shoe has been transformed into the Old Couple, this fertile pair, furthermore, being chastised for not having a plan to have fewer children. Birth control in a nursery rhyme!

Religious-minded writers have used the familiarity of Mother Goose rhymes as a means of conveying their beliefs, sometimes stretching literary license to the utmost in order to make their points. The intentions of the writers, as well as their poetic skills, of course, bear upon the effectiveness of the results.

In 1949, Geoffrey Hall attempted to "reform" what he considered the most objectionable rhymes in *New Nursery Rhymes for Old*. The world took little note of such as:

Ding, dong bell,
Pussy's at the well.
Who took her there?
Little Johnny Hare.
Who'll bring her in?
Little Tommy Thin.
What a jolly boy was that
To get some milk for pussy cat,
Who ne'er did any harm,
But played with the mice in his father's barn.

— *Geoffrey Hall 1949*

Sara Levy's *Mother Goose Rhymes for Jewish Children* (1951) is aimed primarily at presenting Hebrew words (with a glossary) in the context of the customs in which they appear. The following is representative:

Little Jack Horner
Sat in the corner,
Eating a *haman tash*.†
He stuck in his thumb,

†*Three-cornered cake eaten on* purim, *filled with poppy seeds.*

And took out some *mohn,*†
And said: "I'm a good boy, by gosh."

—*Sara Levy 1951*

†*Poppy seeds.*

Marjorie Decker's self-published *The Christian Mother Goose* (1977) and
its sequel *The Christian Mother Goose Treasury* (1980) were written in protest
to the traditional rhymes. The moralizing, however, tends to be heavy-
handed, and secular booksellers and children's literature scholars deplore the
books as badly written, of poor quality, and monotonously sentimental. The
rhymes have the rhythms of the originals, but otherwise bear little relation to
them, merely cashing in on the appeal of the Mother Goose name and the
nursery characters who populate her realm.

"Little Jack Horner" reads his Bible; "Miss Muffet" thanks Jesus for her
curds and whey; "Old King Cole" calls to the Lord to save his soul; and
"Humpty Dumpty" shouts "Amen" for "God will put him back together
again." The "Three Blind Mice" are up to good deeds:

Three kind mice,
   See what they've done!
They helped a lost chick
   to find Mother Hen,
They brought some food
   to the church mice, then
They cleaned up the tree house
   For Jenny Wren,
Those three kind mice.

—*Marjorie Decker 1977*

Educators, too, have looked to the familiarity of the Mother Goose
rhymes in order to use them as a teaching tool. Some have been content to
simply teach the rhymes. Others have used the nursery characters and themes
as a base on which to build. *The Young and Field Literary Readers: Book One;
A Primer and First Reader* (Boston: Ginn, 1916) is an example. It begins with
a story of three "parts," each containing either four or five "chapters," with
the overall title "How the Children Went to See Mother Hubbard." The first
chapter begins:

(Memorize)

Jack and Jill
Went up the hill
To get a pail of water.

Jack fell down
And broke his crown
And Jill came tumbling after.

I see Jack.
I see Jill.
I see Jack and Jill.
  Here is the pail.
  Here is the hill.
  Here is Jack.
  Here is Jill.
    Jack went up the hill.
    Jill went up the hill.
    Jack and Jill went up, up, up.
    Jack and Jill went to get water.
    Jack and Jill went up the hill to get water.

Jack: Can you run, Jill?
       Can you run up the hill?
       Can you run with me?
Jill: I can run up the hill.
       I can run and run and run.
       I can run with you.
Jack: Run with me.
       Run with me, Jill.
       Run up the hill with me.
Jill: Jack, I see Mother Goose.
Jack: Jill, I see Mother Goose.
Jill: Run to Mother Goose, Jack.
Jack: You run, Jill.

—and so on for 23 more lines. Next, the children are exhorted to memorize "Tom Tinker's Dog," and the story goes on with the dog joining Mother Goose and Jack and Jill, all paraphrased in lines reminiscent of the original nursery verses. In progression, they join or incorporate, "Little Bo-Peep," "Jack-a-Nory," "Three Wise Men of Gotham," "Little Miss Muffet," "Humpty Dumpty," "Little Boy Blue," "Hey Diddle Diddle," "Old Mother Hubbard," "Little Jack Horner," "One, Two, Buckle My Shoe," "Jack, Be Nimble; Jack Be Quick," and "Higgledy-Piggledy, My Black Hen."

The contemporary educator has to ask, "Is this a mere use, a misuse, or an abuse of Mother Goose?" Is the child exposed to such distortions apt to feel the same nursery verse nostalgia most people do, or will the rhymes and rhythms of the traditional pieces be forever imbued with the memory of a hodgepodge of redundant and boring lines to read?

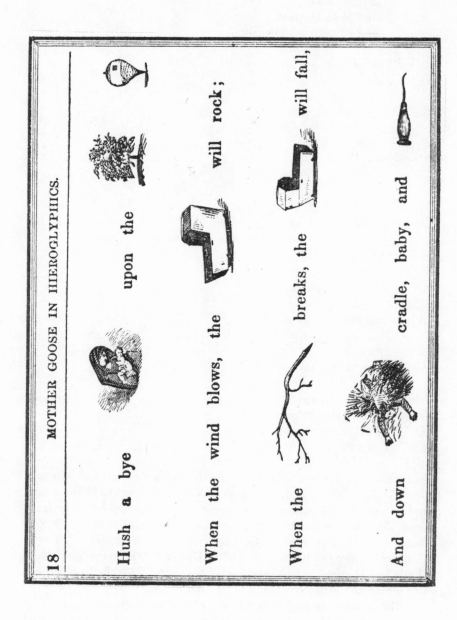

18   MOTHER GOOSE IN HIEROGLYPHICS.

Hush a bye ⬦ upon the ⬦ will rock;

When the wind blows, the ⬦

When the ⬦ breaks, the ⬦ will fall,

And down ⬦ cradle, baby, and ⬦

Music, too, has been taught through the use of the familiar tunes to which many of the rhymes have been set. Even middle-grade youngsters have been introduced to instruments via Mother Goose melodies, and many a parent has had to listen to "Mary Had a Little Lamb" practiced ad infinitum, from hesitant first notes to polished performance.

Where foreign languages have been taught in the early grades, Mother Goose rhymes which occur in similar form are set on facing pages, the English version on one side, and the French, Spanish, German, or whatever, on the opposite. The familiarity of the story in the verse makes the new language come alive easier.

With the computer-age of the late twentieth century, it is inevitable that Mother Goose should appear for use in this electronic media. Such programs are designed to teach young children classical nursery rhymes through pictures and music. The writers of these programs claim that each verse is created to enhance the relationship between pictures and words. If nothing else, the association of the computer screen with the television screen no doubt creates a familiarity with the media, and through that, may lead children to learn to read. The effect of the visual aspects cannot be denied.

Perhaps a word or two should be said about the illustrations that accompany the words in various Mother Goose editions. Except in scholarly treatises or reference books for the use of teachers, there are always drawings of some kind. Some are so ineptly executed that one has to wonder why the publisher bothered to print them — surely, in any age, artists with sufficient skills to draw decent pictures have been available. The work done on earlier woodcuts is somewhat cruder than later, but reproduction methods were more primitive also. Since printing methods have become more sophisticated, there is hardly any excuse for some of the poor artistry foisted on young readers. Children deserve better, as do the adults who read to them.

In truth, most of the art work is adequate to good. Some publications are extraordinary — these are noted in the appendix, Chronological Bibliography of Important Nursery and Mother Goose Books.

On another visual level, there was an interesting edition of rebuses, *Mother Goose in Hieroglyphics*, in 1849. Actually the cover title of the original used a rebus for "Goose" and the word was spelled "Hieroglyphic*ks*." On each page, certain words of the rhymes were replaced with rebuses. The 52 verses were followed by a "Key" which explained the drawings, a necessary inclusion in that some of the rebuses strained thought if one did not already know the verses.

A child could peer for some time at illustrations trying to translate an unknown verse shown as the following:

There was an [woman with cane] sold puddings and
[cloth-covered table with pie with piece out] s,

She went to the [mill that looks more like a barn] and
   The dust flew in her [two eyes].
While through the [several houses on both sides of
   street stretching into distance] to [awl] she meets,
She ever [man carrying vague square object in right hand and
   holding aloft a bell with the left] Hot Pies!
Hot [table holding two pies].

The key reads: *Old Woman, Pies, Mill, Eyes, Street, Awl, Cries, Pies.*

A 1967 double spoof by Jack Roche utilizes "The Mother Goose Report" to make fun of both social workers and Mother Goose. It purports to be a report from an investigator to the director of the Department of Social Assistance, ascertaining that investigation into the Mother Goose community "revealed ingrained pattern of unusual habits, psychological maladjustment, and symptoms of mental instability."

The "Old Woman in the Shoe" needs new housing; "Nimble, Jack B." (sic) is compulsive and furthermore the family can't afford to keep buying candles for him to jump over; "Peep, Bo" is suffering severe depression and apathy, saying of the lost sheep, "Leave them alone and they'll come home, wagging their tails behind them"; "Simon, Simple" is an under-achiever in school and his parents should give him an allowance so he wouldn't have to admit he hadn't a penny, etc. All are presented as "cases," as the following:

Case No. 734

Horner, Jack: Boy of indeterminate age. Parents report failure to motivate him toward normal participation in family life. Boy sits constantly in corner with pie. Occasionally sticks thumb in pie, pulls out plum and shouts, "Wha a good boy am I." Conduct indicates extra-rigid behavioral standard set by parents. Condition could induce hyper-emotional penitential psychosis with potential suicidal tendencies. Recommend adult educational program in child supervision for parents to orient them toward relaxation of abnormal disciplinary techniques. Boy should be given dietary motivation toward food other than pie.

Don Sandburg's 1978 *Legal Guide to Mother Goose* spoofs the rhymes by way of mock-legalese. "Jack Spratt" and wife are treated as a divorce agreement; "Humpty Dumpty" is presented as an inquest; Mary of "Mary's Little Lamb" is given the police report treatment; and "Baa, Baa, Black Sheep" is handled like a last will and testament. "Wee Willie Winkie" (see pages 185–86) is indicted:

1 "WILLIE WINKIE"
2 Indictment
3 The defendant, known as Wee Willie
4 Winkie, has been observed speeding
5 in a congested area, thereby vio-
6 lating Section 22350 of the Vehicle
7 Code.
8 He has further been cited
9 under Section 311 of the Penal Code
10 for indecent exposure and is
11 additionally accused of
12 violating Sections 602 and 647 of the
13 Penal Code for trespassing and dis-
14 orderly conduct.
15 We, nevertheless, request that the
16 court grant clemency in respect to
17 the above charge in view of the
18 defendant's conscientious efforts
19 in helping to enforce the mis-
20 demeanor statute of the Municipal
21 Code dealing with the nocturnal
22 curfew for juveniles.

—Don Sandburg

In 1985, Meg Brigantine's *The Compleat Amethyst Goose*, a bizarre little self-published paperback, tediously (and self-consciously) changed any male names in the nursery rhymes to female ones, so that the verses say such as, "Tammy Lou Blue, come blow your horn..."; "Little Sue Horner sat in a corner..."; "Barbie Shafto's gone to sea..."; "Dear Tammy Tucker sings for her supper..."; and "Jill Spratt could eat no fat...." Other rhymes were rewritten to reflect lesbianism, some of them rather crudely. An interesting dichotomy is the use of the term *wimmin* (for *women*) in the preface.

Counting on the recognition factor of Mother Goose allusions, comics link them to modern modes to get a laugh:

1. Jack: "How did Mother Goose ever manage to write so much?"
   Jill: "She used a word-processor."
2. Jill: "They've rewritten Mother Goose to eliminate sexism."
   Jack: "It won't sound the same."
   Jill: "What won't?"
   Jack: "Goose Person."

In contemporary times, sexuality and other slightly risqué interpretations are a frequent theme, and even late-night talkshow host Johnny Carson did a long skit in October 1985. He pretended to read from an enormous "Mother Goose" book, stopping to create innuendos, among them, "Jack and Jill went up the hill. . . and Jack broke his 'crown'. . . obviously, this is about a teenage transvestite"; "Hey diddle diddle. . . some degenerate farmer is 'mooning' his livestock. . . is this what we want our kids to read?"; "One little, two little. . . ten little Indians. . . do you see what I see in this disgusting rhyme?. . . it's about an ethnic orgy," and "Wee Willie Winkie runs through the town. . . in his nightgown. . . how many think we have a 'flasher' on our hands here?"

There is also the quaint joke in which certain words of the old familiar rhymes are "censored"—that is, left out. Sometimes they are seen with lines indicating the missing words, and sometimes with large black blocks to indicate "censored" material. The element of amusement here seems to be in the assumption that everyone must be reading unprintable words into the censored spaces. By omission, the unprinted somehow becomes tinged with an aura of implicit vulgarity. One example should suffice:

Mary, Mary, quite ____,
How does your ____ ____?
With ____ ____ and ____ ____,
And ____ ____ all in a ____.

The wide range of uses, misuses, abuses, distortions, parodies, and such to which Mother Goose verses have been subjected only points up the large place they hold in the world of literature. A few of the manipulations are works of literature themselves, which add to the eminence of the originals.

At the beginning of the twentieth century, Carolyn Wells published *A Parody Anthology* (1902). Among the interesting inclusions were some nursery rhymes redone in the literary style of well known poets. Readers were treated to such intriguing curiosities as these:

Mary's Lamb à la Henry Wadsworth Longfellow

Fair the daughter known as Mary,
Fair and full of fun and laughter,
Owned a lamb, a little he-goat,
Owned him all herself and solely.
White the lamb's wool as the Gotchi—
The great Gotchi, driving snowstorm.
Hither Mary went and thither,
But went with her to all places,
Sure as brook to run to river,
Her pet lambkin following with her.

—*A.C. White*

Mary's Lamb à la Robert Browning

You knew her? — Mary the small,
How of a summer, — or, no, was it fall?
You'd never have thought it, never believed,
But the girl owned a lamb last fall.
Its wool was subtly, silky white,
Color of lucent obliteration of night,
Like the shimmering snow or — our Clothild's arm!
You've seen her arm — her right, I mean —
The other she scalded a-washing, I ween —
How white it is and soft and warm!

Ah, there was soul's heart-love, deep, true, and tender,
Wherever went Mary, the maiden so slender,
There followed, his all-absorbed passion, inciting,
That passionate lambkin — her soul's heart delighting —
Ay, every place that Mary sought in,
That lamb was sure to soon be caught in.

— A.C. White

Little Miss Muffet à la Alfred Tennyson (as an Arthurian Idyl)

Upon a tuffet of most soft and verdant moss,
Beneath the spreading branches of an ancient oak,
Miss Muffet sat, and upward gazed,
To where a linnet perched and sung,
And rocked him gently, to and fro.
Soft blew the breeze
And mildly swayed the bough,
Loud sung the bird,
And sweetly dreamed the maid;
Dreamed brightly of the days to come —
The golden days, with her fair future blent.
When one — some wondrous stately knight —
Of our great Arthur's "Table Round";
One, brave as Launcelot, and
Spotless as the pure Sir Galahad,
Should come, and coming choose her
For his love, and in her name,
And for the sake of her fair eyes,
Should do most knightly deeds.
And as she dreamed and softly sighed,
She pensively began to stir,
With the tiny golden spoon

Within an antique dish upon her lap,
Some snow-white milky curds;
Soft were they, full of cream and rich,
And floated in translucent whey;
And as she stirred, she smiled,
Then gently tasted them.
And smiling, ate, nor sighed no more.
Lo! as she ate — nor harbored thought of ill —
Near and nearer yet, there to her crept,
A monster great and terrible,
With huge, misshapen body — leaden eyes —
Full many a long and hairy leg,
And soft and stealthy footstep.
Nearer still he came — and Miss Muffet yet,
All unwitting his dread neighborhood,
Did eat her curds and dream.
Blithe, on the bough, the linnet sung —
All terrestrial natures, sleeping, wrapt
In a most sweet tranquillity.
Closer still the spider drew, and —
Paused beside her — lifted up his head
And gazed into the face.
Miss Muffet then, her consciousness alive
To his dread eyes upon her fixed,
Turned and beheld him.
Loud screamed she, frightened and amazed,
And straightaway sprung upon her feet,
And letting fall her dish and spoon,
She — shrieking — turned and fled.

—Anonymous

Jack and Jill à la Algernon Charles Swinburne

The shudd'ring sheet of rain athwart the trees!
The crashing kiss of lightning on the seas!
   The moaning of the night wind on the wold,
That erstwhile was a gentle, murm'ring breeze!

On such a night as this went Jill and Jack
With strong and sturdy strides through dampness black
   To find the hill's high top and water cold,
Then toiling through the town to bear it back.

The water drawn, they rest awhile. Sweet sips
Of nectar then for Jack from Jill's red lips,

And then with arms entwined they homeward go;
Till mid the mad mud's moistened mush Jack slips.

Sweet heaven, draw a veil on this sad plight,
His crazed cries and cranium cracked; the fright
　　Of gentle Jill, her wretchedness and wo!
Kind Phoebus, drive thy steeds and end this night!
　　　　　　　　　　　　　—*Charles Battell Loomis*

Jack and Jill à la (Henry) Austin Dobson

Their pail they must fill
　　In a crystalline springlet,
Brave Jack and fair Jill.
Their pail they must fill
At the top of the hill,
　　Then she gives him a ringlet.
Their pail they must fill
　　In a crystalline springlet.

They stumbled and fell,
　　And poor Jack broke his forehead,
Oh, how he did yell!
They stumbled and fell,
And went down pell-mell—
　　By Jove! it was horrid.
They stumbled and fell,
　　And poor Jack broke his forehead.
　　　　　　　　　　　　　—*Charles Battell Loomis*

Little Bo-Peep à la Andrew Lang

Unhappy is Bo-Peep,
　　Her tears profusely flow,
Because her precious sheep
　　Have wandered to and fro,
　　Have chosen far to go,
For "pastures new" inclined,
　　(See Lycidas)—and lo!
Their tails are still behind!

How catch them while asleep?
　　(I think Gaboriau
For machinations deep
　　Beats Conan Doyle and Co.)
　　But none a hint bestow

Save this, on how to find
    The flocks she misses so—
"Their tails are still behind!"
This simple faith to keep
    Will mitigate her woe,
She is not Joan, to leap
    To arms against the foe
    Or conjugate (A Greek row);
Nay, peacefully resigned
    She waits, till time shall show
Their tails are still behind!

Bo-Peep, rejoice! Although
    Your sheep appear unkind,
Rejoice at last to know
    Their tails are still behind!

                            —*Anthony C. Deane*

Three Blind Mice à la Sir William Watson

Three mice—three sightless mice—averse from strife,
Peaceful descendants of the Armenian race,
Intent on finding some secluded place
Wherein to pass their inoffensive life;

How little dreamt they of that farmer's wife—
The Porte's malicious minion—giving chase,
And in a moment—ah, the foul disgrace!—
Shearing their tails off with a carving-knife!

And oh, my unemotional countrymen,
Who choose to dally and to temporize,
When once before with vitriolic pen
I told the tale of Turkish infamies,
Once more I call to vengeance,—now as then,
Shouting the magic word, "Atrocities!"

—Anthony C. Deane

Cat and Fiddle à la Oscar Wilde

(Our nurseries will soon be too cultured to admit the old rhymes in their Philistine and unaesthetic garb. They may be redressed somewhat on this model.)

Oh, but she was dark and shrill,
(Hey-de-diddle and hey-de-dee!)
The cat that (on the first April)
Played the fiddle on the lea.
Oh, and the moon was wan and bright,
(Hey-de-diddle and hey-de-dee!)
The Cow she looked nor left nor right,
But took it straight at a jump, pardie!
The Hound did laugh to see this thing,
(Hey-de-diddle and hey-de-dee!)
As it was parlous wantoning,
(Ah, good my gentles, laugh not ye,)
And underneath a dreesome moon
Two lovers fled right piteouslie;
A spooney plate with a plated spoon,
(Hey-de-diddle and hey-de-dee!)

—Anonymous

Even some well known poets themselves, not content to write only serious poetry or clever original verses, evidently saw some value or fun in this exercise and tried their hands at mocking nursery rhymes. Among some are:

Coleridge's The House That Jack Built

And this reft house is that the which he built,
Lamented Jack! and here his malt he piled.
Cautious in vain! these rats that squeak so wild,
Squeak not unconscious of their father's guilt.
Did he not see her gleaming through the glade!
Belike 'twas she, the maiden all forlorn.
What though she milked no cow with crumpled horn,
Yet, aye she haunts the dale where erst she strayed:
And aye before her stalks her amorous knight!
Still on his thighs their wonted brogues are worn,
And through those brogues, still tattered and betorn,
His hindward charms gleam an unearthly white.

By Samuel Taylor Coleridge (1772–1834): Coleridge, English poet, critic, and philosopher, was a leader of the romantics. His *Poems on Various Occasions* appeared in 1796. In 1798, he and William Wordsworth published *Lyrical Ballads*, the single most important work of the romantic movement; it included Coleridge's "Rime of the Ancient Mariner." He also wrote "Christabel," "Kubla Khan" and "Dejection: An Ode."

Herford's Song of a Heart

Upon a time I had a Heart,
And it was bright and gay;
And I gave it to a Lady fair
To have and keep alway.

She soothed it and she smoothed it
And she stabbed it till it bled;
She brightened it and lightened it
And she weighed it down with lead.

She flattered it and battered it
And she filled it full of gall;
Yet had I Twenty Hundred Hearts,
Still should she have them all.

By Oliver Herford (1863–1935): Although born in England, Herford crossed the Atlantic to become known as an American humorist, author, and illustrator of many popular volumes of light verse, including *A Child's Primer of Natural History* (1899).

There are few English-speaking people who do not have exposure to Mother Goose nursery rhymes in their backgrounds. It would probably be safe to say that there have been no schools of formal education that have not drawn on them in some form. In addition, from parent toward child, and that child grown to parent, there is an endless circle of appreciation and reaffirmation of the old, familiar pattern of these simple rhymes. The longer the rhymes have circulated, the more they have become known, and the more they have become a logical subject for study in the scholarly traditions of academia.

Mother Goose may have started in the nursery, but there is no question that today her works are considered an important aspect of literature. But even more than literary importance—from century to century—from generation to generation—from season to season—from day to day—Mother Goose has been an important part of our lives. Two quotations say it well:

A Scottish Chapbook of 1817 showed a woodcut of an ancient dame seated on a chair bending forward to read from an open book on the table, below which was the couplet,

> Here Mother Goose on Winter Nights
> The old and young she both delights.

The other appeared in the preface to *The Only True Mother Goose Melodies* (1843). The illustration showed an old crone patting two toddlers on the head. Underneath were the words:

> Hear What Ma'am Goose Says!
> My dear little blossoms, there are now in this world, and always will be, a great many grannies besides myself, both in petticoats and pantaloons, some a deal younger to be sure; but all monstrous wise, and of my own family name. These old women, who never had chick nor child of their own, but who always know how to bring up other people's children, will tell you with very long faces, that my enchanting, quieting, soothing volume, my all-sufficient anodyne for cross, peevish, won't-be-comforted little bairns, ought to be laid aside for more learned books, such as they could select and publish. Fudge! I tell you that all their batterings can't deface my beauties, nor their wise pratings equal my wiser prattlings; and all imitators of my refreshing songs might as well write a new Billy Shakespeare as another Mother Goose: we two great poets were born together, and we shall go out of the world together.
> No, no, my Melodies will never die,
> While nurses sing or babies cry.

Chronological Bibliography of Important Nursery and Mother Goose Books

The books listed here are either important in the history of nursery rhyme books for children, or noted for their illustrations.

Songs for the Nursery, or Mother Goose's Melodies. Boston: Thomas Fleet, 1719. (The "ghost volume," purported in 1860 to have been written in 1719. No copy is known to exist. The possibility of its existence is minimal, and its listing here is only for speculative interest.)

Tommy Thumb's Pretty Song Book: Volume II. London: Mary Cooper, c1744. (The first known-to-exist book of nursery rhymes.)

A Little Pretty Pocket-Book. London: John Newbery, 1744. (Significant as Newbery's first children's book.)

Nurse Truelove's New-Year's Gift; or the Book of Books for Children. London: John Newbery, 1755.

The Famous Tommy Thumb's Little Story-Book. London: Stanley Crowder and Benjamin Collins, c1760.

The Top Book of All, for Little Masters and Misses. London: Crowder, Collins, and R. Baldwin, c1760.

Simple Simon. London: Cluer Dicey and Richard Marshall, 1764.

Mother Goose's Melody: or, Sonnets for the Cradle. London: John Newbery, c1765, 1780. Reprint: Worcester, Mass.: Isaiah Thomas, 1786, 1794. (Established the term "Mother Goose" as a synonym for "nursery rhymes." In all likelihood edited by Oliver Goldsmith. Reprinted in its entirety herein as Chapter 4. No complete copy of either the Newbery or 1786 Thomas editions exist. Facsimiles were produced from the 1794 Thomas edition: William H. Whitmore, 1889; W.F. Prideaux, 1904; Frederic Melcher, 1954. Reprints of the 1889 Whitmore [Joel Munsell's Sons] edition: Detroit: Singing Tree Press/Gale, 1969.)

The Fairing: or a Golden Toy for Children. London: John Newbery, 1765.

Mirth without Mischief. London: C. Sheppard, c1780.

Nancy Cock's Pretty Song Book for All Little Misses and Masters. London: John Marshall, c1780.

Gammer Gurton's Garland or The Nursery Parnassus. Edited by Joseph Ritson. London: R. Christopher, 1784. Enlarged editions: Christopher and Jennett, c1799; R. Triphook, 1810.

Tommy Thumb's Song Book for All Little Masters and Misses. Worcester, Mass.: Isaiah Thomas, 1788.

A Choice Collection of Riddles, Charades, Rebuses, &c. Edited by Peter Puzzlewell, Esq. London: Elizabeth Newbery, 1792.

Infant Institutes, part the first: or a Nuserical Essay on the Poetry, Lyric and Allegorical, of the Earliest Ages, &c. Compiled by the Rev. Baptist Noel Turner. 1797. (Probably the first satire of nursery rhymes.)

Life and Death of Jenny Wren. London: T. Evans, c1800.

The Comic Adventures of Old Mother Hubbard and Her Dog. London: John Harris, 1805.

Songs for the Nursery Collected from the Works of the Most Renowned Poets. London: Benjamin Tabart & Co., 1805; Revised: William Darton, 1818.

Original Ditties for the Nursery. London: John Harris, c1805.

The Happy Courtship, Merry Marriage and Pic-nic Dinner of Cock Robin and Jenny Wren. London: John Harris, 1812.

Little Rhymes for Little Folks. London: John Harris, 1812.

Old Mother Goose or, The Golden Egg. London: T. Batchelar, c1815.

The History of Sixteen Wonderful Old Women. London: John Harris, 1821. (The first known book of limericks.)

Anecdotes and Adventures of Fifteen Gentlemen. London: John Marshall, c1822. (The second known book of limericks.)

Mother Goose's Quarto: Or Melodies Complete. Boston: Munroe and Francis, c1825.

Nurse Lovechild's Ditties for the Nursery. London: D. Carvalho, c1830.

Sarah Josepha Hale. *Poems for Our Children.* 1830. (Includes Hale's famous "Mary had a little lamb....")

London Jingles. Banbury: J.G. Rusher, c1840.

Nursery Poems. Banbury: J.G. Rusher, c1840.

Nursery Rhymes from the Royal Collections. Banbury, J.G. Rusher, c1840.
Nursery Songs. Banbury: J.G. Rusher, c1840.
Poetic Trifles. Banbury: J.G. Rusher, c1840.
James O. Halliwell. *The Nursery Rhymes of England.* London: Published for the Percy
    Society by T. Richards, 1842. Revised and enlarged: 1843, 1844, 1846, 1853,
    c1860.
The Only True Mother Goose Melodies. With Introduction by Edward Everett Hale.
    Boston: Munroe & Francis, c1843. Reprint: Boston: Lothrop, Lee and Shepard,
    1905; this edition has original publication date incorrectly given as 1833. (Con-
    tains most of *Mother Goose's Melody, Mother Goose's Quarto,* and the longer
    pieces of *Gammer Gurton's Garland.*)
Eliza Follen. *New Nursery Songs for All Good Children.* c1843. (Includes "Three little
    kittens....")
Edward F. Rimbault. *Nursery Rhymes with the Tunes to Which They Are Still Sung.*
    1846.
James O. Halliwell. *Popular Rhymes and Nursery Tales.* London: John Russell Smith,
    1849. Revised and enlarged: c1860.
The Mother Goose: Containing All the Melodies the Old Lady Ever Wrote. "Edited
    by Dame Goslin." Philadelphia: G.S. Appleton, 1851.
Sing a Song of Sixpence. Illustrated by Walter Crane. London and New York:
    Frederick Warne, 1867.
Christina Rossetti. *Sing-Song.* 1872. Reissued, New York: Macmillan, 1942. (Rossetti's
    classic nursery volume; includes several of her poems sometimes perceived to be
    Mother Goose.)
The Baby's Opera: A Book of Old Rhymes with New Dresses. Illustrated by Walter
    Crane. London and New York: Frederick Warne, 1877.
The Baby's Bouquet: A Fresh Bunch of Old Rhymes and Tunes. Illustrated by Walter
    Crane. London and New York: Frederick Warne, 1879.
*Mother Goose's Melodies, Containing All That Have Ever Come to Light of Her
    Memorable Writings.* Philadelphia: J.B. Lippincott, 1879.
Mother Goose; or the Old Nursery Rhymes. Illustrated by Kate Greenaway. London
    and New York: G. Routledge and Sons, 1881. Reprint: Frederick Warne, c1910.
    (A small book; with soft colors and the delicate and distinctive illustrations of
    Kate Greenaway.)
William Wells Newell. *Games and Songs of American Children.* New York: Harper
    & Brothers, 1884. Revised and enlarged: 1903.
*Mother Goose's Nursery Rhymes: A Collection of Alphabets, Rhymes, Tales, and
    Jingles.* With 220 illustrations by Walter Crane, Sir John Gilbert, John Tenniel,
    Harrison Weir, et al. New York: Williams, 1886.
A Apple Pie. Illustrated by Kate Greenaway. London: Routledge & Sons, 1886. (Tradi-
    tional text. A departure from Greenaway's usual pale drawings, this is a bigger
    book, bright and colorful.)
A Book of Nursery Songs and Rhymes. Edited by Sabine Baring-Gould. Illustrated by
    members of the Birmingham Art School, directed by A.J. Gaskin. London:
    Methuen, 1895.
The Nursery Rhyme Book. Edited by Andrew Lang; illustrated by L(eonard) Leslie
    Brooke. London: Frederick Warne, 1897.
Randolph Caldecott's Picture Books. Illustrated by Randolph Caldecott. Four-volume
    set. London and New York: Frederick Warne, [190?] (most drawn 1880–1886).
    As a two volume set: *Randolph Caldecott's Collection of Pictures and Songs.* Also
    published individually in 16 separate paperbound volumes: *John Gilpin; House*

that Jack Built; Babes in the Woods; Elegy on a Mad Dog; Three Jovial Hunts-
men; Sing a Song of Sixpence; Queen of Hearts; The Farmer's Boy; The
Milkmaid; Hey Diddle Diddle and Baby Bunting; A Frog He Would A-Wooing
Go; The Fox Jumps over the Parson's Gate; Come, Lasses and Lads; Ride a Cock
Horse; Mrs. Mary Blaize; The Great Panjandrum Himself. (Caldecott, 1846–1886,
was an esteemed English illustrator for children. The prestigious Caldecott Medal
is awarded annually for excellence in picture book illustration.)

Mother Goose's Nursery Rhymes. With 240 illustrations by Gordon Browne, R. Mar-
riott Watson, L. Weedon, et al. New York: A.L. Burt, [190?].

The Big Book of Nursery Rhymes. Edited by Walter Jerrold; illustrated by Charles
Robinson. London: Blackie and Son, [190?], 1911.

Denslow's Mother Goose: Being the Old Familiar Rhymes and Jingles of Mother Goose
Edited and Illustrated by W.W. Denslow. Rhymes hand-lettered by Fred W.
Goudy. New York: McClure, Phillips, 1901.

75 British Nursery Rhymes. Edited by Frank Kidson. London: Augener, 1904.
("[W]ith the melodies which have always been associated with them.")

The Golden Goose Book. Illustrated by L(eonard) Leslie Brooke. London: Frederick
Warne, 1905.

Pinafore Palace; a Book of Rhymes for the Nursery. Edited by Kate Douglas Wiggin
& Nora Archibald Smith. New York: Doubleday, 1907. (Includes Mother Goose,
verses by Edward Lear and others.)

Complete Version of Ye Three Blind Mice. Edited by John William Ivimey. Illustrated
by Walter Corbould. London: Frederick Warne, 1909.

The Complete Mother Goose. Illustrated by Ethel Franklin Betts. New York: Frederick
A. Stokes, 1909.

Old Mother Goose's Nursery Rhymes. Illustrated by E. Stuart Hardy. London: E.
Nister, 1910.

Our Old Nursery Rhymes. Harmonized by Alfred Moffat; illustrated by H.W. le Mair.
New York: David McKay, 1911.

Jolly Mother Goose Annual. Illustrated by Blanche Fisher Wright. Chicago: Rand
McNally, 1912.

Mother Goose's Nursery Rhymes. With 10 full-color plates and 424 woodcuts by
Walter Crane, Sir John Gilbert, W. McConnell, John Tenniel, Harrison Weir,
J.B. Zuecker, et al. Philadelphia: David McKay, 1912.

Mother Goose: The Old Nursery Rhymes. Illustrated by Arthur Rackham. London:
William Heinemann; New York: Century Co., 1913. (The great English artist's
illustrations are of three types: pen-and-ink sketches, silhouettes, and full-page
color.)

The Little Mother Goose. Illustrated by Jessie Wilcox Smith. New York: Dodd, Mead,
1914, 1916.

Nurse Lovechild's Legacy: Being a Mighty Fine Collection of the Most Noble,
Memorable and Veracious Nursery Rhymes. Illustrated by C. Lovat Fraser. London: Poetry Bookshop, 1916. Reprint: New York: Henry Holt, 1924. (18th and
19th century chapbook rhymes.)

Nursery Rhymes. Illustrated by Grace G. Drayton. New York: Charles Scribner's Sons,
1916. (Drayton created the famous "Campbell Kids" for the Campbell Soup
Company.)

The Real Mother Goose. Illustrated by Blanche Fisher Wright. Chicago: Rand-
McNally, 1916, 1965. (Pictures on every page, well-suited to illustrate the verses,
ranging from clear washes to soft, pale tones, and to bright and lively ones.)

The Boyd Smith Mother Goose. Edited by Lawrence Elmendorf; illustrated by E. Boyd

Smith. London and New York: G.P. Putnam's Sons, 1919. (Heavily illustrated in black and white, and color.)

Nursery Rhymes. Illustrated by C. Lovat Fraser. London: T.C. and E.C. Jack, 1919. Reprint: New York: Alfred A. Knopf, 1946.

Mother Goose's Nursery Rhymes. Edited by L.E. Walter; illustrated by Charles Folkard. New York: Macmillan, 1922.

Ring o' Roses; A Nursery Rhyme Picture Book. Illustrated by L(eonard) Leslie Brooke. London: Frederick Warne, 1922. (Humorous illustrations with the characters in English period costumes.)

The Less Familiar Nursery Rhymes. Edited by Robert Graves. London: Ernest Benn, 1926.

Jack Horner's Pie: A Book of Nursery Rhymes. Illustrated by Lois Lenski. New York: Harper & Brothers, 1927. (Lenski won the Newbery Medal in 1946 for *Strawberry Girl*, which she also illustrated.)

Come Hither; a Collection of Rhymes and Poems for the Young of All Ages. Compiled by Walter de la Mare. New York: Alfred A. Knopf, 1928. (England's great children's writer de la Mare won the 1947 Carnegie Medal for *Collected Stories for Children*. The author's notes in *Come Hither*, "written about and roundabout the poems," are of unusual interest.)

Willy Pogany's Mother Goose. Illustrated by Willy Pogany. New York: T. Nelson & Sons, 1928.

Ring-a-Round, a Collection of Verse for Boys and Girls. Compiled by Mildred Harrington; illustrated by Corydon Bell. New York: Macmillan, 1930.

Rhymes from Mother Goose. Compiled by Charles Welch. New York: D.C. Heath, 1930.

The Land of Nursery Rhyme. "As seen by Alice Daglish [sic: Dagleish?] and Ernest Rhys, with a map and pictures by Charles Folkard." London: J.M. Dent & Sons; New York: E.P. Dutton, 1932.

Mother Goose: A Comprehensive Collection of Rhymes. Edited by William Rose Benet; illustrated by Roger Duvoisin. New York: Heritage Illustrated Book Shelf, 1936. (Duvoisin won the Caldecott Medal for *White Snow, Bright Snow* in 1948.)

Four & Twenty Blackbirds, Nursery Rhymes of Yesterday Recalled for Children of Today. Edited by Helen Dean Fish; illustrated by Charles Lawson. New York: Frederick A. Stokes, 1937. (Fish's *Animals of the Bible* won the 1938 Caldecott Medal for its illustrations by Dorothy P. Lathrop.)

The Gay Mother Goose. Selected by Alice Dalgliesh; illustrated by Margot Austin. New York and London: Charles Scribner's Sons, 1938.

The Tenggren Mother Goose. Illustrated by Gustaf Tenggren. Boston: Little, Brown, 1940.

Mother Goose Rhymes. Edited by "Watty Piper"; illustrated by Margot Austin. New York: Platt & Munk, 1940.

Ride a Cock Horse and Other Nursery Rhymes. Illustrated by Mervyn Peake. London: Chatto and Windus, 1940.

A Book of Nursery Rhymes. Illustrated by Enid Marx. London: Chatto and Windus, 1941.

The Tall Book of Mother Goose. Illustrated by Feodor Rojankovsky. London and New York: Harper & Brothers, 1942. (Rojankovsky won the 1956 Caldecott Medal for *Frog Went A-Courtin'*. This "tall book" is 5" by 12" high; depicts husky everyday children and animals that almost appear to have realistic textures.)

Mother Goose: Seventy-Seven Verses.... Illustrated by Tasha Tudor. New York: Oxford University Press, 1944.

Mother Goose. Illustrated by Tasha Tudor. New York: Walck, 1944. (Cozy, domestic drawings.)

Sing Mother Goose. Music by Opal Wheeler; illustrated by Marjorie Torrey. New York: E.P. Dutton, 1945.

The Rooster Crows; A Book of American Rhymes and Jingles. Compiled and illustrated by Maud and Miska Petersham. New York: Macmillan, 1945. (This book won the Caldecott Medal for 1946; the illustrations are cheerful, round, and full.)

The Mother Goose Book. Illustrated by Sonia Roetter. Mount Vernon, N.Y.: Peter Pauper Press, 1946. (Few illustrations; though the Pennsylvania Dutch–style prints are interesting, they may be too static.)

The Oxford Dictionary of Nursery Rhymes. Edited by Iona and Peter Opie. New York: Oxford University Press, 1951. (Scholarly history of the rhymes; sparsely illustrated with old prints and drawings, the book is really meant for adults.)

The Family Goose: Little Goose, Mother Goose, Father Goose. Illustrated by Leonard Weisgard. New York: Harper & Brothers, 1951. Three volumes. (Weisgard won the Caldecott Medal in 1947 for *The Little Island*.)

Mother Goose Riddle Rhymes. Edited by Joseph and Ruth Low; illustrated by Joseph Low. New York: Harcourt Brace Jovanovich, 1953. (Clever modern rebuses.)

Marguerite de Angeli's Book of Nursery and Mother Goose Rhymes. With 260 illustrations by Marguerite de Angeli. Garden City, N.Y.: Doubleday, 1954. (A very large book, with lively, active drawings. De Angeli won the Newbery Medal in 1950 for *The Door in the Wall*, which she also illustrated.)

Lavender's Blue. Compiled by Kathleen Lines; illustrations by Harold Jones. New York: Franklin Watts, 1954. (Illustrations suggest old engravings; black and white, and color.)

Ditties for the Nursery. Compiled by Iona Opie; illustrated by Monica Walker. New York: Walck, 1954.

The Oxford Nursery Rhyme Book. Compiled by Iona and Peter Opie; illustrations by Joan Hassall. New York: Walck, 1955. (Also has illustrations from old chapbooks.)

Frog Went A-Courtin'. Edited by John Langstaff; illustrated by Feodor Rojankovsky. New York: Harcourt Brace Jovanovich, 1955. (This book won the Caldecott Medal for 1956.)

Nursery Rhymes for Certain Times. Introduction by Walter de la Mare; illustrations by Elinor Darwin and Moyra Leatham. London: Faber and Faber, 1956. (De la Mare's *Collected Stories for Children* won the Carnegie Medal for 1947.)

The House That Jack Built. Illustrated by Antonio Frasconi. New York: Harcourt Brace Jovanovich, 1958.

Nursery Rhymes. Illustrated by A.H. Watson. London: J.M. Dent & Sons; New York: E.P. Dutton, 1958.

The Annotated Mother Goose. Edited by Ceil and William S. Baring-Gould. New York: Bramhall House/C.N. Porter, 1962. (Generously illustrated with black and white reprints from numerous earlier Mother Goose books; artists are identified, but not the rhymes to which the pictures apply; really an adult reference.)

Mother Goose and Nursery Rhymes. Illustrated with woodcut engravings by Philip Reed. New York: Atheneum, 1963. Reprint: Chicago: Regnery, 1979.

A Family Book of Nursery Rhymes. Compiled by Iona and Peter Opie; illustrations by Pauline Baynes. New York: Oxford University Press, 1964. (Delicate work by Baynes, whose illustrations for *Dictionary of Chivalry* won the Kate Greenaway Medal for 1968.)

Brian Wildsmith's Mother Goose. Illustrated by Brian Wildsmith. New York: Franklin

Watts, 1965. (Rich colors, some as geometric figures, and period clothing. Brian Wildsmith's *ABC* won the Kate Greenaway Medal in 1962.)

The Mother Goose Treasury. Illustrated by Raymond Briggs. New York: Coward McCann, 1966. (This book won the Greenaway Medal for 1966; drawings range from bold to delicate, from restrained to humorous, Briggs' *Father Christmas* won the Kate Greenaway Medal in 1973.)

The Charles Addams Mother Goose. Illustrated by Charles Addams. New York: Harper, 1967.

London Bridge Is Falling Down. Illustrated by Peter Spier. New York: Doubleday, 1967. (Minute and humorous detail; also includes historical notes about the bridge. Spier won the 1978 Caldecott Medal for *Noah's Ark.*)

London Bridge Is Falling Down: The Song and Game. Illustrated by Ed Emberley. Boston: Little, Brown, 1967. (Emberley won the 1968 Caldecott Medal for *Drummer Hoff.*)

Mother Goose Lost. Compiled by Nicholas Tucker; illustrations by Trevor Stubley. New York: Crowell, 1971. (Gay and colorful.)

The House That Jack Built. Illustrated by Seymour Chwast. New York: Random House, 1973. (Clever variation has each board page larger than the last.)

Three Jovial Huntsmen. Illustrated by Susan Jeffers. Scarsdale, N.Y.: Bradbury, 1973.

Cakes and Custard: Children's Rhymes Chosen by Brian Alderson. Illustrations by Helen Oxenbury. New York: William Morrow, 1975. (Witty, carefully detailed illustrations; Oxenbury won a double Kate Greenaway Medal for her illustrations for *The Quangle-Wangles Hat* by Edward Lear, and *Dragon of an Ordinary Family* in 1969.)

The Mother Goose Book. Illustrated by Alice and Martin Provensen. New York: Random House, 1976. (The Provensens won the 1984 Caldecott Medal for *The Glorious Flight.*)

Gregory Griggs and Other Nursery Rhyme People. Illustrated by Arnold Lobel. New York: Greenwillow, 1978. (Lobel won the 1981 Caldecott Medal for *Fables.*)

Granfa' Grig Had a Pig and Other Rhymes Without Reason from Mother Goose. Illustrated by Wallace Tripp. Boston: Little, Brown, 1976. (Filled with humorous details.)

Popular Nursery Rhymes. Edited by Jennifer Mulherin; Art Director, Tom Deas. New York: Grosset & Dunlap, 1983. (Illustrations from numerous earlier editions of Mother Goose; brief historical notes.)

Annotated Secondary Bibliography

The annotations here either indicate the relevance of the sources to Mother Goose history, or show what they offered in the way of research for this reference.

Abbey, Stella K. "Mother Goose Sweeps History" (pamphlet). [United States]: Stella K. Abbey, 1940, 1967. (A slim, self-published pamphlet, with laborious language, and too many gratuitous digressions from subject under discussion.)

Amis, Kingsley. *The New Oxford Book of English Light Verse.* New York: Oxford University Press, 1978. (Some interesting comments in the introduction re Cowper and Mother Hubbard.)

Appleton, George S. *Mother Goose in Hieroglyphics.* Boston: Frederick A. Brown, 1849. (Mother Goose rhymes with rebuses.)

Arbuthnot, May Hill. *Children and Books.* Chicago: Scott, Foresman, 1947. Revised: Zena Sutherland, Dianne L. Monson, May Hill Arbuthnot, Dorothy M. Broderick. Glenview, Ill.: Scott, Foresman, 1981. (Classic treatise on children's reading, with some historical notes about the origins of Mother Goose.)

Barchilon, Jacques, and Henry Pettit. *The Authentic Mother Goose Fairy Tales and Nursery Rhymes.* Denver: Swallow, 1960. (Postulates a different date for the first publication of Newbery's *Mother Goose's Melody.*)

Baring-Gould, William S. and Ceil. *The Annotated Mother Goose.* New York: Bramhall House/C.N. Potter, 1962. (A fascinating volume with primary emphasis on annotations that explain the obscure and archaic words and expressions found in Mother Goose rhymes. Some of the historical notes contain errors, and the use of only a first-line index detracts from the usefulness of the book.)

Bett, Henry. *Nursery Rhymes and Tales: Their Origin and History.* New York: Henry Holt, 1924.

Bettelheim, Bruno. "Violence: A Neglected Mode of Behavior." *Surviving and Other Essays.* New York: Alfred A. Knopf, 1979. (The essay on violence makes some points that refute the claims of those upset by "violence" in nursery rhymes.)

Bodger, Joan. "Mother Goose: Is the Old Girl Relevant?" *Wilson Library Bulletin,* December 1969, pp. 402–408. (Scholarly article, written from viewpoint of relevance in working with disadvantaged children.)

Brigantine, Meg. *The Compleat Amethyst Goose.* Radnor, Penn.: Seedlings Publications, 1985. (Self-published; a pointless exchange of female names for male ones in the verses, plus some rewrites to make the rhymes reflect lesbianism.)

Burns, Robert. *The Poetical Works of Robert Burns.* Edited by J. Logue Robertson. London: Oxford University Press, 1923. (All of Burns' poems, with a helpful glossary of Scottish words.)

Chukovsky, Kornei. *From Two to Five.* Translated and edited by Miriam Morton. Berkeley: University of California Press, 1966. (Observations and introspective of early childhood.)

Daiches, David. *Robert Burns.* New York: Macmillan, 1950. (Insightful biography of Burns and his works.)

Decker, Marjorie. *The Christian Mother Goose.* Grand Junction: Decker Press, 1980. (Self-published; sanctimonious recastings of the original verses.)

Delamar, Gloria T., compiler and writer. *Children's Counting-Out Rhymes, Fingerplays, Jump-Rope and Bounce-Ball Chants and Other Rhythms: A Comprehensive English-Language Reference.* Jefferson, N.C.: McFarland & Company, Inc., Publishers, 1983. (Intended for teachers and parents to use with children; includes Mother Goose material, many in forms of fingerplays, chants, etc.)

_____, compiler and writer. *Rounds Re-Sounding: Circular Music for Voices and Instruments; An Eight-Century Reference.* Jefferson, N.C.: McFarland & Company, Inc., Publishers, 1987. (Among other rounds, includes musical rounds based on Mother Goose rhymes, plus history of "Three Blind Mice. . . .")

Eckenstein, Lina. *Comparative Studies in Nursery Rhymes.* London: Duckworth, 1906, 1911. (A study of the ancient folk origins of the Mother Goose verses and their European counterparts.)

Ellis, Geraldine. "Biography of Sarah Josepha Hale." Unpublished manuscript, Jenkintown, Penn., 1985. (Full story of Hale's writing of "Mary Had a Little Lamb" and the legal and literary arguments over her authorship of it.)

Fenton, Edward. "Blind Idiot: The Problems of Translation." *The Horn Book,* October, 1977, pp. 505–513. (Effects of literature on language; mentions pervading influence of "Mother Goose," etc.)

Field, Walter Taylor. *A Guide to Literature for Children.* Boston: Ginn, 1928. (Chapter X is on Mother Goose.)

Frazer, James, Sir. *The Golden Bough.* England: 1890. Abridged edition: New York: Macmillan, 1958. *The New Golden Bough.* Abridged revision, edited by Theodor H. Gaster. New York: Mentor/New American Library, 1964. (Mythology connected with some of the rhymes.)

Glazer, Tom. *A Treasury of Folk Songs.* New York: Bantam, 1961. (Comparison of ballad stanzas.)

Halliwell, James O. *The Nursery Rhymes of England.* London: Published for the Percy Society by T. Richards, 1842. (The first comprehensive collection, with selected notes about history and origins.)

_____. *Popular Rhymes & Nursery Tales.* London: John Russell Smith, 1849. (A sequel to the 1842 collection.)

Haviland, Virginia, and Coughlan, Margaret N., compilers. *Yankee Doodle's Literary Sampler of Prose, Poetry & Pictures: Being an Anthology of Diverse Works Published for the Edification and/or Entertainment of Young Readers in America before 1900.* New York: Thomas Y. Crowell, 1974. (A large, beautifully constructed book. Contents selected from the Rare Book Collections of the Library of Congress. Contains the original "claim" script and comments about the origins of the Boston Mother Goose myth; includes a few rhymes.)

Headland, Isaac Taylor. *Chinese Mother Goose Rhymes.* Revell, 1900.

Jerome, Judson. "Poetry: Nursery Versery." *Writer's Digest*, October, 1984, pp. 12–14. (Comments about Mother Goose as serious poetry.)

Johnson, Edna; Scott, Carrie E.; and Sickels, Evelyn R. *Anthology of Children's Literature.* Cambridge, Mass.: Houghton Mifflin, 1935, 1948. (Reference book for teachers; includes some nursery rhymes and comments about origins. Also has author biographies.)

Johnson, Mason P. *History and Gossip in Mother Goose Rhymes.* Detroit: Harlo Press, 1981, 1983. (A small, self-published book. Although well-written, it arbitrarily presents material as historic fact, despite evidence to the contrary.)

Ker, John Bellenden. *An Essay on the Archaiology of Popular English Phrases and Nursery Rhymes.* London: Black, Young, and Young, 1834. (Strained attempt to trace origins of rhymes to Low-Saxon.)

Levy, Sara G. *Mother Goose Rhymes for Jewish Children.* New York: Block, 1951. (The old rhymes recast to teach the Jewish heritage.)

Lindberg, Stanley W. *The Annotated McGuffey: Selections from the McGuffey Eclectic Readers, 1836–1920.* New York: Van Nostrand Reinhold, 1976. (Some background on the "Mary's Little Lamb" controversy.)

Lomax, John A. and Alan. *Best Loved American Folk Songs.* New York: Grosset & Dunlap, 1947. (Comparison of ballad stanzas; some historical notes.)

Lukens, Rebecca. "In Defense of Mother Goose." *PTA Magazine,* June 1973, pp. 21–23. (Makes the point that the activities in many Mother Goose rhymes have counterparts in real life.)

MacDougall, J.B. *The Real Mother Goose: The Reality Behind the Rhymes.* Toronto: Ryerson Press, 1940. (Small pedantic volume, with a number of flights of conjecture and several inexcusable errors.)

Minnich, Harvey C., editor. *Old Favorites from the McGuffey Readers: 1836–1936.* New York: American Bk. Co., 1936. (Shows limited use of Mother Goose in McGuffey.)

Moore, Annie E. *Literature Old and New for Children.* Cambridge, Mass.: Houghton Mifflin, 1934. (Chapter II, "Mother Goose," has history of the book and some analysis of the verses.)

Mother Goose's Melody. Probably edited by Oliver Goldsmith. London: John Newbery, c1765, 1780. Reprint: Worcester, Mass.: Isaiah Thomas, 1786. Reprint: Boston: Houghton Mifflin, 1869.

    Reissues edited by William A. Wheeler, with Wheeler's byline omitted: 1872 — illustrations by Henry Stephens and Gaston Fay; 1884 — color illustrations by Alfred Kappes.

    Reprint: *The Original Mother Goose's Melody As First Issued by John Newbery of London, About A.D. 1760.* Reproduction of c1885 edition as reprinted by Isaiah Thomas of Worcester, Mass. Introductory notes by William H. Whitmore. Albany: Joel Munsell's Sons, 1889. Reprints: W.F. Prideaux, 1904; Frederic G. Melcher, 1954. Whitmore-edited reissue: Detroit: Singing Tree Press/Gale, 1969.

    Reprint: *The Original Mother Goose's Melody As First Issued by John Newbery of London, About A.D. 1760.* Repr. of 1889 edition. Detroit: Gale, 1969. (An important edition; entire text reprinted herein as Chapter 4.)

Nikoforuk, Andrew. "God Meets Mother Goose." *MacLeans,* November 23, 1981, p. 60. (Negative review of Decker's Christianized version of Mother Goose.)

Niles, John Jacob. *The Ballad Book.* New York: Bramhall House/C.N. Potter, 1960. (Comparison of ballad stanzas; some historical notes.)

Opie, Iona and Peter. *The Oxford Dictionary of Nursery Rhymes.* New York: Oxford University Press, 1951. (Thorough, scholarly book, well-written and conceived, that traces the origins of almost every traditional nursery rhyme of the English language. The first such since Halliwell. Comprehensive index. The casual use of the term "nigger" in narrative text is an unfortunate offense.)

—————. *The Lore and Language of Schoolchildren.* Oxford, England: Clarendon Press, 1960. (Superb scholarly research — marginally useful for specific Mother Goose study.)

Parker, Patricia. "What Comes After Mother Goose?" *Education Digest,* October 1969, pp. 46–49. (Discusses the importance of exposing children to poetry, beginning with Mother Goose rhymes.)

Robbins, Peggy. "History's Slighter Side: The American Mother Goose." *American History, Illustrated,* July 1981, p. 6. (Lightweight, slim filler-article accepting as fact the discredited claims about Boston's "Mother Goose.")

Roche, Jack. "The Mother Goose Report." *Saturday Evening Post,* October 7, 1967, p. 22. (Spoof: Mother Goose as social work cases.)

Rossetti, Christina. *Sing-Song.* 1872. Reprint: New York: Macmillan, 1942. (Rossetti's classic nursery volume; includes several of her poems sometimes perceived to be Mother Goose.)

Sackville-West, Vita. *Nursery Rhymes.* London: Michael Joseph, 1950. (Critical study of traditional nursery rhymes.)

Sandburg, Don. *Legal Guide to Mother Goose.* Los Angeles: Price/Stern/Sloan, 1978. (Spoof: Mother Goose as legal cases.)

Seeger, Ruth Crawford. *American Folk Songs for Children.* Garden City, N.Y.: Doubleday, 1948. (Comparison of ballad stanzas.)

Sharp, Cecil J., and Maud Karpeles. *Eighty English Folk Songs from the Southern Appalachians.* Cambridge, Mass.: Massachusetts Institute of Technology Press, 1968. (Comparison of ballad stanzas.)

Starrett, Vincent. "Much Ado About Mother Goose," in *Bookman's Holiday,* pp. 146–166. Freeport, N.Y.: Books for Libraries Press, 1942, 1971. (Presents as fact the discredited history of Boston's Elizabeth Goose, with tracing of claims that she was the real "Mother Goose.")

Stevenson, Burton Egbert. *The Home Book of Verse for Young Folks.* N.Y.: Henry

Holt, 1915. (Contains Cowper's "John Gilpin"; helpful listing of authors' dates.)

Thomas, Katherine Elwes. *The Real Personages of Mother Goose*. Boston: Lothrop, Lee & Shepard, 1930. (Interesting, but somewhat fancifully interpreted treatise; the writing style constantly switches from pedantic and awkward to flights of fancy and picturesque speech. Despite its shortcomings, and sometimes because of them, it is quoted by almost every later researcher in the field.)

Wells, Carolyn, compiler. *A Nonsense Anthology*. New York: Charles Scribner's Sons, 1902, 1919. (Includes Mother Goose parodies.)

_____, compiler. *A Parody Anthology*. New York: Blue Ribbon Books, 1904. (Includes Mother Goose parodies.)

Winn, Marie. *The Fireside Book of Children's Songs*. New York: Simon and Schuster, 1966. (Comparison of ballad stanzas.)

Withers, Carl, compiler. *A Rocket in My Pocket: The Rhymes and Chants of Young Americans*. New York: Henry Holt, 1948. (Helpful for comparing traditional/Mother Goose rhymes with American child lore.)

Wood, Ray. *American Mother Goose*. Philadelphia: J.B. Lippincott, 1938. (Misleading title; includes traditional and American child-lore.)

_____. *Fun in American Folk Rhymes*. Philadelphia: J.B. Lippincott, 1952. (More American rhymes.)

"Wrigley's 'Mother Goose'—Introducing the Sprightly Spearmen" (booklet). Chicago: Wm. Wrigley Jr. Co., 1915. (Advertisements incorporating Mother Goose rhymes and chewing gum.)

Young, Ella Flagg, and Field, Walter Taylor. *The Young and Field Literary Readers: Book One; A Primer and First Reader*. Boston: Ginn, 1916. (Primer, with short sentences, that invokes the characters and themes of traditional Mother Goose rhymes.)

Index

Titles of books, magazines, newspapers; *Titles of verses, short stories, ballads, broadsides;* "First lines..."; Names, pseudonyms, nicknames; MISCELLANY.